Wordsworth's Vocabulary in *The Prelude*

WORDSWORTH'S VOCABULARY IN *THE PRELUDE*

KEN NAKAGAWA

KEISUISHA
Hiroshima, Japan
2018

First published in 2018

Nakagawa, Ken, 1947-
Wordsworth's Vocabulary in *The Prelude* / Ken Nakagawa
Includes bibliographical references, appendix, and index
ISBN 978-4-86327-437-2   C3098

Copyright © 2018 Ken Nakagawa

All rights reserved. No part of this book may be reprinted or reproduced or utilised in any form or by any electronic, mechanical, or other means, now known or hereafter invented, including photocopying and recording, or in any information storage or retrieval system, without permission in writing from Keisuisha Publishing Company.

Printed by
Keisuisha Co. Ltd., 1-4 Komachi, Naka-ku, Hiroshima 730-0041

Printed in Japan

For Chitose, Chie, and Mari

Contents

List of Tables   x
List of Figures   xi
List of Charts   xii
Acknowledgements   xiii

Introduction   1

Chapter 1
Vocabulary that Constitutes *The Prelude*
  1.0 Introduction   7
  1.1 Noun class   8
    1.1.1 Nouns under Division 1.1 and Division 1.5   9
    1.1.2 Nouns under Division 1.2   15
    1.1.3 Nouns under Division 1.3   18
  1.2 Verb class   20
  1.3 Adjective class   21
  1.4 Other word classes   25
  1.5 Summary   28

Chapter 2
Words Combined with 'Weight' in *The Prelude*
  2.0 Introduction   31
  2.1 Purpose   33
  2.2 Categorization of the examples of 'weight' in *The Prelude*   34
    2.2.1 How to read the chart   36
    2.2.2 Fourteen extracts   37
  2.3 Examples of (A) Negative Value   37
  2.4 Examples of (B) Positive Value   39
    2.4.1 How to intensify the degree of 'pleasure'   40
    2.4.2 Finite verbs used in citation (3)   40
    2.4.3 'Even' prefixed to '*with*-phrase'   40
    2.4.4 Brief mention of citations (9), (10), and (11)   41
  2.5 Example of (C) Neutral Value   41
  2.6 Observation   42
  2.7 Summary   44

Chapter 3
Verbs of Perception and Cognition in *The Prelude*
   3.0 Introduction   45
   3.1 Verbs appearing more than ten times in *The Prelude*   46
   3.2 Verbs of visual perception   48
   3.3 Objects of verbs of visual perception   49
   3.4 Adverbial modifiers around verbs of visual perception   54
      3.4.1 The poet's persistent attitude toward objects   54
      3.4.2 The poet's emotional state while seeing   57
   3.5 Modifiers of 'eye' and 'eyes'   58
   3.6 Verbs of auditory perception   59
   3.7 Objects of verbs of auditory perception   60
      3.7.1 The poet's keen interest in obscure 'sound' and 'voice'   61
      3.7.2 'Sound (s)' and 'voice' tend to be qualified   62
      3.7.3 The poet's feeling while hearing   63
   3.8 Modifiers of 'ear' and 'ears'   66
   3.9 Co-occurring pattern of verbs of perception and cognition:
      'saw'→'heard'→'felt'   66
   3.10 Summary   68

Chapter 4
'Mighty' in *The Prelude*
   4.0 Introduction   69
   4.1 Adjectives in the comparative and superlative degrees   69
   4.2 Polarized adjectives   70
   4.3 Rearrangement of adjectives   71
   4.4 Mirror-image relation between 'in' and 'out'   72
   4.5 Close adhesion of 'mighty' and 'mind'   74
      4.5.1 How close 'mighty' and 'mind' stand to each other   74
      4.5.2 Sound structure of 'mighty mind'   75
   4.6 Summary   75

Chapter 5
'Through' in *The Prelude*
   5.0 Introduction   77
   5.1 Unusual rank order of 'through' in *The Prelude*   77
   5.2 Distribution of objects for occurrences of 'through'   82
      5.2.1 Abstract nouns or concrete nouns?   82
      5.2.2 "Abstract locative" nouns   83
   5.3 Co-occurrence of 'through' with verbs   84
      5.3.1 Combination of 'roam' with other words   84

    5.3.2 Combination of other verbs of motion with 'through'   86
    5.3.3 Semantic components of verbs of motion   88
    5.3.4 Other similar examples of verbs of motion
         co-occurring with 'through'   89
    5.3.5 Example of a verb of visual perception
         co-occurring with 'through'   90
  5.4 Image schema of 'through'   90
  5.5 Further observations of 'through'   91
  5.6 Reasons for the frequent use of 'through'   91
  5.7 'Through' in the Snowdon passage   92
  5.8 Summary   95

Chapter 6
Multi-Layered Structure of Expression in *The Prelude*
  6.0 Introduction   97
  6.1 Threefold structure   97
  6.2 Enhancing   98
  6.3 Deepening   101
  6.4 Introduction to the Snowdon passage   103
  6.5 First half of the Snowdon passage   106
    6.5.1 Triple-layered structure representative of 'crack'   108
    6.5.2 Co-referential double structure   109
    6.5.3 Subtle difference of meaning in "isotopy"   111
  6.6 Second half of the Snowdon passage   112
    6.6.1 Nominal equivalent structure   113
    6.6.2 Verbal equivalent structure   118
  6.7 Summary   121

Conclusion   125

Works Cited   129

Select Bibliography   135

Appendix
  List 1.1 Alphabetical frequency list for *The Prelude*   155
  List 1.2 Rank frequency list for *The Prelude*   170

Subject Index   193

Personal Name Index   197

List of Tables

1.1 Framework of the *Word List by Semantic Principles*	8
1.2 Classification of 'cherry-trees'	9
1.3 Classification of nouns	10
1.4 Presence or absence of *of*-phrase modifying 'forms'	14
1.5 Nouns referring to <mind>	16
1.6 Distribution of vocabulary of emotion	19
1.7 Verbs of perception and cognition	20
1.8 Quantitative classification of adjectives	22
1.9 *The Prelude* rank list	26
3.1 Verbs of perception and cognition and their frequency count	45
3.2 Verb list in *The Prelude*	47
3.3 Verbs of visual perception	48
3.4 Presence or absence of *of*-phrase modifying 'sound' and 'voice'	62
4.1 *Mighty*'s proximity to *mind*	74
5.1 *The Prelude* rank list	78
5.2 Abstract nouns vs. concrete nouns	82
5.3 Combination of 'roam' with other words	85

List of Figures

1.1 Conceptual diagram of distribution of chapters	3
4.1 Rearranged adjectives	71
4.2 Mirror-image relation between 'in' and 'out'	73
5.1 Semantic components	88
5.2 Image schema of 'through'	90
5.3 Two sets of appositives: synonymous representations of 'crack'	93
6.1 Triple-structured expression	108
6.2 Co-referential double-structured expression	109
6.3 Graphic description of post-modifying structures	111
6.4 Double-layered structure	114
6.5 Configuration of verbs	118
6.6 Structures of subject and complement	120

List of Charts

2.1 'Weight' and its surroundings	35
3.1 Objects of verbs of visual perception	50
3.2 Objects of verbs of auditory perception	64
5.1 Distribution of objects of 'through'	80
6.1 Analytical syntax of the Snowdon passage	104
6.2 Division between major and minor sentences	122

Acknowledgements

I am particularly grateful to Professor Akiyuki Jimura, Graduate School of Letters, Hiroshima University, who has encouraged me to complete the doctoral dissertation from which this monograph grew. His suggestions have been of great value.

I gratefully express my gratitude to the late Professors Emerita of Hiroshima University, Michio Masui, Michio Kawai, and Toshiro Tanaka. Professor Masui first guided me to the language of Wordsworth, Professor Kawai taught me 18th century English literature, and Professor Tanaka led me into English philology.

My hearty thanks are due to the late Professor Masatsugu Matsuo of Hiroshima University, who helped me with computational works and Professor Keisuke Kouguchi of Yasuda Women's University, who has given me invaluable comments after reading my manuscript. My thanks should also go to my colleagues, Professor P. Timothy Ervin, Associate Professors Richard Gabbrielli and John McLean, who have spared no pains proofreading my dissertation.

The moral support and encouragement from the late Professors Sadao Ando and Masahiko Kanno and Professors Kiichiro Nakatani and Masahiko Agari are highly appreciated.

I would also like to mention three of my pupils: Mayumi Dogishi, Tomoko Yamashina, and Rie Taira, who have helped me with the Bibliography, proofreading, and Appendix, respectively.

In publishing this monograph, Professor Osamu Imahayashi of Hiroshima University spared no effort in editing my drafts, and Associate Professors John McLean and Taras Sak greatly helped me with my English. I am also indebted to Lecturer Katsuya Shima, who helped me with compiling the Index. My thanks should also go to Itsushi Kimura, president of Keisuisha Publishing Company. All the remaining errors in this book are, of course, my own.

Last but not least, I have to express my hearty thanks to Toshio Seyama, President of Yasuda Women's University and Hiromi Yasuda, chairman of the board of directors of the Yasuda Educational Foundation for financial support for the publication of this monograph.

Hiroshima, March 2018

K. N.

Introduction

It was in 1971 that I wrote my master's thesis entitled "Some Aspects of Expression in *The Prelude*." At that time, I approached the language of *The Prelude* from four perspectives: (1) Repetitive Expression, (2) Appositive Expression, (3) Negative Expression, and (4) Wordsworthian Combination of Words. This linguistic approach to the great work of William Wordsworth (1770-1850) was encouraged by Professor Michio Masui, who suggested that, in contrast to the study of the poetic thoughts of the long poem, very few studies had been made on the language of *The Prelude*.

As is suggested by the chapter title (1) Repetitive Expression, Wordsworth has a tendency to qualify a word when it is repeated. Arguably, he feels something is lacking in his expression, so he gives a more concrete and detailed meaning to the word by the craft of repetition. By using (2) Appositive Expression, he tries to express his deeper, more poetical and philosophical thoughts. I believe that in *The Prelude* Wordsworth wrestles to describe the indescribable. In such a quest, his soul never fails to have recourse to (3) Negative Expression (e.g. undistinguishable motion (Book 1, line 331); unknown modes of being (1, 420)). Perspective (4) looks at the combinations of words by means of the preposition 'of.' They are classified into four types according to the following forms: N(oun) + of + N (e.g. motions of delight (11, 9)); A(djective) + N + of + N (e.g. perfect joy of heart (4, 125)); A + N + of + A + N (e.g. a gentle shock of mild surprise (5, 407)); and N + of + A + N (e.g. The soil of common life (9, 168)).

As can be seen in the title of my master's thesis and the individual names of the chapters, my greatest concern then was in the expression itself of *The Prelude*. In other words, at that time, I was clearly more interested in 'how something is said' in *The Prelude* than 'what is said.'

Forty-six years have passed since I wrote my MA thesis, and during those years my interests have changed. To put it concretely, my concern has turned to the vocabulary *per se* which forms the foundation of expression. When we express something through language, we necessarily select and combine words out of the vocabulary of the language, i.e. the body of words in the language.

While I was an undergraduate student, I came across a novel approach to the academic study of vocabulary in the *Asahi Shimbun* newspaper. It was a short introductory note concerning how to analyze the entire corpus of Japanese vocabulary. The title of the study note was '13 Words is a Prototype for Intellectual Activity.' It was written by Shirou Hayashi, a member of the National Institute for Japanese Language. The Institute had conducted vocabulary surveys of the Japanese language four times in the 89 years spanning from 1877 (Meiji 10) to 1966 (Showa 41). Each time, the following 13 words were in the top 100 positions for occurrence: 1 *koto* (thing), 2 *mono* (object), 3 *aru* (be), 4 *naru* (become), 5 *toki* (time), 6 *tokoro* (place), 7 *iu* (say), 8 *yoru* (by), 9 *tame* (for), 10 *mata* (and), 11 *kore*, (this), 12 *kono* (this), and 13 *sono* (that).

Hayashi initially asserted that these words seem to be used almost unconsciously as if they were air and water. Later, however, he argued that the prototype for mental activity of human beings is deeply rooted in these 13 words. He concluded that tens of thousands of words are all a realization of these prototypical 13 words. I was greatly impressed with Hayashi's reasoning, which led me to investigate the network of the vocabulary employed in *The Prelude*.

Prompted by Hayashi's innovative approach to linguistic analysis, I have taken my own bold approach to the vocabulary that constitutes *The Prelude*. I have made investigations into the network of the body of words in the long poem. The question is which words are selected or chosen and how they are combined or intertwined. The poem's vocabulary turned out to comprise a total of 62,707 words. It would be impossible to examine the entire corpus, so I have focused on those lexical items which appear more than ten times. These terms make up nearly 80 percent of the whole vocabulary of *The Prelude*. I believe they are sufficient to supply the basic data for the present discussion.

The conceptual diagram of chapters in this study is shown below. As seen in Figure 1.1, Chapter 1 offers a few general remarks on the "vocabulary" of *The Prelude* from four perspectives; Chapters 2 to 5 each pick up one particular word and enlarge upon the lexical item singled out from each section of Chapter 1 (i.e. §§1.1-1.4), (dependences of sections to other chapters are shown by arrows); and Chapter 6 observes *The Prelude* syntactically from another perspective of "expression." As a result of the conceptual distribution of this study, there are cases of overlapped descriptions found in successive chapters. I ask for readers' understanding of my duplicate explanations.

Introduction

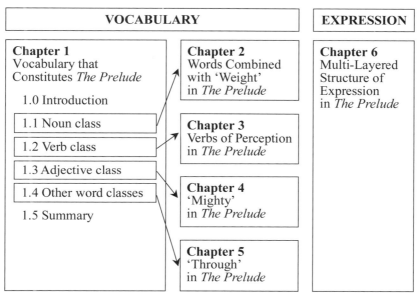

Figure 1.1: Conceptual diagram of distribution of chapters

The first chapter deals with the general view of the vocabulary realized in *The Prelude*, which is surveyed from four perspectives, or rather word classes: nouns, verbs, adjectives, and others (i.e. prepositions).

The second to the fifth chapters are concerned with a particular word or words seen from the aforementioned four perspectives. To be more specific, the second chapter pays special attention to the noun 'weight' and how uniquely it combines with 'pleasure.' The third chapter deals with verbs of perception. The former part of the chapter describes the verbs of visual perception and the latter part treats those of auditory perception. The fourth chapter concerns the adjective 'mighty.' Wordsworth is attracted by something grand and strong. As a representative adjective expressing <strength>, I investigate 'mighty' co-occurring with 'mind.' The fifth chapter is about the preposition 'through.' The frequency of 'through' appearing in *The Prelude* deviates noticeably from the norm of the English language. This deviation impelled me to survey every occurrence of 'through' in the long poem. The object nouns which 'through' takes are surveyed first and then the verbs which precede 'through' are scrutinized.

In the foregoing chapters, words are dealt with in terms of four word classes, that is, four parts of speech. This way of approaching the vocabulary of *The Prelude* is destined to be static. In order to make up for this deficiency and investigate the dynamic movement of the poem, in the sixth and final chapter, the multi-layered structure of expression is syntactically observed and the function of a triple structure is particularly discussed.

Concerning the source text and some notational conventions used in this book, all quotations are taken from the 1805 edition of *The Prelude* (1959) edited by Ernest de Selincourt and revised by Helen Darbishire, published by Clarendon Press in Oxford. I chose the 1805 edition rather than the 1850 edition because the former edition is full of the young poet's powerful and unrestrained writing style. All italics and underlines are mine unless otherwise mentioned. Book and line numbers are cited parenthetically in the quoted passage, as in "(1, 420)" meaning "(book 1, line 420)." The superscript on the left side of a word indicates the line number as in "^{42}immense" which refers to "line 42."

Next, concerning the punctuation in this monograph, as a general rule, single quotation marks indicate citations from texts and the title of an academic paper. Double quotation marks indicate the title of a poem and technical terms. Angle brackets (< >) are used around SEMEMES (i.e. semantic components) as in "<SEMEMES>."

Before proceeding, I would like to take this opportunity to share a behind-the-scenes story. I have already mentioned the scope of the vocabulary to be investigated. I have narrowed it down to those lexical items which occur more than ten times. These words make up nearly 80 percent of the whole vocabulary. The reason for reducing the number of vocabulary to be investigated was that I first needed to make my investigation less complicated, and second to seek accurate figures of occurrence of words. For the purpose of obtaining the exact frequency of occurrence, I made use of a personal computer instead of sorting information on cards by hand. As a matter of fact, I spent the whole summer vacation of 1988 inputting the entire text of *The Prelude* (1805 version) into my personal computer by hand. Needless to say, it was a really tough job, literally full of perspiration. If I had had a scanner or used a ready-made electronic text commercially available, it would have been an easier task. However, I would not have received the inspiration which happily led me to a deeper understanding of 'through' in *The Prelude*. Therefore, the perspiration of one hot summer, I believe, did more for my understanding of *The Prelude* than what I could ever have expected. The happy result of the sweat of my labours will be fully described in Chapter 5: 'Through' in *The Prelude*.

Sources of each chapter

The first chapter is based on my paper with the same title in *Studies in Modern English: The Twentieth Anniversary Publication of the Modern English Association* (2003), which first appeared in Japanese in *Studies in Modern English* 6 (1990), and then in *Eigo Eibungaku Kenkyū to Konpyūta* [*Studies of English Language and English Literature and Computers*] edited by T. Saito (1992).

The content of the second chapter first appeared in Japanese in *Eigo Eibei Bungaku Ronshū* [*Journal of English Language and Literature*] 7 published by English Language and Literature Society, Yasuda Women's University in 1998. A revised and enlarged version then appeared in *"FUL OF HY SENTENCE": Papers on English Vocabulary* edited by M. Kanno (2003). The content of this chapter was read at an international conference: PALA (Poetics And Linguistics Association) 2006, Joensuu University, Finland. It was accepted as a chapter (pp.413-26) in PALA book 5: *The State of Stylistics* edited by G. Watson (2008). The title was 'On the Phrase "Even with a Weight of Pleasure" in *The Prelude* (Bk 2, 178),' which Joanna Gavins mentioned as one of the most excellent papers in 'The year's work in stylistics 2008' (*Language and Literature*, Vol. 18, No 4, November 2009, p. 377).

The first part of the third chapter (i.e. verbs of visual perception) comes from 'What Wordsworth saw in *The Prelude*' in *Eigo Eibei Bungaku Ronshū* 3 (1994) and 'The Eyes of Wordsworth in *The Prelude*' in *Essays on Poetry* 10 (1994) published by the Chugoku-Shikoku Association of English Romanticism; and the second part comes from 'On Verbs of Auditory Perception in *The Prelude*' in *Eigo Eibei Bungaku Ronshū* 6 (1997).

The fourth chapter is newly added to the present book and discusses the adjective 'mighty' in the hope that the exquisite nature of the phrase, 'mighty mind' can be explicated phonetically and semantically. The content of this chapter was read at PALA 2007, Kansai Gaidai University, Hirakata, Japan.

The fifth chapter is included in *Voyages of Conception: Essays in English Romanticism* published by the Japan Association of English

Romanticism (2005). This is an abridged English version of my article that first appeared in Japanese in *Eigo Eibei Bungaku Tenbyō* [*Sketches of English Language and Literature*] edited by R. Kumagawa (1991). This was also read at PALA 2000, Goldsmiths College, London University and then at the Wordsworth Summer Conference 2001, Grasmere, England with subsidiary aid called a 'Travel Grant' from the English Literary Society of Japan.

The sixth and last chapter appeared first as an essay, 'Multi-layered Structure of Expression in *The Prelude*' in *Journal of Yasuda Women's University* 12 (1984). Part of this chapter was read at PALA 2013, Heidelberg University, Heidelberg, Germany. A revised version of this appears in *Studies in Modern English: The Thirtieth Anniversary Publication of the Modern English Association* edited by K. Nakagawa (2014).

The first, third, fifth, and sixth chapters are also included in my small book (in Japanese), *The Language of William Wordsworth: A Linguistic Approach to the Poetic Language* (1997), Monograph Series No. 2, published by the Research Institute for Language and Culture, Yasuda Women's University.

Chapter 1
Vocabulary that Constitutes *The Prelude*

1.0 Introduction
The aim of this chapter is to describe the stratificational network of the vocabulary of *The Prelude*. If its network is well defined, it allows us to obtain a Wordsworthian way of grasping the outer world.

The vocabulary of *The Prelude* (1805 edition) by William Wordsworth (1770-1850) is made up of a total of 62,707 words (tokens), consisting of 8,287 distinct words (types), out of which I will consider 769 types that appear more than ten times in the text. These words correspond to 75.43% of the total number of words in *The Prelude*. Consequently, I can confidently describe the general tendency of the vocabulary found in *The Prelude*. I am fully aware of the view that a poet's use of rarely occurring words or neologisms (such as 'Under-powers' (1, 163) and 'under-thirst' (6, 489) among others) reveals the distinctive characteristics of an opus. In this chapter, however, I have purposefully avoided dealing with such words or phrases.

I first made the entire text of *The Prelude* machine-readable and sought an accurate frequency count of each word by using the search program, PC-KWIC, developed by M. Matsuo and S. Suzuki.

As a model of classification, I consulted the *Word List by Semantic Principles* (1989: 5, 165-67) compiled by the National Japanese Language Research Institute. Before deciding to rely on the *Word List*, I had tried to seek an appropriate model among the Western lexical works, such as Roget's *International Thesaurus* (4th ed.) and McArthur's *Longman Lexicon of Contemporary English*. Unfortunately, I found those works unsuitable for my present study.

The framework of the classification of the *Word List* is shown in Table 1.1. Japanese vocabulary is divided into four parts. The whole numbers (1, 2, 3 and 4) refer to, in this order, nouns, verbs, adjectives, and others (conjunctions, interjections, etc.), and the decimals (0.1, 0.2, 0.3, 0.4 and 0.5) refer to the semantic fields. For example, in the third row (HUMAN ACTIVITY—MIND AND DEED), I can assign the 'joy' in Division 1.3, the verb 'enjoy' in 2.3, the adjective 'joyful' in 3.3, and the interjection 'oh' in 4.3.

Table 1.1: Framework of the *Word List by Semantic Principles*

	nouns	verbs	adjectives	others		
ABSTRACT RELATION	1.1	2.1	3.1	4.1		
AGENT OF HUMAN ACTIVITY	1.2	—	—	—	subject	
HUMAN ACTIVITY —MIND AND DEED	1.3	2.3	3.3	4.3	predicate (action)	
PRODUCTS FROM HUMAN ACTIVITY	1.4	—	—	—	object	artificial
NATURE—NATURAL THINGS AND PHENOMENA	1.5	2.5	3.5	—		natural
	entities	events	abstracts	relational		

* The divisions attached to the bottom of the list (entities, events, abstracts, relational) come from Nida (1975: 178-86); those on the right, which show the syntagmatic relationship (i.e. subject + predicate + object), are devised by the present writer.

1.1 Noun class

In this section, I describe the distribution of nouns realized in *The Prelude*. For convenience of explanation, I will first deal with Division 1.5 (i.e. NATURE—NATURAL THINGS AND PHENOMENA) together with 1.1 (i.e. ABSTRACT RELATION), then Division 1.2 (i.e. AGENT OF HUMAN ACTIVITY), and finally Division 1.3 (i.e. HUMAN ACTIVITY— MIND AND DEED).

Incidentally, it is indeed rather easy to seek hyponymy in a limited aggregate, as seen, for example, in a set of cherry trees. Table 1.2, which I transcribed from the Japanese original, is a table that Kunihiro (1980: 244-45) compiled:

Chapter 1   Vocabulary that Constitutes *The Prelude*   9

Table 1.2: Classification of 'cherry trees'

(1)	**vegetable**	animal	mineral ...				
(2)	**tree**	plant	flower	moss ...			
(3)	**cherry**	pine	plum	peach	cedar	*shii*	*hinoki* ...
(4)	*yama-zakura**	*yae-zakura*	*shidare-zakura*	*higan-zakura*	*somei-yoshino*		
(5)	*ooyama-zakura*	*nara-yae-zakura*					

* *zakura* (sakura)=Japanese word for cherry tree

Kunihiro remarks that every language has five or six strata and that more often than not level (3) is used in daily life. Hyponymy is easily recognized in a specific part of vocabulary, specifically in a limited area of words denoting the names of plants and animals.

When it comes to the vocabulary comprised of a wide range of natural objects, however, it is difficult to find an appropriate model to divide them into an elaborate system of classification. Despite this difficulty, I managed to complete Table 1.3. The left-hand figures in boldface type in the Table (i.e. numbers **1.1, 1.2, 1.3,** and **1.5**) correspond to the figures of Table 1.1. In Table 1.3 below, Division 1.4 (i.e. PRODUCTS FROM HUMAN ACTIVITY) is empty. The reason simply comes from the fact that such words very rarely occur in the poem. Physical and material products (such as 'tools,' 'goods,' 'dwellings') are artificial and therefore vulgar to the poet's sensitivity and consequently do not appear so often in the poetic world of *The Prelude*. The figure on the right side of each word (for instance object '16' in hyponymous subdivision FACT) indicates its frequency count.

1.1.1 Nouns under Division 1.1 (ABSTRACT RELATION) and Division 1.5 (NATURE—NATURAL THINGS AND PHENOMENA)

First, as mentioned above, I analyzed *The Prelude*'s vocabulary to identify words that fit into Division 1.5—nouns that depict NATURE surrounding human beings—and seek hyponymy among the vocabulary pertaining to NATURE. NATURE is a superordinate concept, i.e. hypernym, under which lie MATERIAL, HEAVEN, WEATHER, TOPOGRAPHY, SCENERY, PLANTS, and ANIMALS.

Wordsworth's Vocabulary in *The Prelude*

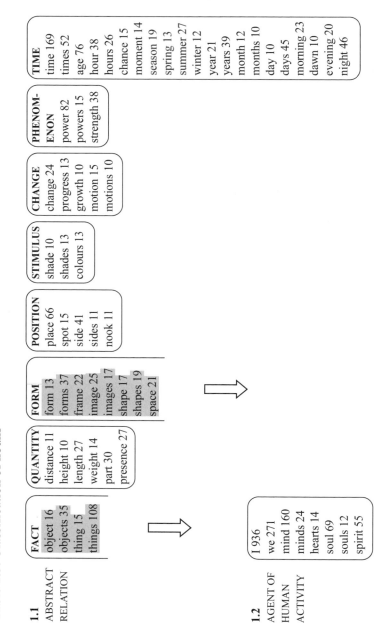

Table 1.3: Classification of nouns

1.1 ABSTRACT RELATION

FACT	QUANTITY	FORM	POSITION	STIMULUS	CHANGE	PHENOMENON	TIME
object 16	distance 11	form 13	place 66	shade 10	change 24	power 82	time 169
objects 35	height 10	forms 37	spot 15	shades 13	progress 13	powers 15	times 52
thing 15	length 27	frame 22	side 41	colours 13	growth 10	strength 38	age 76
things 108	weight 14	image 25	sides 11		motion 15		hour 38
	part 30	images 17	nook 11		motions 10		hours 26
	presence 27	shape 17					chance 15
		shapes 19					moment 14
		space 21					season 19
							spring 13
							summer 27
							winter 12
							year 21
							years 39
							month 12
							months 10
							day 10
							days 45
							morning 23
							dawn 10
							evening 20
							night 46

1.2 AGENT OF HUMAN ACTIVITY

I 936
we 271
mind 160
minds 24
hearts 14
soul 69
souls 12
spirit 55

Chapter 1 Vocabulary that Constitutes *The Prelude*   11

1.3 HUMAN ACTIVITY

MIND AND DEED
- thought 60
- thoughts 73
- remembrances 10
- imagination 16
- fancy 17
- memory 19
- feeling 34
- feelings 18
- sense 50

1.4 ∅

1.5 NATURE (117)

NATURAL THINGS AND PHENOMENA

MATERIAL
- water 13
- air 25
- crags 13
- rock 17
- rocks 19
- stone 16

HEAVEN
- universe 11
- heaven 31
- sky 22
- sun 37
- moon 18
- stars 14

WEATHER
- breeze 10
- storm 24
- wind 25
- winds 19
- clouds 25

TOPOGRAPHY
- earth 62
- ground 24
- land 23
- hill 14
- hills 37
- mountain 22
- mountains 24
- vale 20
- field 17
- fields 29
- plain 14
- sea 31
- waters 17
- lake 16
- river 13
- stream 29
- shore 10
- island 14

SCENERY
- prospect 14
- scene 20
- scenes 12
- sight 44
- sights 13
- spectacle 13
- view 20
- groves 19
- woods 28
- turf 10
- way 57
- ways 10
- road 18
- roads 11
- streets 11

PLANTS
- tree 15
- trees 21
- wood 12
- grass 13
- flowers 17

ANIMALS
- creature 13
- creatures 11
- birds 17
- flock 11

⇐

⇐

Of all seven hyponyms in Division 1.5, SCENERY is the most noticeable. It seems to me that words expressing SCENERY can be divided into two types according to the degrees of abstraction: one that stretches from 'groves' to 'streets' and another that ranges from 'prospect' to 'view.'

The former (i.e. the lower half of SCENERY) represents the concrete aspects of nature when the poet directly sees natural objects with his own eyes. In contrast, the latter (i.e. the upper half of SCENERY) abstracts and summarizes the former as well as the words located on both sides (i.e. TOPOGRAPHY and PLANTS). These latter words arise in reminiscence when their individual concrete details blur and disappear. That is to say, as indicated by the two upward-pointing arrows on the Table 1.3, the upper group of words—'prospect' to 'view'—proceeds towards Division 1.1 representing ABSTRACT RELATION.

I would now like to point out a tendency which is quite opposite to the above. Most readers of *The Prelude* will notice the high frequency words such as 'thing(s)' and 'object(s)' that appear throughout the work. In most cases, these words are to be included under the subdivision entitled FACT in Division 1.1 (i.e. nouns expressive of ABSTRACT RELATION). However, these so-called abstract nouns seem to be charged, in the case of Wordsworth, with a great deal of <concreteness>. Individual aspects of nature, such as 'hill(s),' 'mountain(s),' 'field(s),' 'stream,' 'tree(s),' and 'wood(s)' converge into 'thing(s)' and 'object(s).' Wordsworth must have expressed the essence of the concrete natural objects with the use of 'thing' and 'object,' the highest-ranking superordinate terms.

If I may be allowed to slightly alter the above-cited classification by Kunihiro (Table 1.2) and to boldly add a level (0), then I can say that Wordsworth dared to use the language in stratum (0), i.e. terms of the highest degree of abstraction. For Wordsworth, words at level (0) are not what are called abstract words. They are words full of <concreteness> with the meaning of levels (1) to (5) integrated into that of level (0): 'thing' and 'object.'

All things in nature sometimes approach the poet with their horrifying aspects and sometimes surround him with their gentle phases. Nothing natural around him fails to contribute to his human growth. Pushing away the individual attributes of natural things, the poet collectively calls their general and intrinsic essence 'thing' and 'object.' This attitude itself constitutes a Wordsworthian way of grasping the outer world.

Moreover, the poet calls human beings 'thinking things' ("Tintern Abbey" 101). What first gives him respect for human beings is a shepherd, and it is noteworthy that he refers to a shepherd living in nature as 'A solitary object and sublime' (8, 407).

Let us observe the same kind of tendency which shows a parallel relationship to the above. In particular, let us pay attention to Wordsworth's marked preference for words of higher degree of abstraction in expressing concrete objects. When he describes concrete natural things such as 'hills' and 'mountains,' he tends to use abstract terminology. He prefers the vocabulary expressing FORM, which is a subdivision of 1.1 ABSTRACT RELATION on Table 1.3. He chooses such words as 'form,' 'frame,' 'image,' 'shape' and 'space' rather than concrete words. Indeed, there is no doubt that these are abstract nouns, but when it comes to Wordsworth, the situation turns out to be a little different. As a matter of fact, lexical items belonging to Division 1.1 (ABSTRACT RELATION) tend to shift to those pertaining to 1.5 (NATURAL THINGS AND PHENOMENA) as shown by the two downward-pointing arrows in Table 1.3. In other words, a conversion from an abstract to a concrete entity is observed in his use of these seemingly abstract words.

To make the point clearer, let us cite an example of 'forms,' which shows the highest frequency count among the FORM group, the third subdivision from the left along the horizontal axis of 1.1 ABSTRACT RELATION on Table 1.3. Let us make a closer observation, particularly, of the elements which come after 'forms,' that is to say, the post-modifiers of 'forms.'

In daily English use, the 'form of ~' pattern is a usual word combination. In other words, 'form' is usually followed by an '*of*-phrase.' West (1953: s.v. 'form') illustrates such patterns as 'Clock made in the *form* of a globe,' 'the *form* of man,' and 'A diamond is one *form* of carbon.' West's illustrative examples total 14, out of which seven examples (50%) have an '*of*-phrase,' one example (7.1%) has a post-modifying (contact) relative clause, and six examples (42.9%) have no 'post-modifiers.' The percentage of 'form' without post-modification in West's examples is 42.9%, which means the remaining 57.1% of his examples are post-qualified by a phrase or a clause.

Incidentally, it is interesting that no plural form, i.e. 'forms,' is seen in West's examples. In *The Prelude*, however, Wordsworth uses the plural 'forms' 37 times and the singular 'form' 13 times. One of the reasons for this frequent use is that Wordsworth tries to exploit 'forms' in order to represent concrete natural things rather than to delineate the abstract shape of things.

An investigation of 'forms' in various contexts of *The Prelude* reveals the following (Table 1.4):

Table 1.4: Presence or absence of *of*-phrase modifying 'forms'

of-phrase	+	−	total
forms (natural)	3	28	31
forms (others)	3	3	6
total	6 (16.2%)	31 (83.8%)	37 (100%)

First, there are 31 examples of 'forms' pertaining to natural things, while there are only six examples of 'forms' of those other than natural objects (e.g. 'man,' 'house' and the like). Furthermore, the above-mentioned pattern, 'forms' + 'of ~,' appears in only six out of a total of 37 examples. What is clear from Table 1.4 is that, unlike common usage exemplified by West (1953), the addition of an *of*-phrase is relatively scarce (16.2%) in *The Prelude*. In contrast, 'forms' without an *of*-phrase reach the high percentage of 83.8%.

Look at the rare examples of nature-related 'forms' appearing with an '*of*-phrase' (cf. vulgar *forms* / Of houses, pavements, streets (8, 695-96)):

    the beauteous *forms* / Of Nature   (2, 51-52)
    the *forms* / Perennial of the ancient hills   (7, 725-26)
    the *forms* / Of Nature   (12, 289-90)

These 'forms of ~' patterns are only three in number, and two of them collocate with 'Nature' which carries extensively strong and vast connotations. Again, the percentage of this pattern's occurrence is 16.2%, which is rather small, compared with the general tendency (50%) of 'form of ~' collocations shown by West.

These findings suggest that the '*of*-phrase' in itself in 'forms of ~' does not appeal to Wordsworth and consequently he does not find it necessary to express that part followed by 'of.' It is the very 'forms' rather than individual attributes that are important to the poet's poetic mind.

How about other ways to post-modify 'forms' except by using an '*of*-phrase'? There are only two cases, in which relative clauses post-modify 'forms,' whose number of occurrences is rather small in the same way as the above-mentioned '*of*-phrase' case. At any rate, it is certain that post-modification of 'forms' by a phrase or a clause is scarcely seen in *The Prelude*. This is one of the striking stylistic features of *The Prelude*.

At first I thought the reason such abstract nouns as 'form,' 'frame,' 'image,' 'shape' and 'space' are used so often in *The Prelude* derives from the fact that the poet deconstructs concrete natural objects into abstract elements such as <form>, <colour>, <weight>, <quality>, and then directs his attention to one element <form>. On second thought, however, I came to realize that he recognizes an object (e.g. mountain) as a concrete form, not as an abstract element. Wordsworth is elated by the way a material object occupies its firm and steady position in space. His peculiar way of expression in delineating natural things in such a way may result from retrospection, which is one operation of his poetical mind. That is to say, when he expresses what is recollected in tranquility, then the superficial and redundant attributes of things are cleared away by the filter of time. After that the real and essential things emerge. In other words, what appeals most strongly to the poet's mind will appear in his expression, i.e. come out in his words. Until now, I have not dealt with pre-modification of 'forms.' What comes before 'forms' in syntagmatic relation is also important, which will be treated later in Chapter 4, '"Mighty" in *The Prelude*,' of this monograph.

1.1.2 Nouns under Division 1.2 (AGENT OF HUMAN ACTIVITY)

Next, I describe Division 1.2: nouns expressing AGENT OF HUMAN ACTIVITY. They are basically 'I' and 'we,' the frequency count of which is 937 and 272, respectively. To these agents I would like to add the words referring to 'mind,' although they are usually grouped into Division 1.3 (HUMAN ACTIVITY—MIND AND DEED) according to the *Word List by Semantic Principles*. It is no exaggeration to say that 'mind' is a main character of *The Prelude*, because, first, the subtitle of the poem is, as a matter of fact, 'Growth of a Poet's <u>Mind</u>'; second, Wordsworth traces faithfully 'The workings of a youthful <u>mind</u>' (10, 944); and, third and last, his theme for *The Prelude* is 'No other than the very <u>heart</u> of man' (12, 240), which is the emotional side of his mental faculties.

Table 1.5: Nouns referring to <mind>

	human	natural	other	Total
mind	160	1	—	161
minds	24	—	—	24
heart	107	6	—	113
hearts	13	—	1	14
soul	58	11	—	69
souls	11	1	—	12
spirit	39	16	—	55

First of all, 'mind' and 'minds' are used to describe intellectual mental activities of human beings. The singular form solely refers to the human mind with the exception of 'the one great mind' (2, 272), which means 'Nature Herself.' Mind equals Nature—this recognition is closely related to a theory of imagination peculiar to Wordsworth. (This point will be dealt with further in Chapters 3 and 6 of this monograph.) In contrast, all of the plural forms signify human minds or the possessors of them.

Next, I move on to 'heart' and 'hearts.' Six cases of singular 'heart' refer to 'the innermost or central part of anything; the centre, middle' (*OED2*) as in 'the heart / Of London' (6, 288-89). (Incidentally, London is here considered as one aspect of nature surrounding the poet.) The remaining 107 examples refer to 'the seat of the emotions generally; the emotional nature, as distinguished from the intellectual nature placed in the *head*' (*OED2*). Wordsworth's emotional heart enjoys the pleasure and benefit from Nature extravagantly and immensely. One case of 'hearts' in plural is used in relation to card games. All others refer to human hearts and their possessors.

While 'mind' and 'heart' are mainly exploited with reference to humans, 'soul,' 'souls,' and 'spirit' are often used for the description of nature as well as for humans. For example, 11 out of 69 occurrences of 'soul' refer to the soul of Nature, and one out of 12 occurrences of 'souls' is 'Souls of lonely places!' (1, 492), which definitely describes one aspect of nature. 'Spirit' occurring 55 times in total refers to Nature in 16 cases. Sometimes 'soul' and 'spirit' are employed as synonyms as is shown in the following passage:

(1) In progress through this Verse, my mind hath look'd
 Upon the speaking face of earth and heaven
 As her prime Teacher, intercourse with man
 Establish'd by the sovereign Intellect,
 Who through that bodily Image hath diffus'd
 A soul divine which we participate,
 A deathless spirit. (5, 11-17)

In this passage, as mentioned above, we can observe that 'mind' works as an agent, in other words, as a "sensor" of the 'process of sensing' (i.e. 'look'd') (Halliday: 1985: 106).

A similar example of synonymous use is seen in:

(2) The Spirit of Nature was upon me here;
 The Soul of Beauty and enduring life (7, 735-36)

Here I need to explain why I divide the vocabulary of mental working into two uses: one belonging to the human world and the other belonging to the natural world. It is because I would like to find in what mutual relationships both Wordsworth's inner world (lexical items of 1.2 in the *Word List* above) and the outer world of Nature (those of 1.5) are retained. The point is succinctly expressed in:

(3) The mountain's outline and its steady form
 Gives a pure grandeur, and its presence shapes
 The measure and the prospect of the soul
 To majesty; (7, 722-25)

The outward form of the mountain gives the poet a pure splendor. The existence of its steady form enlarges the capacity of the poet's soul correspondingly to the dignity of Nature. It is on this very point that I am most impressed when reading through *The Prelude*. Nature enhances human beings in dignity.

1.1.3 Nouns under Division 1.3 (HUMAN ACTIVITY—MIND AND DEED)

Next, I investigate the nouns pertaining to mental workings of man which are to be included in 1.3 of the *Word List by Semantic Principles*. Here I will make special mention of what Miles (1942, rpt. 1965) calls vocabulary of emotion, which appears so frequently in this poem. Wordsworth gazes at natural objects and feels joy. The following lines come from Book 1, where he describes the growth of his mind by comparing his soul to the growth of a plant, likening his inner soul to part of the outer world:

(4) Fair seed-time had my soul, and I grew up
Foster'd alike by **beauty** and by **fear**;   (1, 305-06)

And similar content is seen at the end of *The Prelude*, Book 13:

(5) early intercourse,
In presence of sublime and lovely Forms,
With the adverse principles of **pain** and **joy**,   (13, 145-47)

Putting these two pairs of shaded words in the center, I made Table 1.6, which shows the distribution of Wordsworth's "vocabulary of emotion." I arranged words expressive of pleasant feelings on the left side of the table and those of unpleasant feelings on the right.

It is difficult to say that 'beauty' is an antonym of 'fear.' Therefore, I selected 'love' as the antonym of 'fear.' When I think of an antonym of 'love,' 'hatred' occurs to me first. Yet, Wordsworth uses 'hatred' only once throughout *The Prelude*. He uses its related words, 'hate,' four times and 'hater,' only once. All human beings are susceptible to feelings of hatred. Wordsworth cannot be an exception. He seems, however, to refrain from expressing feelings of hatred.

On the contrary, as seen in the Table below, 'joy' appears as many as 69 times in total. Wordsworth is often said to be a 'nature poet,' but when we pay attention to his frequent use of "vocabulary of emotion," we can say he is also a 'poet of love, joy, and passion.' This point is clearly illustrated by the amplitude of the total area on the left side on the bar graph below, which indicates pleasant feelings. His mind was full of pleasant feelings.

Chapter 1　Vocabulary that Constitutes *The Prelude*　　　19

Table 1.6: Distribution of vocabulary of emotion

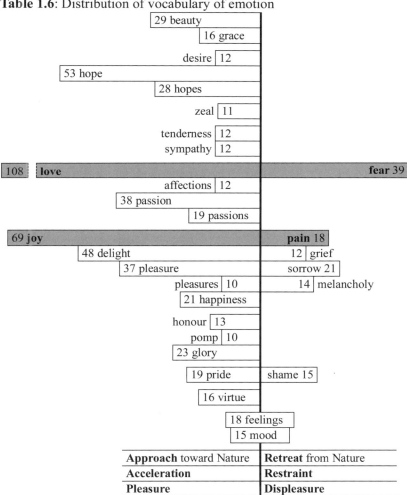

Look at the bottom of the graph. If I turn my eyes to the poet's attitude towards Nature from the point of dynamics, I find his approach to Nature revealed on the left side of the graph and his retreat from Nature on the right. Kanou (1969: 16), using a car-related metaphor, refers to the beauty of Nature as the "accelerator" and the admonishing aspect of Nature as the "brake."

Let us observe some actual examples. A good illustration of the former—the poet's movement towards Nature—is revealed in the sentence: 'surely I was led by her (=Nature)' (1, 372). A good example of a cause of the latter movement—the poet's retreat or withdrawal from Nature—is shown in the phrases: 'huge and mighty Forms' (1, 425) of 'unknown modes of being' (1, 420). These phrases describe 'a huge cliff' that admonished young Wordsworth for his wrong deed of stealing a shepherd's boat. Both are from the famous stolen boat episode.

Wordsworth says in the preface of *Lyrical Ballads* (1800: 263-64) that '[t]he end of Poetry is to produce excitement in coexistence with an overbalance of pleasure.' The high percentage of nouns denoting <pleasure> such as 'joy' and 'pleasure' would therefore be quite natural in a work where he practiced his own poetic theory.

1.2 Verb class

Following the classification of nouns, I will proceed to a brief discussion of verbs. One characteristic of verbs in *The Prelude* is that the verbs of perception and cognition appear in large quantities. They are grouped into 2.3 (verbs referring to HUMAN ACTIVITY—MIND AND DEED) of the *Word List by Semantic Principles*. Their frequencies are shown in Table 1.7:

Table 1.7: Verbs of perception and cognition

Verbs of perception		Verbs of cognition	
feel	29	*seem*	24
felt	49	*seems*	11
see	44	*seem'd*	64
sees	10	*appear'd*	19
saw	58	*think*	21
seen	44	*thought*	21
look	20	*know*	19
look'd	30	*knew*	15
behold	22	*find*	30
beheld	24	*found*	51
hear	18	*learn'd*	11
heard	42		

The following is a sentence structure with the second most frequent verb of perception, 'felt.'

I | felt | X.

This S(ubject) + P(redicate) + O(bject) structure is the formula used when the poet perceives all things existing around him. The vertical axis of 'felt' is realized by such verbs as 'see,' 'look,' and 'hear.' The axis of 'X' is realized by anything that gives some sort of stimulus to the young poet. The lexical items to be filled in X are represented by 'thing' and 'form.' The left side of the axis 'felt' is to be supplied with agents, whose typical examples are 'mind' and 'heart' as well as 'I.' The nouns which occupy the slot of S and O have been minutely discussed in the Noun section (§1.1) of this chapter.

Another characteristic behavior of verbs is that the pattern 'saw → heard → felt' is often observed throughout *The Prelude*. Look at a typical example in the next lines:

...even the grossest minds must <u>see</u> and <u>hear</u>
And cannot chuse but <u>feel</u>.   (13, 83-84)

This point will be discussed in detail in Chapter 3, Verbs of Perception in *The Prelude*.

One more characteristic of the verbs in *The Prelude* is seen in the frequent use of verbs of motion, especially those concurring with 'through.' These verbs bear the semantic components of <gradual progress>, <expansion>, or <pervasiveness>. This topic will be dealt with in some detail in Chapter 5, 'Through' in *The Prelude*.

1.3 Adjective class
In this section I will extract the adjectives that modify natural things and then investigate which nouns (expressive of the human 'mind') those adjectives tend to modify in turn. The figures in Table 1.8 indicate frequency counts:

Table 1.8: Quantitative classification of adjectives

POSITION		
23 distant	near 31	
23 outward	inner 12	
27 high		
17 higher	low 13	
13 highest		
11 lofty		
36 deep		
11 deeper		

SHAPE		
70 great	small 23	
15 large		
13 huge		
14 wide		
12 vast		
36 open		
40 long	short 21	

AMOUNT		
30 full	vain 16	
352 all	one 188	
11 endless	little 40	

SUBSTANCE		
	simple 17	
34 strong	weak 12	
23 mighty		
21 young	old 59	
33 new	ancient 21	
12 fresh		

STIMULUS		
	quiet 17	
11 loud	silent 30	
	still 15	
12 bright	dark 13	
23 visible	invisible 14	
	unknown 19	
green 24		
golden 11		

TIME		
36 first	last 34	
19 early	later 14	
daily 14		
21 present	past 22	
12 steady		

Chapter 1 Vocabulary that Constitutes *The Prelude*

STATE	18 divine / 11 holy / 11 busy / 14 awful / 13 sublime / 20 naked / 34 living		human 63 / gentle 21 / wild 26 / dead 16
VALUE	38 good / 26 better / 27 best / 22 true / 11 real / 14 glorious / 23 pure / 14 beauteous / 10 beautiful / 20 fair / 13 perfect / 10 worthy		false 18 / plain 16 / vulgar 14 / mean 15
TYPE	32 common / 12 universal / 40 same / 13 kindred		individual 15 / different 20
DEGREE	10 utter		
TOTAL NUMBER	1,467		855

This classification depends on the framework of *Kadokawa's New Dictionary of Synonyms* (1981). The dictionary classifies the whole vocabulary of Japanese into three large groups (i.e. NATURE (0-2); HUMAN AFFAIRS (3-6); CULTURE (7-9)) and then groups them into 100 smaller items. In the dictionary, items 10-19 (which make up an intermediate group PROPERTY) in the first large group NATURE deal with adjectives related to Nature surrounding human beings; and small items 60-69 (which comprise an intermediate group DISPOSITION) in the second large group, HUMAN AFFAIRS, deal with adjectives relevant to humans themselves. The names of the ten classified items printed in bold (i.e. 10 **POSITION**...19 **DEGREE**) correspond to those of 10-19 in the *Kadokawa* dictionary.

In the above classification, adjectives that solely express human emotions, such as 'delighted' and 'pleased,' are omitted. Moreover, determiners such as 'a,' 'this,' and 'those' are also omitted with the exception of 'all' and 'one.' When a word can be used across two or more word classes as in 'open,' 'present,' and 'utter,' I closely examined each word's context and selected the adjectival use only.

The left row displays ten smaller groupings and on its right are shown antonyms corresponding to each category, in which, roughly speaking, positive-image words are put on the left side. Some words do not have their pair words. Non-existence of such pairs signifies that their frequency count is less than ten and does not necessarily mean zero. The adjectives with a positive image are 1,467 and those with a negative one are 855 in number. When calculating a total, I excluded the number of neutral adjectives, 'green,' 'golden,' and 'daily,' which are displayed neutrally with the center of their boxes on the vertical heavy line of Table 1.8.

What is clear from this table is that Wordsworth is attracted by something 'great (70),' 'strong (34),' 'mighty (23),' 'sublime (13),' 'solid (9),' and 'grand (6).' (The last two adjectives, 'solid' and 'grand' do not appear in the above table because they occur nine and six times respectively. As I mentioned earlier, I narrowed down the scope of my survey to the 769 words which appear more than ten times in *The Prelude*).

To be more specific, on the shadowed lexical items in Table 1.8: 'Outward' in **POSITION** is exploited when a natural thing acts on the poet's inner world, and 'high' is relevant to his ascending inclination towards something noble and eternal, as seen also in the famous phrase: 'plain living and high thinking' ("Written in London, September, 1802," 11).

'Great,' 'large,' 'huge,' 'wide,' and 'long' in **SHAPE** are used in relation to the grandeur and magnificence that are involved in both nature and the poet's mind.

'Strong' and 'mighty' in **SUBSTANCE** are relevant to <power>. In particular, 'mighty' culminates in a phrase 'a mighty Mind' (13, 69), which might be called the most important word combination in *The Prelude*. This point will be specifically investigated in Chapter 4, 'Mighty' in *The Prelude*.

'Invisible' and 'unknown' in **STIMULUS** are made use of when what is mysterious and inscrutable to ordinary people can be seen by the poet. Wordsworth is able to conceive of things that would never occur to ordinary people.

'Steady' in TIME shows the poet's firm attention when he concentrates his mind upon the real state of affairs.

'Living' and 'dead' in STATE are seen respectively in 'ye who are fed / By the dead letter' (8, 431-32) and 'Mighty indeed, supreme must be the power / Of living Nature' (5, 166-67).

What can I extract from the above observations? There are at least two findings. One is a tendency for the poet to use identical adjectives to qualify both natural things and human temperaments. In other words, a correspondence is recognized between the adjectives describing natural objects and those that describe human minds so that you see the same adjectives appear in both Division 3.5 (NATURE) and Division 3.3 (HUMAN ACTIVITY—MIND AND DEED) of Table 1.1. To give a representative example, 'mighty' forms (1, 425) of Nature deeply influence Wordsworth's mind, hence his 'mighty' mind (13, 69). I cannot help feeling the poet's deepest debt to Nature is condensed into this phrase, 'mighty mind.'

The other finding is that Wordsworth uses the adjectives 'heavy, thick, long, large' rather than those of 'light, thin, short, small.' This must be a natural consequence of the poet's way of looking at things. He takes a broad and wide view of things around him. He shows more interest in the real state of affairs than in the superficial appearance of affairs. He is a poet who looks into the essence rather than the surface of things.

Incidentally, in §1.1, the Noun class in Table 1.4: Presence or absence of *of*-phrase modifying 'forms,' I briefly referred to the unique linguistic situation of post-modification of 'forms.' Wordsworth tends *not* to post-modify 'forms.' Unlike common usage, the addition of an *of*-phrase is relatively scarce in *The Prelude*.

Pre-modification of 'forms' is important to survey as well. What form of adjective comes before 'forms' in syntagmatic relation? What kind of adjectives precedes 'forms'? The behavior of these *forms*-modifying adjectives, about which there is also something unique, will be treated in Section 1 of Chapter 4 entitled 'Adjectives with or without comparative and superlative degree.'

1.4 Other word classes
Now, I will move on to the last word type. In the *Word List by Semantic Principles*, the 'other word class' category includes conjunctions, interjections, and certain types of adverbs. Here I focus on the

preposition 'through.' Table 1.9 illustrates where 'through' stands in *The Prelude* rank list. It appears 203 times. It is ranked at 36th if I include the abbreviated form 'thro.'

Table 1.9: *The Prelude* rank list

1 the	3,221	*27* is	292	*52* there	159	*78* first	104
2 and	2,715	*28* it	285	*52* those	159	*78* own	104
3 of	2,378	*29* he	276	*54* no	158	*80* could	103
4 a	1,420	*30* we	272	*55* then	155	*81* might	100
5 to	1,322	*31* when	251	*56* did	152	*81* thus	100
6 in	1,269	*32* have	248	*57* like	147	*83* far	93
7 I	937	*33* their	237	*58* its	142	*84* them	92
8 that	909	*34* be	236	*59* man	141	*85* how	88
9 with	779	*35* more	223	*60* these	137	*86* out	86
10 was	558	*36* **through**	**203**	*61* so	135	*86* would	86
11 my	538	(thro'	4)	*62* up	133	*88* power	83
12 as	477	*37* her	203	*63* love	132	*89* here	82
13 by	447	*37* upon	203	*64* him	130	*90* thought	81
13 from	447	*39* were	200	*64* some	130	*91* before	80
15 which	441	*40* one	188	*66* life	128	*91* less	80
16 for	399	*41* such	186	*67* are	126	*93* hath	79
17 or	365	*42* yet	174	*67* if	126	*93* into	79
18 not	364	*43* what	172	*69* than	124	*93* men	79
19 his	354	*44* our	170	*70* where	123	*93* other	79
20 all	352	*45* time	169	*71* among	121	*97* long	78
21 had	349	*46* an	167	*71* nor	121	*97* still	78
22 this	343	*47* who	166	*73* day	118	*99* every	77
23 at	334	*48* now	165	*74* nature	117	*100* truth	75
24 but	322	*49* been	162	*75* heart	113		
25 on	316	*49* they	162	*76* even	108		
26 me	295	*51* mind	161	*76* things	108		

Let me make a comparison of the frequency rank of 'through' in *The Prelude* with other references. Its ranking in the Lancaster-Oslo/Bergen Corpus of British English (hereafter LOB) is 120th; that in the Brown University Corpus of American English (hereafter Brown) is 102nd; and those of *Word Frequencies in Written and Spoken English* are 192nd (written) and 108th (spoken). Its rank in *The Prelude* is at a much higher 36th. This difference is considerable. This, I argue, is where the secret of the interpretation of *The Prelude* lies.

It may be dangerous to completely ignore the time difference between the age of Wordsworth (1770-1850) and the present day, but if we stand on the following assumption, the danger may be reduced. We can assume there are words that are often used or realized in any text and in any age despite the time difference. Indeed, it is expected that content words may take a different rank order depending on the content of a given text, but when it comes to function words, especially prepositions, alterations of the rank order deriving from texts' differences seem to be rather small. Prepositions are by nature the words expressing the relation of dependence and the cause and effect between objects, so they are presupposed to appear in any text rather regularly and steadily regardless of individual rank order differences. According to Davies (1986: 58), high-frequency words like prepositions 'are imposed on him [the writer] by the laws of chance, in the sense that they result from the simple fact that he has to choose to write in a language in which these words have these probabilities of occurrence.'

Why is 'through' used so often in *The Prelude*? My first impression on reading through the poem is that the poet's way of recognizing the outer world is highly extensive and on a grand scale. He generally tries to take a higher and broader view of things around him. Talking through the axis of time, he retraces the growth of his poetic mind from early childhood to manhood. From the axis of space, he might be said to travel extensively as far as France and Germany. As the sentence 'I walked with Nature' (2, 377) clearly indicates, he is a wandering poet. Such is his movement in time and space that 'through' representing <motion> rather than 'in, at' representing a <stationary state> appears more frequently in the work.

Let us turn to several interesting verbal expressions co-occurring with 'through.' First, 'rough and smooth' combines with 'through' rather than with 'over,' as seen in '*through* rough and smooth / We scamper'd homeward' (2, 137-38). Second, when describing the figure of a shepherd, he catches him 'stalking *through* the fog' (8, 401), not stalking 'in' the fog. Third, '*Through* Paris' (9, 40) is preferred to 'in Paris.' Fourth, 'under all conditions' seems to be normal usage, but when it comes to Wordsworth's hand, it becomes: 'Nature *through* all conditions hath a power / To consecrate' (12, 282-83). All these examples of the use of 'through' emphasize his habit of wandering about.

The next quotation is the most famous passage in *The Prelude*, where Wordsworth states an interrelation between Man and Nature and the procedure of establishing the theory of Imagination peculiar to the poet himself. 'Through' in this case is stylistically 'marked,' because it has a relative pronoun as its object. The total number of instances of 'through' taking a relative pronoun as object is four, and indeed half of these appear in this single passage, which is stylistically quite noteworthy.

```
1   …and from the shore
2   At distance not the third part of a mile
3   Was a blue chasm; a fracture in the vapour,
4   A deep and gloomy breathing-place *through* which
5   Mounted the roar of waters, torrents, streams
6   Innumerable, roaring with one voice.
7   The universal spectacle *throughout*
8   Was shaped for admiration and delight,
9   Grand in itself alone, but in that breach
10  *Through* which the homeless voice of waters rose,
11  That dark deep *thorough*fare had Nature lodg'd
12  The Soul, the Imagination of the whole.      (13, 54-65)
```

From this description of the majestic scene, I only tally the word 'through' twice (lines 4 and 10). However, I can even say three times, because 'throughout' is used in line 7 as well, which equals 'all through.' Furthermore, if I add 'thoroughfare' from the eleventh line (which is etymologically composed of 'through' and 'fare'), I get a total number of four. It is quite surprising that 'through' and its related words appear as many as four times in only twelve lines. In a word, 'through' functions as a medium that connects the poet's inner world and the outer world of Nature.

1.5 Summary

Thus far I have observed the vocabulary that constitutes *The Prelude* from four perspectives: nouns, verbs, adjectives, and others (prepositions).

Close observation of the poet's use of nouns reveals that his use of hypernyms such as 'thing(s)' and 'object(s)' is conspicuous and that his abstract nouns tend to take on a concrete quality, and his concrete nouns, on the contrary, an abstract one.

Concerning the verb class, verbs of perception and cognition are used abundantly, and the pattern 'saw → heard → felt' is often observed throughout *The Prelude*.

The consideration of the adjective class shows that the poet uses identical adjectives for describing both nature and the human mind. He also uses adjectives with heavy and serious meanings such as 'great,' 'high,' 'strong,' and 'sublime' rather than those with light and frivolous meanings.

From the last word class, I singled out the preposition 'through,' for it reveals an unusually marked difference in frequency count, compared with the general trend of 'through' observed in several other corpora available.

From these four perspectives, I have investigated in what mutual relationship the poet's inner world and the outer world of Nature are retained. The greatness of Nature enhances human beings to a higher and mightier existence 'through' its lofty and mighty forms. The mind of Wordsworth grew even greater and mightier 'through' those mighty forms.

Chapter 2
Words Combined with 'Weight' in *The Prelude*

2.0 Introduction
The foregoing chapter took a bird's-eye view of the vocabulary of *The Prelude* from four perspectives: nouns, verbs, adjectives, and others. In this chapter, I will focus on one particular word, 'weight' from the noun class and demonstrate how one of Wordsworth's uses of 'weight' deviates from the norm of the English language.

Before we look at the poet's deviational usage of 'weight,' let us turn our attention to the non-deviational, conventional use of 'weight.' The following passage appears in Wordsworth's Poem "Tintern Abbey"

```
                    that blessed mood,
    In which the burthen of the mystery,              A   of   B
    In which the heavy and the weary weight                A'
    Of all this unintelligible world,                   Of   B'
    Is lightened:            (T. A. 37-41)
```

The A of B structure, 'the burthen of the mystery' in line 2, is repeated appositionally and amplified to the A' of B' structure, 'the heavy and the weary weight / Of all this unintelligible world' in lines 3-4. Wordsworth regards the shackles of this world as a 'weight.' This is certainly one of the most famous passages in English literature, and *The Oxford Dictionary of Quotations* gives it as the first of eight instances for the item 'weight.' *Collins Dictionary of Quotations*, too, quotes this passage for one of its six citations.

Let us attempt to appreciate a little bit of Wordsworth's linguistic artistry in this passage. First, 'mystery' and 'burthen' are, as it were, forcibly connected, which enables us to get a glimpse into the working of the poet's imagination. He begins the grammatical subject of the relative clause, 'In which ~' with 'the burthen of mystery' (A of B). He appears to have felt some confusing hesitation about the boldness of A's connection with B and the obscure meaning of the phraseology, so he resumes his expression by replacing 'burthen' (A) with 'weight' (A'), which is much easier to understand. At the same time, by adding two adjectives, he expands 'burthen' (A) to 'the heavy and weary weight' (A'), thus emphasizing the two aspects of meaning of the burthen: intrinsic <heaviness> and connotative <weariness>. He also

31

expands 'mystery' (B) into 'all this un·in·tel·li·gi·ble world' (B') by adding a long polysyllabic adjective, thus turning the abstract meaning of 'mystery' into the concrete yet inscrutable meaning of 'this world.'

Let us turn to the phonetic aspect of the phrase, A' of B'. What is striking at first is the alliteration of the 'w' sound in 'weary,' 'weight,' and 'world.' Then, we should notice that the simple vowels /i/, /e/, and /ə/ appear frequently. With these keynote vowels and the alliterative consonant as an undercurrent, the diphthongs /iə/ in 'weary' and /ei/ in 'weight' sound conspicuous. The poet's use of these three words and this sequence of two diphthongs serves to reinforce the meaning of <heaviness> and <weariness> in the lines.

Meanwhile, the diphthong /ai/ in 'lightened' appears just once in the passage and the /a/ sound, first element of the /ai/, is an 'open front unrounded vowel' (Wells 2000). It is the least interrupted and therefore the most free, open vowel of all vowels. It is also the 'clearest' vowel in the lines discussed. Accordingly, it can be argued that the appearance of the /a/ sound is a 'marked' phonetic phenomenon in terms of phonetic value and occurrence rate.

The /l/ sound in 'lightened' is a 'clear' sound, too. In contrast, the /l/ sound in 'unintelligible' is a 'dark' sound, /ɫ/ by narrow transcription. (The /l/ sound in 'unintelligible' too seems to be relatively 'dark,' compared with that in 'lightened.') The same applies to the /l/ sound in 'all' and 'world.'

The four lines under discussion as a whole signify our burden is "lightened," that is to say, is "made lighter or less heavy" (*OED2*). The meaning of the passage, speaking in the abstract, is that 'things turn for the better and the situation is looking up.' The choice of the word 'lightened' there, thanks to the phonetic value of its clear /l/ sound, is quite appropriate both phonetically and semantically. The word 'lightened' is indeed suitable to describe a situation in which things take a favorable turn.

What essentially expresses the same purport as the above is the next passage from *The Prelude*:

>   (0)   Though doing wrong, and suffering, and full oft
>   Bending beneath <u>our life's mysterious</u> **weight**
>   <u>Of pain and fear</u>; yet still in happiness
>   Not yielding to the happiest upon earth.   (5, 441-44)

Chapter 2 Words Combined with 'Weight' in *The Prelude* 33

Here Wordsworth states one aspect of his image of an ideal child. Here, too, 'weight' is used. The noun form 'mystery' in "Tintern Abbey" has been transformed into the adjective form 'mysterious.'

Incidentally, Shakespeare (1564-1616) has Albany speak on the sad occasion of King Lear's death in similar terms:

The **weight** of this sad time we must obey,
Speak what we feel, not what we ought to say.
(*Lear* 5. 3. 324-25)

Japan's own Tokugawa Ieyasu (1543-1616), originator of the Tokugawa shogunate, is quoted to have said:

A man's life is like a long journey with a heavy **load** on his back.
(Watanabe *et al*: 2003, s.v. *omoni*)

Lakoff and Turner (1989: 25-26, 52) proposed a metaphorical proposition:

LIFE IS A **BURDEN**.

From what I have discussed, the conception that 'the shackles of this world are regarded as *weight*' is true for all ages and in all places. There is general agreement on the notion that carrying on with our work and surviving in our life is a burden that necessarily falls upon human beings. Put simply, the notion that LIFE IS A BURDEN is a universally acknowledged truth.

2.1 Purpose

Now, the purpose of this chapter, as previously stated, is to argue that Wordsworth sometimes uses 'weight' in a deviant way from other writers. Let me explore where and how he uses 'weight' in *The Prelude* (1805) and scrutinize his unique use of 'weight' in *The Prelude*.

There are a total of 14 examples of 'weight' in *The Prelude*, which is far fewer than I expected. For the first step of a working procedure I printed out each 19 lines with a line containing 'weight' in the center (i.e. in the tenth line, below).

For example:

34   Wordsworth's Vocabulary in *The Prelude*

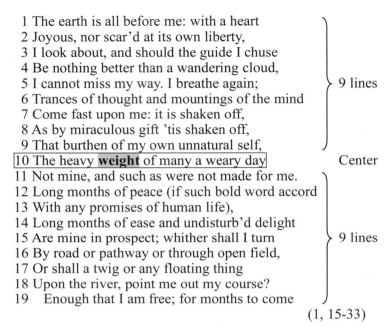

```
 1 The earth is all before me: with a heart
 2 Joyous, nor scar'd at its own liberty,
 3 I look about, and should the guide I chuse
 4 Be nothing better than a wandering cloud,
 5 I cannot miss my way. I breathe again;          9 lines
 6 Trances of thought and mountings of the mind
 7 Come fast upon me: it is shaken off,
 8 As by miraculous gift 'tis shaken off,
 9 That burthen of my own unnatural self,
10 The heavy weight of many a weary day           Center
11 Not mine, and such as were not made for me.
12 Long months of peace (if such bold word accord
13 With any promises of human life),
14 Long months of ease and undisturb'd delight
15 Are mine in prospect; whither shall I turn      9 lines
16 By road or pathway or through open field,
17 Or shall a twig or any floating thing
18 Upon the river, point me out my course?
19    Enough that I am free; for months to come
                                                   (1, 15-33)
```

The reason for such a long citation was to illuminate its meaning in a broad context. I scrutinized the sense in which 'weight' is exploited in the context of each extract and discovered that all of them carry more or less figurative meanings.

2.2 Categorization of the examples of 'weight' in *The Prelude*

Next, I tried to categorize the 14 examples according to various criteria. In so doing, I had difficulty in finding an appropriate criterion. *OED2*'s five larger groupings and twenty-four smaller groupings seemed too complicated, while *Longman Lexicon*'s seven classifications or *Roget's II The New Thesaurus*'s six classifications did not sit well with my purpose. Finally, I decided to divide the 14 instances of 'weight' into three categories in terms of 'value,' that is, according to whether it is valuable to the poet or not:

(A) Negative Value
(B) Positive Value
(C) Neutral Value

Here let us find a synonym suitable for each value. Synonyms corresponding to 'weight' with (A) Negative Value are, as previously

Chapter 2   Words Combined with 'Weight' in *The Prelude*

stated in Section 2.0, 'burden' and 'affliction'; those expressing the meaning of (C) Neutral Value are 'counterpoise,' that is to say, a 'counterbalancing weight' (*OED2*) and 'restraint.' When it comes to choosing synonyms for (B) Positive Value, I am quite at a loss because I cannot find any appropriate synonyms however hard I try. Is there any other way of expressing it than 'weight'? It is rather easy to find synonyms for (A) and (C), but difficult to allocate a proper synonym for (B), which is quite strange to me. Perhaps in everyday English 'weight' does not carry a "positive value," whereas Wordsworth does use this term in referring to such an agreeable and pleasant meaning.

Chart 2.1 displays the semantic and syntactic features of the 14 examples according to the criteria explained above. In other words, it shows how each instance of 'weight' behaves semantically and syntactically in its own context. In making the chart, I followed an example from Carter (1987: 172).

Chart 2.1: 'Weight' and its surroundings

	(A) Negative Value (burden, affliction)	(B) Positive Value (?)	(C) Neutral Value (counterpoise, restraint)	mind	heart	power	joy, delight, pleasure, happiness	appositive	preposition	verb combination
(1)	+			+	+		+	burthen		is shaken off
(2)		+		+			+		by	
(3)		+		+	+				with	
(4)			+							hang on days
(5)	+			+				woes		
(6)	+			+		+	+		beneath	
(7)	+							some personal concerns		
(8)	+			+	+				against	
(9)		+		+	+					descend / Up-on my heart
(10)		+				+				
(11)		+				+			with	
(12)	+						+		like	
(13)	+			+			+		of	
(14)	+			+					under	

(1) The heavy **weight** of many a weary day (1, 24 (A))
(2) by its own **weight** (1, 625 (B))   <ACCOMPANIMENT>
(3) Even with a **weight** of pleasure (2, 178 (B))   <COOPERATIVENESS>
(4) A **weight** (3, 419 (C))
(5) that **weight** (5, 6 (A))
(6) Beneath our life's mysterious **weight** / Of pain and fear (5, 442-43 (A))
(7) no heavy **weight** (6, 36 (A))
(8) Against the **weight** of meanness, selfish caress, / Coarse manners, vulgar passions (8, 454-55 (A))
(9) A **weight** of Ages (8, 703 (B))
(10) no ~ but **weight** of power (8, 705 (B))
(11) Power growing with the **weight** (8, 706 (B))
(12) there lay it like a **weight** (10, 252 (A))
(13) aught of heavier or more deadly **weight**, / In trivial occupations, and the round / Of ordinary intercourse (11, 262-64 (A))
(14) under all the **weight** / Of that injustice (12, 102-03 (A))

2.2.1 How to read the chart

Let me explain how to look at the Chart 2.1. Bracketed figures in the leftmost side of the chart correspond to the phrases quoted just below the chart itself. The sequence follows the order of occurrence of 'weight' in *The Prelude* (1805 version), which is comprised of 13 books. There are fourteen 'weight' phrases in total. Roughly speaking, one example of 'weight' appears in each book.

The next group of three columns indicates, in terms of semantics, or rather synonyms, whether each example is valuable or not. Or, to put it another way, whether each example is favourable to the poet or not.

The following group of four shaded columns represents, in terms of syntax, how each 'weight' co-occurs with 'mind,' 'heart,' 'power,' and 'joy, delight, pleasure, and happiness' in its own context covering the 19 lines. These lexical items are all key words for understanding Wordsworth's poetry. The first and second lexes, 'mind' and 'heart' are recipients that feel diverse emotions caused by surrounding objects. The third, 'power' is one of Wordsworth's favorite words (Havens 472), and the poet uses it (including its plural form 'powers') 99 times in *The Prelude*. This frequency count corresponds to 83rd in *The Prelude* rank list (Table 1.9). The fourth column displays 'joy,' 'delight,' 'pleasure,' and 'happiness.' These four words are examples of what Josephine Miles (1942, rpt. 1965) calls the "vocabulary of

Chapter 2 Words Combined with 'Weight' in *The Prelude*   37

emotion." Such emotions must be intense and <u>powerful</u> when they first arise in the poet's mind and heart. In his Preface to the *Lyrical Ballads*, Wordsworth defines poetry as follows: 'Poetry is the spontaneous overflow of <u>powerful</u> feelings: it takes its origin from emotion recollected in tranquility.' That is why words denoting 'emotion' coexist with those signifying 'power.'

In the following three columns of the chart, in terms of syntax as well, we find: first, with what appositional lexical item each 'weight' occurs; second, with what preposition (also shaded) each 'weight' co-occurs; and third and last, with what verb each 'weight' combines. Let us pay special attention to the prepositions listed in the right-hand shaded column. They are prepositions which stand before 'weight.' I have two points to make: 1) human beings have to endure 'beneath' or 'under' a heavy burden; 2) relations between human beings and such examples of a heavy 'weight' are hostile, which is most noticeably realized by 'against.'

What I want to discuss earnestly here is the prepositions, 'by' and 'with' which are relevant to the (B) Positive Value group. There are five instances in all, of which (2) 'by its [joy's] own **weight**' and (3) 'Even with a **weight** of pleasure' are worthy of special mention. They both describe the inner feelings of Wordsworth, that is to say, the poet's joy and pleasure. One is preceded by the preposition 'by' and the other by 'with,' both of which entail the meaning of <ACCOMPANI- MENT> and <COOPERATIVENESS>. Both meanings are favorable to human beings.

2.2.2 Fourteen Extracts
In order to ascertain whether the semantic classification above is appropriate, let us observe concrete examples. We will examine the three groups in order of occurrence: eight examples of (A) Negative Value, five of (B) Positive Value, and one of (C) Neutral Value.

2.3 Examples of (A) Negative Value (8 instances)
Examples of (A) Negative Value, which are relevant to the idea that 'life is a burden,' are (1), (5), (6), (7), (8), (12), (13), and (14).

(1)   it is shaken off,
    As by miraculous gift 'tis shaken off,
    That burthen of my own unnatural self,
    <u>The heavy **weight** of many a weary day</u>
    Not mine, and such as were not made for me. (1, 21-25)

(5)   ..., it grieves me for thy state, O Man,
Thou paramount Creature! And thy race, while ye
Shall sojourn on this planet; not for woes
Which thou endur'st; that **weight**, albeit huge,
I charm away; but for those palms atchiev'd
Through length of time, by study and hard thought,
The honours of thy high endowments, there
My sadness finds its fuel.   (5, 3-10)

(6)   Though doing wrong, and suffering, and full oft
Beneath our life's mysterious **weight**
Of pain and fear; yet still in happiness
Not yielding to the happiest upon earth.
                              (5, 441-44, the same as (0))

(7)   and [I] should have been
Even such, but for some personal concerns
That hung about me in my own despite
Perpetually, no heavy **weight**, but still
A baffling and a hindrance, a control   (6, 33-37)

(8)   And thus
Was founded a sure safeguard and defence
Against the **weight** of meanness, selfish cares,
Coarse manners, vulgar passions, that beat in
On all sides from the ordinary world
In which we traffic.   (8, 452-57)

(12) Now had I other business for I felt
The ravage of this most unnatural strife
In my own heart; there lay it like a **weight**
At enmity with all the tenderest springs
Of my enjoyments.   (10, 250-54)

(13) There are in our existence spots of time,
Which with distinct pre-eminence retain
A vivifying Virtue, whence, depress'd
By false opinion and contentious thought,
Or aught of heavier or more deadly **weight**,
In trivial occupations, and the round
Of ordinary intercourse, our minds
Are nourished and invisibly repair'd,

Chapter 2   Words Combined with 'Weight' in *The Prelude*   39

>   A virtue by which pleasure is enhanced
>   That penetrates, enables us to mount
>   When high, more high, and lifts us up when fallen.
>   (11, 258-68)

(14)   … how much of *real* worth
>   And genuine knowledge, and true power of mind
>   Did at this day exist in those who liv'd
>   By bodily labour, labour far exceeding
>   Their due proportion, <u>under all the **weight**
>   Of that injustice</u> which upon ourselves
>   By composition of society
>   Ourselves entail. [my italics]   (12, 98-105)

All of the eight examples above show negative vectors in a downward direction. As I mentioned in the introduction to this chapter, the conception that LIFE IS A BURDEN is universal to all mankind for all times and places, so I will not deliberate further about this group.

2.4 Examples of (B) Positive Value (5 instances)

Contrary to the above, I can give examples (2), (3), (9), (10), and (11) as those with (B) Positive Value, which are favorable to human existence. Let us observe the examples:

(2)   ―And if the vulgar joy <u>by its own **weight**</u>
>   Wearied itself out of the memory,
>   The scenes which were a witness of that joy
>   Remained, in their substantial lineaments
>   Depicted on the brain, and to the eye
>   Were visible, a daily sight;   (1, 625-30)

(3)   Oh! then the calm
>   And dead still water [lay] upon my mind
>   <u>Even with a **weight** of pleasure</u>, and the sky
>   Never before so beautiful, [sank] down
>   Into my heart, and [held] me like a dream. (2, 176-80)

(9), (10), (11)
>   The very moment that I seem'd to know
>   The threshold now is overpass'd, Great God!
>   That aught *external* to the living mind
>   Should have such mighty sway! Yet so it was

> <u>A **weight** of Ages</u> did at once descend
> Upon my heart; no thought embodied, no
> Distinct remembrances; but **weight** and power,
> <u>Power growing with the **weight**</u>: alas! I feel
> That I am trifling: [original italics]   (8, 699-707)

First, let us look at the most Wordsworthian (so it seems at least to me) examples in (2) and (3). Unlike the representative example (0) with 'pain' and 'fear' illustrated at the beginning of this chapter, 'weight' here is used together with 'joy' and 'pleasure,' which bears a positive meaning, not a negative one.

2.4.1 How to intensify the degree of 'pleasure'
Next, I will make a special mention of citation (3) above. When one wants to intensify the degree of 'pleasure,' what kind of expression will he or she use? It would seem normal to modify 'pleasure' with an adjective such as 'great,' 'genuine,' 'real' or 'much.' Instead, here, 'weight' is used in the expressive form of '<u>a weight of</u> pleasure.' Wordsworth combines 'weight' with 'pleasure.' His purpose is to heighten the intensity of 'pleasure,' although there seems to be little semantic affinity between 'weight' and 'pleasure.' I cannot help thinking that, hidden in Wordsworth's use of the expression 'weight of pleasure,' there is a strong desire of Wordsworth to be *vertically* connected with the earth, to be a part of Nature.

2.4.2 Finite verbs used in citation (3)
At the same time, I have to point out the meanings of the finite verbs used in this citation: 'Oh! then the calm / And dead still water **lay** upon my mind / … and the sky / Never before so beautiful, **sank** down / Into my heart, and **held** me like a dream.' All these verbs, especially the first two, combine suitably with 'weight.' The verbs 'lie,' 'sink,' and 'hold' perform their functions most properly when they collaborate with 'weight,' in other words, when they are given an added load, that is to say, 'weight.'

2.4.3 'Even' prefixed to '*with*-phrase'
One cannot ignore the fact that 'Even' is prefixed to a *with*-phrase in Book 2 line 178, 'Even with a weight of pleasure.' *Oxford Advanced Learner's Dictionary* refers to 'even' as 'used to emphasize something unexpected or surprising in what one is saying or writing.' When he

wrote this phrase, Wordsworth must have wanted to emphasize the expression (i.e. 'with a weight of pleasure') as something unexpected or surprising. In addition to this, *Collins Dictionary of the English Language* defines 'even' as an 'intensifier; used to suggest that the content of a statement is unexpected or paradoxical (my underline).' There is something paradoxical in the combination of 'weight' and 'pleasure.' 'Weight' is easily associated with <DOWN>, while 'pleasure' is always thought of in connection with <UP> (cf. 'orientational metaphor' in Lakoff and Johnson: 1980; 14-21). There is an obvious contradiction in the combination of these two words. This is an extremely *marked* linguistic phenomenon. This is why Wordsworth must have inserted a word of emphasis 'even,' which will be dealt with in more detail later in §2.6.

2.4.4 Brief mention of citations (9), (10), and (11)

Next, in the examples of (9), (10), and (11) (Section 2.4), I can see a conspicuous convergence of three occurrences of 'weight.' Here, too, 'weight' is charged with a positive meaning which carries favorable implications. Wordsworth is overwhelmed by 'A weight of Ages,' when the poet sets foot in the metropolis of London for the first time in his life. His heart is overpowered by the human lives which have lived assiduously and strenuously there for thousands of years. The poet's urban life in London contributes to awaken his interest in human beings and his esteem for them.

2.5 Example of (C) Neutral Value (1 instance)

Finally, I will give an example of (C) Neutral Value, of which there is only one example:

(4) **A weight** must surely hang on days begun
And ended with worst mockery: be wise,
Ye Presidents and Deans, and to your Bells
Give seasonable rest;   (3, 419-22)

Wordsworth feels outrage over the archaic system of management that has not changed over the years in the University of Cambridge. He does not want to be forced to attend formal morning and evening services which have remained unchanged for a long time. In this case he insists that such an old custom should be abolished by placing on it such a 'weight.'

2.6 Observation

Thus far I have cited fourteen examples of 'weight' that appear in *The Prelude* and divided their meanings into three major categories, and explained them partially.

The first category, (A) Negative Value is the stress that unavoidably accompanies human life. The heavy burden and strong pressure inevitably befalls human beings who come into this world and lead a social life. The perception that LIFE IS A BURDEN is common to people of all ages and countries. This usage of 'weight' with an unfavourable and uncooperative sense accounts for as many as eight out of fourteen examples. Therefore, the first group with negative meaning can be said to be the normal and ordinary usage of 'weight.' That is why little explanation has been made on the (A) usage.

Incidentally, I have put a question mark in the diagonal column of (B) Positive Value on the chart, because I was unable to find a corresponding synonym when I was making the chart. Why? It occurs to me that these word combinations, 'weight' with '*joy*' and '*pleasure*' are notably peculiar to Wordsworth. That must be the very reason why I cannot think of a proper synonym. If combining 'weight' with 'joy' and 'pleasure' is a common practice in English, perhaps I could have hit upon a synonym commonly used with this positive meaning.

In order to examine whether my speculation is right or wrong, I investigated whether the same collocation might be found in the works of other writers. Take Shakespeare (1564-1616), for example, who flourished prior to Wordsworth (1770-1850). According to a concordance of Shakespeare's works, there are nine examples under the item 'weight of ~' in his works. None of these, however, could be considered positive. Tracing further back to Chaucer (1340?-1400), I was not able to find any similar positive combinations in his concordance, either.

Extending the scope of my search, I consulted the *Gutenberg Files*. This file, as of August 1997, contained 550 copies of English books, both verse and prose. Among these books were twentieth century novels, to say nothing of the Bible and Shakespeare. In total, 1281 examples which include 'weight of ~' were found, and out of these there were only four instances of 'weight' being used with 'pleasure' or 'joy.' These concrete examples are:

> the whole **weight** of her dis<u>pleasure</u>, was obvious.
> (Hardy, *The Return of the Native*, 1878)

Chapter 2 Words Combined with 'Weight' in *The Prelude*   43

> the want of an army saved France from the full **weight** of his dis<u>pleasure</u>. (Schiller, *The History of the Thirty Years' War*, 1789?, Translated by Morrison)

> would let Plato feel the **weight** of her dis<u>pleasure</u>.
> (Chesnutt, *The House Behind the Cedars*, 1900)

> bear the **weight** of a secret <u>joy</u> or of a secret sorrow,
> (Defoe, *Moll Flanders*, 1722)

As one can see in the above quotations, 'weight' is combined, however, not with 'pleasure' but with '*dis*pleasure.' When it comes to 'joy,' it is most commonly united with '*secret*,' not with 'genuine.' In either case, 'weight' does not tie well with 'pleasure' or 'joy.' 'Weight' collocates with words of a negative meaning (i.e. 'pleasure' prefixed by <u>dis</u>, and <u>secret</u> 'joy'). What these four examples reveal is that 'weight' is hard to combine directly with either 'pleasure' or 'joy.' In everyday English, 'weight' is semantically in harmony with words carrying negative, passive, and regressive meanings. In short, 'weight' does not go well with 'joy' and 'pleasure.'

Now, let us consider the matter from another viewpoint. To use Lakoff and Johnson's (1980: 14-21) "orientational metaphor" <UP> and <DOWN> again, 'weight' usually goes with 'down.' In Wordsworth's case, however, there is one exception: 'a weight of pleasure.' 'Pleasure' is <up> and 'weight' is <down>. The two words clash in meaning. This idiosyncratic or oxymoronic combination of words would appear to be a uniquely Wordsworthian turn of phrase.

Now, let us turn back to the quotations from Wordsworth discussed in the second section of this chapter: '<u>[M]any a weary</u> day' in citation (1) '<u>pain and fear</u>' in (6), '<u>meanness, selfish cares, / Coarse manners, vulgar passions</u>' which appear quadruply in (8), and '<u>that injustice</u>' in (14). All of these underlined phrases have negative, passive, and regressive meanings. Such words with negative significance are, in almost all cases, easily combined with 'weight' in the way they are actually presented.

Furthermore, in order to investigate words that may fit in the slot of 'weight of ~,' I referred to *Collins COBUILD Wordbanks Online*. I found only one 'weight of <u>joy</u>' combination in all 525 examples of 'weight of ~.' This, from its context, seems to be part of a translation from a Greek version of *Oedipus Rex*. Regardless, the combination of 'weight' with 'pleasure' was nowhere to be found in the 525 examples.

Other evidence to reinforce my argument comes from the *Nineteenth-Century Fiction: Full-Text Database*. It reveals 646 examples of the 'weight of ~' combination, but 'weight of pleasure' could be found nowhere.

On the other hand, Wordsworth uses a combination of 'Even with a weight of pleasure' (2, 178) contrary to the above-mentioned general tendency of popular usage. He, as it were, forcibly and directly unites 'weight' with 'pleasure' without the intervention of 'dis-' and 'secret.' He combines in this way: 'weight of Ø pleasure.' For the so-called poet of Joy, 'pleasure' must not be a 'secret' one but must be a 'true' and 'genuine' one. If I am allowed to supply an epithet to 'pleasure,' I would like to add, among others, 'real' which is actually used by William Wordsworth in citation (14).

It is said that reaching through sufferings to a higher perception is a great step of Wordsworth poetry. It is akin to the theme of Beethoven's music: reaching through affliction to joy. Wordsworth (1770-1850) and Beethoven (1770-1827) have something in common with each other. This world is filled with heavy pressure and distress. The poet captures that aspect of the world in the word 'weight.' He compensates a downward vector component ↓ of 'weight' with an upward vector component ↑ of 'joy.' What is more, he overwhelms such a 'weight' lying heavily on human beings with his feeling of 'pleasure' and 'joy.'

2.7 Summary

It is apparent from the discussion above that Wordsworth is the one and only poet in English literature who boldly connected 'weight' and 'pleasure' with the use of the particle 'of.' He captures the strong feeling of joy not from the direction of <intensity> but from the direction of <weight>. He is the first poet in English literature that realized 'the weight of pleasure' deep down in his heart. Therefore, I can conclude that this oxymoronic word combination 'Even with a weight of pleasure,' which seems to break the selectional restriction between lexical items, is actually an expression peculiar to Wordsworth, poet of nature and joy.

Chapter 3
Verbs of Perception and Cognition in *The Prelude*

3.0 Introduction
In the first chapter, 'Vocabulary that Constitutes *The Prelude*,' I set up what might be called 'an equation (i.e. I ⌐felt¬ X)' to capture Wordsworth's realization of the outer world. In Section 1 of Chapter 1, I examined the nouns used as subjects and objects, and in Section 2 the verbs between the subjects and objects. In this chapter, I present the findings of an investigation concerning what kinds of verbs are mainly used to embody those subject-object relations. First, I chose verbs of perception and those of cognition. Then, I separated the verbs of perception into visual and auditory verbs. In this chapter, I regard 'feel' as a verb of cognition because in *The Prelude* in almost all cases 'feel' turned out to describe a mental activity, not a physical one. Table 3.1, which is a revised version of Table 1.7 where I had grouped 'feel' into verbs of perception, not into verbs of cognition, shows examples of verbs of perception and cognition and their frequency count:

Table 3.1: Verbs of perception and cognition (appearing more than ten times) and their frequency count

Verbs of perception			Verbs of cognition	
see		44	feel	29
sees		10	felt	49
saw		58	seem	24
seen		44	seems	11
seeing	272	10	seem'd	64
look		20	apear'd	19
look'd		30	think	21
looking		10	thought	20
behold		22	know	19
beheld		24	knew	15
			known	22
hear	60	18	find	30
heard		42	found	51
			learn'd	11
Total 272+60	= 332			385

In the first chapter, I stated very simply to the effect that one of the features of verbs appearing in *The Prelude* is that verbs of perception and cognition are large in number. These verbs are correspondent to the entry of 2.3 (i.e. verbs referring to HUMAN ACTIVITY—MIND AND DEED) in the *Word List by Semantic Principles.* I proposed the following sentence structure by using the second most frequent verb of perception, 'felt.'

I | felt | X.

This S(ubject) + P(redicate) + O(bject) structure is the formula employed when Wordsworth perceives all things in the universe. The vertical axis of 'felt' is realized by verbs such as 'see,' 'look,' and 'hear.' The axis of 'X' is realized with anything that stimulates the young poet emotionally and spiritually.

Following the introductory sketch of the verb class, this chapter investigates what Wordsworth saw and heard in the world of *The Prelude*; to put it the other way round, what (things and phenomena) he was attracted to. The question will be addressed by observing verbs of visual and auditory perception and their surroundings. What comes before and after these verbs syntactically? What objects do they take lexically and what adverbial expressions co-occur with them?

3.1 Verbs appearing more than ten times in *The Prelude*

Before going into a detailed study of verbs of visual and auditory perceptions, let us look at Table 3.2 below and get a glimpse of all the verbs that appear more than ten times in *The Prelude*:

Chapter 3 Verbs of Perception and Cognition in *The Prelude* 47

Table 3.2: Verb list in *The Prelude* (more than 10 frequency)

1	was	593	*30*	took	31	*61*	put	19	*89*	didst	12
2	had	348	*32*	find	30	*61*	spread	19	*89*	held	12
3	is	318	*32*	look'd	30	*62*	comes	18	*89*	hung	12
4	have	248	*32*	went	30	*62*	hear	18	*89*	return	12
5	be	236	*35*	feel	29	*62*	return'd	18	*95*	fell	11
6	were	200	*35*	take	29	*62*	wrought	18	*95*	gives	11
7	been	162	*37*	gone	28	*67*	began	17	*95*	laid	11
8	did	152	*38*	let	27	*67*	pleas'd	17	*95*	learn'd	11
9	are	126	*39*	rose	25	*67*	stand	17	*95*	makes	11
10	hath	79	*39*	live	25	*70*	gave	16	*95*	mean	11
11	left	64	*39*	brought	25	*70*	lost	16	*95*	met	11
11	seem'd	64	*39*	love	25	*70*	turn'd	16	*95*	move	11
13	made	62	*39*	lov'd	25	*73*	add	15	*95*	rear'd	11
14	saw	58	*40*	beheld	24	*73*	am	15	*95*	seems	11
15	found	51	*40*	sate	24	*73*	knew	15	*95*	stirr'd	11
16	come	50	*40*	say	24	*73*	liv'd	15	*106*	become	10
17	felt	49	*40*	seem	24	*73*	pass	15	*106*	born	10
18	see	44	*41*	doth	23	*73*	turn	15	*106*	being	10
18	seen	44	*41*	led	23	*79*	bring	14	*106*	does	10
20	came	42	*41*	read	23	*79*	done	14	*106*	fill'd	10
20	heard	42	*51*	behold	22	*79*	has	14	*106*	hast	10
22	make	41	*51*	call'd	22	*79*	mov'd	14	*106*	looking	10
23	having	40	*51*	known	22	*83*	art	13	*106*	seeing	10
24	pass'd	39	*54*	set	21	*83*	lie	13	*106*	sees	10
25	speak	38	*54*	think	21	*83*	sent	13	*106*	sit	10
26	lay	35	*54*	told	21	*83*	sought	13	*106*	taught	10
26	stood	35	*57*	look	20	*83*	tell	13	*106*	wanting	10
28	given	34	*57*	thought	20	*83*	touch'd	13			
29	give	33	*59*	appear'd	19	*89*	breathe	12	**117**	*in Total*	
30	said	31	*60*	know	19	*89*	call	12			

Notes:
(1) 'was' includes ''twas' (36).
(2) 'is' includes ''tis' (26).
(3) When verb form and auxiliary form are identical as in 'was, had, is', the auxiliary forms are excluded.
(4) In case of words ending with '~ing' as in 'being,' the number of nouns is excluded.
(5) When verb form (present tense) and noun form are identical as in 'look' and 'love,' the number of nouns is excluded.
(6) When verb forms (past and past participle) and noun forms are identical as in 'thought,' the number of nouns is excluded.
(7) When verb form and adjective form are identical as in 'live,' the number of adjectives is excluded.

3.2 Verbs of visual perception

There are 117 kinds of verbs in total which appear more than ten times in *The Prelude*. In the list above, there are 10 verbs, marked by shaded boxes, which represent 272 verbs (in total) of visual perception. (For future reference, I added bordering (☐) to verbs of auditory perception, 'hear' and 'heard,' and underlining (___) to verbs of cognition, 'feel' and 'felt,' respectively). In addition to these verbs of visual perception, for the present investigation, I also deal with the next 59 verbs whose occurrence is less than ten times, which is shown in Table 3.3:

Table 3.3: Verbs of visual perception (331 verbs in total (=272+59))

see	44	look	20	behold	22	watch	6	view	4
seest	1	looketh	1						
sees	10	looks	8	beholds	3				
saw	58	look'd	30	beheld	24	watch'd	9	view'd	2
seen	44	looked	5						
seeing	10	looking	10	beholding	2	watching	2		
subtotal	167		74		51		17		6
gaze	1			glance	1	stare	1		
		observes	1						
gazed	1			glanced	3				
gaz'd	2	observ'd	3			star'd	1	peep'd	1
								peeping	1
subtotal	4		4		4		2		2

As a working procedure I printed out eleven lines containing each verb of visual perception in the center (i.e. in the sixth line). (See a similar example shown in §2.1.) I investigated a total of 331 verbs of visual perception in their own immediate contexts.

I placed some restrictions in order to make the inquiry easier. One of the restraints was on the scope of my investigation. My research covered the verbs of visual perception with 'I, we, the poet's mind, and his eye' as subject. In other words, I investigated only the examples with Wordsworth functioning as a grammatical subject since I believed that it would be sufficient to capture what the poet himself is interested in and what his object of visual cognition is.

Next, I examined each verb in its context by making use of Spitzer's (1967: 25) method of "philological circle." In so doing, I found that the semantic content of each eleven-lined passage was sometimes obscure and not easily understood. It is because the average number of lines in a paragraph in *The Prelude* is 36 and the average number of words is 262. In this long blank verse, Wordsworth is loquacious. He tries to describe or portray one thing after another in rapid succession, using appositional expressions. This use of appositives will be fully discussed in the last chapter.

3.3 Objects of verbs of visual perception

Next, in order to grasp what the poet saw, it is convenient to see what comes syntactically as the objects of verbs of visual perception. Thus I extract those objects, specifically their head words, and examine what types of nouns appear and what distribution they have. Here again, I imposed some restrictions for the work to go smoothly:

(1) I do not mention the distinction between their appearance in the main clause or subordinate clause;
(2) I do not mention the tense nor voice in which the object appears;
(3) I cite the object of the relative pronoun;
(4) I cite the object of the infinitive;
(5) I cite all elements of objects in appositional arrangement, that is to say, I cite not only A1 but also A2, A3,...;
(6) when an object appears in pronominal form, I cite it and show it in parentheses (e.g. her (=dame)) on the chart;
(7) 'behold' is often used as an interjection of attention, but when it is followed by an object, I count it in the list, because the poet himself beholds the object; and
(8) finally, in a passive voice construction where the agent Wordsworth is expressed explicitly or implicitly, the subject is cited as the object because the poet saw it.

Chart 3.1 is the result of my observation. It is based on the framework of *Kadokawa's New Dictionary of Synonyms* (1981), which divides the entire Japanese vocabulary into three broad categories:

        NATURE which surrounds us
        HUMAN AFFAIRS in which we live
        CULTURE which we produce

These three categories are further divided into 100 subcategories, beginning with (upper left) item 00 ASTRONOMY and ending with (lower right) 99 MACHINERY.

Chart 3.1: Objects of verbs of visual perception

		00 ASTRONOMY	01 CALENDAR	02 WEATHER	03 TOPOGRAPHY	04 SCENERY
NATURE	NATURE	sun 13.4 stars 4.235 moon 4.79 him (=sun) 2.188 her (=moon) 2.198 — 4.81	spring 11.24 summers 1.311 years 5.575		fields 1.83 — 13.152 pool 11.304 earth 5.538 — 9.523 mountain 2.190 vale 6.448 brook 10.911 summit 6.453 cavern 7.485 himself 4.41 (=child, brook) 4.46 him (=child, brook)	sight 8.551 — 8.83 sights 5.476 — 7.248 — 10.49 spectacle 1.418 — 8.581 — 10.487 spectacles 7.245 prospect 13.379 grove 3.442 pomp 4.331 — 9.527 shows 4.265 grave 5.422 scene 6.628 — 7.139
		10 POSITION	11 FORM	12 QUANTITY	13 SUBSTANCE	14 STIMULUS
	PROPERTY	something 9.70 — 11.331	form 3.124 shape 4.402 — 7.620 patch 8.562 line 12.148 appearance 7.102 appearances 6.106 — 8.428	parts 7.711 all 2.296 — 3.128 — 10.517 — 13.255 — 13.219 much 1.266 nothing 13.21 nought 1.91		visions 6.105
CHANGE		20 SHAKING	21 MOVEMENT	22 MEETING/PARTING	23 APPEARING	24 TRANSFORMATION
HUMAN AFFAIRS	BEHAVIOUR	30 ACTION	31 TRAFFIC	32 EXPRESSION	33 OBSERVATION glimpse 8.347	34 STATEMENT
	AFFECTION	40 SENSE sense 9.394	41 THOUGHT plans 12.75 spirit 8.828 discretion 7.335 opinions 7.336	42 LEARNING	43 INTENTION continence 9.394	44 DEMAND power 9.528
	PERSON	50 PERSON	51 AGE maiden 7.328 babe 7.381 woman 7.418 man 4.408 — 8.451 — 8.844 — 12.86 girl 11.306 youths 3.221 boy 7.395 dame 4.208 her (=dame) 4.209 — 4.218 her (=maiden) 7.335 him (=man) 8.852 him (=boy) 7.395	52 RELATIVES mother 13.155 pair 7.374 — 13.154 bachelor 7.546	53 FRIENDS creatures 10.295 the people 9.531 Italian 7.229 Jew 7.231 Turk 7.231 strangers 9.280 men 9.281 — 12.321 Briton 12.322 him 3.288 (=our blind poet) 6.246 thee (=Coleridge)	54 SOCIAL STATUS Book 8: Retrospect – Love of Nature Leading to Love of Mankind –
	DISPOSITION	60 PHYSIQUE body 7.102	61 COUNTENANCE face 7.217 — 7.621 — 9.223 — 13.296 faces 4.84 eyes 7.621	62 FIGURE figure 4.468	63 GESTURE	64 ATTITUDE modesty 7.336
CULTURE	SOCIETY	70 REGION sanctuary 3.440 domain 3.449 haunt 3.450 tract 8.325 village 4.450 spots 9.501 world 9.24 recess 6.448 place 7.74	71 GROUP congregation 3.222 troops 7.246	72 FACILITIES habitation 3.448 dwelling 4.30 abodes 6.445	73 RULE	74 TRANSACTION
	Art & Science	80 SCHOLARSHIP work 7.652	81 LOGIC confirmation 9.389	82 SIGNAL	83 LANGUAGE	84 DOCUMENT
	GOODS	90 COMMODITIES	91 MEDICINE	92 FOOD	93 CLOTHING garments 5.461	94 BUILDING house 1.83 chapel 3.4 church 4.13 spire 6.418 beacon 11.305 antechapel 3.58 village church 5.424 towers 2.117
			no interest in vulgar and 'superficial things' (11, 159) 'unassuming things' (12,51)			

Chapter 3   Verbs of Perception and Cognition in *The Prelude*   51

(Numbers: Book.Line)

05 FLORA	06 FAUNA	07 PHYSIOLOGY	08 MATERIAL	09 PHENOMENON
fruit 3.124 — 3.530 turf 10.503 trees 2.117	glow-worm 7.39 dog 10.935 lamb 13.154 hen 5.246 cattle 8.19 sheep 8.19 birds 7.246 beasts 7.246 'general' or 'superordinate' words	life 2.430	rock 3.124 — 8.566 stones 3.125 things 3.151 — 3.110 — 6.694 — 6.694 — 7.513 — 7.513 — 10.37 — 12.51 — 10.872 — 12.354 metal 10.666 object 12.379 them (=things) 10.736	light 2.186 — 6.318 taper 7.41 lustre 8.571

15 TIME	16 STATE	17 VALUE	18 TYPE	19 DEGREE
past 12.320	solemnity 3.455 frailties 10.821 shades 3.158	truths 12.59 depth 12.166	samples 7.311	little 3.654 — 4.150 — 8.427 — 12.47 — 13.15 enough 8.214

25 CHANGE IN QUALITY	26 FLUCTUATION	27 SITUATION	28 PROGRESS	29 RELEVANCE
			tempests 10.422	

35 BED & BOARD	36 WORK SERVICE	37 GIVE & RECEIVE	38 OPERATION	39 PRODUCTION
			props 7.492	produce 8.208

45 INDUCEMENT	46 STRIFE	47 HONOUR & DISGRACE	48 LOVE & HATE	49 JOY & SORROW
	resistance 10.594 sea-fight 7.313		love 9.393	blessings 2.414 passions 3.513 those (=passions) 3.535

55 SOCIAL FUNCTION	56 MANUFACTURE	57 SERVICE SECTOR	58 PEOPLE	59 GODS
	woodman 4.206 shepherd 4.207 — 8.105 him (=shepherd) 8.391 — 8.400	singers 7.293 rope-dancers 7.293 giants 7.293 dwarfs 7.293 clowns 7.294 conjurors 7.294 posture-masters 7.294 harlequins 7.294 knights 9.456 teachers 12.349 nature 7.297	bedlamites 12.158 vagrants 12.159	monsters 10.36

The Bartholomew Fair
Book 7: Residence in London

65 BEHAVIOUR	66 CHARACTER	67 ABILITY	68 CIRCUMSTANCES	69 MENTAL STATE
retiredness 7.337	patience 7.337	faculties 9.245	things 7.313 incident 7.314	

75 NEWS	76 MANNERS & CUSTOMS	77 CONDUCT	78 SOCIAL LIFE	79 MORALITY
	ways 8.205 manners 8.206 institutes 9.526			self-sacrifice 9.393 virtues 9.392 — 10.579

85 LITERATURE	86 ART	87 MUSIC	88 ENTERTAINMENT	89 AMUSEMENT
chronicle 9.100			dances 6.381 — 6.382 dramas 7.312	

95 FURNITURE	96 STATIONERY	97 LANDMARK	98 TOOLS	99 MACHINERY
	her (=kite) 1.523	garland 3.226 marks 7.566		vessels 10.294 them (=vessels, creatures) 10.296

Let us look at what can be extracted from Chart 3.1. First, the NATURE category reveals that 03 TOPOGRAPHY, 04 SCENERY and 08 MATERIAL are large in number, the columns of which are marked by shading. Looking at these words comprising TOPOGRAPHY, SCENERY and MATERIAL, I can say that 'general' or 'superordinate' words, or 'hypernyms' (to be specific, 'things') are particularly noticeable.

Second, Wordsworth's abundant use of words constituting 11 FORM shows that he is attracted to the out**line**s of things, and furthermore, to those solid and grave out**line**s. Incidentally, bearing this in mind, Pottle's (1950, 1985: 19) comment is sharp and interesting:

> You will know that you are dealing with imagination when the edges of things begin to waver and fade out.

In other words, it is the very moment when the outlines of things begin to disappear that your imagination begins to work.

Wordsworth's handling of 'the edges or outlines of things,' in this connection, reminds me of Miyagawa's (2007: 128) opinion. He points out that Wordsworth uses the word 'something' rather frequently. Miyagawa's understanding of the poet's use of 'something' is as follows: 'it is a thing which he believes the poet eventually tracked down from his association with Nature, and which he is able to really feel but unable to fix in particular words. "Something" is the word which Wordsworth has to rely on at the moment of expressing *signifié* without *signifiant*' (my translation from his original Japanese).

Third, I can say Wordsworth is a poet who abstracted inner recesses or depths of things from the surface of individual things. He was able to recognize *motion* in seemingly static things, *unity* in miscellany, *universal* in the common, and the *invisible* in the visible. Let us pay attention to 'shades' in 16 STATE and 'depth' in 17 VALUE:

> (1)   I had an eye
> Which in my stronger workings, evermore
> Was looking for the *shades* of difference
> As they lie hid in an exterior forms,
> Near or remote, minute or vast, ...   (3, 156-60)
>
> (2) There [I] saw into the depth of human souls,
> Souls that appear to have no *depth* at all
> To vulgar eyes.   (12, 166-68)

Chapter 3   Verbs of Perception and Cognition in *The Prelude*   53

Both passages clearly show that Wordsworth's eyes have an ability to see through things whose depth cannot possibly reach ordinary eyes.

Let us next move to the HUMAN AFFAIRS category. One characteristic here is that words pertaining to human beings are abundantly exploited. As the title of Book 8 of *The Prelude*, 'Retrospect—Love of Nature Leading to Love of Mankind' suggests, the object of the poet's observation covers not only Nature but also Man. He chooses to describe 'plain-living People' (4, 204) who live freely among mountains. He does not like to portray eccentric and gorgeous people nor men of imposing appearance. As is seen in the following citation, it is a shepherd who first arouses Wordsworth's admiration for human beings:

(3)   one Evening I beheld,
    And at as early age (the spectacle
    Is *common*, but by me was then first seen)
    A Shepherd in the bottom of a Vale   (8, 102-05)

And he feels a certain deity in the shepherd:

(4) Have I beheld him, without knowing why
    Have felt his presence in his own domain,
    As of a *Lord and Master*; or a *Power*
    Or *Genius*, under Nature, under God,
    Presiding;   (8, 391-95)

In addition, the poet chooses to talk about vulnerable or marginalized people, such as elderly men, ladies, infants, and babies, as seen in 51 AGE. Prior to writing Book 7, 'Residence in London,' Wordsworth saw a variety of curious performers and entertainers at the Bartholomew Fair. He vividly described these people in Book 7; hence column 57 SERVICE SECTOR abounds with various lexical items.

Let us now proceed to the CULTURE category. What is striking in this category is that I find no artificial or vulgar things. Take, for example, the lexical items in 70 REGION. All of them are the settings of activities of ordinary people who live ordinary lives. 94 BUILDING includes 'churches' and 'chapels' which are not vulgar at all, either. They are sacred. Wordsworth shows no interest in vulgar and 'superficial things' (11, 159). Let us remember that the poet sheds tears at the sight of 'the meanest flower that blows' ("Immortality Ode," 203). To generalize, he is a poet who sets a high value on 'unassuming things' (12, 51).

Thus far, I have explored the objects of the poet's steady gaze and observation by looking at all the objects of his verbs of visual perception. Consequently, I can say Wordsworth is a poet who was able to recognize:

something visible	in	hidden and invisible things
depth		something that appears to have no depth at all
uniqueness		a common spectacle
deity		an ordinary shepherd

Not to change the subject, but, when one divides and classifies something on a plane, the result inevitably tends to be static, as if pushed, by force, into the columns, or pigeonholes of a chart. There are, however, dynamic aspects I have found during the exploration, which will be discussed in the following sections.

3.4 Adverbial modifiers around verbs of visual perception

The following sub-sections supplement the previous part, where the verbs of visual perception and their objects were closely examined for the purpose of discovering what Wordsworth saw and consequently what he was attracted to. In other words, §3.3 focused attention on the 'Predicate + Object' structure. In this section, §3.4, I will examine: (1) the poet's persistent attitude toward objects; and (2) the poet's emotional state while seeing them. Furthermore, I will investigate the linguistic phenomenon concerning visual verbs which Wordsworth abundantly uses.

3.4.1 The poet's persistent attitude toward objects

When Wordsworth sees something around him, with what intensity does he see it? Here I would like to recognize the persistent power accompanying his perceptual process of 'seeing.' He, however, does not necessarily see objects with the same intensity or power in all the passages where verbs of perception appear. The following three examples are relatively simple:

(5) It is not wholly so to him who looks
     In steadiness,   (7, 709-10)

(6)   now all eye
     And now all ear;   (11, 143-44)

Chapter 3   Verbs of Perception and Cognition in *The Prelude*   55

(7)   I watch'd,
            Straining my eyes intensely,   (11, 361-62)

The next example is arguably the most highly persistent and tenacious passage in *The Prelude*. The passage is from Book 3 'Residence in Cambridge,' which abounds with as many as fourteen verbs (nine finite verbs and five non-finite verbs, indicated by an underline and a bordering line respectively).

(8)   As if awaken'd, summon'd, rous'd, constrain'd,
      I look'd for universal things; perused   110
      The common countenance of earth and heaven;   111
      And, turning the mind in upon itself,   112
      Pored, watch'd, expected, listen'd; spread my thoughts 113
      And spread them with a wider creeping; felt   114
      Incumbences more awful, visitings
      Of the Upholder of the tranquil Soul,   (3, 109-16)

This is the passage where Wordsworth feels his own strength more clearly than before. Leaving the natural setting of his birthplace, he now encounters Nature for the first time in a long time. As many as nine finite verbs are used in only five lines (between lines 110-14) and the way the poet fixes his eyes upon earth and heaven is expressed persistently. The insatiable spirit of inquiry working and moving in the poet's mind when he endeavors to internalize the impressions from the outer world can be seen in the structure of equivalence consisting of these nine finite verbs.

The four "past participles" appearing successively in the first line express the energy with which Nature awakens the poet's mind which has been inactive. A participial clause followed by 'turning' at the fourth line describes the poet's vigilant attention to his inner self. Moreover, three nouns in the last three lines (i.e. 'creeping,' 'visitings,' and 'Upholder') are full of verbal characteristics. It is interesting to note the poet himself declares elsewhere 'let me dare to speak / A higher language' (3, 106-07) by using so-called metalanguage.

The passage above which is conspicuous for multitude of verbs reminds me of the passage of Mount Snowdon in the last book of *The Prelude*, where the poet builds up his unique theory of imagination. It is no exaggeration to say that the Snowdon passage shows every aspect of his way of expression. Although it is rather difficult to understand what Wordsworth tries to convey because of the content's high abstractness, let me analyze the passage linguistically:

(9) above all
One function of such mind had Nature there　　74
Exhibited by <u>putting forth</u>, and that　　　　　75
With circumstance most awful and sublime,　 76
That domination which she oftentimes　　　　77
Exerts upon the outward face of things,　　　　78
So <u>moulds</u> them, and <u>endues</u>, <u>abstracts</u>, <u>combines</u>, 79
Or by abrupt and unhabitual influence
Doth make one object so <u>impress</u> itself
Upon all others, and <u>pervade</u> them so
That even the grossest minds must see and hear
And cannot chuse but feel.　　　　(13, 73-84)

Looking down from the moonlit summit of Mount Snowdon, the poet sees a sea of clouds. In that majestic scene there is a fracture, from which he finds a homeless voice ascending. The last word 'there' at line 74 in the citation refers to the scene with '[56]a blue chasm' as its focal point of description. After the grand and magnificent scene disappears completely, the poet sinks into deep meditation. He then recollects what he saw with his inner eyes.

What Nature particularly presents to the poet is one 'function' of a poetic mind, imagination. The way Nature uses her dominant power when presenting is so strong and powerful that it is minutely and analytically described in line 75, with the use of the 'by putting forth …'-phrase and what follows. Wordsworth describes, under the 'most awful and sublime' circumstances, how Nature exercises 'domination' on 'the outward face of things,' by exploiting a phrase with a meaning of special emphasis, i.e. 'and that' (l. 75), which has a similar function to 'above all' (l. 73). She 'exerts' that domination upon the outward face of things. She 'moulds' the outward face of things, 'endues' them, 'abstracts' them, and 'combines' them, or she, 'by abrupt and unhabitual influence,' 'makes' one object 'impress' itself on all others, and 'pervade' them. Therefore, any observer of the magnificent scene *cannot help but see, hear and feel.*

In the above example, Wordsworth describes the dynamic way of presentation and the tremendous energy when Nature causes a spectacular natural phenomenon to manifest itself. To put it another way, the situation of a voice ascending through a fracture in a sea of mist is analytically verbalized by using a series of verbs of high "transitivity." In this connection, Ward's (1984: 93) remark is noteworthy:

Chapter 3   Verbs of Perception and Cognition in *The Prelude*   57

the passage's syntax gives the words not so much meaning as energy, an energy which however yields even stronger charges of meaning.

Just after the passage, Wordsworth states that the very scene is a perfect image of a mighty Mind, and that the process by which Nature causes a voice to rise through a fracture in a sea of mist is exactly the same as that by which the imagination is aroused in a poetic mind. What is more, he recognizes that Nature's creative power producing an admirable, grand natural phenomenon is one and the same with the poetic imagination working within a great poet's mind. To put it simply, he identifies Nature's creative power with the poetic imagination.

In order to make the poet's powers of expression match Nature's tremendous influence on him, it must be inevitably necessary for Wordsworth to use one verb after another in rapid succession.

3.4.2 The poet's emotional state while seeing

In most cases Wordsworth sees objects with feelings of joy. The very beginning of *The Prelude* starts with a joyous feeling. Feeling a breeze on his cheek, he looks around 'with a heart / Joyous' (1, 15-16). Furthermore, in Book 2, we encounter the following lines: 'I ... / Saw blessings spread around me like a sea' (2, 414-15), and 'with bliss ineffable / I felt the sentiment of Being spread / O'er all ....' (2, 419-21). These are followed by the next passage:

> (10)   Wonder not
>   If such my transports were; for in all things
>   I saw one life, and felt that it was joy.   (2, 428-30)

As mentioned above, it is a shepherd that causes Wordsworth to first recognize his love for mankind. The emotion with which he saw the shepherd is 'with those motions of delight' (8, 80), 'with what joy and love!' (8, 83), and 'With delight / As bland almost' (8, 101-02).

Wordsworth sympathized with the ideals of the French Revolution. He and his charismatic friend, Michel Beaupuy (1755-96) saw, in the French people who rose to action, an indomitable resolution to make a new nation:

> (11)   elate we look'd
>   Upon their virtues, saw in rudest men
>   Self-sacrifice the firmest, generous love
>   And continence of mind, and sense of right
>   Uppermost in the midst of fiercest strife.   (9, 391-95)

Similar examples:

(12)   Oh! What <u>joy</u> it were
To <mark>see</mark> a Sanctuary for our Country's Youth,   (3, 439-40)

(13) Great <u>joy</u> was mine to <mark>see</mark> thee once again,   (4, 29)

(14) Among the faces which it <u>pleas'd</u> me well
To <mark>see</mark> again, was one,   (4, 84-85)

(15) I <mark>looked upon</mark> the real scene,
Familiarly perus'd it day by day
With keen and lively <u>pleasure</u>   (7, 139-41)

All these examples show that *The Prelude* is full of the emotions of joy and pleasure. As for the vocabulary pertaining to 'joy' and 'pleasure' appearing more than ten times throughout *The Prelude* (see Table 1.6 in Chapter 1). Wordsworth is indeed a poet of joy.

3.5 Modifiers of 'eye' and 'eyes'

So far I have observed the depth with which the poet faces objects and the emotion with which he watches things. In this section, I would like to explore with what eyes he looks at objects by investigating the modifiers of 'eye' and 'eyes':

(16)   a <u>watchful</u> eye,
Which with the outside of our human life
Not satisfied, must read the inner mind: (8, 66-68)

(17) Again I look the <u>intellectual</u> eye
For my instructor, studious more to see
Great Truths, than touch and handle little ones. (12, 57-59)

(18)   I had an eye
<u>Which in my strongest workings, evermore
Was looking for the shades of difference
As they lie hid in all exterior forms,</u>   (3, 156-59)

In (16) the poet states his gratitude for what he owes to Nature even while in the great city of London. He says that without being satisfied with the outward face of human life he is gifted with an eye which penetrates the inner mind. Citation (17) tells how he comes to regard the 'intellectual' eye as his teacher in proportion as 'the horizon of his mind' (12, 56) broadens. Example (18) is not an example with an adjective but instead with a relative clause. From (18) I can see the poet has an eye to detect a subtle difference on the invisible surface of things.

In addition to the above, there are other expressions modifying the poet's eyes:

>   (19) <u>bodily</u> eyes (2, 369), <u>fix'd</u> eyes (4, 81), my <u>inner</u> eye (5, 475), <u>quick and curious</u> eye (7, 580), my <u>untaught</u> eyes (8, 439), an eye <u>so rich</u> (8, 595)

The first example in (19) appears in a context where 'I forgot / That I had <u>bodily eyes</u>, and what I saw / Appear'd like something in myself, a dream, / A prospect in my mind.' An antonymous expression to 'bodily eyes' is 'inner eyes.' *Roget's Thesaurus* quotes 'that <u>inward</u> eye which is the bliss of solitude' from "Daffodils" under item 535 imagination (405). I think the poet's '<u>inner</u> eyes' could certainly be added there, as well.

The above-mentioned phrases have a positive image, but the following are negative-image expressions: an <u>over-anxious</u> eye' (1, 249) and '<u>truant</u> eyes' (3, 529).

Next are expressions representing the eyes of people in general. It is useful to quote them here as contrastive expressions to Wordsworth's watchful eyes:

>   (20) to the <u>common</u> eyes, / No difference is (2, 319-20)
>   to the <u>human</u> eye / Invisible, yet liveth to the heart
>   (2, 423-24)

>   Souls that appear to have no depth at all / To <u>vulgar</u> eyes
>   (12, 167-68)

All these examples reveal that Wordsworth's eyes can see what is invisible to the eyes of ordinary people; in other words, the poet's eyes can transform the invisible into the visible.

3.6 Verbs of auditory perception

In the preceding sections (§§3.2-3.4), I investigated the verbs of visual perception in *The Prelude*. In this section, I discuss the findings of a survey of the verbs of auditory perception. What linguistic behavior could I perceive around the auditory verbs: 'hear' and 'listen'? More specifically, I made a close investigation as to what kinds of objects 'hear' and 'listen' take. In so doing, I was able to realize what sound the poet's ears listened to and heard. If the sounds which attracted the poet, or rather the kinds of sound the poet was interested in become clear, I can grasp the poet's auditory approach towards the outer world.

First, let us go back to Table 3.2 and see the bordered verbs of auditory perception which occur more than 10 times in *The Prelude*. Table 3.2 shows us that 'hear' and 'heard' appear 18 and 42 times respectively. If I add 'hearing' which occurs five times, I get 65 words related to <hear>. I did not include 'listen'-related words in the table because they occurred less than 10 times. Actually, 'listen'd' occurs five times, and 'listening' seven times, 12 times in total. Consequently, the number of aural verbs totals 77 (= 65 + 12).

Incidentally, the total number of verbs of visual perception is 331. The ratio is 331 vs. 77. The total number of visual verbs (331) is 4.3 times as many as that of auditory verbs (77). This figure clearly shows the predominance of the sense of sight over other human sensory organs.

3.7 Objects of verbs of auditory perception

Chart 3.2 shows the classification of the objects governed by verbs of auditory perception. By classifying the objects of auditory verbs into 100 subcategories from 00 ASTRONOMY to 99 MACHINERY, I found that the words belonging to NATURE total 32 and is the largest in number; those related to HUMAN AFFAIRS total 26; and those pertaining to CULTURE total 14. The most frequently appearing words are 'sound(s)' in 09 PHENOMENON and 'voice' in 32 EXPRESSION. Both 'sound' and 'voice' are very common words for the objects of verbs of auditory perception and each of them occurs eight times. These words, compared with the other object words, are highly abstract, and may be called "superordinate" words. What is in parallel with this linguistic phenomenon in terms of both the words' frequency and their degree of abstraction is that 'thing(s)' appear most frequently as the object of visual perception. We can say the typical object of auditory verbs is 'sound(s) and voice' and that of visual verbs is 'things.' The poet's use of "general" or "superordinate" words seems to be relevant to the poet's way of grasping the outer world. Wordsworth tries to transcend individuality and pursue universality. His way of conceiving objects becomes evident in his use of highly abstract words.

Chapter 3   Verbs of Perception and Cognition in *The Prelude*   61

3.7.1 The poet's keen interest in obscure 'sound' and 'voice'
Here, let me present what I particularly became aware of when I examined the contexts in which 'sound(s)' and 'voice' occurred. Though my observation is not entirely without a tinge of impressionism, it seems to me that Wordsworth is keenly interested in dim, faint, and undifferentiated sounds. The next quotation describes Nature remonstrating the young boy's theft of his friend's game (i.e. birds):

> (21)   when the deed was done
> I heard among the solitary hills
> <u>Low</u> *breathings* coming after me, and *sounds*
> Of <u>undistinguishable motion</u>, *steps*
> Almost as <u>silent</u> as the turf they trod.   (1, 328-32)

The threefold objects repeated appositionally are qualified by 'low,' 'of undistinguishable motion,' and 'silent' respectively. Here, a horrible sound made by something huge and gigantic which far exceeds the young boy's recognition is expressed. The polysyllabic epithet 'un·dis·tin·guish·a·ble,' among others, sounds odd along with its meaning. This quotation never fails to remind me of the next famous scene. As a boy, Wordsworth uses a shepherd's boat without permission and rows out on a lake:

> (22)   and after I had seen
> That spectacle, for many days, my brain
> Work'd with a <u>dim</u> and <u>undetermin'd</u> sense
> Of <u>unknown</u> modes of being;   (1, 417-20)

Here the aftereffect of Nature's harsh treatment of the boy's behavior is expressed. This example does not include any auditory verbs, but the same (as in (21)) holds true in the use of threefold adjectives of 'dim,' 'undetermined,' and 'unknown.'

The next quotation describes an incident during a solitary walk:

> (23)   and I would stand,
> Beneath some rock, listening to sounds that are
> The <u>ghostly</u> language of the <u>ancient</u> earth,
> Or make their <u>dim</u> abode in the distant winds
> Thence did I drink the visionary power.   (2, 326-30)

This passage depicts the poet's mysterious interrelationships with Nature through his auditory sense. From such an experience with

Nature Wordsworth draws on imagination. The poet uses 'ghostly' to describe the language of the 'ancient' earth which is far and distant in <time> and 'dim' to delineate the abode of winds which is far and distant in <space>. From this it is evident that the poet is charmed by undistinguishable sounds.

3.7.2 'Sound(s)' and 'voice' tend to be qualified

If I suppose 'sound' and 'voice' are the objects for auditory verbs, I can safely assert that 'forms' is the counterpart for verbs of visual perception. Let me make a comparison between the contexts in which both verbs actually occur. As I have already indicated in Table 1.3, 'forms' appear 37 times throughout *The Prelude*. It is interesting that, in almost all cases, 'forms' are not post-modified. To be concrete, 31 examples are followed by none, and only six examples are followed by an '*of*-phrase.' Two examples are accompanied by relative clauses. In short, 'forms' is rarely modified in *The Prelude*. In contrast, what about 'sound(s)' and 'voice'?

Table 3.4: Presence or absence of *of*-phrase modifying 'sound' and 'voice'

post-modifier	sound(s)	voice	total
none	1	2	3
prepositional phrase	3	3	6
relative clause	4	3	7
total	8	8	16

The table above shows that 13 out of 16 instances of both words are qualified by post-modifiers. The word 'sounds' without a post-modifier appears in the form of 'What sounds are those…?' and the sentence actually seeks to find out the origin of the sounds. In brief, 'sound(s)' and 'voice' tend to be qualified from behind when they are the objects of auditory verbs.

In contrast, as is mentioned above, 'forms' is scarcely post-modified when it is the object of visual verbs. What a difference! Why? The following is my hypothesis: What is significant to Wordsworth's sight is the exterior forms of things in Nature, above all else, 'mighty' forms. After superfluous parts are cut off, the essential core of things appeals to his sight and imagination. In other words, mighty forms of Nature form and mould his mighty mind. It is this idea which lies at the root of Wordsworth's perception.

3.7.3 The poet's feeling while hearing

Next, I will investigate what kind of feeling accompanies his process of 'hearing' and 'listening.' What is striking is that the words that show <joy> and <delight> are not to be found around the verbs of auditory perception. It is quite a surprising result, compared with the cases of verbs of visual perception, where joyful feelings are abundant.

Let me investigate what happens in his mind or heart when he hears or listens to something around him. The scene below depicts a naval port, Portsmouth, where an English fleet is at anchor:

> (24)   there I heard
> Each evening, walking by the still sea-shore,
> A monitory <u>sound</u> that never fail'd,
> The sunset Canon. While the Orb went down
> In the tranquillity of Nature, came
> That <u>voice</u>, ill requiem! seldom heard by me
> Without a spirit overcast, a deep
> Imagination, thought of woes to come,
> And sorrow for mankind, and pain of heart.   (10, 299-307)

Whenever he hears the roar of a gun, he feels sad and trembles with fear about what may happen in the future. He receives an auditory stimulus and it elicits a mental reaction from him.

In the next quotation, unlike the serious one in (24), the topic is a cheerful song of redbreasts:

> (25)   But I heard,
> After the hour of sunset yester even,
> Sitting within doors betwixt light and dark,
> A voice that <u>stirr'd</u> me. 'Twas a little Band,
> A Quire of Redbreasts gather'd somewhere near
> My threshold, ….   (7, 20-25)

The next depicts a time full of hope when the French Revolution was under way yet well before the period known as the Reign of Terror:

> (26)   the fife of War
> Was then a spirit-<u>stirring</u> sound indeed,
> A Blackbird's whistle in a vernal grove.   (6, 685-87)

In both (25) and (26), it is interesting to find that the word, 'stir' and the voice of 'birds' are used together.

Wordsworth's Vocabulary in *The Prelude*

Chart 3.2: Objects of verbs of auditory perception

		00 ASTRONOMY	01 CALENDAR	02 WEATHER	03 TOPOGRAPHY	04 SCENERY
NATURE	NATURE			wind 4.76 rain 4.77	stream 7.10 cataracts 7.125	groves 7.124
		10 POSITION	11 FORM	12 QUANTITY	13 SUBSTANCE	14 STIMULUS
	PROPERTY			Nought 1.91 nothing 7.641 — 13.21		solitude 4.390
		20 SHAKING	21 MOVEMENT	22 MEETING/PARTING	23 APPEARING	24 TRANSFORMATION
	CHANGE					
HUMAN AFFAIRS		30 ACTION	31 TRAFFIC	32 EXPRESSION	33 OBSERVATION	34 STATEMENT
	BEHAVIOUR			voice 1.64 — 7.23 — 7.417 — 9.405 — 10.76 — 10.304 — 12.324 — 13.376	'general' or 'superordinate' words	
		40 SENSE	41 THOUGHT	42 LEARNING	43 INTENTION	44 DEMAND
	AFFECTION		notions 9.198			
		50 PERSON	51 AGE	52 RELATIVES	53 FRIENDS	54 SOCIAL STATUS
	PERSON		Maids 8.193 Man 8.213 Woman 10.909		Traveller 9.449 ladies 7.125	
		60 PHYSIQUE	61 COUNTENANCE	62 FIGURE	63 GESTURE	64 ATTITUDE
	DESPOSITION					
CULTURE		70 REGION	71 GROUP	72 FACILITIES	73 RULE	74 TRANSACTION
	SOCIETY					
		80 SCHOLARSHIP	81 LOGIC	82 SIGNAL	83 LANGUAGE	84 DOCUMENT
	Art & Science		images 8.211	name 1.257 — 7.525 term 7.526		
		90 COMMODITIES	91 MEDICINE	92 FOOD	93 CLOTHING	94 BUILDING
	GOODS					

Chapter 3 Verbs of Perception and Cognition in *The Prelude* 65

(Numbers: Book.Line)

05 FLORA	06 FAUNA	07 PHYSIOLOGY	08 MATERIAL	09 PHENOMENON
flowers 6.231 grass 6.231	Popinjays 3.457	breathings 1.330	whate'er 6.469 — 6.672 things 6.694 — 12.252 what 9.644 that cl. 10.469 matter 12.253 'general' or 'superordinate' words	echo 1.65 sound 10.301 — 10.349 — 13.175 sounds 1.330 — 2.327 — 5.429 — 8.1 — 12.183 hubbub 9.56 canon 10.302
15 TIME	16 STATE	17 VALUE	18 TYPE	19 DEGREE
25 CHANGE IN QUALITY	26 FLUCTUATION	27 SITUATION	28 PROGRESS	29 RELEVANCE
			tempests 10.422	
35 BED & BOARD	36 WORK SERVICE	37 GIVE & RECEIVE	38 OPERATION	39 PRODUCTION
45 INDUCEMENT	46 STRIFE	47 HONOUR & DISGRACE	48 LOVE & HATE	49 JOY & SORROW
salutation 7.638				
55 SOCIAL FUNCTION	56 MANUFACTURE	57 SERVICE SECTOR	58 PEOPLE	59 GODS
	Quarry-man 8.504	Hawkers 9.56 Haranguers 9.56 Factionists 9.57 Builders 9.59 Subverters 9.59	Him 3.278 (=Chaucer) Carra 9.178 Gorsas 9.178	
65 BEHAVIOUR	66 CHARACTER	67 ABILITY	68 CIRCUMSTANCES	69 MENTAL STATE
			events 9.553	
75 NEWS	76 MANNERS & CUSTOMS	77 CONDUCT	78 SOCIAL LIFE	79 MORALITY
85 LITERATURE	86 ART	87 MUSIC	88 ENTERTAINMENT	89 AMUSEMENT
tale 12.183 tales 1.184 — 8.198		music 2.135 requiem 10.304		
95 FURNITURE	96 STATIONERY	97 LANDMARK	98 TOOLS	99 MACHINERY
lamps 7.124	flute 8.339 flagelet 8.339 fireworks 7.126 Pipe 8.321			

3.8 Modifiers of 'ear' and 'ears'

Now, I would like to share some insights resulting from an investigation of what epithet modifies 'ear(s)' in order to see with what ear(s) Wordsworth perceives objects. I do not deal with a determiner nor a possessive adjective here:

>   (27) jingling in our <u>youthful</u> ears (6, 416)
>   even in a <u>young Man's</u> ear (7, 542)
>   listen'd with a <u>stranger's</u> ears (9, 55)
>   I had but lent a <u>careless</u> ear (10, 777)

We have to pay attention to the meaning of 'careless' in the last example. It is '2. Unconcerned; not caring or troubling oneself' (*OED2*). It is not '3. Not taking due care, not paying due attention to what one does' (*OED2*).

What strikes me as most Wordsworthian, however, is the use of an epithet in the following:

>   (28) One song they sang, and it was audible,
>   Most audible then when the *fleshy* ear,
>   O'ercome by grosser prelude of that strain,
>   Forgot its functions, and slept undisturb'd.   (2, 431-34)

Here is a Wordsworthian paradox: when bodily ears stop functioning, they demonstrate their fullest power, just as when 'fleshy' eyes sleep, their greatest ability is displayed.

3.9 Co-occurring pattern of verbs of perception and cognition: 'saw' → 'heard' → 'felt'

Lastly, I would like to point out a co-occurring expression of three kinds of verbs. The order 'saw' → 'heard' → 'felt' is its basic pattern.

As I keep reading *The Prelude* paying attention to the verbs of visual and auditory perceptions, I notice 'feel' often comes after them. After seeing, the poet feels. This must be the pattern of Wordsworth's process of perception. This is a verbal reflection of his four-level poetry creation process of the 'observation → gazing → contemplation → union.' (See Nakagawa 2005: 95). This pattern is also seen in the above quotations (8) and (9) in §3.4.1 and (10) and (11) in §3.4.2. I can add the following:

Chapter 3   Verbs of Perception and Cognition in *The Prelude*   67

(29)   Finally whate'er
       I saw, or heard, or felt, was but a stream
       That flow'd into a kindred stream, a gale
       That help'd me forwards, did administer
       To grandeur and to tenderness,   (6, 672-76)

(30)   ..., now speaking in a voice
       Of sudden admonition, ... and now
       Seen, heard and felt, and caught at every turn, (10, 910-13)

(31) A Stripling, scarcely of the household then
     Of social life, I look'd upon these things
     As from a distance, heard, and saw, and felt,
     Was touch'd, but with no intimate concern;   (6, 693-96)

Citation (30) depicts how Wordsworth feels when he crosses the military band of the Brabant armies going into battle under the banner of 'Liberty.' As similar examples, I quote the following four passages, of which the first two are partially negated:

(32) I look'd not round, nor did the solitude
     Speak to my eye; but it was heard and felt: (4, 390-91)

(33) Of this I little saw, car'd less for it,
     But something must have felt.   (8, 427-28)

(34) All that I saw, or felt, or communed with
     Was gentleness and peace.   (10, 517-18)

(35) Have I beheld him, without knowing why
     Have felt his presence in his own domain,
     As of a Lord and Master; or a Power
     Or Genius, under Nature, under God,
     Presiding;   (8, 391-95)

As Wordsworth admits that the eye is '[T]he most despotic of our senses' (11, 174), the sense of sight gains an absolute advantage over other senses. Therefore, as seen in the examples above, 'hear' is sometimes deficient between 'see' and 'feel.' The number of visual verbs and that of auditory verbs appearing more than ten times in *The Prelude* is 272 and 60 respectively. The former far exceeds the latter. This figure is also a proof of the poet's statement.

From the above, it is evident the poet gazes at objects with intensity and with persistence. To my surprise 'gaze' and its variants appear only four times in 8,484 lines of the work under examination, while 'gazed' appears two times in no more than 24 lines of a short poem "Daffodils."

3.10 Summary

So far I have observed the linguistic behavior around verbs of visual and auditory perception in *The Prelude* from several viewpoints: the objects of the two kinds of verbs; the poet's emotional state while seeing and hearing; and the modifiers of the two sensory organs. Based on my findings, I could argue that:

(1) Wordsworth is a poet who sets great value on 'unassuming things' (12, 51) whether visual or auditory;
(2) Wordsworth is a poet who is able to see through to the heart of things;
(3) The representative object of visual verbs is 'things' and those of aural verbs are 'sound(s)' and 'voice,' all of which are superordinate words;
(4) The object of visual verbs, 'forms' is rarely post-modified, while 'sound(s)' and 'voice' tend to be specified;
(5) The poet sees objects with feelings of 'joy;'
(6) He is interested in undistinguishable sounds; and
(7) Verbs of visual, auditory, and cognitive perception in this order can form a pattern of co-occurrence. The order 'saw' → 'heard' → 'felt' is its basic pattern.

Additionally, while a key-word study of *The Prelude* has been undertaken by a number of scholars (e.g. Lewis (1964), Miles (1942, rpt.1965), Empson (1967), Ward (1984), Davies (1986), Miyazaki (1988), Austin (1989), Gill (1991), Nakamura (1994), Yamauchi (1994) and Miyagawa (2001, 2007)), I am not aware of any exhaustive and comprehensive study of the objects of the verbs of visual perception in *The Prelude*. Therein lies the raison d'être of this study.

Chapter 4
'Mighty' in *The Prelude*

4.0 Introduction

This chapter supplements a description given in Chapter 1, Section 3, Adjective class. As the reader will recall, in that chapter, I made a table (Table 1.8 entitled 'Quantitative classification of adjectives') which classified the adjectives appearing more than ten times in *The Prelude*, and arranged them according to their semantic fields. Before going into the kernel adjective 'mighty,' which I consider the most important and Wordsworthian of all the epithets in *The Prelude*, let me survey several noteworthy and, hopefully, enlightening linguistic facts about the adjectives modifying the poet's inner 'mind' and Nature's external 'forms.'

4.1 Adjectives in the comparative and superlative degrees

When I scrutinized adjectives modifying 'mind' and 'forms,' I came across an interesting linguistic fact. Those adjectives which modify 'mind' are sometimes expressed in the comparative and superlative degrees. For example, the following comparative combinations are found:

That mellower years will bring a <u>riper</u> mind	(1, 237)
they are kindred to our <u>purer</u> mind	(2, 333)
My <u>wiser</u> mind grieves now for what I saw.	(3, 516)
Add comments of a <u>calmer</u> mind,	(10, 78)
Calling upon the <u>more instructed</u> mind	(13, 297)

Comparative and superlative in essence connote both the process and the result of growth. We might well remember that the subtitle of *The Prelude* is 'Growth of a Poet's Mind.' In this long autobiographical poem, the poet's mental and spiritual development is recorded from his early childhood to manhood. Comparison is an inevitable accompaniment to growth. It is, therefore, quite natural that the poet's 'mind' should be described by means of the comparative degree of adjectives.

Adjectives which modify the 'forms' referring to natural things are not expressed using the comparative or superlative degrees. The following are representative examples:

huge and mighty Forms	(1, 425)
lovely forms	(1, 660; 3, 366)
the beauteous forms / Of Nature	(2, 51-52)
all exterior forms, / Near or remote, minute or vast	(3, 159-60)
mighty forms	(6, 347)
awful Powers, and Forms	(8, 213)
her awful forms	(8, 485)
fair forms	(9, 209)
pure forms and colours	(11, 110)
sublime and lovely Forms	(13, 146)

As shown above, *forms*-modifying adjectives are in the positive degree. This is because Wordsworth adores Nature as an absolute being. 'Form' is one embodiment or manifestation of Nature. Nature is absolute and she admits no comparison. Nature assumes a solemn and grave appearance. She refuses to compromise. However, when it comes to individual elements of Nature, for example 'lake' and 'stream,' they sometimes take the comparative degrees as seen in 'calmer Lakes, and louder Streams' (6, 12). It is interesting to note that such a "superordinate" word as 'forms' does not occur with adjectives of the comparative or superlative degree, while hyponyms such as 'lake' and 'stream' do.

4.2 Polarized adjectives

The above discussion reminds me of the verbal situation of the noun class, in which superordinate nouns, hypernyms, are preferred to hyponyms. I have only to remember that 'things' and 'objects' are used abundantly in *The Prelude*. The same tendency is actually observed in the adjective class. That is to say, adjectives belonging to what may be called superordinate types are preferred to those describing individual, superficial attributes.

What I call superordinate adjectives may be divided into four types: (1) <size>, (2) <height>, (3) <power>, and (4) <others>. Typical examples of each are (1) 'great,' (2) 'high,' (3) 'strong,' and (4) 'sublime.' At the other end of the spectrum are adjectives, such as 'beauteous' and 'good.' One of the reasons for this tendency toward bipolarization may be that the former appeal forcibly to the poet's mind and the latter appeal superficially to his eyes. The intrinsic grandeur of Nature is so great that the superficial beauty of Nature is, so to speak, eclipsed, which I represented by printing with light or faint type in a box marked by a dotted line in the lower right of Figure 4.1.

Chapter 4 'Mighty' in *The Prelude* 71

As argued in §1.3 (and as will be discussed again in §5.6), Wordsworth's way of looking at things is from a broad point of view. He puts the outer world into perspective and assesses situations with a bird's-eye view. Therefore, the above-mentioned four types of adjectives appear frequently because these words, what might be called 'superordinate adjectives,' appeal more strongly to the poet's reason or intellect than to his emotion or sensitivity. He uses adjectives depicting the real state of affairs rather than the superficial appearance of affairs. To state a plain example, Wordsworth prefers to use 'mighty' rather than adopt 'beautiful.' In the next section, I would like to rearrange the adjectives discussed in §1.3 (See Table 1.8) so as to gain another glimpse of the distribution of adjectives.

4.3 Rearrangement of adjectives

In Figure 4.1, I would like to rearrange the adjectives given in Table 1.8 from the four points of view mentioned above: (1) <size>, (2) <height>, (3) <power>, and (4) <others>. These four types are adjectives suggestive of something that goes straight to the poet's mind. They are contrastive to those appealing to his senses. (The number at the right of each word indicates its frequency count.)

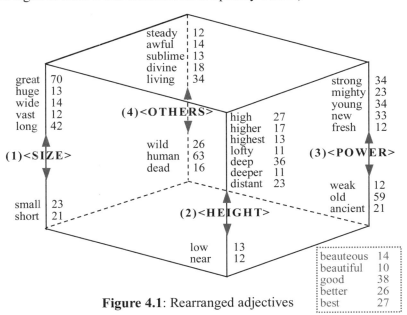

Figure 4.1: Rearranged adjectives

Let me talk a little about the third point <power>. It is traditionally acknowledged that literature aims at the pursuit of truth, goodness, and beauty. In the case of Wordsworth, however, <power> is sought prior to the above three. Havens (1941: 472-73) states as follows: "Power' was a favorite word with Wordsworth; he uses it and its plural over six hundred times in his poetry.... De Quincey's (1785-1859) emphasis on the literature of power as opposed to the literature of knowledge was derived from Wordsworth.'

By way of illustration, I quote one passage which typically illustrates the poet's use of adjectives as well as the poet's thought:

> By influence <u>habitual</u> to the mind
> The mountain's outline and its <u>steady</u> form
> Gives a <u>pure</u> grandeur, and its presence shapes
> The measure and the prospect of the soul
> To majesty;   (7, 721-25)

Here Nature's influence on man is depicted. Nature gives 'pure' grandeur to the mind of man by exerting a 'habitual' influence on it through the mountain's outline and its 'steady' form. Nature shapes the measure and the prospect of man's soul to majesty through the existence of the mountain's outline and its 'steady' form. Here, in this passage, Wordsworth's language reveals that outer forms have a grandiose and majestic effect on the poet's inner mind and soul.

Let me examine each adjective minutely. Nature's influence is 'habitual,' not 'transitory' (7, 739). The mountain's form is 'steady,' not 'meagre' (7, 738). The grandeur is 'pure,' not 'self-destroying' (7, 739). In a word, Nature's influence on man is <CONSTANT>. The mountain's outline and form constantly makes Wordsworth's mind reflect on grandeur, and his soul, on majesty. In other words, the majestic grandeur of the line and form of the mountain is mapped onto Wordsworth's mind and soul. This leads to the mirror-image relationship discussed in the next section.

4.4 Mirror-image relation between 'in' and 'out'

As I mentioned earlier (in §1.3), Wordsworth has a tendency to use the same adjective in order to describe both the poet's mind and natural things. This means that an adjective common to both worlds functions, as it were, as a mirror reflecting both his mind and the world around him. As Shakespeare holds 'the mirror up to nature' (*Hamlet* 3.2.22), Wordsworth uses outer Nature as a mirror so as to measure his inner world. Here is a phrase which contains 'mirror':

Chapter 4 'Mighty' in *The Prelude* 73

<blockquote>
a genuine counterpart
And softening <u>mirror</u> of moral world   (13, 287-88)
</blockquote>

In the passage where the above is included, he declares that, in *The Prelude*, he has barely touched upon the more superficial yet sweet charm, 'Nature's secondary grace, / That outward illustration' (13. 282-83). He acknowledges that he has not fully mentioned nor described that secondary charm, though it actually held forth 'a genuine counterpart / And softening mirror of moral world' (13. 287-88). To put it bluntly, he did not deal with the beauty of woods or fields, but their beauty ('Nature's secondary grace') did give comfort to his mind. Though being secondary and superficial, 'the speaking face of earth and heaven' (5, 12) still has an amazing charm, which is described by means of such adjectives as 'beautiful' and 'beauteous.' A secondary sense of grace is also depicted in the following expression: 'The changeful language of their [hills'] countenances' (7, 727). Wordsworth, however, surpassing the superficial and shallow beauty of nature, always tries to seek something more sublime and divine, which ultimately is connected to God. He regards the grandeur and sublimity of nature as its primary charm.

The adjectives common to both the poet's inner world and Nature's outer world, therefore, are those pertaining to the primary charm, i.e. 'grand,' 'sublime,' 'awful,' and 'great.'

Figure 4.2 represents the corresponding relation between adjectives describing inner and outer worlds. Expressions in the left box depict aspects of the outer world, and those in the right refer to the world of the human mind. Adjectives in the center box are those common to both worlds. The numbers (3.1), (3.3), and (3.5) correspond to those allocated to Table 1.1, which represent 'adjectives' indicative of 'ABSTRACT RELATION,' 'HUMAN ACTIVITY—MIND AND DEED,' and 'NATURE—NATURAL THINGS AND PHENOMENA,' respectively.

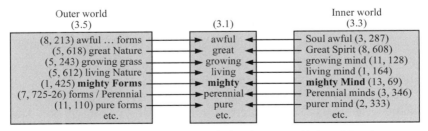

Figure 4.2: Mirror-image relation between 'in' and 'out'

4.5 Close adhesion of 'mighty' and 'mind'

One of the greatest advantages of using a computer for literary study is that we can immediately investigate how close any given two words stand next to each other.

4.5.1 How close 'mighty' and 'mind' stand to each other

I examined the juxtaposition of 'mighty' and 'mind' when they appear within 15 lines of each other in *The Prelude*. The results were as follows:

Table 4.1: *Mighty*'s proximity to *mind*

	mighty	mind
1	1, 425	1, 426
2	6, 73	6, 64
3	6, 73	6, 76
4	6, 178	6, 179
5	6, 347	6, 334
6	6, 459	6, 443
7	8, 702	8, 701
8	9, 383	9, 394
9	10, 952	10, 944
10	12, 302	12, 288
11	**13, 69**	**13, 69**
12	13, 69	13, 74

There are 12 examples in total in which 'mighty' and 'mind' occur within 15 lines of each other. It is not until line 69 of the last and the thirteenth book that both words appear on the same line, adjacent to each other, juxtaposed without any words in between.

> A meditation rose in me that night
> Upon the lonely Mountain when the scene
> Had pass'd away, and it appear'd to me
> The perfect image of a <u>mighty Mind</u>,   (13, 66-69)

The phrase 'Mighty mind' is key to understanding Wordsworth's poetry, and it is well worth scrutinizing.

Wordsworth was brought up surrounded by 'mighty forms' of Nature. He seldom shows interest in things artificial and vulgar. The crudity and shallowness of things are what he dislikes. Mighty forms of the outer world of Nature are mapped onto the mind of the poet, hence his 'mighty mind.'

4.5.2 Sound structure of 'mighty mind'
Let me make a careful examination of the sound structure of the phrase. The two words can be said to be composed of almost the same sounds: /máiti/ and /máind/.

First, alliteration of the 'm' sound is conspicuous: /**m**áiti/ and /**m**áind/. Coincidentally, there is an interesting story by Jakobson (1960: 357) that would seem to apply here.

> A girl used to talk about 'the horrible Harry.' 'Why horrible?' 'Because I hate him.' 'But why not *dreadful, terrible, frightful, disgusting?*' 'I don't know why, but horrible fits him better.' Without realizing it, she clung to the poetic device of paronomasia.

Why mighty? Why not *strong*? Of course Wordsworth certainly realized the poetic effect of paronomasia, that is, alliteration.

Second, the sounds, /t/ and /d/, are identical in the point of articulation and different only in the point of <voiceless> and <voiced>. When pronounced aloud, the /t/ sound in 'migh**t**y' and /d/ sound in 'min**d**' resound to each other. Strength is added and amplified when the chronologically early sound /t/ moves to and meets with the later voiced /d/. Consequently, the total meaning of the word combination gains weight and solidity.

Wordsworth regards the Snowdon passage as the most important episode of all and therefore he must have chosen to put it at the beginning of the last Book 13, titled 'Conclusion.' It is no mere coincidence that the two words 'mighty' and 'mind' co-occur in one and the same line in the important Snowdon passage. Wordsworth must have left the significant phrase 'mighty mind' in the last Book of *The Prelude* consciously and intentionally.

4.6 Summary
I have made a quick survey of adjectives, specifically of 'mighty.' The consideration of the adjective class shows that the poet uses the same adjective for describing both Nature and the human mind. What Wordsworth depicted in *The Prelude* was the workings of his 'mighty mind.' The word combination, 'mighty mind,' is loaded with the best blessings of Nature Wordsworth received from Nature.

Reconsideration of the quantitative classification of adjectives in §1.3 of this book makes me realize Wordsworth's preference for one type of adjective: <heavy, thick, long, large> over another type of adjective: <light, thin, short, small>. He, for example, chooses to use 'great,' 'high,' 'strong,' and 'sublime' rather than 'beautiful' and 'fair' which denote the superficial beauty of Nature.

Chapter 5
'Through' in *The Prelude*

5.0 Introduction
In this chapter, I investigate how distinctively the prepositional particle 'through' functions in *The Prelude*. *The Prelude* is, as we know, an autobiographical poem describing 'the growth of a poet's mind' and Wordsworth's vivid interrelations with Nature. I have focused special attention on 'through' and emphasize that this preposition best embodies the interrelationships between the poet's mind and Nature.

Given the extensive body of scholarship on Wordsworth, there must be critics who argue that a content word such as 'nature,' 'imagination,' or 'sense' rather than a function word, such as 'through,' should be studied when approaching this masterwork. In his "'Sense' in *The Prelude*,' for example, Empson (1967: 289-305) makes a penetrating observation on its position and function appearing as it does so often at the end of a line. He noticed that Wordsworth, in his 1805 edition, used 'sense' 35 times at the end of a given line and 12 times at other places; in 1850 edition, he used 'sense' 31 times at the end of a line and 11 times elsewhere. In either case, the poet tends to use 'sense' at a given line's end. His usage of 'sense' at a line's end in the form of 'a sense of ...' makes readers expect the succeeding word following 'of' at the start of the very next line. They look forward to realizing what comes after 'of,' in other words, what the object of the preposition 'of' is, in each case. Empson (1967: 290) asserts that this type of Wordsworthian use of 'sense' bears within it 'a new kind of sensing' suggested 'from the pause at the end of the line.'

However, I believe that a seemingly inconsequential function word, 'through,' likewise, affords us a key to unlocking *The Prelude*, so this preposition is well worth investigating. I would also like to point out that some parts of the following explanation overlap with my exegesis in §1.4, to which I humbly refer the reader.

5.1 Unusual rank order of 'through' in *The Prelude*
My own statistics of the frequency of occurrences of the word 'through' that appear in *The Prelude* reveal that it occurs 207 times and ranks 36th (See Table 5.1, which is in fact the same as Table 1.9, shown earlier). The rank order of 36th stands a great deal higher than that of

other references. LOB's ranking is 120th (Hofland and Johansson), Brown's is 102nd (Carroll et al.), and those of Leech et al.'s are 192nd (written) and 108th (spoken), all of which represent the general trends of present-day English. This difference is significant: indeed, such an idiosyncratic stylistic deviation from standard word frequency practically impels me to investigate all the contexts of 'through' in *The Prelude*. This divergence from the norm, I argue, is the key to a powerful interpretation of *The Prelude*.

Table 5.1: *The Prelude* rank list

1	the	3,221	27	is	292	52	there	159	78	first	104
2	and	2,715	28	it	285	52	those	159	78	own	104
3	of	2,378	29	he	276	54	no	158	80	could	103
4	a	1,420	30	we	272	55	then	155	81	might	100
5	to	1,322	31	when	251	56	did	152	81	thus	100
6	in	1,269	32	have	248	57	like	147	83	far	93
7	I	937	33	their	237	58	its	142	84	them	92
8	that	909	34	be	236	59	man	141	85	how	88
9	with	779	35	more	223	60	these	137	86	out	86
10	was	558	36	**through**	**203**	61	so	135	86	would	86
11	my	538		**(thro'**	**4)**	62	up	133	88	power	83
12	as	477	37	her	203	63	love	132	89	here	82
13	by	447	37	upon	203	64	him	130	90	thought	81
13	from	447	39	were	200	64	some	130	91	before	80
15	which	441	40	one	188	66	life	128	91	less	80
16	for	399	41	such	186	67	are	126	93	hath	79
17	or	365	42	yet	174	67	if	126	93	into	79
18	not	364	43	what	172	69	than	124	93	men	79
19	his	354	44	our	170	70	where	123	93	other	79
20	all	352	45	time	169	71	among	121	97	long	78
21	had	349	46	an	167	71	nor	121	97	still	78
22	this	343	47	who	166	73	day	118	99	every	77
23	at	334	48	now	165	74	nature	117	100	truth	75
24	but	322	49	been	162	75	heart	113			
25	on	316	49	they	162	76	even	108			
26	me	295	51	mind	161	76	things	108			

It may be inappropriate to completely ignore the time difference between the age of Wordsworth (1770-1850) and the present day that LOB, Brown and Leech et al. cover. However, if we stand on the assumption that there are words that are often used or realized in any text and in any age, the danger of generalization is alleviated. Indeed, it is only to be expected that content words may take a different rank order according to the content of a given text: for example, a love story tends to reveal a high frequency of affection-related lexes, while a tale of chivalry may involve a lot of battle-linked words. However, when it comes to function words, especially prepositions, alterations of the rank order deriving from textual differences are rather small. Prepositions are by nature words expressing a relation of dependence and a cause and effect between objects, so they are presupposed to appear in any text rather regularly and steadily regardless of their individual rank order differences. According to Davies (1986: 58), as briefly mentioned §1.4,

> high-frequency words like prepositions are imposed on him [the writer] by the laws of chance, in the sense that they result from the simple fact that he has chosen to write in a language in which these words have these probabilities of occurrence.

Let us turn our eyes to several individual writers and historically seek their particular figures. The frequency rank order of 'through' in Chaucer's (*c*.1340-1400) *The Canterbury Tales* (1387-1400) is 181st according to the Concordance. That of J. Austen's (1775-1817) novels stands at 318th. That of E. Brontë's (1818-48) *Wuthering Heights* (1847) is 177th. Dickens' (1812-70) 'through' ranks 166th. That of E. Dickinson's (1830-86) poetical works is 125th. All of these figures rank well over 100th; meanwhile, *The Prelude*'s frequency rank order is 36th.

I assert that the abundant use of 'through' results from the frequent interrelations between the poet's inner world and the outer world of Nature. Close observation of the immediate contexts of 'through' will, therefore, lead us to a deeper understanding of *The Prelude*.

Having extracted all 207 examples of 'through' from the text of *The Prelude*, I then looked closely at their contexts and surveyed, first, the object of each occurrence of 'through,' that is to say, what follows each 'through' syntactically; then, I inquired into the syntactic combination of verbs that occur in combination with 'through,' in other words, what precedes each 'through.' For this study, I have made use of Spitzer's (1967: 25) "philological circle" method and have thereby observed "a series of back-and-forth movements" between 'through' and 'the artistic effect of the whole' (Leech & Short: 75) of *The Prelude*.

Wordsworth's Vocabulary in *The Prelude*

Chart 5.1: Distribution of objects of 'through'

		00 ASTRONOMY	01 CALENDAR	02 WEATHER	03 TOPOGRAPHY	04 SCENERY
NATURE	NATURE	heaven 3.281 day 1.279 night 1.279 — 7.465	summer 7.18 — 8.375 year 1.494 — 8.539 years 1.667 — 2.3 — 10.371 month 10.297 months 5.496 — 10.371 days 1.114 seasons 1.610	fog 8.401 storm 12.155	rough 2.137 smooth 2.137 Heights 8.369 heights 5.235 hollows 5.235 bye-spots 5.235 ground 5.236 pastures 5.237 hills 8.372 Alps 11.241 field 1.30 — 12.130 fields 1.253 — 7.587 — 11.9 Desert 5.83 Waste 5.85 waste 12.337 Stream 10.528 Vales 8.12	landscape 7.277 scenes 10.4 spectacle 3.29 sights 7.189 labyrinth 10.923 labyrinths 7.201 maze 7.550 walks 1.253 lanes 5.241 — 6.240 paths 6.365 pathways 6.617 avenue 10.98 strait 8.113 bye-tracts 6.209 tract 8.261 tracts 7.188 groves 1.154 — 1.297 — 5.602 woods 6.241 — 9.453 meadows 1.416 forest 7.42 — 12.130 enclosures 8.368 graves 10.491
		10 POSITION	**11 FORM**	**12 QUANTITY**	**13 SUBSTANCE**	**14 STIMULUS**
	PROPERTY	place 8.163 nook 7.662 — 8.265 — 9.182 recess 7.446 stage 8.545 space 6.229 surface 8.733 depth 8.2 seams 8.116 shades 4.481 abyss 11.63 (breathing-place 13.57) (breach 13.62)	lines 7.738 Image 5.15 image 13.110	length 3.308 hair-breadth 1.607 magnitude 8.629 all 8.731 league 10.914		cold 1.465 colouring 8.653 colours 7.237 — 7.738 darkness 1.465 — 1.481 — 12.155 gloom 5.459 twilight 1.454
	CHANGE	**20 SHAKING**	**21 MOVEMENT**	**22 MEETING/PARTING**	**23 APPEARING**	**24 TRANSFORMATION**
						transmigrations 13.292
HUMAN AFFAIRS	Behaviour	**30 ACTION**	**31 TRAFFIC**	**32 EXPRESSION**	**33 OBSERVATION**	**34 STATEMENT**
						claims 9.225
	AFFECTION	**40 SENSE**	**41 THOUGHT**	**42 LEARNING**	**43 INTENTION**	**44 DEMAND**
		stroke 11.149 impressions 13.111	thought 13.110 thoughts 1.80 mind 1.426 heart 10.210	retrospect 6.296	zeal 3.469 — 10.589 ambition 6.601 faith 10.787 hope 10.788	privilege 7.400
	Person	**50 PERSON**	**51 AGE**	**52 RELATIVES**	**53 FRIENDS**	**54 SOCIAL STATUS**
		me 7.52 myself 1.158				
	Disposition	**60 PHYSIQUE**	**61 COUNTENANCE**	**62 FIGURE**	**63 GESTURE**	**64 ATTITUDE**
			ears 1.349 — 12.238 veins 4.327			negligence 9.753 obliquities 8.542
CULTURE	SOCIETY	**70 REGION**	**71 GROUP**	**72 FACILITIES**	**73 RULE**	**74 TRANSACTION**
		world 3.228 country 3.255 — 9.89 Land 7.315 — 10.440 Lands 3.476 Realms 3.482 Hamlets 6.361 Towns 6.361 City 10.41 Metropolis 9.19 region 8.346 vestiges 12.318 Paris 9.40 France 9.930 Britain 10.639 England 13.349 Wales 13.2 — 13.349	throng 3.319	habitations 11.89 Museum 3.653		
	Art & Science	**80 SCHOLARSHIP**	**81 LOGIC**	**82 SIGNAL**	**83 LANGUAGE**	**84 DOCUMENT**
			causes 9.119			Book 9.306
	GOODS	**90 COMMODITIES**	**91 MEDICINE**	**92 FOOD**	**93 CLOTHING**	**94 BUILDING**
					arras 3.593	Gateways 3.265 wall 7.482 Walls 2.135 windows 3.3 Arch 10.452

Chapter 5 'Through' in *The Prelude*

(Numbers: Book.Line)

05 FLORA	06 FAUNA	07 PHYSIOLOGY	08 MATERIAL	09 PHENOMENON
trees 2.165		birth 2.230 growth 10.786	Nature 8.588 — 8.836 — 10.388 air 6.698 water 1.404 — 1.413 rocks 8.116 objects 8.451	press 7.738 force 1.205 sounds 7.189 hubbub 7.227

15 TIME	16 STATE	17 VALUE	18 TYPE	19 DEGREE
time 8.363 times 10.411 — 10.942 — 10.942 — 11.31 hours 6.84 afternoon 2.168 ages 8.783 youth 3.229 — 8.482 — 11.140 life 10.468 length 2.47 — 5.8 space 7.474 — 9.684 divisions 2.84	conditions 12.282 chance 8.596 punctilios 9.118	impotence 8.537 frailties 10.821	kind 10.388	steps 10.928

25 CHANGE IN QUALITY	26 FLUCTUATION	27 SITUATION	28 PROGRESS	29 RELEVANCE
	want 9.752 — 10.145 — 12.214 lack 3.491	decay 1.560 change 1.502 — 2.279 turnings 5.627	lapse 3.576 course 5.505 tenor 9.222	effect 9.595

35 BED & BOARD	36 WORK SERVICE	37 GIVE & RECEIVE	38 OPERATION	39 PRODUCTION
		intercourse 2.260		

45 INDUCEMENT	46 STRIFE	47 HONOUR & DISGRACE	48 LOVE & HATE	49 JOY & SORROW
hindrance 7.20 help 9.342 (education 7.715)	campaign 1.547 struggle 6.530	compunction 9.749	grace 5.287 — 6.189 dislike 8.673	pain 8.536 — 8.673 fear 9.748 — 11.286

55 SOCIAL FUNCTION	56 MANUFACTURE	57 SERVICE SECTOR	58 PEOPLE	59 GODS

65 BEHAVIOUR	66 CHARACTER	67 ABILITY	68 CIRCUMSTANCES	69 MENTAL STATE
piety 3.469 impiety 10.116 presumption 11.152 humility 11.210 lowliness 11.210	tenderness 6.189 self-submission 7.143	weakness 8.53 ignorance 10.183 immaturity 10.184 knowledge 9.368	happiness 11.211 hardships 10.556 events 9.304	

75 NEWS	76 MANNERS & CUSTOMS	77 CONDUCT	78 SOCIAL LIFE	79 MORALITY
	history 2.230			mistrust 10.144

85 LITERATURE	86 ART	87 MUSIC	88 ENTERTAINMENT	89 AMUSEMENT
Verse 5.11 — 13.341 Romance 9.306 Tale 9.306 dream 9.307				journey 9.880

95 FURNITURE	96 STATIONERY	97 LANDMARK	98 TOOLS	99 MACHINERY
Cabinet 3.652	instrument 5.397			

5.2 Distribution of objects for occurrences of 'through'

The distribution of the objects of 'through' is shown in Chart 5.1. This chart yet again uses the framework of *Kadokawa's New Dictionary of Synonyms* (1981). As explained above, this lexicon divides the entire Japanese vocabulary into three categories:

NATURE which surrounds us;
HUMAN AFFAIRS in which we live;
CULTURE which we produce.

These three categories are divided into 100 subcategories, beginning with item 00 Astronomy and ending with 99 Machinery. What becomes obvious from this chart is that the vocabulary items related to 04 Scenery, 03 Topography, and 01 Calendar on the top row; 10 Position and 15 Time on the second row; and 70 Region are particularly large in number. The merit of this chart is that you can obtain a bird's-eye view of all the objects of 'through.'

5.2.1 Abstract nouns or concrete nouns?

Next, the total number of nouns which follow each occurrence of 'through' is 238, as shown in Table 5.2. The table is based on a distinction drawn between abstract and concrete nouns. Classifying all these nouns into groups, however, causes a problem. There are some borderline cases, such as 'labyrinth' and 'scenes.' I am often at a loss as to which side to put them due to the varying scales of abstraction that can be applied to them.

Table 5.2: Abstract nouns vs. concrete nouns

		Category	Frequency		Examples
Abstract	[1]	abstract words (time)	32	137	*time, times, hours, ages, youth, life, length, days, month, year, years*, etc.
	[2]	abstract words (others)	103		*thought, fear, pain, happiness, hope, faith, ambition, growth, grace, importance, hindrance, retrospect*, etc.
	[3]	relative pronouns	(2)		*which* (=*education*) and *what*
Concrete	[4]	words related to Nature	59	101	*field, fields, stream, vales, trees, woods, hills, heights, forests, meadows, rocks, fog, Waste*, etc.
	[5]	regions; proper nouns	19		*world, country, land, Hamlets, towns, Realms; Paris, Wales, England*, etc.
	[6]	poet; parts of his body	5		*me* and *myself*; *ears* (2 times) and *veins*
	[7]	artificial objects	16		*window, walls, arch, book, Verse, Museum*, etc.
	[8]	relative pronouns	(2)		*which* (=*breathing-place* and *breach*)
		Total	238		

When I examine the above figures from the angle of abstract and concrete nouns, I find the following distribution:

```
           Abstract                           Concrete
    [1]    [2]    [3]            [4]    [5]   [6]   [7]    [8]
   [ 32  + 103 + (2)=] 137 > 101 [= 59 + 19 + 5  + 16 + (2)]
     _____/_____/                          \____/
   time meaning relative pronoun                relative pronoun
```

Two pairs of parentheses ([3] and [8]) in the above chart and in the 'Frequency' column of the Table 5.2 suggest that the antecedent of a relative pronoun is not explicit. That is to say, it is hidden in the relative pronoun.

The number of genuinely abstract nouns marked with number [1] on the Table, and the second category (marked with [2]) is 135, while the number of remaining nouns ranging from the fourth to the seventh category is 99. Wordsworth is often said to be a 'nature' poet, so one may well expect that nouns expressing natural and concrete things would exceed those of abstract things in number. Contrary to this general expectation, however, abstract nouns (137) outnumber the concrete ones (101) and show Wordsworth in a new light.

Lindenberger (1963: 65) points out:

> The closest prose equivalent to Wordsworth's meditative verse, one ventures to say, is perhaps the later style of Henry James.

Moreover, it is still fresh in the author's memory that Chatman (1972: 2-6) clearly explained the abstractness of James's later works.

A full-length poem which traces, in the form of retrospection, the development of the workings of a poet's poetic mind will need many abstract words. The correctness of Lindenberger's assertion is indeed confirmed by these above-mentioned figures.

5.2.2 "Abstract locative" nouns

Of particular relevance here are Leech and Short's (1981: 84) remarks on 'subordination of concreteness to abstraction.' They investigate the nouns in the opening passage of a short story by Joseph Conrad (1857-1924):

> As a physical description, we expect the passage to contain a large number of physical, concrete nouns (*stakes, bamboo, fences, fishermen, ruins*, etc) but what is more striking is that these

concrete nouns are matched by nouns which are more abstract in one way or another. Similarly, these tend to occur as heads of major noun phrases (*'line* of…stakes,' *'system* of…fences), so that concreteness is subordinated to abstraction.

They say such words as 'line' and 'system' may be called "abstract locative" nouns. In fact, the same linguistic feature is found in Wordsworth's *The Prelude*. Let me here quote some examples:

| through every *nook* / Of the wide area | (7, 662-63) |
| through every *nook* of town and field | (9, 182) |

'Nook' appears three times as the object of 'through.' In two out of these three, 'nook' is used in the same sense as Leech and Short's "abstract locative" noun.

Similar examples are:

Through every *hair-breadth* of that field of light	(1, 607)
through a *length* of streets	(3, 308)
through a deep *recess* / Of thick-entangled forest	(7, 446-47)
through that unfenced *tract* of mountain-ground	(8, 261)
through every *stage* of its tall stem	(8, 545)

In these 'A of B' phrase type examples, the degree of A's abstractness is higher than that of B's, so that B's concreteness is lessened by the existence of A. It follows that the expression 'A of B' as a whole takes on an abstract quality.

5.3 Co-occurrence of 'through' with verbs

In sections 5.2, 5.2.1 and 5.2.2, I have looked at the objects of 'through,' in other words, the semantic characteristics of the nouns which follow each occurrence of 'through.' Now, let me examine what precedes 'through.' As might be expected, in most cases, verbs, especially those of motion, are the most commonly observed.

5.3.1 Combination of 'roam' with other words

Here, I would like to draw special attention to one particular verb, 'roam.' 'Roam' appears ten times throughout *The Prelude*. One of them appears in the capacity of a noun. They show the following patterns of combination:

Chapter 5 'Through' in *The Prelude*

Table 5.3: Combination of 'roam' with other words

roam +	*none*	2
	about from ~ to ~	1
	from ~ to ~, from ~ to ~	1
	about	2
	through ~	4

As is shown in the above, two instances of 'roam' have no prepositions nor adverbs; one appears with 'about from ~ to ~'; one occurs with 'from ~ to ~, from ~ to ~'; two have 'about'; while the instances combined with 'through' are, to my amazement, on top with four. The following are illustrative examples:

ROAM'D (five examples)
>I was the Dreamer, they the Dream; I *roam'd*
>Delighted, **through** the motley spectacle; (3, 28-29)

>Yet was I often greedy in the chace,
>And *roam'd* from hill to hill, from rock to rock, (11, 190-91)

>Long afterwards, I *roam'd* about
>In daily presence of this very scene, (11, 319-20)

>At other moments, for **through** that wide waste
>Three summer days I *roam'd*, (12, 337-38)

>   I *roam'd* about from place to place
>Tarrying in pleasant nooks, wherever found
>Through England or through Wales. (13, 347-49)

ROAM (four examples)
>   not to comfort the Oppress'd,
>But, like a thirsty wind, to *roam* about,
>Withering the Oppressor: (1, 209-11)

>When but a half-hour's *roam* (noun) **through** such a place
>Would leave behind a dance of images (8, 163-64)

>Defenceless as a wood where tigers *roam*. (10, 82)

>   and where now I *roam*,
>A meditative, oft a suffering Man, (13, 125-26)

ROAMING (one example)
    And afterwards, when **through** the gorgeous Alps
    Roaming, I carried with me the same heart: (11, 241-42)

In short, four out of 10 instances of 'roam' co-occur with 'through,' all of which bear the semantic components of <penetration> and <passage>.

5.3.2 Combination of other verbs of motion with 'through'

Now, I will quote other typical examples of verbs of motion concurring with 'through.' These quotations especially include verbs with the semantic components of <gradual progress>, <expansion>, or <pervasiveness>.

(1)   And, as I rose upon the stroke, my Boat
      Went heaving *through* the water, like a Swan;
      . . . .
          . . . With trembling hands I turn'd,
      And *through* the silent water stole my way
      Back to the Cavern of the Willow tree.
      There, in her mooring-place, I left my Bark,
      And, *through* the meadows homeward went, with grave
      And serious thoughts; . . .
      . . . .
          . . . , no familiar shapes
      Of hourly objects, images of trees,
      Of sea or sky, no colours of green fields;
      But huge and mighty Forms that do not live
      Like living men mov'd slowly *through* my mind
      By day and were the trouble of my dreams.
                            (1, 403-04, 412-17, 422-27)

This is from the famous boat-stealing episode when Wordsworth rowed out in a shepherd's boat without permission, and Nature passed 'through' the young poet's mind and remonstrated him for his blameworthy conduct. There are as many as four occurrences of 'through' in just 25 lines. The first three are used with external natural objects such as 'water' and 'meadows.' To be more precise, the initial 'through' is employed to describe the boy's access to the beauty of Nature, and the second and the third ones are used to describe his retreat from horrifying and admonishing Nature. In contrast, the last use of 'through' refers to the internal human mind. In order to delineate such 'to-and-fro' movements of the boy's approach toward natural beauty and flight in horror, it is inevitably necessary for Wordsworth to use 'through.'

The next example depicts how deeply the poet's mind looks upon the outward face of Nature:

> (2) In progress ***through*** this Verse, my mind hath look'd
> Upon the speaking face of earth and heaven
> As her prime Teacher, intercourse with man
> Establish'd by the sovereign Intellect,
> Who ***through*** that bodily Image hath <u>diffus'd</u>
> A soul divine which we participate,
> A deathless spirit.   (5, 11-17)

Here Nature, whom the poet admired as his Teacher, spreads freely in all directions 'a divine soul and a deathless spirit' 'through' the medium of her 'speaking face of earth and heaven.'

The following citation represents how the external movement of a cluster of trees causes the internal mental activity in the poet:

> (3)   and my favourite Grove,
> Now tossing its dark boughs in sun and wind
> <u>Spreads</u> ***through*** me a commotion like its own,
> Something that fits me for the Poet's task,   (7, 50-53)

The movement of the boughs of the trees, an aspect of Nature's outward movements, awakes a corresponding exciting movement 'through' his inner self, and enhances his poetic spirit to the stage ready to compose a poem.

The next passage depicts a lasting influence of Nature on the poet:

> (4) The Spirit of Nature was upon me here;
> The Soul of Beauty and enduring life
> Was present as a habit, and <u>diffused</u>,
> ***Through*** meagre lines and colours, and the press
> Of self-destroying, transitory things
> Composure and ennobling Harmony.   (7, 735-40)

Wordsworth, here, states that in London, an 'undistinguishable world' (in his words), Nature gave to his mind 'composure and ennobling Harmony' 'through' the city's superficial and transitory objects.

Next, as was seen in (3), gentle breezes of the external world blow 'through' the fields to reach the bottom of the poet's inner heart:

> (5) Ye motions of delight, that ***through*** the fields
> <u>Stir</u> gently, breezes and soft airs that breathe
> The breath of Paradise, and find your way
> To the recesses of the soul! (11, 9-12)

Things that are moving bring delight to the wandering poet. The expression 'motions of delight,' as seen in this passage, can be said to be characteristically Wordsworthian.

Incidentally, as his sentence, 'I with nature walk'd' (8, 463) clearly demonstrates, walking was his daily habit. Not only things which are moving but also moving itself brings him great delight. Walking, that is to say, moving actively and positively was his daily routine.

5.3.3 Semantic components of verbs of motion

As stated above, the verbs in these quotations ((1) to (5)) as well as the '*roam* through ~' instances mentioned earlier have the semantic components of <gradual progress>, <expansion>, and <pervasiveness>, as shown in Figure 5.1. All of these components are accordant with those involved in the preposition 'through' defined in the *OED2* (s.v. 'through': 1.a.) as follows: 'Expressing movement (or extension) either so as to *penetrate* (my italics) the substance of a thing, or along a passage or opening already existing in it.'

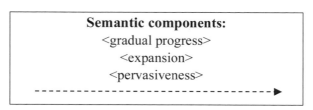

Figure 5.1: Semantic components

The word 'penetrate' reminds me of Lewis's (1967: 206) remark. Lewis calls the imagination of the Middle Ages, 'realizing;' of Shakespeare, 'penetrative;' and of Wordsworth, 'transforming.' Indeed, Wordsworth calls London 'that vast receptacle' (7, 734) and the hustle and bustle of the city, a 'blank confusion' (7, 695). Indeed, these expressions may be called 'transforming,' but we can reasonably state that Wordsworth's is also a 'penetrative' imagination, if we pay particular attention to his frequent and significant use of 'through.'

5.3.4 Other similar examples of verbs of motion co-occurring with 'through'
Similar examples are as follows:

(6)   to <u>stray about</u>
Voluptuously ***through*** fields and rural walks, (1, 252-53)

(7) To <u>gallop</u> ***through*** the country in blind zeal
Of senseless horsemanship,   (3, 255-56)

(8)   I could not always lightly <u>pass</u>
Through the same Gateways; sleep where they had slept,
Wake where they wak'd, range that enclosure old
That garden of great intellects undisturb'd.   (3, 264-67)

(9)   What wonder then if sounds
Of exultation <u>echoed</u> ***through*** the groves!   (5, 601-02)

(10) ***Through*** those delightful pathways we <u>advanc'd</u>,
                                       (6, 617)

(11) Mine eyes have glanced upon him, few steps off,
In size a giant, <u>stalking</u> ***through*** the fog,
His Sheep like Greenland Bears;   (8, 400-02)

(12)   for there,
There chiefly, hath she feeling whence she is,
And, <u>passing</u> ***through*** all Nature rests with God.
                                       (8, 834-36)

(13) Free as a colt at pasture on the hill,
I <u>ranged</u> at large, ***through*** the Metropolis   (9, 18-19)

(14) To Paris I returned. Again I <u>rang'd</u>
More eagerly than I had done before
Through the wide City,   (10, 39-41)

(15)   Great God!
Who <u>send'st</u> thyself into this breathing world
Through Nature and ***through*** every kind of life,
And mak'st Man what he is, Creature divine, (10, 386-89)

(16) The bliss of <u>walking</u> daily in Life's prime

> ***Through*** field or forest with the Maid we love, (12, 129-30)

(17) In one of these excursions, <u>travelling</u> then
> ***Through*** Wales on foot, and with a youthful Friend,
> I left Bethkelet's huts at couching-time, (13, 1-3)

The above are only a few of the examples which include verbs of motion together with 'through.'

5.3.5 Example of a verb of visual perception co-occurring with 'through'

Next is a passage which includes a verb of visual perception. Unlike the quotations (1) through (17) which syntactically show a 'verb' + 'through ~' pattern, passage (18) shows a pattern of 'verb' + object + 'through ~.' The poet's matter of concern is not only natural objects but also human beings, as is indicated in the title of Book 8 of *The Prelude*, 'Retrospect—Love of Nature Leading to Love of Mankind.' He becomes increasingly interested in mankind after experiencing his university life at Cambridge, his residence in London, and his stay in Paris during the French Revolution.

(18) first I look'd
> At Man ***through*** objects that were great and fair,
> First commun'd with him by their help. (8, 450-52)

Here Wordsworth says that in his childhood he was happy to be able to look at mankind, not through 'the deformities of crowded life' (8, 465) but through the great and fair natural objects surrounding him, and that he was happy to be able to come into close spiritual contact with humanity through the help of those great and fair natural objects.

5.4 Image schema of 'through'

Now, let us take a brief look at the image schema of 'through.'

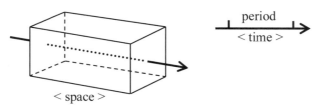

Figure 5.2: Image schema of 'through'

According to R. A. Close (1968: 154), as Figure 5.2 clearly shows, <time> is captured as a linear 'period,' and <space> is schematized as a 'three-dimensional form.'

An arrow penetrating the box represents the agent of movement: it is sometimes the poet himself and at other times Nature; sometimes, physical agents, at other times, spiritual agents.

The contents of the box are sometimes both natural objects and natural phenomena in the outer world of Nature, and at other times the heart and mind of the poet. In one word, 'through' functions as a medium that connects the inner and outer worlds.

5.5 Further observations of 'through'

Next, let us turn to other interesting verbal expressions occurring with 'through':

- First, 'rough and smooth' combines with 'through' rather than with 'over,' as is seen in '*through* rough and smooth / We scamper'd homeward' (2, 137-38).
- Second, when describing the figure of a shepherd, he catches him 'stalking *through* the fog' (8, 401), not stalking 'in' the fog.
- Third, not 'in Paris' but '*Through* Paris' (9, 40) is preferred.
- Fourth, 'under all conditions' seems to be normal usage, but when it comes to Wordsworth's hand, it becomes: 'Nature *through* all conditions hath a power / To consecrate' (12, 282-83).

All these uses illustrate and emphasize his habit of wandering, which the sentence 'I walked with Nature' (2, 377) clearly suggests. All these uses must be considered an important point to understanding Wordsworth and the poem.

5.6 Reasons for the frequent use of 'through'

Let us now consider possible reasons why 'through' is used so often in *The Prelude*. We may reasonably conclude that the poet's way of recognizing the outer world is highly extensive and on a grand scale. He thus generally tries to take a higher and broader view of things around him.

Talking through the axis of time, he retraces the growth of his poetic mind from early childhood to manhood. From the axis of space, he can be said to travel extensively, as far afield as France, Germany, and Switzerland. To be more specific, he was born in Cockermouth, moved to Hawkshead, where he spent his school days, and when he grew older, studied at Cambridge. During his university days, he went on a walking tour of the Alps. After graduating, he lived in London, went to Wales, and across to France where the Revolution was at its prime. He also visited the Isle of Wight and Goslar, Germany. He moved residence several times in England. In short, he was a wandering poet.

Such was his own movement in time and space, that 'through' of <motion> rather than 'in, at' of <stationary state> appears quite frequently in the work under consideration.

5.7 'Through' in the Snowdon passage

Let us now move to the last and most important quotation in this chapter. 'Through' in this case is stylistically 'marked,' because, unlike the preceding usages, it has a relative pronoun as its object. The total number of 'through' phrases taking a relative pronoun as object is four throughout *The Prelude*, and indeed two of these appear in this single passage, which is stylistically quite noteworthy.

Wordsworth states in this famous passage the interrelation between Man and Nature, and the procedure of establishing a theory of Imagination which is peculiar to himself.

```
1              ...and from the shore
2   At distance not the third part of a mile
3   Was a blue chasm; a fracture in the vapour,
4   A deep and gloomy breathing-place through which
5   Mounted the roar of waters, torrents, streams
6   Innumerable, roaring with one voice.
7   The universal spectacle throughout
8   Was shaped for admiration and delight,
9   Grand in itself alone, but in that breach
10  Through which the homeless voice of waters rose,
11  That dark deep thoroughfare had Nature lodg'd
12  The Soul, the Imagination of the whole.     (13, 54-65)
```

The poet stands at the summit of Mt. Snowdon, the highest mountain in Wales, in order to see the sunrise from its top. He finds himself on the 'shore' of a huge 'sea' of mist. The sea of mist at his feet is so grand and majestic that the real sea far behind fades into insignificance. The moon looks down on this sight in single glory.

With this scene as background, several "foregrounded"—'highlighted' or 'made prominent'—expressions appear: *chasm*, *fracture*, *breathing-place*, *breach*, and *thoroughfare*. 'Chasm' is foregrounded

Chapter 5 'Through' in *The Prelude* 93

in that it is expressed in an alternative way; it is rephrased in as many as five different ways through parallelism. 'Parallelism has been defined by Leech (1969) as 'foregrounded regularity' (Wales, 1989: 335-36).

As I mentioned in Section 1.4 of Chapter 1, in the description of the majestic scene, 'through' is used twice: in lines 4 and 10. A compound noun *'through*fare' is used in line 11; this word is etymologically composed of 'through' and 'fare.' Furthermore, adding an adverb *'through*out,' which equals 'all through' (*OED2* s.v. 'throughout' 2. b.), from the seventh line, the total number comes up to four. It is quite surprising that 'through' and its related words appear as many as four times in only twelve lines.

Next, I shall draw attention to the development in the variation of the near-synonyms expressing the crack in 'a huge sea of mist:' *chasm, fracture, breathing-place; breach, thoroughfare*.

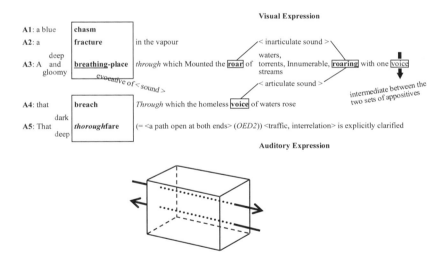

Figure 5.3: Two sets of appositives: synonymous representations of 'crack'

Let me represent the passage graphically. See Figure 5.3. Two sets of appositives are exploited in the Figure 5.3: marked A1, A2, A3, and A4, A5. The space occupied for expression to delineate the entity of the crack grows wider and wider in this order in the former set: A1, A2, A3. More specifically, A1 is composed of three words, A2 is comprised of five words, and A3 is made up of five words plus a long relative clause.

At the same time, notice the change from visual to auditory expressions. The first element of variation is only 'a <u>blue</u> chasm,' the second is 'a fracture <u>in the vapour</u>,' both of which are simply related to the visual. However, notice the rather elaborate third element:

> A deep and gloomy <u>breathing</u>-place through which
> Mounted the **roar** of waters, torrents, streams
> Innumerable, **roaring** with one **voice**, (13, 57-59)

This is closely related to an auditory expression ('roar,' 'roaring,' 'voice'). Note also the subtle change of description from visual to auditory expression in the use of 'breathing,' which is evocative of <sound>. It thus becomes evident that the poet's 'struggle toward definition' (Lindenberger, 1963: 51) here is elaborated dexterously by this twofold representation appealing both to the eyes and the ears.

A4 and A5 are slightly different from the former set: A1, A2, and A3. The sound of the former is captured as 'roar,' while that of the latter is 'voice.' There is a distinct difference between the two in that the former is an <<u>in</u>articulate sound>, while the latter is an <articulate sound>. 'Voice' at the very end of A3 functions as an intermediate (which is diagrammatically illustrated by a broad down arrow) between the two sets of appositives. Returning to the top of the appositional elements and observing them oriented downward, I see that the key word 'chasm' is reworded to 'fracture' and then 'breathing-place;' it is then rephrased to 'breach' and finally 'thoroughfare.' 'Thoroughfare' has the meaning of <a path open at both ends> (*OED2* 1.c.) and <an unobstructed channel> (*OED2* 1.d.). As the box-shaped image schema indicates the meaning of <coming and going; traffic; interrelation> is explicitly clarified in the final appositive, A5. Notice the difference of the number and the direction of arrows. Those of Figure 5.2 are one and <u>uni</u>directional, while those of Figure 5.3 are two and <u>bi</u>directional, the prefix of which signifies 'interactive actions' themselves. Through that 'thoroughfare,' the poet heard mighty Nature's articulate and recognizable 'voice.' In other words, he received a message full of revelations. Conversely, Nature brought a revelational message hitherto unknown to the poet.

Taking the above-mentioned differences into consideration, I conclude that what was nothing but a 'chasm,' from which an inarticulate 'roar' arose, eventually develops into a 'thoroughfare,' through which a somewhat meaningful, positive 'voice' ascends without obstacle, and, through which, this time conversely, the poet Wordsworth is able to, the more easily, find his way back into the 'thoroughfare' because it is <open at both ends>. In this way, the poet freely uses his technical skill of giving a slight and subtle change of meaning to each appositional element. Here is manifested one of the poetic crafts of Wordsworth; here is demonstrated one aspect of the Wordsworthian imagination.

To use Roman Jakobson's (cited in Sebeok 1960: 358) words, one might say Wordsworth is a poet who 'shows the axis of selection.' He is a poet who realizes that he can only make himself understood to his readers by showing 'the axis of selection,' which comprises 'the sequential elements of apposition.'

The poet, upon looking at this marvelous scene, becomes lost in meditation. Then, as mentioned earlier in §3.4.1, he derives the revelation that (1) The very scene is a perfect image of a mighty Mind. He knows by intuition that (2) The process by which Nature causes to raise a 'homeless voice' *through* the breach in the sea of mist is exactly the same as that by which imagination arises in a poetic mind. Furthermore, he recognizes that (3) Nature's creative power producing an admirable, grand natural phenomenon is one and the same with the poetic imagination working within a great poet's mind.

5.8 Summary

Thus far, I have closely observed several contexts around 'through,' stimulated by the "marked" deviation of its occurrence from that in the LOB, Brown, and other Corpora. Firstly, I paid attention to the object of each occurrence of 'through.' In other words, I focused on what syntactically follows each 'through.' I have made a chart (5.1) that displays the distribution of objects of preposition 'through.' As a result, it turned out that abstract noun objects outnumber concrete noun ones, which attests to the abstractness of *The Prelude*. Secondly, I inquired into the syntactic combination of verbs with 'through,' focusing on what precedes each 'through.' Verbs of 'motion' tend to come before the preposition. They all have semantic components of <gradual progress>, <expansion>, and <pervasiveness>. To illustrate the penetrating function of 'through,' I introduced two kinds of box-shaped image schema. Lastly, in §5.7, I pointed out a few interesting linguistic facts realized in the well-wrought Snowdon passage of *The Prelude*. I have also directed attention to the question of the interrelations between the poet's inner world and the outer world of

Nature. As a consequence, I conclude: the greatness of Nature enhances human beings '**through**' its mighty Forms, and the mind of Wordsworth grew even greater and mightier '**through**' the mighty forms. Though only a small indeclinable preposition, I can safely assert that '**through**' fulfills a vital role in *The Prelude*.

Notes
Very few studies have been made upon 'through' in *The Prelude*. Gill's (1991: 31) observation is sharp.

Chapter 6
Multi-Layered Structure of Expression in *The Prelude*

6.0 Introduction
The foregoing five chapters are chiefly concerned with 'the vocabulary of *The Prelude*' per se. In this sixth and final chapter, I deal with expressions in which the vocabulary is manipulated in particular contexts. More specifically, I discuss 'the way words, phrases and clauses are ordered and formally grouped' (Wales 2001: s.v. syntax). I would like to seek a distinguishing feature of expressions used in *The Prelude*, among others, in its multi-layered structure.

When we read a literary work, we often come across certain characteristics appearing repeatedly in the work. The repeated characteristic in *The Prelude* is a multi-layered structure, particularly the triple structure. By "triple structure" I mean one such as 'I felt X1, X2, X3' when an ordinary expression, 'I felt X' is more common. In this chapter, I call each X1, X2, and X3 an 'element.'

In the former part (§§6.1-6.3) of this chapter, I examine in particular the nature of the triple structure which seems to be one of the most dominant stylistic features of *The Prelude* from two perspectives: (1) Enhancing and (2) Deepening. In the latter part (§§6.4-6.5), I observe the function of the triple structure in detail, analyzing the famous Snowdon passage in *The Prelude*.

6.1 Threefold structure
First, let us look at what is called the preamble of *The Prelude*:

(1) For I, methought, while the sweet breath of Heaven
     Was blowing on my body, felt within
     A corresponding mild creative breeze,   A1
     A vital breeze which travell'd gently on A2
     O'er things which it had made, and is become
     A tempest, a redundant energy,   B1, B2
     Vexing its own creation. 'Tis a power   C1
     That does not come unrecognized, a storm,   C2
                                              (1, 41-48)

This passage well describes how Wordsworth's imagination arises internally corresponding to the breeze blowing from the outside. Here, one direction of the movement of the poet's mind which we often encounter as we read *The Prelude* is manifested. Double structures are repeated three times in total: A1 'A mild creative breeze' is enhanced to A2 'A vital breeze'; B1 'A tempest' is changed to B2 'a redundant energy;' and C1 'a power' is altered to C2 'a storm.' In each pair the expressive power of the former is increasingly heightened in that of the latter. In brief, an external 'breeze' is strengthened to an internal 'storm.' The outward breeze in the natural world gives rise to a poem inside Wordsworth's poetical mind.

Expressions by means of these multi-layered structures are stylistic characteristics of *The Prelude*, and can be regarded as what is called by formalists "foregrounding." Double structures such as *the poet, Wordsworth* and *my friend, Bob* are commonly used in our daily life. In *The Prelude* as well, appositional double expressions like *Child of the mountains, I* (10, 1007-08), and *God, the Giver of all joy* (6, 614) are quite often observed. Those consisting of triple elements, however, are not so common in ordinary language except in expressions such as proverbs and advertisements. Therefore, when we come across these threefold structures in *The Prelude*, we cannot help being attracted by the unique expressions themselves. This is "foregrounding" itself, and it is this very technique that Wordsworth employs when he finds it difficult to communicate his mystical experiences to his readers. '[T]he poet's verbal struggle to define his moment of spiritual illumination' (Lindenberger 1963: 53) must require such multi-layered expressions.

We will be able to divide the triple-structures into two types according to their meanings: Enhancing and Deepening.

6.2 Enhancing

By Enhancing I mean that the content of the third appositional element A3 is heightened as compared with those of A2 and A1. I can indicate the expressive force by a rising curve like this: →→↗. At the last element of the sequence, the superlative degree of an adjective and 'God' and words related to Him tend to appear in almost all examples.

The next example is a passage in which Wordsworth declares that the theme of *The Prelude* is nothing less than the Imagination, after realizing a theory of imagination peculiar to him at the top of Mt. Snowdon. By 'its progress' in line 182, the poet means 1) his Imagination's progression from early childhood, 2) its impairment after many twists and turns, especially during and just after the French

Chapter 6   Multi-Layered Structure of Expression in *The Prelude*

Revolution, and 3) its final restoration:

> (2)   And lastly, from its progress have we drawn
> The feeling of life endless, the great thought   A1,   A2
> By which we live, Infinity and God.   A2,   A3
>   (13, 182-84)

A1, 'The feeling of life endless' is incrementally heightened to A3, 'Infinity and God.' Here is expressed the poet's emotional heightening which increases gradually according as A1 develops to A2 and A2 develops to A3. The poet's mind seems to try to reach a certain ultimate height leading to God.

As a boy, Wordsworth borrowed a shepherd's boat without the owner's permission and rowed out on a lake. He is horrified at 'unknown modes of being' (1, 420) and hears Nature remonstrate with him about his dishonest deed. Wordsworth addresses the spirit presiding over the universe:

> (3)   Wisdom and Spirit of the universe!
> Thou Soul that art the Eternity of Thought!
> That giv'st to forms and images a breath
> And everlasting motion! not in vain,
> By day or star-light thus from my first dawn
> Of Childhood didst Thou intertwine for me
> The passions that build up our human Soul,
> Not with the mean and vulgar works of Man,
> But with high objects, with enduring things,   A1,   A2
> With life and nature, purifying thus   A3
> The elements of feeling and of thought,
> And sanctifying, by such discipline,
> Both pain and fear, until we recognize
> A grandeur in the beatings of the heart.   (1, 428-41)

The universe feeds the poet's mind with its wise spirit from his early childhood. He offers thanks to Nature for all the work it has done in favor of him. Here, he expresses how and by what means he is cherished and educated by Nature. To be exact, Nature intertwines the passions of Wordsworth's soul with 'high objects,' 'enduring things,' and 'life and nature.' Nature influences the young poet not by using 'the mean and vulgar works of Man,' but by employing 'high' and 'enduring' natural things full of life. What the first and second appositional elements (A1 and A2) depict might be all the living things around human beings (e.g. 'rocks,' 'stones,' and 'trees'), whether they are grand or unknown. What is expressed by the third element (A3) might be life-giving Nature that provides him with 'everlasting motion' and vitality.

In the next citation, the poet expresses his pleasure gained from studying geometry. He tries to find a similitude between the simple and genuine symmetry in geometry and the structure and ordering in Nature:

(4) Yet from this source more frequently I drew
A pleasure calm and deeper, a still sense   A1,   A2
Of permanent and universal sway
And paramount endowment in the mind,
An image not unworthy of the one   A3
Surpassing Life, which out of space and time,
Nor touch'd by welterings of passion, is,
And hath the name of God.   (6, 150-57)

The word 'pleasure' in A1, which belongs to the stratum of everyday personal feelings, is enhanced to 'image' in A3, which transcends time and space and is not influenced by human passions. It is even worthy of the name of God. In A2, or rather in 'a still sense / Of permanent and universal sway / And paramount endowment in the mind' particularly, '[A]n illustration of Wordsworth's cravings for "enduring things"' (Havens 1967: 411) is observed. In this way the poet draws something metaphysical from physical matter or the law of Nature.

The next example comes just after the scene where he felt sad at the sight of Mont Blanc, which was not as grandiose as he had expected:

(5)   the wondrous Vale
Of Chamouny did, on the following dawn,
With its dumb cataracts and streams of ice,   A1
A motionless array of mighty waves,   A2
Five rivers broad and vast, make rich amends,   A3
And reconcil'd us to realities.   (6, 456-61)

Here, Wordsworth tells us that the Vale of Chamonix makes up for his disappointment when he saw Mont Blanc. The sight of the Vale of Chamonix is expressed in three ways. A1: 'dumb cataracts and streams of ice' (*dumb* because the cataracts and streams were frozen) is appositionally developed to A2: 'A motionless array of mighty waves' (*motionless* because the waves were frozen, too) and furthermore is

Chapter 6 Multi-Layered Structure of Expression in *The Prelude*

expanded and elaborated with two postposed adjectives, up to A3: 'Five rivers broad and vast.' It might be said that A1 is an acoustically motivated expression, while A2 and A3 are optically motivated expressions. The poet's sense of admiration is explicitly depicted in his choice of adjectives: 'mighty' in A2 and 'broad and vast' in A3. Mighty and vast forms, among others, stimulate Wordsworth's poetic mind.

6.3 Deepening

By Deepening I mean that the purport of the third appositional element A3 is deepened in proportion as the appositional element expands from A1 to A3. As often as not, a progressive change in this category of Deepening is observed from depiction of outward things to that of inward things. The expressive force is diagrammatically shown as follows: →→↘.

The example below describes the poet's impression when he saw the din and bustle of a market called St. Bartholomew's Fair. The poet says the hustle and bustle of the fair does not differ in the least from that of London. This is a rare example of a four-layered structure:

(6) Oh, blank confusion! and a type not false   A1! A2
Of what the mighty City is itself
To all except a Straggler here and there,
To the whole Swarm of its inhabitants;
An undistinguishable world to men,   A3
The slaves unrespited of low pursuits,
Living amid the same perpetual flow
Of trivial objects, melted and reduced
To one identity, by differences
That have no law, no meaning, and no end;
Oppression under which even highest minds   A4
Must labour, whence the strongest are not free; (7, 695-706)

First, Wordsworth captures the hustle and bustle of St. Bartholomew's Fair as 'blank confusion.' After expressing his general impression of the fair in the two words, he compares the confusion of the fair to that of 'the mighty City,' London. He refers to the state of congestion as 'a type' which is identical with the hurly-burly of London. This, in turn, transforms into 'An undistinguishable world' at the stage of A3 and lastly is deepened into 'Oppression' under which 'even the highest minds' must suffer and from which 'the strongest' minds cannot escape.

To each appositional element is added a two-layered recipient: 'To all, To the whole Swarm…' in A2 and 'to men, The slaves…' in A3 respectively. In A4, one relative clause contains two recipients with superlative-degree expressions: 'highest minds' and 'the strongest (minds).'

The next quotation depicts Wordsworth's feelings before leaving for France. His only regret is that he has to give up browsing through books at his favorite secondhand book-stalls in London:

> (7) A year thus spent, this field (with small regret
> Save only for the Book-stalls in the streets,   A1
> Wild produce, hedge-row fruit, on all sides hung   A2, A3
> To tempt the sauntering traveller from his track)
> I quitted, and betook myself to France,   (9, 31-35)

The real 'book-stalls' are likened to natural things, that is, 'Wild produce, hedge-row fruit,' both of which are unmistakably natural products. The 'Book-stalls,' 'Wild produce,' and 'hedge-row fruit' are all concrete nouns, but they differ in that the former is an artifact and the latter two are not artifacts.

The following passage describes the ecstatic emotion he felt during his early morning walk at the age of ten:

> (8) Oft in those moments such a holy calm
> Did overspread my soul, that I forgot
> That I had bodily eyes, and what I saw
> Appear'd like something in myself, a dream,   A1, A2
> A prospect in my mind.   A3
> (2, 367-71)

An obscure 'something in myself' gradually takes a definite shape and becomes 'a dream' and develops into 'A prospect in my mind.' In this way, when the poet forgets the existence of his own bodily eyes, an outward landscape turns to a scene reflected in his mind through his inward eyes.

As seen above, Wordsworth makes frequent use of triple appositive structures. He strives to make his impression gained from the outside world more articulate and definite by using one expression after another in rapid succession. In so doing, what he endeavours to express turns eventually either to (1) Enhancing or (2) Deepening. It is this 'struggle toward definition' (Lindenberger 1966: 51) that gives rise to multi-layered expression peculiar to Wordsworth's literary style.

6.4 Introduction to the Snowdon passage

So far I have explained triple structures characteristic of *The Prelude* in two ways: Enhancing and Deepening. The contexts of the passages I quoted, however, are limited and narrow. Here in §6.4, I would like to cite a longer passage describing the poet's ascent of Snowdon and closely investigate how the multi-layered structure functions in a wider context. This passage, I believe, is the most apt illustration of multi-layered expressions in *The Prelude*.

First, in order to observe the movement of syntax explicitly, it is best to make diagrammatic illustrations. Chart 6.1 shows the syntax, i.e. 'the skeleton framework of the sentences' (Wales 2001: s.v. syntax) realized in the Snowdon passage. The diagrammatic Chart 6.1 is based on Chart 6.2 given at the end of this chapter, in which the Snowdon lines are cited with two kinds of numbering added to them.

Then, an explanation of Chart 6.1 is required. The heavy horizontal line in the center of the chart represents the division of stanzas. Here, I call a sentence (beginning with a capital letter and ending with a full stop, colon, or semicolon) a "major sentence," and to the major sentences I give a sequential serial number with broad figures, **1** to **8**. The division between them is shown by the second thickest horizontal lines on the chart. I call subdivided sentences within a major sentence "minor sentences," which are numbered with smaller figures from 1 to 19. The division between them is shown by a thin horizontal line.

I arrange P (predicate verb) in the center of the chart, S (subject) on its left side, and O (object), C (complement) on its right. On the left side of S is M (modifier). M is also arranged on the right side of O and C. M is further divided into either Mcl (Modifier in the form of a clause) or Mph (Modifier in the form of a phrase). At the left side is placed Cj (conjunction). A vertical broken line between P and O, C indicates that the P before the line is an intransitive verb. The reverse slash marks (i.e. \ ) indicate that what follows these marks is a subordinate clause.

The greatest advantage of this chart is that we can obtain, at a glance, a clear view of the syntactic movement in the passage. For example, we can understand that, in the former half which depicts the poet's objective outward description of Nature, almost all the minor sentences have conjunctions; while the latter half which describes his meditation after seeing a marvelous scene has only one conjunction. Even a casual glance at the chart is enough to understand the "depth-ordered or recursive" structure (Otsuka 1970: 998) realized in sentences 6-15

Chart 6.1: Analytical syntax of the Snowdon Passage

Maj.	Min.	Cj	M	S	P
1	1	When	at my feet / with a step or two	the ground	appear'd / And / seem'd
	2	Nor		I	had
	3	For	instantly	a Light	Fell
2	4			I	looked about,
	5	and lo!		The Moon	stood
	6	and		I	found
3	7			A hundred hills	upheaved
	8	and	beyond, Far, far beyond,	the vapours	shot
4	9	Meanwhile,		the Moon	look'd down upon
	10	and		we	stood,
	11	and	from the shore At distance not the third part of a mile	a blue chasm; a fracture in the vapour, deep A and breathing-place gloomy	Was
5	12			The universal spectacle throughout	Was shaped
	13	but	that breach \Through which the homeless voice of waters rose, in dark That thoroughfare deep	Nature	had lodg'd
6	14			A meditation	rose
	15	and	to me	it	appear'd
	16		above all there	Nature	had Exhibited

Arrows with dotted lines indicate the original location of the lexical item in question within Wordsworth's writing.

7	17		\ which these Acknowledge when thus moved, The Power \ which Nature thus Thrusts forth upon the senses,		is
8	18			That	is
	19		from their native selves for themselves \ whene'er it is Created for them,	They	Can send abroad create and, catch

Chapter 6   Multi-Layered Structure of Expression in *The Prelude*   105

O	C	M	
to brighten, brighter still;			
time to ask the cause of this,			
upon the turf	like a flash:		
naked in the Heavens, at height Immense above my head,			
myself	on the shore	of a huge sea of mist, \ Which, meek and silent, rested at my feet:	
their dusky backs	All over this still Ocean,		
themselves,	In headlands, tongues, and promontory shapes,	Into	the Sea, the real sea,	\ that seem'd To give up	dwindle, and	its majesty, Usurp'd upon \ as far as sight could reach.
this shew	In single glory,		
the mist Touching our very feet;			
\ through which Mounted the roar of torrents, Innumerable, roaring with one voice.	waters streams		
for	admiration and delight,	Grand in itself alone,	
The Soul, the Imagination of the whole.			
in me that night	Upon the lonely Mountain \ when the scene Had pass'd away,		
The perfect image	of a mighty Mind, Of one	\ that feeds upon infinity, an under-presence, \ That is exalted by	The sense of God, or \ whatsoe'er is Or vast	dim in its own being,
One function by putting forth, …and that	of such mind That domination With circumstance most	\ which she oftentimes awful and sublime,	Exerts upon the outward face of things, moulds and them, endues, abstracts, combines, Or
			Doth make one object so impress itself Upon all others, and
		by	abrupt and influence unhabitual	pervade them	\ so That even the grossest minds	see must and And hear cannot chuse but feel.
the express Resemblance,			
a genuine	Counterpart And Brother in the fulness of its strength Made visible,	of the glorious faculty \ Which higher minds bear with them as their own.	
the very spirit \ in which they deal With all the objects of the universe;			
Like transformation, A like existence,			
it		by an instinct;	

and 6-16. The fact that the occupied space in 6-15 and 6-16 extends lengthwise greatly shows that the two sentences are extremely long and complicated. In other words, the poet makes so much use of equivalent structures that its syntax becomes complex and intricate. Inversions such as PS and OP are not represented as the original word order because of the restriction that P is located in the center of the diagram. The original order is shown by using ⌊⎯⎯⎯↑ after the manner of Bolton (1982: 177).

The passage in question is said to be written based on the poet's real experience. Wordsworth climbs Mount Snowdon, the highest mountain in Wales (1,085 m), with his friend, Robert Jones, on a sultry summer night. Before the quotation, there appear four descriptions expressing their ascending movement: '[13-14]on we went / Uncheck'd,' '[20]Thus did we breast the ascent,' '[28]on we wound,' and '[31]I panted up.' (Hereafter, superior figures in front of each expression indicate line number.) It is as if to hint that the poet's upward movement to the summit, surpassing physical height, reaches metaphysical height, the stage of his realizing an astounding revelation. Put simply, Wordsworth here depicts the interrelationship between man and Nature and how he establishes his unique theory of imagination revealed in the interaction of his mind with surrounding Nature.

From the content of expression, I can split this passage into two parts: the first half makes a detailed description of the nature seen from the summit; and the second half describes the profound influence of Nature on the poet's mind. (Again, the division is marked by a thick horizontal line in Chart 6.1.) The relationship between man and Nature, as mentioned above, is a reciprocal one so that, seen from the pattern of description, the expressions of both parts have much in common. Both can be seen to form a mirror-image relation in which one part reflects the other and vice versa. Now, I will consider "isotopy" (Riffaterre 1978: 172) which are seen in both worlds, and then extract the corresponding expressions. Katie Wales (1989: 265) defines the term thus: 'Isotopy refers to a level of meaning which is established by the recurrence in a text of SEMES belonging to the same **semantic field**, and which contributes to our interpretation of the THEME.' Moreover, I will conduct an investigation into the movement of syntax in this passage.

6.5 First half of the Snowdon passage

What impresses me most after a single perusal of the Snowdon passage

Chapter 6   Multi-Layered Structure of Expression in *The Prelude* 107

is the <vastness> of the moon-lit scene watched afar from the summit. The tremendousness can be summarized by <immensity> (cf. [42]Immense):

The spatial upper limit of <immensity> is expressed in the sentence 2-5: '[41-42]The Moon stood naked in the Heavens at height / Immense above my head.'

The horizontal expansion is rendered by '[42-43]on the shore / I found myself of a huge sea of mist' in 2-6; '[45-46]A hundred hills their dusky backs upheaved / All over this still Ocean' in 3-7; and '[46-48]beyond, / Far, far beyond, the vapours shot themselves / In headlands, tongues, and promontory shapes' in 3-8.

The spatial lower limit is expressed by '[49-51]Into the Sea, the real Sea, that seem'd / To dwindle, and give up its majesty, / Usurp'd upon as far as sight could reach' in 3-8.

All these are expressions appealing to visual perception. Auditory expression, as well, is employed in 4-11: '[57-59]through which / Mounted the roar of waters, torrents, streams / Innumerable, roaring with one voice.'

The total scene is summarized by and culminated in the expression: '[60]The universal spectacle throughout' in 5-12.

In order to give a contrastive emphasis to the <vastness> of the sight, the poet seems to consciously employ the expressions of spatial and temporary <nearness>. They are, from a spatial point of view, '[36-37]at my feet the ground appear'd to brighten, / And with a step or two seem'd brighter still' in 1-1; '[41-42]The Moon stood naked in the Heavens, at height / Immense above my head' in 1-5; '[44]Which, meek and silent, rested at my feet' in 2-6; and '[53-54]and we stood, the mist / Touching our very feet' in 4-10.

Viewed in the light of temporal <nearness>, the <instantaneousness> is expressed by '[38]Nor had I time to ask the cause of this' in 1-2; and '[39-40]For instantly a Light upon the turf / Fell like a flash' in 1-3.

In this connection we have to take notice of the expressive force of 'not' in 4-11: '[54-56]from the shore / At distance not the third part of a mile / Was a blue chasm.' The literal meaning of the sentence might be paraphrased as: 'the blue chasm was less than 536 meters (⅓ mile) from the shore (of mist where the poet stood).' The <nearness> expressed here is not so intense (or proximate) as that associated with '[36]at my feet,' '[44]at my feet,' and '[54]our very feet.' The chasm could not be so far away when we consider it is the chasm itself that is the central core of description here; in other words, it is the very chasm that is foregrounded in this context. The distance between the chasm and the observer has to be appropriate enough for him to observe the circumstances. The chasm could be said to lie at a moderate distance. One cannot see an object minutely at this distance, but can hear the sound emitted from the object. In this case, it is unnecessary for the details of the chasm to be observed fully by the poet's eyes, because its details can be captured aurally by the poet's ears.

6.5.1 Triple-layered structure representative of 'crack'

The triple-structured expression realized in the minor sentence 4-11 is noteworthy. Let me express it schematically once again here:

A1: a blue   chasm,
A2: a   fracture   in the vapour,
    deep   waters
A3: a and   breathing-place, through which Mounted the roar of torrents Innumerable, roaring with one voice
    gloomy   streams

A1:   M   H
A2:   H   Qph
A3:   M   H   Qcl

(M=Modifier=pre-modifier; H=Head word; Q=Qualifier=post-modifier; ph=phrase; cl=clause)

Figure 6.1: Triple-structured expression

The first element of the multi-layered structure, A1, to use Halliday's (1970: 59) terminology, is M H. It expresses a broad and general sketch of the scene: 'a <u>blue</u> chasm.' The second element, A2, unlike the first A1, has a post-modifying prepositional phrase: 'a fracture <u>in the vapour</u>.' Both A1 and A2 are visual representations of the crack. However, the third element, A 3 contains both M and Q, each of which modifies the head word, 'breathing-place' from the front, and qualifies it from the rear, respectively. The coordinated M consists of 'deep,' which represents its form, not its color nor its place; and of 'gloomy,' which bears the meaning suggestive of <mysteriousness>. The Q consists of a rather long post-modifying relative clause filled with detailed information.

Here, we have to notice a subtle 'elegant variation' of head words. According as they vary from A1 to A3, visual A1 and A2 turn and deepen into auditory A3, also seen in a fine piece named "To the Cuckoo," where the cuckoo is captured as 'a wandering Voice' (l. 4) and 'A voice, a mystery' (l. 16).

Let us look at A3. The head, 'breathing-place,' belongs to an auditory expression rather than a visual expression, for breathing is closely associated with <sound>. Moreover, 'roar,' 'roaring,' and 'one voice' all definitely belong to the same lexical set <sound>. It is therefore evident that what is expressed in the triple structure (A1, A2, A3) shifts from visual to auditory perception. This threefold variation still develops into another variation of dual structure, which will be discussed in the next section.

6.5.2 Co-referential double structure

The co-referential double structure appears in the sentence 5-13. Both <u>A1, A2, A3</u> and <u>A4, A5</u> refer to the same 'chasm,' and hence are co-referential. The structure may be schematized as follows:

A4: that   <u>breach</u>   Through which the homeless voice of waters rose
        Dark
A5: That   <u>thoroughfare</u>
        deep

A4:   <u>H</u>   Qcl
       M
A5:   <u>H</u>
       M

(M=Modifier=pre-modifier; H=Head word; Q=Qualifier=post-modifier; cl=clause)

Figure 6.2: Co-referential double-structured expression

The grammatical subject of the qualifying clause (Qcl) in A4 is the same 'voice' as the last word in A3, 'voice,' so that, despite the intervening minor sentence 5-12, the shift from A3 to A4 runs smooth.

Incidentally, the space allocated for each expression (i.e. the total length of its H with M and Q) is 'small, medium, large, large, and medium' in the order of A1, A2, A3, A4, and A5. That is to say, A1: A2: A3: A4: A5 = S: M: L: L: M.

I have just mentioned that the shift goes smoothly from A3 to A4. Why, however, does a sentence followed by an adversative conjunction, '^{62}but,' intervene between A3 and A4? Furthermore, why does '^{62}but' try to interrupt the smooth movement of the lines? (Incidentally, if you look at Chart 6.1, you will notice almost all the conjunctions used for the minor sentences are copulative, not adversative. The above-mentioned '^{62}but' is an exception and thus it is "marked.")

The decisive factor in answering the question is the meaning of the sentence 5-12 between A3 and A4. It runs as follows: 'The universal spectacle throughout / Was shaped for admiration and delight, / <u>Grand</u> in itself alone.' Each of the natural things comprising the universal spectacle is given its own attribute. Take '[43]a huge sea of mist,' for example. It is given super-<[50]majesty> because '[49-50]the Real sea seem'd / To ... give up its majesty.' '[52]The Moon' is given <[53]glory>, and the whole scene is given <grandeur> (cf. [62]Grand).

In such a '[62]grand' natural phenomenon, the poet cannot but feel '[61]admiration and delight.' The agent who experiences the 'admiration' and 'delight' is human, so the 'admiration' *for* and 'delight' *in* natural things are personal human feelings.

It is true that the view spread out before the poet's eyes is <grand> enough to demand 'delightful admiration' from him, **but** Nature does more than instill a sense of 'admiration' into the beholder, the poet Wordsworth. (This is an explication of the meaning of '[62]but.') It is not until we come to the minor sentence 5-13 that we encounter a mind-stirring, not heart-stirring, spectacle. In fact, Nature *had* lodged 'in that breach,' in 'That dark deep thoroughfare' 'The Soul, the Imagination of the whole.'

The position of the phrase, 'Imagination of the whole' in the sentence 5-13 is noteworthy. It is syntactically placed at the end of a sentence, where its meaning (i.e. new information) is highlighted through the principle of "end focus." The meaning is doubly emphasized because it is both at the end of the line and at the end of the stanza.

We should also be aware of the grammatical fact that the predicate is depicted in the past perfect tense: the tense expressed by 'had lodg'd' implies that, while his bodily eyes functioned, the poet did not recognize the poetic truth that Nature revealed the picture of imaginative faculty's welling up to the poet, himself. In point of fact, 'Nature had' <u>already</u> 'lodg'd the Imagination of the whole' there 'in that breach' <u>before</u> the poet realized it.

So far I have pointed out that the triple (A1, A2, and A3) and double (A4 and A5) appositional and equivalent structures are employed in the Snowdon passage and that their content of expressions changed from visual into auditory. I have clarified why the minor sentence of 5-12 exists and also explained that '[58]roar,' '[59]roaring,' '[59]voice,' in A3 and '[63]voice' in A4 constitute "isotopy" in which lexical items belong to the same semantic field.

6.5.3 Subtle difference of meaning in "isotopy"

I believe that it is important to be aware of the subtle difference of meaning between the appositional elements constituting the "isotopy." In order to trace the relationship, or rather fill up the break, between the former appositional group and the latter one, here again I give a graphic description of the post-modifying structures in A3' and A4'. Both of them are partially taken from the original A3 and A4 and followed by 'through which (i.e. the chasm),' hence A3' and A4' with the addition of a prime symbol.

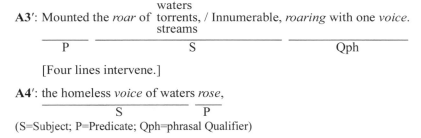

Figure 6.3: Graphic description of post-modifying structures

In A3', the head word of S is 'roar,' which, together with 'roaring,' forms "polyptoton" (a figure of rhetoric in which…words are repeated derived from the same root, Wales: 364-65). The participial phrase 'roaring with one voice' is given "end-weight" and qualifies 'Mounted.' The 'voice' in turn suddenly appears again in A4' at the subject position, which is a position of due prominence in a clause. The 'roar' is not a 'voice.' The former signifies an inarticulate and meaningless sound, but the latter signifies an articulate and meaningful sound. This is an important difference.

Furthermore, it is significant that 'breach' in A4 (See Figure 6.2) is further rephrased to 'thoroughfare' in A5. Let me go back to the first appositional element and review how a series of appositional expressions develops. The head of A1 'chasm' becomes 'fracture' in A2 and 'breathing-place' in A3; and then in A4 'breach' and finally in A5 'thoroughfare.' At the last element, the original 'chasm' evolves into 'thoroughfare,' to which *OED2* gives a definition: 'a public way unobstructed and open at both ends.' From this I can surmise that the meaning of <traffic; coming and going> becomes conspicuous at the last stage of description. In other words, taking the above-mentioned two kinds of difference of meaning (i.e. roar ≠ voice; chasm ≠ thoroughfare) into consideration, I can recognize one clear intention of expression in Wordsworth's handling of words and phrases: his expression changes from nothing but a 'chasm' (from which a meaningless 'roar' arises) to a 'thoroughfare' (from which the somewhat meaningful 'voice' comes up easily). In this way Wordsworth is successful in using, to the full, every expressive means available.

One more thing to be noticed in A3 is that there is a part which is parallel to the above-mentioned mode of expression.

A3: a deep and breathing-place, through which Mounted the roar of waters torrents Innumerable, roaring with one voice
gloomy streams

That is to say, <nearness> is interspersed among <immensity> so as to emphasize the <immensity>. More specifically, the three nouns in plural forms, 'water**s**,' 'torrent**s**,' and 'stream**s**,' (which are compatible with <immensity> in expressing the weight of numbers) are given <limitation> by the use of 'one' in 'roaring with **one** voice.' Speaking in the abstract, <divergence> tends to turn into <convergence>.

This tendency which can be seen in A3 corresponds to the gradual change of scope of expression from something huge to something small, or rather one particular point. The poet's object or target of expression changes from the vast landscape to 'a chasm.' The vast and grand landscape seen from the summit of Mt. Snowdon consists of the moon upwards, of the sea of mist around, and the real sea downwards. The particular point is verbalized with the method of "elegant variation." In other words, it is verbalized with the equivalent expressions of A1, A2, A3 in 4-11 plus those of A4, A5 in 5-13. The 'chasm' forms a core of expression in the first half of the Snowdon passage. This tendency in expression is seen in the second half as well.

6.6 Second half of the Snowdon passage

Now, let us proceed to the second half. Sentence 6-14 begins, not with '*I meditated ...*' but with

(9)   A meditation *rose in me* that night
        Upon the lonely Mountain when the scene
        Had pass'd away,   (13, 66-68)

Here again 'rose' is used just as if the poet had been charmed by the same word 'rose' used at 5-13 in the first half. The verb 'rose' has a semantic feature of intransitive <spontaneity>. Citation (9) is an objective way of expression given with proper detachment. 'I meditated' would be a subjective expression and constitutes a flat and dull description. What the poet performs here is his famous poetic principle: 'Poetry is the spontaneous overflow of powerful feelings: it takes its origin from emotion recollected in tranquility' (Wordsworth, Vol. II, Preface, 400). It is not coincidental that the identical word 'rose' is used in both sentences 5-13 and 6-14. It is precisely because the poet, Wordsworth recognizes the identity between the process in both the manifestations of a natural phenomenon and in the workings of a human mind.

6.6.1 Nominal equivalent structure

In 6-15, the seemingly initial main clause, 'it appear'd to me (that)...' may cause difficulty when interpreting the meaning of the sentence. If we suppose that the conjunction 'that' is omitted after 'it appear'd to me,' then we usually expect the main clause will be followed by the subject of a subordinate '(*that*-) clause.' We expect such sentence structure as 'it appear'd to me (*that*) Subject + Predicate...' will arise. However, this is not the case here. Our expectation does not materialize. The fact is '[69]The perfect image of a mighty Mind' is not the subject which introduces the subordinate '(*that*-) clause,' but the subject complement to the verb '[68]appear'd' in 'it appear'd to me.' The pronoun '[68]it' is not 'a formal subject referring to (*that*-) clause,' but 'an anaphoric *it*' referring to the very scene the poet witnessed. After all, the correct reading is this: 'it (i.e. the scene) appear'd' to the poet 'the perfect image of a mighty Mind.' One must avoid misinterpreting '[69]The perfect image of a mighty Mind' as an inverted object of '[75]Exhibited' which appears six lines later. As a matter of fact, the inverted object of '[75]Exhibited' is 'one function of such mind' which appears just in front, in line 74.

The Prelude: The Four Texts (1798, 1799, 1805, 1850) offers one proof of this interpretation. In the corresponding lines of its 1805 text, there is a period placed between '[68-73]and it appear'd to me... whatsoe'er is dim / Or vast in its own being' and '[73-84]Above all / One function of such mind... / That even the grossest minds must see and hear / And cannot chuse but feel.' Given the situation, we decidedly have to take 'The perfect image...in its own being' as a subject complement which follows the linking verb, 'appear'd.' We have no alternative but to interpret the pronoun '[68]it' as an anaphoric use which refers to 'the scene.'

Figure 6.4 shows the double-layered structure of the above-mentioned complement in minor sentence 6-15 and the object in 6-16. As a matter of fact, the subject complement (B1) and the inverted object (B2) refer to the same thing, seen from two different angles. 'B' is adopted, in contrast from the aforementioned A, to stand for a different appositional element. From one angle, Wordsworth sees the whole picture, and from the other angle, he captures one particular aspect of the whole image. Here, as well, is seen the poet's way of expressing things: from <divergence> to <convergence>.

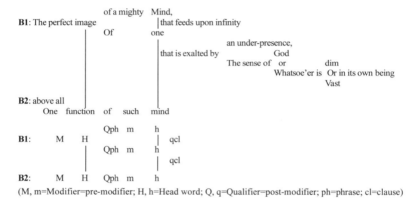

(M, m=Modifier=pre-modifier; H, h=Head word; Q, q=Qualifier=post-modifier; ph=phrase; cl=clause)

Figure 6.4: Double-layered structure

One of the most complicated manifestations in the double-layered structure of the Snowdon passage is seen on the right in the latter part of B1. The vertical axis of 'mind' consists of three parts: 'Mind,' 'one,' and 'mind,' that is, three h(ead)'s. The second 'h' element, 'one (i.e. mind)' is qualified by double '*that*-clauses.' In the second '*that*-clause,' in turn, the preposition 'by' takes double objects (i.e. 'an under-presence' and 'The sense of…'), and further the preposition 'of' in the second prepositional object (i.e. 'The sense of…') takes double objects (i.e. 'God' or 'whatsoe'er is…') as well.

A further investigation of the multi-layered structure will lead to a more detailed explanation of the passage. Let me begin with B1. 'The perfect image' is qualified by double '*of*-phrases.' The former '*of*-phrase' is simply 'of a mighty Mind,' the structure of which is 'of + determiner + modifier + head.' The latter, however, is rather complex.

Chapter 6 Multi-Layered Structure of Expression in *The Prelude*

Wordsworth must have felt that his favorite epithet, 'mighty' is not clear enough to describe fully his own meditative thought awakened at the Snowdon summit. Consequently, he must have amplified the referent of 'mighty' by giving variation and accuracy to the former expression. He employs double-structured, post-modifying qualifiers to extend the meaning of 'mighty.' He is anxious to express the condensed meaning of <majesty>, <glory>, <grandeur> which are minutely described earlier with reference to <immensity> in §6.5, 'First half of the Snowdon passage.' <Immensity> is strongly related to 'infinity.' This is exactly why the word 'infinity' appears in the first '*that*-clause, (i.e. that feeds upon infinity)' which is in itself an amplified expression of 'mighty.' In other words, the adjective 'mighty' signifies dual and reciprocal meanings: one is 'intensity with which Nature and her external manifestations (i.e. the moon, a huge sea of mist, etc.) impress on the poet'; and the other is 'intensity with which the poet receives the deep and lasting impressions when his mind is stirred.' As a matter of fact, the poet may insist that his mind can become 'mighty' just when he concentrates his mind upon 'infinity.'

We should pay attention to the "voice" of the double *that*-clauses as well. The former is "active" and the latter is "passive." The mind 'that *feeds upon* infinity' is, in fact, the mind 'that *is exalted by* an under-presence, / The sense of God or whatsoe'er is dim / Or vast in its own being.' The poet chooses both active and passive "voice" forms, and at the same time the "present tense" which describes 'general timeless statements, or so-called "eternal truths"' (Quirk, et al, 179). Incidentally, all the sentences after 6-15 and 6-16 are in the present tense with the exception of '[68]and it appear'd to me' in 6-15 and '[74,75]had… / Exhibited' in 6-16. Lindenberger (1963: 52), in this connection, makes an interesting remark:

> The grammatically parallel phrases and clauses—'under-presence,' 'sense of God,' 'whatsoe'er is dim'—do not function primarily to add descriptive detail about the object but, rather, to suggest new perspectives (the traditionally religious dimension in 'sense of God,' the hidden, mysterious depths in 'under-presence,' a word which Wordsworth coined himself) through which the object may be viewed.

The word, 'under-presence,' as Lindenberger points out, is coined by the poet. It is not recorded even in *OED2*. Poets boldly coin new words when they feel the existing language code is not sufficient enough to express their feelings. Herbert Read (1948: 170) is quite right when he says 'Expression knows no law.' What the coined word means is obscure, but I would like to think it refers literally to an existence presiding under '$^{64,\ 74,\ 85}$Nature,' namely '^{72}God.' It seems to me that in Wordsworth's mind there is a cognitive stratum which comprises 'natural phenomenon' (i.e. the moon, sea of mist, sea, hills) → 'Nature' → 'dim or vast existence, God.'

Let us go on to an explanation of B2 in 6-16 shown by Figure 6.4. 6-16 is the longest sentence as is clearly seen from the diagram of Chart 6.1. It consists of as many as 12 lines. There is a phrase, '^{73}above all' before B2. The 'such' in '^{74}One function of such mind' summarizes the referential meaning of both 'mighty' and double-structured post-modifying '*that*-clauses' in B1. '^{74}One function' is identical with '^{65}Imagination.' In this use of 'above all' and 'one,' there can be seen a parallelism with the above-mentioned tendency of movement from <divergence> to <convergence>. In this way, Wordsworth tends to first express something big and then proceeds to focus on a kernel point. Additionally, if we use his so-called spots of time, he may well be called a poet who is interested in and clings to 'spots of place.'

Until this point I have analyzed the multi-layered structure of B1 and B2 in sentences 6-15 and 6-16. Which does this structure belong to: (1) Enhancing or (2) Deepening? To me it seems to belong to (1) Enhancing. I say this because the main purport of B1, '^{69}image' is centripetally enhanced, eventually reaching '^{74}function,' in B2. This 'function' then turns to '^{84}Power' and finally ascends to '^{89}the glorious faculty' in 7-17. It is noteworthy that a static 'image,' changing its phase of meaning, turns to a dynamic 'faculty' in the end.

Let us move on to 7-17. It is also worthwhile to notice that the epithet 'glorious' is used here in 7-17. Its related word 'glory' is used in the first half at line 53 in 4-9, describing the situation of the moon in the form of 'In single glory.' On one hand 'glory' is used to describe part of Nature, and on the other 'glorious' is used to describe the workings of the human mind. This is why I pointed out that, in the description, the first half and the second half establish a mirror-image relationship with each other. The same is true of the word 'Nature.' 'Nature' appears three times in the Snowdon passage. Its derived lexical form 'native' appears in the form of 'native selves' in line 93. There is Nature deep down in the poet's mind.

Next, I would like to draw attention to the head word 'image' in B1. It is changed in the 1850 version into 'type, emblem,' so it might be possible to interpret it as its synonym, 'symbol.' However, I would like to regard it as just a 'picture, image' whose form is really visible to man. The reason is that 'the universal spectacle' 'appears' as such to the poet, not 'seems.' It is really visible to Wordsworth as a poetic truth. He actually uses both 'appear' and 'seem' in the very first sentence 1-1. If he wanted to emphasize 'seem,' he could have chosen an expression such as 'it <u>seemed</u> to me.' On top of that, the co-existence of '[36]appear'd' and '[37]seem'd' in sentence 1-1 may be thought of as the foreshadowing of the poet's shift from the description of <u>external</u> Nature to that of <u>internal</u> ability, that is, 'one function of a human mind.'

Now, let us investigate more minutely the ascending tendency from B1 'image' to B2 'function.' Here too we must pay attention to the use of the verbs in the pluperfect tense. Just as '[64]Nature' works as a subject to '[64]<u>had...lodg'd</u>' in the former descriptive part, so the same '[74]Nature' works as a subject to '[74-75]<u>had... / Exhibited</u>' in the latter meditative part. This parallel linguistic structure naturally results from these: the latter part is a meditative representation of the former physical description of Nature, and the minor sentence 6-16 (including '[74-75]had... / Exhibited') fulfills the duty of amplifying the purport of 5-13 (including '[64]had...lodg'd'). However, the energy of verbs 'expressing an action which passes over to an object (*OED2* s.v. 'transitive')' is quite different. In other words, the "transitivity" of the two verbs differs to a great degree. The former is 'lodg'd' and the latter is 'Exhibited.' 'Exhibited' outdoes 'lodg'd' in transitive intensity. The difference runs directly parallel to the one between the two noun phrases: B1 'The perfect <u>image</u> of a mighty Mind' and B2 'One <u>function</u> of such mind.' I could safely assert that, metaphorically, B1 is 'a static picture' and that B2 is 'a dynamic movie.'

What Nature 'had exhibited' actively to the poet is B2 as described above. The phases and circumstances of Her exhibition are depicted powerfully and minutely with the use of '[75]by putting forth...' and the description that follows. Nature 'puts forth domination.' Wordsworth adds strength to his argument by using '[75]and that' which has the same meaning of particular emphasis as '[73]above all.' Nature often 'exerts' that domination upon the outward face of things, 'moulds' them, 'endues,' 'abstracts,' 'combines,' or by sudden and unexpected influence 'makes' one object so impress itself upon all others, and 'pervades' them so. To put it simply, Wordsworth here gives us an explanation of Nature's powerful processes in action. He explains analytically the tremendous energy Nature employs when she presents a 'universal spectacle,' and at the same time the poet makes an analytical explanation of processes as to how Nature produces the spectacular scene.

6.6.2 Verbal equivalent structure

So far, we have encountered several nominal equivalent structures, but we can also see an example of a verbal equivalent structure in B2 and what follows, on which I briefly touched at the end of the preceding section. Let us make a diagram to show the configuration of a series of verbs (also mentioned in §3.4.1):

S	M	P	O
	oftentimes	Exerts	upon the outward face of things
she	So	moulds and endues abstracts combines Or	them
	abrupt By and influence unhabitual	make Doth and pervade	one object *so* impress itself Upon all others them
	So		see must and *That* even the grossest minds hear And cannot chuse but feel

(S=subject, M=modifier, P=predicate, O=object)

Figure 6.5: Configuration of verbs

The vertical column P consists of a total of seven verbs in present form. The subject of those predicate verbs is decidedly '[77]she' (i.e. Nature) and the object of the verbs is '[79]them' (i.e. the outward face of things), except in the case of 'Doth make,' which is a causative verb, and has a different and more complicated sentence structure: '[81-82]make one object so impress itself / Upon all others.'

What is the antecedent of the relative pronoun, 'which' in line 77? It is '[77]domination.' Placing the antecedent noun in its original position, we get the sentence: 'She oftentimes exerts <u>domination</u> upon the outward face of things.' The subsequent sentence is an elliptical one: 'So moulds them.' If we supplement this with a subject, we can get the following sentence: 'So she moulds them.' This is in itself a complete sentence, and accordingly is free from restraint of the relative pronoun,

Chapter 6   Multi-Layered Structure of Expression in *The Prelude*   119

'which.' Therefore, 'which...she moulds them' is a non-sentence. There seems to be something crooked and distorted in its syntactic structure. Thinking in this way, '[79]So moulds them' and the following are anacoluthic in that the connection of 'which' and 'So moulds them' is redundant. It is this anacoluthon that shows Wordsworth's vigorous writing ability and his unrestrained writing style when his poetic mind reaches its highest in the 1805 version of *The Prelude*. The 1850 version alters the expression to 'So moulded, joined, abstracted, so endowed,' whose past perfect verb forms post-modify the preceding 'the face of outward things' adequately and appropriately. In the 1805 version, the portion (consisting of five and a half lines in total) from 'So moulds them, ...' in line 79 to '... / And cannot chuse but feel' in line 84 gives an analytical description of the way Nature creates a universal spectacle—half independently; in other words, without qualifying the preceding part with grammatical precision. This, to put it the other way around, is the way the poet's imagination functions. That is to say, the way Nature creates a universal spectacle is itself a dynamic mode of working of the '[74]One function' of 'such' a mighty 'mind' in B2.

Look at lines 80-82 in 6-16: 'by abrupt and unhabitual influence / Doth make one object so impress itself / Upon all others, and pervade them so.' The former part, '[80]by abrupt and unhabitual influence' describes something like the same circumstance as '[75-77]by putting forth, ... / That domination...' in lines 75-77, because there is an overlapped meaning between 'influence' and 'domination.' The latter part, '[81]Doth make <u>one</u> object so impress itself / Upon <u>all</u> others' is exploited to emphasize a particular thing as more important than other things, i.e. 'one object' among other things. These lines depicted in meditation accurately correspond to the part where 'a blue chasm' is particularly highlighted in the physical description of Nature in the first half of the Snowdon passage. Speaking in the abstract again, <divergence> tends to turn into <convergence>.

Here let us observe the stream of syntactical movement of 6-15 and 6-16 and take notice of a series of subordinate clauses. The subject complement of '[68]it appear'd to me' contains twofold recursive subordinate clauses (i.e. two '*that*-clauses' and one '*whatsoe'er*-clause'). In 6-16 the object of '[75]putting forth,' that is 'That domination' is followed by twofold subordinate clauses (i.e. '*which*-clause' and '*That*-clause'). The subject of these dependent clauses is either 'mind' or 'Nature' and they in order appear alternately, which is particularly appropriate to the fact that the mutual relationship between the poet and Nature is depicted here. However, as if to break the alternating order, the above-mentioned "anacoluthic" sentence emerges:

(10) ***So*** moulds them, endues, abstracts, combines,
Or by abrupt and unhabitual influence
Doth make one object *so* impress itself
Upon all others, and pervade them *so*
That even the grossest **minds** must see and hear
And cannot chuse but feel.   (13, 79-84)

The subject of the last subordinate clause is '[83]minds.' This clause is followed by a correlative 'that' which corresponds to the threefold 'so' (in lines 79, 81, 82) in the preceding long clause which has 'Nature' as subject. Even 'the grossest minds' cannot help feeling. How much more should the common people? Here again is Wordsworth's rhetoric: part of the whole (the lowest border of sensitivity in this case) suggests the whole situation (even the highest border).

Now, let us move to the last part: 7-17, 8-18, and 8-19. Here at last a very simple equation, 'X is Y' presents itself. By exploiting the complicated 6-15 and 6-16, the poet tries to convey to the reader the truth he intuitively grasped at the summit of Mt. Snowdon. At that moment, he endured the pains of creation because the content of his intuitive truth was such a mysterious revelation, which was peculiar to the poet. Therefore, he uses idiosyncratic multi-layered structures containing "coinage" and "anacoluthon."

On the contrary, 7-17 is extremely well-balanced, in that the subject 'Power' is qualified by double '*which*-clauses'; and one of the double-structured, appositional complements is qualified by one '*which*-clause.' Let us schematize this SPC structure for clarity:

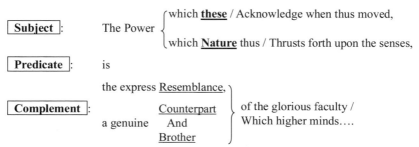

Figure 6.6: Structures of subject and complement

In the subject position, the double '*which*-clauses,' referring to one antecedent, 'power,' take, as a subject, '[84]these (i.e. the grossest minds)' and '[85]Nature,' thus complementarily describing a mutual relationship between a human mind and Nature. In the complement position, symmetrically, the double head words are postmodified by one '*of*-phrase.'

In the transition from a complicated syntactic structure in 6-15 and 6-16 down to an extremely well-balanced expression of 7-17, the reader can feel the poet's hard and painful breathing turning to a soft and restful one. Remember minor sentence 6-15 and 6-16 consist of 6 lines and 12 lines respectively, and both contain twofold subordinate clauses. Major sentence 7 has basically a simple X is Y structure. To this end, we should bear in mind what Donald Davie (1976: 111) has pointed out:

> In short, this [*The Prelude*] is poetry where the syntax counts enormously, counts for nearly everything.

8-18 is an even shorter sentence. In the last sentence 8-19, the poet declares that the power with which Nature thrusts forth natural phenomena is quite the same as that which the strongest minds bear with them when moved emotionally. That is to say, the creative power of Nature *is* exactly the same as the imaginative power of poets. It is this epiphanic revelation 'X *is* Y' that Wordsworth acquired at the summit of Mt. Snowdon.

Additionally, in the second half of the Snowdon passage, there appear numerous words denoting <perfection>: '[69]perfect,' '[76]most,' '[86]express (i.e. exact),' '[87]fulness,' '[88]genuine,' '[91]the very' and '[92]all.' This suggests that the workings of Nature and those of human minds are one hundred percent identical in character and nature.

6.7 Summary

Thus far, I have observed only part of the expressions in *The Prelude* which runs as long as 8,484 lines, but it becomes clear that a key stylistic feature of *The Prelude* is its use of 'multi-layered expression.' Wordsworth's poetic thought sometimes turns to 'Enhancing' and sometimes to 'Deepening,' depending on the content of the appositives and according to the variation of the appositional elements in this multi-layered structure.

Wordsworth tends to express, first, something big and then goes on to focus on a kernel point. Abstractly, whether in terms of the object of description or the mode of expression, he tends to move from <divergence> to <convergence>. In a word, we can clearly see a centripetal tendency in the poet's way of grasping the world.

In *The Prelude*, Wordsworth states, 'I should need / Colours and words that are unknown to man (11, 309-10)' and 'It [heroic argument] lies far hidden from the reach of words (3, 185).' In such a situation, it is the use of 'multi-layered expression' that he can rely on when he struggles to delineate something beyond the phenomenal world.

Chart 6.2: Division between major and minor sentences
First half of the Snowdon passage (13, 36-65) (**1**-1~**5**-13)

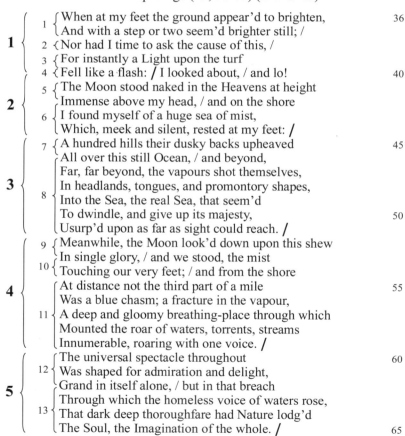

Chapter 6 Multi-Layered Structure of Expression in *The Prelude* 123

Second half of the Snowdon passage (13, 66-96) (**6**-14~**8**-19)

```
       ┌     ┌  A meditation rose in me that night
       │  14 ┤  Upon the lonely Mountain when the scene
       │     ├  Had pass'd away, / and it appear'd to me
       │     │  The perfect image of a mighty Mind,
       │  15 ┤  Of one that feeds upon infinity,                70
       │     │  That is exalted by an under-presence,
       │     │  The sense of God, or whatsoe'er is dim
       │     ├  Or vast in its own being, / above all
       │     │  One function of such mind had Nature there
    6  ┤     │  Exhibited by putting forth, and that            75
       │     │  With circumstance most awful and sublime,
       │     │  That domination which she oftentimes
       │     │  Exerts upon the outward face of things,
       │  16 ┤  So moulds them, and endues, abstracts, combines,
       │     │  Or by abrupt and unhabitual influence           80
       │     │  Doth make one object so impress itself
       │     │  Upon all others, and pervade them so
       │     │  That even the grossest minds must see and hear
       └     └  And cannot chuse but feel. / The Power which these
       ┌     ┌  Acknowledge when thus moved, which Nature thus  85
       │     │  Thrusts forth upon the senses, is the express
    7  ┤  17 ┤  Resemblance, in the fulness of its strength
       │     │  Made visible, a genuine Counterpart
       │     │  And Brother of the glorious faculty
       └     └  Which higher minds bear with them as their own. /  90
       ┌  18 ┌  That is the very spirit in which they deal
       │     └  With all the objects of the universe; /
    8  ┤     ┌  They from their native selves can send abroad
       │  19 ┤  Like transformation, for themselves create
       │     │  A like existence, and, whene'er it is           95
       └     └  Created for them, catch it by an instinct; /
```

(A thick oblique line in the quotation on this Chart 6.2 indicates a division between major sentences and a thin oblique line indicates one between minor sentences.)

Conclusion

In the first chapter of this monograph, I investigated the vocabulary in *The Prelude* in general. I considered 769 words that appear more than ten times in the text. By observing the vocabulary, I was able to gain a Wordsworthian way of grasping the outer world. The poet perceives things from a broad perspective. He looks beneath the surface of matters.

I approached *The Prelude* vocabulary from four perspectives, or rather four word classes: nouns, verbs, adjectives, and others (i.e. prepositions).

1) What is most striking about the poet's use of nouns is that his abstract nouns tend to take on a concrete quality; his concrete nouns, on the contrary, take on an abstract one. General words such as 'thing' and 'object' are abundantly used in *The Prelude*, which is a lexical reflection of the poet's broad perception of the outer world of Nature.

2) Concerning the verb class, abundant use of verbs of perception and cognition is conspicuous. 'I $\boxed{\text{felt}}$ X' is a representative equation when Wordsworth perceives the surrounding world.

3) The observation of the adjective class reveals that he uses the same adjectives to describe both Nature and the human mind. Mutual interaction between the poet's mind and the surrounding Nature is realized in the use of those identical adjectives. 'Mighty' Nature, for example, is mapped onto 'mighty' mind.

4) With reference to prepositions, I extracted 'through,' which shows a considerable frequency difference in comparison with other literary works, both modern and classical, catalogued in various corpora. The frequent use of 'through' corresponds to the frequent interrelation of the poet's mind with outer Nature. The frequent appearance of 'through' is a natural consequence of his frequent and intimate contacts with Nature. 'Through' is in fact key to the interpretation of *The Prelude*.

In the second chapter, I narrowed down the coverage of the noun category described in Chapter 1 and focused on the noun 'weight.' Usually, 'weight' combines with words of negative association such as 'responsibility' and 'care.' Meanwhile, Wordsworth uses 'weight' in an unusual way. He connects 'weight' with 'pleasure.' He is the only English poet who coined such a striking phrase: 'Even with a weight of pleasure' (12, 178).

In the third chapter, I dealt with verbs of perception, which appear in large quantities in *The Prelude*. I set up an equation, 'I felt X,' and examined the verbs to fill the slot of felt. By observing the verbs and their contexts, I found, among other things, the following five points:

1) As might be expected from the main topic of *The Prelude*, the poet's interaction with Nature, verbs of perception and those of motion are frequently exploited;

2) Wordsworth is a poet who makes much of 'unassuming things' (12, 51) whether visual or auditory;

3) The poet sees objects with feelings of joy;

4) He is interested in undistinguishable sounds; and

5) Verbs of visual, auditory, and cognitive perception in this order (e.g. saw → heard → felt) can form a pattern of co-occurrence.

In Chapter 4, I briefly described, among others, the adjective 'mighty.' 'Mighty' is the most appropriate word to collocate with 'mind' semantically and phonetically. It was the very workings of his 'mighty mind' that Wordsworth depicted in *The Prelude*. In this chapter, I also described the mirror-image relation seen between adjectives denoting the poet's inner self and the outer world of Nature. I rearranged the quantitative classification of adjectives in §1.3 (Table 1.8) in order to obtain another view of the *Prelude* adjectives.

In the fifth chapter, I shed light on the unusually frequent use of 'through' in *The Prelude*. Compared with other corpora, the frequency count of 'through' deviates noticeably from that of the general trend of English. I argue that the reason for this deviation comes solely from the poet's frequent interaction with Nature. The frequent interrelations between 'in' of his mind and the 'out' of the Nature are shown by the frequent appearances of 'through' in *The Prelude*.

Unlike the foregoing chapters, in the sixth and last chapter, I dealt with the syntactic structure of *The Prelude*. One of the stylistic features of this major poem is its "multi-layered" expression. Studying its multiple structure leads to clarification of the true structure of its syntax. Wordsworth seeks to describe the indescribable, 'which lies far hidden from the reach of words' (3, 185). In such a quest, what he can rely on is nothing but multi-layered expression, in particular, a triple structure. This triple structure is divided into two types according to the mode of expression: Enhancing and Deepening.

If I were asked to select the most Wordsworthian words from each word class, in other words, one word each from Chapters 2 to 5, then I would choose the following: 'weight' from the noun class, 'felt' from the verb class, 'mighty' from the adjective class, and 'through' from other word classes. By using these words, I can then make a sentence which summarizes the theme of *The Prelude*:

> Wordsworth **felt mighty** Nature **through** his **mighty** mind with a **weight** of pleasure.

Allow me to repeat part of the summary of §1.5:

> The greatness of Nature enhances human beings to a higher and **mightier** existence **through** its lofty and **mighty** forms. The mind of Wordsworth grew even greater and **mightier through** those **mighty** forms.

Lastly, I would like to end this monograph, which is the fruit of many patient years of devoted study to one of the masters of English verse, by quoting three phrases that strongly reveal the poet's union with Nature:

the horizon of my mind	(12, 56)
the suburbs of the mind	(7, 506)
Caverns there were within my mind.	(3, 246)

The first two phrases unite words, rather forcibly, that belong to different worlds with the use of the preposition 'of.' That is to say, the two phrases combine together 'mind,' belonging to a mental world, and 'horizon, suburbs,' belonging to the natural world. The last sentence reveals that Nature undeniably exists within the poet's mind. These unique phrases testify that Nature indeed resides inside Wordsworth's mind, magisterially. External Nature literally exists in his internal mind.

Works Cited

(following the style of *Language and Literature: Journal of the Poetics and Linguistics Association* (2005))

Text

Wordsworth, W. (1959) *William Wordsworth: The Prelude or Growth of a Poet's Mind* (2nd edn). de Selincourt, E. (ed.) and Darbishire, H. (rev.) Oxford: Clarendon Press.

Books

Austin, F. (1989) *The Language of Wordsworth and Coleridge.* London: Macmillan Education.

Blake, N.F., Burnley, D., Matsuo, M. and Nakao, Y. (eds) (1994) *A New Concordance to* The Canterbury Tales *Based on Blake's Text Edited from the Hengwrt Manuscript.* Okayama: University Education Press.

Bolton, W.F. (1982) *A Living Language: The History and Structure of English.* New York: Random House.

Carroll, J.B., Davies, P. and Richman, B. (1971) *The American Heritage Word Frequency Book.* New York: American Heritage.

Carter, R. (1987) *Vocabulary: Applied Linguistic Perspectives.* London: Allen & Unwin.

Chatman, S. (1972) *The Later Style of Henry James.* Oxford: Basil Blackwell.

Close, R. A. (1968) *English as a Foreign Language.* London: George Allen & Unwin.

Davie, D. (1955, 1976^2) 'Syntax in Blank Verse of Wordsworth's *Prelude*' in *Articulate Energy: An Inquiry into the Syntax of English Poetry.* London: Routledge & Kegan Paul.

Davies, H.S. (1986) *Wordsworth and the Worth of Words.* Kerrigan, J. and Wordsworth, J. (eds) Cambridge: Cambridge University Press, p. 58.

Empson, W. (1967) 'Sense in *The Prelude*' in *The Structure of Complex Words.* Ann Arbor: The University of Michigan Press, pp. 289-305.

Gill, S. (1991) *Wordsworth* The Prelude, *Landmarks of World Literature.* Cambridge: Cambridge University Press, p. 31.

Halliday, M.A.K. (1970) 'Descriptive Linguistics in Literary Studies' in Freeman, D.C. (ed.) *Linguistics and Literary Style.* New York: Holt, Reinhart & Winston, p. 59.
Havens, R.D. (1967) *The Mind of a Poet*, Vol. 2, The Prelude, *A Commentary.* Baltimore: The Johns Hopkins University Press.
Hofland, K. and Johansson, S. (1982) *Word Frequencies in British and American English.* Bergen: The Norwegian Computing Centre for the Humanities.
Jakobson, R. (1960) 'Closing Statement: Linguistics and Poetics' in Sebeok, T.A. (ed.) *Style in Language.* Cambridge, MA: MIT Press, pp. 350-77.
Kanou, H. (1969) *Wordsworth* (10th edn). Tokyo: Kenkyusha, p. 16.
Kokuritsu Kokugo Kenkyusho [The National Language Research Institute] (1964, 1989) *Bunrui Goi-Hyo* [*Word List by Semantic Principles*]. Tokyo: Shuei Shuppan.
Kunihiro, T. (1980) *Gengo no Kouzou* [*The Structure of Languages*] in Shibata, T. (ed.) *Kouza Gengo*, [*Languages Series*] Vol. 1. Tokyo: Taishukan, pp. 244-45.
Lakoff, G. and Johnson, M. (1980) *Metaphors We Live By.* Chicago: The University of Chicago Press.
—— (1989) *More than Cool Reason: A Field Guide to Poetic Metaphor.* Chicago: The University of Chicago Press.
Leech G., Rayson, P. and Wilson, A. (2001) *Word Frequencies in Written and Spoken English.* London: Pearson Education.
Leech, G.N. and Short, M. (1981) *Style in Fiction: A Linguistic Introduction to English Fictional Prose.* Quirk, R. (gen. ed.) *English Language Series.* London: Longman.
Lewis, C.S. (1964, rpt. 1967) *The Discarded Image: An Introduction to Medieval and Renaissance Literature.* Cambridge: Cambridge University Press.
Lindenberger, H. (1963) *On Wordsworth's* Prelude. Princeton: Princeton University Press.
Miles, J. (1942, rpt. 1965) *Wordsworth and the Vocabulary of Emotion.* New York: Octagon Books.
Miyagawa, K. (2001) 'Wāzuwasu to "Something" no Shigaku' ['Wordsworth and the Poetics of "Something"'] in *The Rising Generation*, July & Aug. Tokyo: Kenkyusha.
—— (2007) 'Something to Vijyon' ['Something and Vision'] in *Shizen to Vijyon no Shigaku—Wāzuwasu, Kōrurijji and Eriotto—* [*The Poetics of Nature and Vision—Wordsworth, Coleridge and Eliot—*]. Tokyo: Eihōsha.

Miyazaki, Y. (1988) '*Jokyoku* Dansou' ['Fragmentary thoughts on *The Prelude*'] in Oka, S. (ed.) *Wordsworth* Jokyoku *Ronshu [Collected Essays on Wordsworth* The Prelude]. Tokyo: Kokubun-sha, pp. 43-76.
Nakagawa, K. (1990) 'On the Vocabulary of *The Prelude*' (in Japanese), *The Bulletin of Modern English Association of Japan* 6, 23-43.
—— (1992) 'On the Vocabulary of *The Prelude*' (in Japanese) in Saito, T. (ed.) *Eigo Eibungaku Kenkyū to Conpyutā [A Study of English and English Literature and Computers]*. Tokyo: Eichosha, pp. 93-113.
—— (1997) *The Language of William Wordsworth: A Linguistic Approach to Poetic Language* (in Japanese). Hiroshima: Research Institute for Language and Culture, Yasuda Women's University.
—— (2003) 'The Vocabulary that Constitutes *The Prelude*' in Editorial Committee of the Modern English Association (ed.) *Studies in Modern English: The Twentieth Anniversary Publication of the Modern English Association*. Tokyo: Eichosha, pp. 457-71.
—— (2005) '"Through" in *The Prelude*' in Japan Association of English Romanticism (ed.) *Voyages of Conception: Essays in English Romanticism*. Tokyo: Kirihara Shoten, pp. 118-33.
—— (2008) 'On the Phrase "Even with a Weight of Pleasure" in *The Prelude*' in G. Watson (ed.) *PALA book 5: The State of Stylistics*. Amsterdam-New York: Rodopi, pp. 85-96.
—— (2014) 'Multi-Layered Structure of Expression in *The Prelude*' in Nakagawa, K. (ed.) *Studies in Modern English: The Thirtieth Anniversary Publication of the Modern English Association*. Tokyo: Eihōsha, pp. 401-16.
—— (2016) 'Some Aspects of Adjectives in *The Prelude*' in Nakagawa, K., Jimura, A. and Imahayashi, O. (eds) *Language and Style in English Literature*. Hiroshima: Keisuisha, pp. 137-148.
Nakaoka, H. (1983) *A Concordance to* Wuthering Heights. Tokyo: Kaibunsha.
Nida, E.A. (1975) *Componental Analysis of Meaning: An Introduction to Semantic Structures*. The Hague: Mouton.
Pottle, F.A. (1985) 'The Eye and the Object in the Poetry of Wordsworth' in Bloom, H. (ed.) *Modern Critical Views: William Wordsworth*. New York: Chelsea House, pp. 9-21.

Quirk, R. et al. (1985) *A Comprehensive Grammar of English Language.* London: Longman.
Read, H. (1930, 1948²) *Wordsworth.* London: Faber & Faber.
Riffaterre, M. (1978) *Semiotics of Poetry. Advances in Semiotics.* Sebeok, T.A. (gen. ed.) Saito, Y. (trans.) (2000) Bloomington: Indiana University Press.
Rosenbaum, S.P. (1964) *A Concordance to the Poems of Emily Dickinson.* Ithaca: Cornell University Press.
Sebeok, T.A. (ed.) (1960) *Style in Language.* Cambridge, MA: MIT Press.
Shakespeare, W. (1997) *The Riverside Shakespeare* (2nd edn). Evans, G.B. (ed.) Boston: Houghton Mifflin Company.
Spitzer, L. (1967) *Linguistics and Literary History: Essays in Stylistics.* Princeton: Princeton University Press.
Ward, J.P. (1984) *Wordsworth's Language of Men.* Brighton: The Harvester Press.
West, M. (1953) *A General Service List of English Words with Semantic Frequencies and a Supplementary Word-List for the Writing of Popular Science and Technology.* London: Longman.
Wordsworth, W. (1968) *The Prelude, or Growth of a Poet's Mind.* Oka, S. (trans.) Tokyo: Kokubun-sha.
—— (1907) *The Poetical Works of William Wordsworth: With Introductions and Notes.* Hutchinson, T. (ed.) London: Oxford University Press.
—— (1995) *The Prelude: The Four Texts (1798, 1799, 1805, 1850).* Wordsworth, J. (ed.) London: Penguin Books.
Wordsworth, W. and Coleridge, S.T. (1991) '*Lyrical Ballads, 1798*' in Brett, R.L. and Jones, A.R. (eds) *Lyrical Ballads* (2nd edn). London: Routledge, pp. 263-64.

Dictionaries
Crowther, J. et al. (eds) (2000) *Oxford Advanced Learner's Dictionary of Current English* (6th edn). Oxford: Oxford University Press.
Hanks, P. et al. (eds) (1979) *Collins Dictionary of the English Language.* London: Collins.
Jeffares, A.N. and Gray, M. (eds) (1995) *Collins Dictionary of Quotations.* Glasgow: Harper Collins Publishers.
McArthur, T. (1981) *Longman Lexicon of Contemporary English.* London: Longman.
Ohno, S. and Hamanishi, M. (1981) *Kadokawa's New Dictionary of Synonyms.* Tokyo: Kadokawa Shoten.

Works Cited

Otsuka, T. (ed.) (1970) *Shin Eibunpou Jiten [Sanseido's New Dictionary of English Grammar]* (2nd edn). Tokyo: Sanseido.
Roget's II The New Thesaurus. (1980) Boston: Houghton Mifflin Company.
Shakespeare, W. (1970) *A Complete and Systematic Concordance to the Works of Shakespeare.* Vol. 6. Spevack, M. (ed.) Hildesheim: Georg Olms.
The Oxford English Dictionary (2nd edn) on CD-ROM Version 3.0. (2002) New York: Oxford University Press.
The Oxford Dictionary of Quotations (3rd edn). (1979) Oxford: Oxford University Press.
Wales, K. (2001) *A Dictionary of Stylistics* (2nd edn). Harlow: Pearson Education.
Watanabe, T., Skrzypczak, E.R. and Snowden, P. (2003) *Kenkyusha's New Japanese-English Dictionary* (5th edn). Tokyo: Kenkyusha.
Wells, J.C. (2000) *Longman Pronunciation Dictionary.* Harlow: Pearson Education.

Software
Collins COBUILD Wordbanks Online service.
Gutenberg Files.
Matsuo, M. and Suzuki, S. *A Search Program, PC-KWIC.*
Nineteenth-Century Fiction: Full-Text Database.

Select Bibliography

Books

Abraham, A.P. (1920) *Some Portraits of the Lake Poets and Their Homes*. Keswick: G. P. Abraham.

Abrams, M.H. (ed.) (1972) *Wordsworth: A Collection of Critical Essays*. Englewood Cliffs, NJ: Prentice-Hall.

Adams, V. (1973) *An Introduction to Modern English Word-Formation*. London: Longman.

Aitchison, J. (1994) *Words in the Mind: An Introduction to the Mental Lexicon* (2nd edn). Oxford: Blackwell.

Alexander, J.H. (1987) *Reading Wordsworth*. London: Routledge & Kegan Paul.

Allen, B. (1995-a) *Best Walks on the Lower Lakeland Fells: In the North-West*. London: Michael Joseph.

—— (1995-b) *Best Walks on the Lower Lakeland Fells: In the North-East*. London: Michael Joseph.

Allen, B. and Linney, P. (1995) *Walking the Ridges of Lakeland: According to* Wainwright's Pictorial Guides *Books 1-3*. London: Michael Joseph.

Ando, K. (1983) *Igirisu-romanha to Furansukakumei: Burēku, Wāzuwasu, Korurijji to 1790nendai no Kakumei Ronsou* [*British Romantics and the French Revolution: Blake, Wordsworth, Coleridge and the Revolution Controversy in the 1790s*]. Tokyo: Kirihara Shoten.

Ando, S. (1983) *Eigo Kyoushi no Eibunpou Kenkyu* [*A Study of English Grammar for Teachers of English*]. Tokyo: Taishukan.

Austin, T.R. (1984) *Language Crafted: A Linguistic Theory of Poetic Syntax*. Bloomington: Indiana University Press.

Baayen, R.H. (2001) *Word Frequency Distributions*. Dordrecht: Kluwer Academic.

Baker, C. (ed.) (1954) *William Wordsworth's* The Prelude*: With a Selection from the* Shorter Poems, the Sonnets, The Recluse *and* The Excursion*: And Three Essays on the Art of Poetry*. New York: Reinhart.

Barfield, O. (1962) *History in English Words*. London: Faber & Faber.

—— (1973) *Poetic Diction: A Study in Meaning* (3rd edn). Middletown: Wesleyan University Press.

Bate, J. (2000) *Romantic Ecology: Wordsworth and the Environmental Tradition*. Oda, T. and Ishihata, N. (trans.) Tokyo: Shohakusha.

Batten, G. (1998) *The Orphaned Imagination: Melancholy Commodity Culture in English Romanticism*. Durham: Duke University Press.

Beaugrande, R.de and Dressler, W.U. (1981) *Introduction to Text Linguistics*. London: Longman.

Beer, J. (1978) *Wordsworth and the Human Heart*. London: Macmillan.

Beers, H.A. (1968) *A History of English Romanticism in the Eighteenth Century*. New York: Dover.

Benis, T.R. (2000) *Romanticism on the Road: The Marginal Gains of Wordsworth's Homeless*. Basingstoke: Macmillan.

Berry, F. (1974) *Poets' Grammar: Person, Time and Mood in Poetry*. Westport, CT: Greenwood Press.

Biber, D. et al. (eds) (1999) *Longman Grammar of Spoken and Written English*. Harlow: Pearson Education.

Bloom, H. (ed.) (1986) *William Wordsworth's* The Prelude, *Modern Critical Interpretations*. New York: Chelsea House.

—— (ed.) (1999) *William Wordsworth: Comprehensive Research and Study Guide*. New York: Chelsea House.

Bloom, H. and Trilling, L. (1973) *Romantic Poetry and Prose*. New York: Oxford University Press.

Bradford, R. (1997) *Stylistics*. London: Routledge.

Branford, W. (1980) *Structure, Style and Communication: An English Language Manual*. Cape Town: Oxford University Press.

Brewer, D.S. (1958) *Proteus: Studies in English Literature*. Tokyo: Kenkyusha.

Bromwich, D. (1998) *Disowned by Memory: Wordsworth's Poetry of the 1970s*. Chicago: The University of Chicago Press.

Brooke-Rose, C. (1958) *A Grammar of Metaphor*. London: Secker & Warburg.

Brooks, C. (1971) *A Shaping Joy: Studies in the Writer's Craft*. London: Methuen.

Brooks, C. and Warren, R.P. (1960) *Understanding Poetry* (3rd edn). New York: Holt, Rinehart and Winston.

Brumfit, C. and Carter, R. (eds) (1986) *Literature and Language Teaching*. Oxford: Oxford University Press.

Bush, D. (1963) *English Poetry: The Main Currents from Chaucer to the Present*. New York: Oxford University Press.

Byatt, A.S. (1970) *Wordsworth and Coleridge in Their Time*. London: Nelson.

Select Bibliography

Byron, M. (n.d.) *A Day with William Wordsworth*. London: Hodder & Stoughton.

Campbell, P. (1991) *Wordsworth and Coleridge* Lyrical Ballads*: Critical Perspectives*. Basingstoke: Macmillan.

Carter, R. (1982-a) 'Sociolinguistics and the Integrated English Lesson' in Carter, R. (ed.) *Linguistics and the Teacher.* London: Routledge & Kegan Paul, p. 179.

—— (ed.) (1982-b) *Language and Literature: An Introductory Reader in Stylistics*. London: George Allen & Unwin.

—— (ed.) (1990) *Knowledge about Language and the Curriculum: The LINC Reader*. London: Hodder & Stoughton.

—— (1995) *Keywords in Language and Literacy*. London: Routledge.

—— (1997) *Investigating English Discourse: Language, Literacy and Literature*. London: Routledge.

—— (1998) *Vocabulary: Applied Linguistic Perspectives* (2nd edn). London: Routledge.

—— (2004) *Language and Creativity: The Art of Common Talk*. London: Routledge.

Carter, R. and Long, M.N. (1987) *The Web of Words: Exploring Literature through Language*. Cambridge: Cambridge University Press.

—— (1991) *Teaching Literature*. Harlow: Longman.

Carter, R. and McCarthy, M. (1988) *Vocabulary and Language Teaching*. Candlin, C.N. (gen. ed.) *Applied Linguistics and Language Study*. Harlow: Pearson Education.

—— (1997) *Exploring Spoken English*. Cambridge: Cambridge University Press.

Carter, R. and McRae, J. (1997) *The Routledge History of Literature in English: Britain and Ireland*. London: Routledge.

Carter, R. and Nash, W. (1990) *Seeing through Language: A Guide to Styles of English Writing*. Oxford: Basil Blackwell.

Carter, R. and Simpson, P. (eds) (1989) *Language, Discourse and Literature: An Introductory Reader in Discourse Stylistics*. London: Unwin Hyman.

Chapman, R. (1973) *Linguistics and Literature: An Introduction to Literary Stylistics*. London: Edward Arnold.

Clancey, R.W. (2000) *Wordsworth's Classical Undersong: Education, Rhetoric and Poetic Truth*. Basingstoke: Macmillan.

Close, R.A. (1975) *A Reference Grammar for Students of English*. London: Longman Group.

Colville, D. (1984) *The Teaching of Wordsworth*. New York: Peter Lang.

Coulthard, M. (1977) *An Introduction to Discourse Analysis*. Candlin, C.N. (gen. ed.) *Applied Linguistics and Language Study*. London: Longman.
Cowell, R. (ed.) (1973) *Critics on Wordsworth*. London: George Allen & Unwin.
Cummings, M. and Simmons, R. (1983) *The Language of Literature: A Stylistic Introduction to the Study of Literature*. Oxford: Pergamon Press.
Culler, J. (1981) *The Pursuit of Signs: Semantics, Literature, Deconstruction*. London: Routledge & Kegan Paul.
Curtis, J. (ed.) (1993) *The Fenwick Notes of William Wordsworth*. London: Bristol Classical Press.
Danby, J.F. (1963-a) *The Simple Wordsworth: Studies in the Poems 1797-1807*. London: Routledge & Kegan Paul.
—— (1963-b) *William Wordsworth:* The Prelude *and Other Poems*. Daiches, D. (gen. ed.) *Studies in English Literature* 10. London: Edward Arnold.
Davie, D. (1955, 1976^2) *Articulate Energy: An Inquiry into the Syntax of English Poetry*. London: Routledge & Kegan Paul.
Davies, H. (1980) *William Wordsworth: A Biography*. London: Weidenfeld & Nicolson.
Deguchi, Y. and Yakushigawa, K. (eds) (1994) *Igirisu Shiki to Seikatsu no Shi* [*English Poems of Four Seasons and Everyday Life*]. Tokyo: Kenkyusha.
van Dijk, T.A. (1977) *Text and Context: Explorations in the Semantics and Pragmatics of Discourse*. London: Longman.
Dillon, G.L. (1978) *Language Processing and the Reading of Literature: Toward a Model of Comprehension*. Bloomington: Indiana University Press.
Drabble, M. (ed.) *The Oxford Companion to English Literature* (6th edn). Oxford: Oxford University Press.
Durrant, G. (1969) *William Wordsworth*. Cambridge: Cambridge University Press.
Easthope, A. (1983) *Poetry as Discourse*. London: Methuen.
Everyman's Library Pocket Poets (1995) *Wordsworth: Poems*. London: David Campbell.
Fabb, N. and Durant, A. (1993) *How to Write Essays, Dissertations and Theses in Literary Studies*. London: Longman.
Ferguson, F. (1977) *Wordsworth: Language as Counter-Spirit*. New Haven: Yale University Press.

Ferguson, M., Salter, M.J. and Stallworthy, J. (1996) *The Norton Anthology of Poetry* (4th edn). New York: W.W. Norton & Company.
Fowler, R. (ed.) (1966) *Essays on Style and Language: Linguistic and Critical Approaches to Literary Style*. London: Routledge & Kegan Paul.
—— (1975) 'Language and the Reader: Shakespeare's Sonnet 73' in Fowler, R. (ed.) *Style and Structure in Literature*. Oxford: Basil Blackwell, pp. 79-122.
—— (1986) *Linguistic Criticism*. Oxford: Oxford University Press.
Fulford, T. (1996) *Landscape, Liberty and Authority: Poetry, Criticism and Politics from Thomson to Wordsworth*. Cambridge: Cambridge University Press.
Fukuchi, A. (1998) *Wāzuwasu no* Intonsha*: Uchinaru Rakuen e no Michi* [*Wordsworth's* The Recluse*: A Way toward His 'Paradise Within'*]. Tokyo: Shohakusha.
Garrod, H.W. (ed.) (1958) *The Poetical Works of John Keats* (2nd edn). Oxford: Clarendon Press.
Gill, S (1989) *William Wordsworth, A Life*. Oxford: Clarendon Press.
Graham, W. (1983) *Notes on English Literature: The Prelude I & II*. Whitstable: Basil Blackwell.
Grierson, H.J.C. (1963) *Milton and Wordsworth: Poets and Prophets—A Study of Their Reactions to Political Events*. London: Chatto & Windus.
Gutierrez, D. (1987) *Subject-Object Relations in Wordsworth and Lawrence*. Michigan: UMI Research Press.
Haiman, J. (1985) *Iconicity in Syntax*. Amsterdam: John Benjamin.
Halliday, F.E. (1970) *Wordsworth and His World*. London: Thames & Hudson.
Halliday, M.A.K. (1985) *An Introduction to Functional Grammar*. London: Edward Arnold.
Halliday, M.A.K. and Hasan, R. (1976) *Cohesion in English*. Ando, S. et al. (trans.) (1997). London: Longman.
Hamilton, P. (1986) *Wordsworth*. Sussex: The Harvester Press.
Hara, I. (1983) *Wordsworth Kenkyū: Shikon no Tenpen no Ato o Otte* (rev. edn) [*A Study of Wordsworth: In Search of Traces of Changes in His Poetic Mood*]. Tokyo: Hokuseido.
Harada, T. (1997) *Wordsworth no Shizen-shinpishisou* [*Nature-mysticism of Wordsworth*]. Tokyo: Nan'undo.
Harada, T. (1990) *Nihon ni okeru Wāzuwasu Bunken* (I) [*An Annotated Critical Bibliography of William Wordsworth in Japan*] (I). Tokyo: Kirihara Shoten.

Harada, T. (2013) *Nihon ni okeru Wāzuwasu Bunken* (II) [*An Annotated Critical Bibliography of William Wordsworth in Japan* (II)]. Kyoto: KyotoShūgakusha.

Harper, G.M. (1967) *Wordsworth's French Daughter: The Story of Her Birth, With the Certificates of Her Baptism and Marriage*. New York: Russell & Russell.

Hartman, G.H. (1971) *Wordsworth's Poetry 1787-1814*. New Haven: Yale University Press.

Harvey, W.J. and Gravil, R. (eds) (1972) *Wordsworth* The Prelude. Dyson, A.E. (gen. ed.) *Casebook Series*. London: Macmillan.

Hayden, J.O. (ed.) (1988) *William Wordsworth: Selected Prose*. Harmondsworth: Penguin Books.

Hebron, S. (2000) *William Wordsworth*. London: The British Library.

Heffernan, J.A.W. (1969) *Wordsworth's Theory of Poetry: The Transforming Imagination*. Ithaca: Cornell University Press.

Hill, A.G. (ed.) (1978) *The Letters of William and Dorothy Wordsworth* (2nd edn). III. Part I 1821-1828. Oxford: Clarendon Press.

—— (ed.) (1979) *The Letters of William and Dorothy Wordsworth* (2nd edn). V. Part II 1829-1834. Oxford: Clarendon Press.

—— (ed.) (1988) *The Letters of William and Dorothy Wordsworth* (2nd edn). VII. Part IV 1840-1853. Oxford: Clarendon Press.

—— (ed.) (1993) *The Letters of William and Dorothy Wordsworth*. VIII. Oxford: Clarendon Press.

Hirata, T. (trans.) and Ogawa, K. (rev.) (1982) *Kindai Eishisen* [*The Modern English Poets*] (new edn). Tokyo: Eikōsha.

Holenstein, E. (1976) *Roman Jakobson's Approach to Language: Phenomenological Structuralism*. Schelbert, K. and Schelbert, T. (trans.). Bloomington: Indiana University Press.

Holt, T. and Gilroy, J. (1983) *A Commentary on Wordsworth's* Prelude: *Books I-V*. London: Routledge & Kegan Paul.

Huddleston, R. and Pullum, G.K. (2002) *The Cambridge Grammar of the English Language*. Cambridge: Cambridge University Press.

Hulbert, H.R. (1950) *In the Footsteps of William and Dorothy: An Illustrated Anthology*. Kendal: Titus Wilson.

Hunter, J.P. (ed.) (1973) *The Norton Introduction to Literature: Poetry*. New York: W. W. Norton and Company.

Hutchinson, T. (ed.) (1934) *The Complete Poetical Works of Percy Bysshe Shelley*. London: Oxford University Press.

Ikegami, Y. (1967) *Eishi no Bunpou: Gogakuteki Buntairon* [*A Grammar of English Poetry: Linguistic Stylistics*]. Tokyo: Kenkyusha.

Select Bibliography

Ishibashi, K. (ed.) (1973) *Gendai Eigogaku Jiten* [*Seibido's Dictionary of English Linguistics*]. Tokyo: Seibido.

Iwasaki, T. (2002) *Roman Shugi no Shi to Kaiga: Burēku, Wāzuwasu, Tānā, Konsutaburu* [*Poems and Paintings of Romanticism: Blake, Wordsworth, Turner, and Constable*]. Tokyo: Eichosha.

Jackson, H. (2002) *Grammar and Vocabulary: A Resource Book for Students*. London: Routledge.

Jackson, H. and Zé Amvela, E. (2000) *Words, Meaning and Vocabulary: An Introduction to Modern English Lexicology*. Fawcett, R. (series ed.) *Open Linguistics Series*. London: Cassell.

Jakobson, R. (1985) *Verbal Art, Verbal Sign, Verbal Time*. Pomorska, K. and Rudy, S. (eds) Oxford: Basil Blackwell.

Johansson, S. and Hofland, K. (1989) *Frequency Analysis of English Vocabulary and Grammar Based on the LOB Corpus*. Vol. I and II. Oxford: Clarendon Press.

Johnston, K.R. (1984) *Wordsworth and* The Recluse. New Haven: Yale University Press.

Jones, M. (1995) *The 'Lucy Poems': A Case Study in Literary Knowledge*. Toronto: University of Toronto Press.

Jones, S. (2002) *Antonymy: A Corpus-Based Perspective*. London: Routledge.

Kaneda, M. (1972) *Wāzuwasu no Shi no Hensen: Utopia Soushitsu no Katei* [*Changes in Wordsworth's Poems: The Process of the Loss of Utopia*]. Tokyo: Hokuseido Shoten.

Kasahara,Y. (ed.) (2004) *Chishi kara Jojō e: Igirisu Roman-shugi no genryū o tadoru* [*From Denham to English Romanticism: How Arose the Lyric from Loco-descriptive Poetry*]. Tokyo: Meisei University Press.

Katamba, F. (1994) *English Words*. London: Routledge.

Kawamoto, S. (gen. ed.) (1976) *Ippan Gengogaku* [*General Linguistics*]. Tokyo: Misuzu Shobo.

Kawamura, M. (2014) *Wāzuwasu* Lyrical Ballads *Saidoku* [*Rereading Wordsworth's* Lyrical Ballads]. Tokyo: Eihōsha.

Kawasaki, T. (1988) 'Tintan Souin no Fuukei: Pikucharesuku kara Romanshugi e no Ikou' ['The Landscape of Tintern Abbey: Transition from the Picturesque to Romanticism'] in Kawasaki, T. (ed.) *Igirisu Romanshugi ni Mukete: Shisou, Bungaku, Gengo* [*Towards English Romanticism: Thoughts, Literature, and Language*]. Nagoya: Nagoya University Press.

Keen, J. (1978) *Teaching English: A Linguistic Approach*. London: Methuen.

Keith, W.J. (1980) *The Poetry of Nature: Rural Perspectives in Poetry from Wordsworth to the Present*. Toronto: University of Toronto Press.
Kelley, T.A. (1988) *Wordsworth's Revisionary Aesthetics*. Cambridge: Cambridge University Press.
Kennedy, X.J. and Gioia, D. (1998) *An Introduction to Poetry* (9th edn). New York: Longman.
Kermode, F. (2002) *Romantic Image*. London: Routledge.
Kermode, F. et al. (eds) (1973) *The Oxford Anthology of English Literature, Vol. I: The Middle Ages through the Eighteenth Century*. New York: Oxford University Press.
—— (eds) (1973) *The Oxford Anthology of English Literature, Vol. II: 1800 to the Present*. New York: Oxford University Press.
Kneale, J.D. (1988) *Aspects of Rhetoric in Wordsworth's Poetry: Monumental Writing*. Lincoln: University of Nebraska Press.
Knight, G.W. (1959) *The Starlit Dome: Studies in the Poetry of Vision*. London: Methuen.
Koguchi, I. (ed.) (2015) *Romanshugi Ekorojī no Shigaku: Kankyou Kanjyusei no Mebae to Tenkai* [*The Poetics of Romantic Ecology: The Emergence and Development of Environmental Sensibility*]. Tokyo: Otowashobou-TsurumiShoten.
Kuki, S. (1967) *"Iki" no Kouzou* [*The Structure of "Iki"*]. Tokyo: Iwanami Shoten.
Kumagawa. R. (ed.) (1991) *Eigo Eibei Bungaku Tenbyo* [*Sketches of English Language and English and American Literature*]. Hiroshima: Keisuisha.
Kunihiro, T. (1970) 'Kouzouteki Imiron no Senkusha: Kuki Shuzo' [Shūzō KUKI: A Pioneer in Structural Semantics] in *Imi no Shosou* [*Aspects of Meaning*], *ELEC Gengo Sousho* [*ELEC Language Series*]. Tokyo: Sanseido, pp. 255-66.
Kuriyama, M. (1981) *Wāzuwasu* Jokyoku *no Kenkyu* [*A Study of Wordsworth's* The Prelude]. Tokyo: Kazama Shobo.
Labbe, J.M. (1998) *Romantic Visualities: Landscape, Gender and Romanticism*. Basingstoke: Macmillan.
Lee, V. (1968) *The Handling of Words and Other Studies in Literary Psychology*. Lincoln: University of Nebraska Press.
Leech, G.N. (1969) *A Linguistic Guide to English Poetry*. Quirk, R. (gen. ed.) *English Language Series*. London: Longman.
Leech, G. and Svartvik, J. (2002) *A Communicative Grammar of English* (3rd edn). London: Pearson Education.

Select Bibliography

Legouis, É. (1922) *William Wordsworth and Annette Vallon*. London: J. M. Dent & Sons.

—— (1965) *The Early Life of William Wordsworth 1770-1798: A Study of The Prelude*. Matthews, J.W. (trans.) New York: Russell & Russell.

Leisi, E. (1961) *Der Wortinhalt: Seine Struktur im Deutschen und Englischen*. Suzuki, T. (trans.) (1974) *Imi to Kouzou* [*Meaning and Structure*] (3rd edn) (rev. and enl.) Tokyo: Kenkyusha.

—— (1985) *Praxis der Englischen Semantik*. Ito, H. and Koga, Y. (trans.) (2002) *Eigo Imiron Jissen* [*English Semantics in Use*]. Tokyo: Aratake Shuppan.

Lennard, J. (1996) *The Poetry Handbook: A Guide to Reading Poetry for Pleasure and Practical Criticism*. Oxford: Oxford University Press.

Levin, S.R. (1962) *Linguistic Structures in Poetry*. The Hague: Mouton.

Levinson, M. (1986) *Wordsworth's Great Period Poems: Four Essays*. Cambridge: Cambridge University Press.

Lodge, D. (1981) *Working with Structuralism: Essays and Reviews on Nineteenth- and Twentieth-Century Literature*. Boston: Routledge & Kegan Paul.

Maekawa, S. (1967-a) *Wakaki Wāzuwasu: Shishin no Seichou to Henreki* [*The Young Wordsworth: Progress and Change of His Poetical Spirit*]. Tokyo: Eihōsha.

—— (trans.) (1967-b) *Jojou Minyoushu Jobun* [*Preface to Lyrical Ballads*] *Eibei Bungeiron Sousho* [*English and American Literature Series*] 4. Tokyo: Kenkyusha.

McCalman, I. et al. (eds) (1999) *An Oxford Companion to the Romantic Age: British Culture 1776-1832*. Oxford: Oxford University Press.

McCarthy, M. (1991) *Discourse Analysis for Language Teachers*. Cambridge: Cambridge University Press.

McConnell, F.D. (1974) *The Confessional Imagination: A Reading of Wordsworth's Prelude*. Baltimore: The Johns Hopkins University Press.

McCracken, D. (1984) *Wordsworth and the Lake District: A Guide to the Poems and Their Places*. Oxford: Oxford University Press.

Mead, M. (1964) *Four Studies in Wordsworth*. New York: Haskell House.

Miles, J. (1974) *Poetry and Change: Donne, Milton, Wordsworth, and the Equilibrium of the Present*. Berkeley: University of California Press.

Miller, J.H. (1985) *The Linguistic Moment: From Wordsworth to Stevens*. Princeton: Princeton University Press.

Miyagawa, K. (1994) *Shizen to Shishin no Undou: Wāzuwasu to Diran Tōmasu* [*Motion of Poets and Poetical Spirits: Wordsworth and Dylan Thomas*]. Osaka: Osaka University Press.

Moore, G. (1992) *The Illustrated Poets: William Wordsworth*. London: Aurum Press.

Mori, G. (1988) *Suukou to Meisou to Jiga: Eikoku 18-Seiki Suukouron to Wāzuwasu* [*Sublime and Meditation and Ego: The18th-century English Conception of the Sublime and Wordsworth*]. Nagoya: Chubu Nippon Kyouiku Bunkakai.

Mori, H. (1995) *Wāzuwasu no Kenkyu: Sono Joseizou* [*A Study of Wordsworth: His Image of Women*]. Tokyo: Kokusho Kankokai.

Muramatsu, S. (1980) *Kindai Eishi no Shosou: Midoku to Kousatsu* [*Some Aspects of Modern English Poems: Appreciation and Consideration*]. Tokyo: Hokuseido Shoten.

Nagasawa, J. (ed.) *Dorothy Wordsworth: Journal of My Second Tour in Scotland, 1822*. Tokyo: Kenkyusha.

Nakagawa, K. (1991) '"Through" in *The Prelude*' in *Language and Style in English Literature: Essays in Honour of Dr. Michio Masui*. Tokyo: Eihōsha, pp. 655-70.

―― (1994-a) '*Jokyoku* ni oite Wāzuwasu no Mita Mono (sono 1): Shikaku-doushi wo Chushin ni' ['What Wordsworth Saw in *The Prelude* (1): With Special Reference to Verbs of Visual Perception']. *Eigo Eibei Bungaku Ronshū* [*Journal of English Language and Literature*] 3, 121-30.

―― (1994-b) '*Jokyoku* ni okeru Wāzuwasu no Manazashi' ['Wordsworth's Eyes in *The Prelude*']. *Essays on Poetry* 10, 60-70.

―― (2005) 'A Structural Analysis of Wordsworth's "Daffodils"' in Caldas-Coulthard, C.R. and Toolan, M. (eds) *The Writer's Craft, the Culture's Technology*. Amsterdam: Rodopi, pp. 85-96.

Nakamura, H. (1994) '"Chasm" wo Yomu: Wāzuwasu *Jokyoku*' ['A Reading of "Chasm": Wordsworth's *The Prelude*'] in Yoshino, M. (ed.) *Wāzuwasu to* Jokyoku [*Wordsworth and* The Prelude]. Tokyo: Nan'undo, pp. 168-96.

Noyes, R. (1971) *William Wordsworth*. Bowman, S.E. (ed.) *Twayne's English Authors Series*. New York: Twayne.

Oda, T. (trans.) (2010) *Kosuichihou Annai* [*William Wordsworth: Guide to the Lakes*]. Tokyo: Hosei University Press.

O'Dowd, E.M. (1998) *Prepositions and Particles in English: A Discourse-Functional Account*. New York: Oxford University Press.

O'Flinn, P. (2001) *How to Study Romantic Poetry* (2nd edn). Peck, J. and Coyle, M. (eds) *How to Study*. Basingstoke: Macmillan.

Ogawa, J. (1964-a) *Bungaku Ronshu* [*Essays on Literature*]. Hiroshima: Ogawa Jiro 'Chosakushū' Kankoukai.

―――― (1964-b) *Eishi Koudoku* [*Reading of English Poetry*]. Kyoto: Apollon-sha.

Ogawa, K. (1968) *Eishi: Kanshou to Bunseki* [*English Poems: Appreciation and Analysis*]. Tokyo: Kenkyusha.

Oka, S. (1971) *Gyoushi to Musou: Wāzuwasu Ron* [*Gazing and Dreaming: Essays on Wordsworth*]. Tokyo: Kokubun-sha.

―――― (1988) *Wāzuwasu* Jyokyoku *Ronshū* [*Essays on Wordsworth's* The Prelude]. Tokyo: Kokubun-sha.

Okada, A. (1991) *Mahou to Yousei: Igirisu Romanha no Shijintachi* [*Magic and Fairies: Poets of English Romanticism*]. Kyoto: Apollon-sha.

Okamoto, M. (1984) *Wāzuwasu, Kōrurijji to Sono Shuuhen: Shijin Sougo ni okeru Shiteki Eikyou wo Chūshin ni* [*Wordsworth, Coleridge, and Their Surroundings: Their Poetical Influence on Each Other*]. Tokyo: Kenkyusha.

Okuda, K. (1999) *Shizen Shijin William Wordsworth: Shizen to Kami to Ningen no Rei no Majiwari* [*William Wordsworth as the Greatest Poet of Nature: The Converse between Nature and God and Man*]. Hiroshima: Keisuisha.

O'Neil, M. (ed.) (1998) *Literature of the Romantic Period: A Bibliographical Guide*. Oxford: Clarendon Press.

Onorato, R.J. (1971) *The Character of the Poet: Wordsworth in* The Prelude. Princeton: Princeton University Press.

Owen, W.J.B. (1969) *Wordsworth as Critic*. Toronto: University of Toronto Press.

Paffard, M. (1973) *Inglorious Wordsworths: A Study of Some Transcendental Experiences in Childhood and Adolescence*. London: Hodder & Stoughton.

Page, J.W. (1994) *Wordsworth and the Cultivation of Women*. Berkeley: University of California Press.

Palmer, F.R. (1979) *Modality and the English Modals*. London: Longman.

Parker, E. (ed.) (1964) *Poems of William Wordsworth*. New York: Crowell.

Patton, C.H. (1966) *The Rediscovery of Wordsworth*. New York: Gordian Press.

Pinion, F.B. (1976) *Brodie's Notes on Selections from Wordsworth*. London: Pan Educational.

Potts, A.F. (1966) *Wordsworth's* Prelude*: A Study of Its Literary Form*. New York: Octagon Books.

Prickett, S. (1970) *Wordsworth and Coleridge: The Poetry of Growth*. London: Cambridge University Press.

—— (1975) *Wordsworth and Coleridge:* The Lyrical Ballads. London: Edward Arnold.

—— (1976) *Romanticism and Religion: The Tradition of Coleridge and Wordsworth in the Victorian Church.* Cambridge: Cambridge University Press.

Purkis, J. (1970) *A Preface to Wordsworth.* London: Longman.

—— (1986) *A Preface to Wordsworth* (rev. edn). London: Longman.

Quirk, R. (1968) *Essays on the English Language: Medieval and Modern.* London: Longmans.

Quirk, R. et al. (1972) *A Grammar of Contemporary English.* London: Longman.

Rader, M. (1967) *Wordsworth: A Philosophical Approach.* Oxford: Clarendon Press.

Raleigh, W. (1918) *Wordsworth.* London: Edward Arnold.

Reeves, J. (1965) *Understanding Poetry.* London: Heinemann.

Regueiro, H. (1976) *The Limits of Imagination: Wordsworth, Yeats, and Stevens.* Ithaca: Cornell University Press.

Rehder, R. (1981) *Wordsworth and the Beginnings of Modern Poetry.* London: Croom Helm.

Ricks, C. (1984) *The Force of Poetry.* Oxford: Clarendon Press.

Roberts, J.L. (ed.) (1964) The Prelude: *Notes.* Lincoln: Cliff's Notes.

Roe, N. (2002) *The Politics of Nature: William Wordsworth and Some Contemporaries.* Basingstoke: Palgrave.

Rosenblatt, L.M. (1978) *The Reader, the Text, the Poem: The Transactional Theory of the Literary Work.* Carbondale: Southern Illinois University Press.

Saito, Y. (2000) *Eigo no Sahou* [*The Art of English*]. Tokyo: Tokyo University Press.

Sands, R. (1981) *William Wordsworth.* London: Pitkin Pictorials.

Sasaki, T. (1955) *Kindai Eishi no Hyougen* [*Expressions of Modern English Poetry*]. Tokyo: Kenkyusha.

Sato, K. (ed.) (1982) *Goi Genron* [*The Principles of Lexicography*] *Kouza Nihongo no Goi* [*Lectures on the Vocabulary of Japanese*] Vol.1. Tokyo: Meijishoin.

Sato, N. (1986) *Imi no Dansei: Rhetoric no Imiron e* [*Elasticity of Meaning: Toward Semantics of Rhetoric*]. Tokyo: Iwanami Shoten.

Schmitt, N. (2000) *Vocabulary in Language Teaching.* Richards, J.C. (ed.) *Cambridge Language Education.* Cambridge: Cambridge University Press.

Schogt, H.G. (1988) *Linguistics, Literary Analysis, and Literary Translation.* Toronto: University of Toronto Press.

Schröer, A. (1880) *Die Anfänge des Blank-Verses in England*. H. Yamaguchi (trans.), Nakajima, F. (gen. ed.) and Miyabe, K. (ed.) (1962) *Eikoku ni okeru Muinshi no Kigen* [*The Origin of Blank Verse in England*], Fushichou Eigogaku Sensho Series [Phoenix English Linguistics Series]. Tokyo: Nan'undo.

Sebeok, T.A. (gen. ed.) (1994) *Encyclopedic Dictionary of Semantics* (2nd edn), Tome 1-3. Berlin: Mouton de Gruyter.

de Selincourt, E. (1964) *Wordsworthian and Other Studies*. New York: Russell & Russell.

Shackford, M.H. (1976) *Wordsworth's Interest in Painters and Pictures*. Massachusetts: The Wellesley Press.

Sheats, P.D. (1973) *The Making of Wordsworth's Poetry, 1785-1798*. Cambridge, MA: Harvard University Press.

Sherry, C. (1980) *Wordsworth's Poetry of the Imagination*. Oxford: Clarendon Press.

Short, M. (1996) *Exploring the Language of Poems, Plays and Prose*. Harlow: Pearson Education.

Simpson, D. (1987) *Wordsworth's Historical Imagination: The Poetry of Displacement*. New York: Methuen.

Simpson, P. (1997) *Language through Literature: An Introduction*. London: Routledge.

—— (2004) *Stylistics: A Resource Book for Students*. London: Routledge.

Sinclair, J. (1991) *Corpus, Concordance, Collocation*. Sinclair, J. and Carter, R. (eds) *Describing English Language Series*. Oxford: Oxford University Press.

Sinfield, A. (1971) *The Language of Tennyson's* In Memoriam. Oxford: Basil Blackwell.

Singleton, D. (2000) *Language and the Lexicon: An Introduction*. London: Arnold.

Sloane, T.O. (ed.) (2001) *Encyclopedia of Rhetoric*. Oxford: Oxford University Press.

Smith, J.C. (1969) *A Study of Wordsworth*. New York: Kennikat Press.

Soeda, T. (1977) *Wāzuwasu Tenbyo* [*Some Sketches of Wordsworth*]. Osaka: Osaka Kyouiku Tosho.

—— (2004) *Wāzuwasu: Kiri ni Miekakuresuru Yamayama ni Nite*. [*Wordsworth: Like Mountains Glimpsed through Fog*]. Tokyo: Eihōsha.

Speirs, J. (1971) *Poetry towards Novel*. London: Faber & Faber.

Spiegelman, W. (1985) *Wordsworth's Heroes*. Berkeley: University of California Press.

Steen, G. (1994) *Understanding Metaphor in Literature: An Empirical Approach*. London: Longman.
Sullivan, B. (2000) *Wordsworth and the Composition of Knowledge: Refiguring Relationships among Minds, Worlds, and Words*. New York: Peter Lang.
Sutherland, J. (1948) *A Preface to Eighteenth Century Poetry*. London: Oxford University Press.
Talbot, R. and Whiteman, R. (1989) *The English Lakes*. London: Weidenfeld.
Tanaka, A. (1978) *Kokugo Goiron [Japanese Lexicology]*. Tokyo: Meijishoin.
Tannen, D. (ed.) (1984) *Coherence in Spoken and Written Discourse*, Vol. XII. Freedle, R.O. (ed.) *Advances in Discourse Processes*. New Jersey: Ablex Publishing Corporation.
Thompson, T.W. (1970) *Wordsworth's Hawkshead*. Woof, R. (ed.) London: Oxford University Press.
Thwaite, A. (1984) *Six Centuries of Verse*. London: Thames Methuen.
Tillyard, E.M.W. (1955) *Poetry and Its Background*. Fujii, H. (trans.) (1975) Tokyo: Nan'undo.
—— (1963) *The Elizabethan World Picture*. Harmondsworth: Penguin Books.
Todd, F.M. (1957) *Politics and the Poet: A Study of Wordsworth*. London: Methuen.
Todd, P. (1996) *Trailing Clouds of Glory: Poems by William Wordsworth*. London: Pavilion.
Toolan, M. (1998) *Language in Literature: An Introduction to Stylistics*. London: Arnold.
Toyota, M. (1981) *Eigo no Sutairu [Styles in English]*. Tokyo: Kenkyusha.
Trott, N. and Perry, S. (eds) (2001) *1800: The New Lyrical Ballads*. Basingstoke: Palgrave.
Ulmer, W.A. (2001) *The Christian Wordsworth, 1798-1805*. Albany: State University of New York Press.
Vivante, L. (1963) *English Poetry and Its Contribution to the Knowledge of a Creative Principle*. Carbondale: Southern Illinois University Press.
Watson, J.R. (1985) *English Poetry of the Romantic Period, 1789-1830*. London: Longman.
Welsford, E. (1966) *Salisbury Plain: A Study in the Development of Wordsworth's Mind and Art*. Oxford: Basil Blackwell.
Westbrook, D. (2001) *Wordsworth's Biblical Ghosts*. New York: Palgrave.

Select Bibliography

Widdowson, H.G. (1975) *Stylistics and the Teaching of Literature*. London: Longman.
—— (1992) *Practical Stylistics: An Approach to Poetry*. Oxford: Oxford University Press.
—— (1996) *Linguistics*. Oxford: Oxford University Press.
Wiley, M. (1998) *Romantic Geography: Wordsworth and Anglo-European Spaces*. Hampshire: Palgrave.
Williams, J. (ed.) *Wordsworth*. Peck, J. and Coyle, M. (series eds) *New Casebooks*. Basingstoke: Macmillan.
Wilson, D.B. (1993) *The Romantic Dream: Wordsworth and the Poetics of the Unconscious*. Lincoln: University of Nebraska Press.
Wise, T.J. (1916) *A Bibliography of the Writings in Prose and Verse of William Wordsworth*. London: Richard Clay & Sons.
Wordsworth, D. (1987) *The Grasmere Journal*. Wordsworth, J. (rev.) London: Michael Joseph.
—— (1989) *Journal of My Second Tour in Scotland, 1822: A Complete Edition of Dove Cottage Manuscript 98 and Dove Cottage Manuscript 99*. Nagasawa, J. (ed.) Tokyo: Kenkyusha.
Wordsworth, J. (ed.) (1970) *Bicentenary Wordsworth Studies: In Memory of John Alban Finch*. Ithaca: Cornell University Press.
—— (1982) *William Wordsworth: The Borders of Vision*. Oxford: Clarendon Press.
—— (2015) *The Invisible World: Lectures from the Wordsworth Summer Conference and Wordsworth Winter School*. Haynes, R. (ed.) CreateSpace Independent Publishing Platform.
Wordsworth, W. (1975) *The Salisbury Plain Poems of William Wordsworth:* Salisbury Plain, *or* A Night on Salisbury Plain Adventures on Salisbury Plain (*including* the Female Vagrant) Guilt and Sorrow; or, Incidents upon Salisbury Plain. Gill, S. (ed.) *The Cornell Wordsworth*. Ithaca: Cornell University Press.
—— (1977) Home at Grasmere *Part First, Book First, of* The Recluse. Darlington, B. (ed.) *The Cornell Wordsworth*. Ithaca: Cornell University Press.
—— (1977) The Prelude, *1798-1799*. Parrish, S. (ed.) *The Cornell Wordsworth*. Ithaca: Cornell University Press.
—— (1979) The Ruined Cottage *and* The Pedlar. Butler, J. (ed.) *The Cornell Wordsworth*. Ithaca: Cornell University Press.
—— (1981) Benjamin the Waggoner. Betz, P.F. (ed.) *The Cornell Wordsworth*. Ithaca: Cornell University Press.
—— (1982) The Borderers. Osborn, R. (ed.) *The Cornell Wordsworth*. Ithaca: Cornell University Press.

—— (1983) *Poems in Two Volumes, and Other Poems, 1800-1807.* Curtis, J. (ed.) *The Cornell Wordsworth.* Ithaca: Cornell University Press.

—— (1984-a) Descriptive Sketches. Birdsall, E. (ed.) *The Cornell Wordsworth.* Ithaca: Cornell University Press.

—— (1984-b) An Evening Walk. Averill, J. (ed.) *The Cornell Wordsworth.* Ithaca: Cornell University Press.

—— (1985-a) *The Fourteen-Book* Prelude. Owen, W.J.B. (ed.) *The Cornell Wordsworth.* Ithaca: Cornell University Press.

—— (1985-b) Peter Bell. Jordan, J.E. (ed.) *The Cornell Wordsworth.* Ithaca: Cornell University Press.

—— (1986) The Tuft of Primroses, *with Other Late Poems for* The Recluse. Kishel, J.F. (ed.) *The Cornell Wordsworth.* Ithaca: Cornell University Press.

—— (1988) The White Doe of Rylstone; *or* the Fate of the Nortons. Dugas, K. (ed.) *The Cornell Wordsworth.* Ithaca: Cornell University Press.

—— (1991-a) *Sonnet Series and Itinerary Poems, 1820-1845.* Jackson, G. (ed.) *The Cornell Wordsworth.* Ithaca: Cornell University Press.

—— (1991-b) *The Thirteen-Book* Prelude, *Vol. I & II.* Reed, M.L. (ed.) *The Cornell Wordsworth.* Ithaca: Cornell University Press.

—— (1997) *Early Poems and Fragments, 1785-1797.* Landon, C. and Curtis, J. (eds) *The Cornell Wordsworth.* Ithaca: Cornell University Press.

—— (1998) *Translations of Chaucer and Virgil.* Graver, B.E. (ed.) *The Cornell Wordsworth.* Ithaca: Cornell University Press.

—— (1999) *Last Poems, 1821-1850.* Curtis, J. (ed.) *The Cornell Wordsworth.* Ithaca: Cornell University Press.

Wordsworth, W. (1940) *The Poetical Works of William Wordsworth* (2nd edn). Vol. 1. de Selincourt, E. (ed.) and Darbishire, H. (rev.) Oxford: Clarendon Press.

—— (1952) *The Poetical Works of William Wordsworth* (2nd edn). Vol. 2. de Selincourt, E. (ed.) Oxford: Clarendon Press.

—— (1954) *The Poetical Works of William Wordsworth* (2nd edn). Vol. 3. de Selincourt, E. (ed.) and Darbishire, H. (rev.) Oxford: Clarendon Press.

—— (1958) *The Poetical Works of William Wordsworth* (2nd edn). Vol. 4. de Selincourt, E. (ed.) and Darbishire, H. (rev.) Oxford: Clarendon Press.

—— (1949) *The Poetical Works of William Wordsworth*, Vol. 5. de Selincourt, E. (ed.) and Darbishire, H. (rev.) Oxford: Clarendon Press.
Wordsworth, W. (1882) *The Poetical Works of William Wordsworth*, Vol. I-VIII. Knight, W. (ed.) Edinburgh: William Paterson.
—— (1928) *Wordsworth:* The Prelude *Book I, II, and parts of V and XII.* Darbishire, H. (ed.) Oxford: Clarendon Press.
—— (1958) *Selected Poems of William Wordsworth.* Sharrock, R. (ed.) London: Heinemann Educational Books.
—— (1959) *Wordsworth: Selected Poems.* Margoliouth, H.M. (ed.) London: Collins.
—— (1968-a) *William Wordsworth:* The Prelude *and Other Poems.* Danby, J.F. (ed.) London: Edward Arnold.
—— (1968-b) *William Wordsworth:* The Prelude or Growth of a Poet's Mind, Books I-IV. Yarker, P.M. (ed.) London: Routledge & Kegan Paul.
—— (1977) *Wordsworth's* Guide to the Lakes*: The Fifth Edition (1835).* de Selincourt, E. (ed.) Oxford: Oxford University Press.
—— (1979) *William Wordsworth:* The Prelude: *1799, 1805, 1850: Authoritative Texts Context and Reception Recent Critical Essays.* Wordsworth, J., Abrams, M.H. and Gill, S. (eds) New York: W. W. Norton & Company.
—— (1985) *William Wordsworth:* The Pedlar, Tintern Abbey, The Two-Part Prelude. Wordsworth, J. (ed.) Cambridge: Cambridge University Press.
—— (1985) *William Wordsworth:* The Ruined Cottage, The Brothers, Michael. Wordsworth, J. (ed.) Cambridge: Cambridge University Press.
—— (1987) *William Wordsworth: An Illustrated Selection.* Wordsworth, J. (ed.) Grasmere: The Wordsworth Trust.
—— (1989) *Shōyō* [*The Excursion*]. Tanaka, H. (trans.) Tokyo: Seibido.
Wordsworth, W. and Coleridge, S.T. (1940) *The Lyrical Ballads 1798-1805.* Sampson, G. (ed.) London: Methuen.
—— (1969) *Wordsworth and Coleridge: Lyrical Ballads 1798* (2nd edn). Owen, W.J.B. (ed.) Oxford: Oxford University Press.
Wu, D. (ed.) (1995-a) *A Comparison to Romanticism.* Oxford: Blackwell.
—— (1995-b) *Wordsworth's Reading 1800-1815.* Cambridge: Cambridge University Press.
—— (2002) *Wordsworth: An Inner Life.* Oxford: Blackwell.

Yamada, Y. (1999) *Kōrurijji to Wāzuwasu: Taiwa to Souzou (1795-1815)* [*Coleridge and Wordsworth: Dialogue and Creation*]. Tokyo: Hokuseido Shoten.

Yamauchi, S. (1989) 'Wāzuwasu to Hokou' ['Wordsworth and Walking'] in *Igirisu Romanha Kenkyū* [*Essays in English Romanticism*] 14. Tokyo: Igirisu Romanha Gakkai [Japan Association of English Romanticism].

—— (1994) 'Wāzuwasu to "spirit:" *Jokyoku* Dokkai no Tame ni' ['Wordsworth and "Spirit:" For Better Understanding of *The Prelude*'] in Yoshino, M. (ed.) *Wāzuwasu to Jokyoku* [*Wordsworth and The Prelude*], pp. 81-125.

Yamanouchi, H. (ed.) (1998) *Taiyaku Wāzuwasu Shishuu: Igirisu Shijinsen* [*A Bilingual Edition of Wordsworth Poems: English Poet*] 3. Tokyo: Iwanami Shoten.

Yoshimi, S. (1985) *Wordsworthian Pilgrimage*. Tokyo: Kaibunsha.

Yoshino, M. (ed.) (1994) *Wāzuwasu to Jokyoku* [*Wordsworth and The Prelude*]. Tokyo: Nan'undo.

—— (ed.) (2000) *Romanha no Kuukan* [*Space for Romantic Poets*]. Tokyo: Shohakusha.

Zitner, S.P., Kissane, J.D. and Liberman, M.M. (1964) *A Preface to Literary Analysis*. Chicago: Scott, Foresman and Company.

Dictionaries

Amano, N. and Kondo, M. (eds) (1999) *Nihongo no Goi Tokusei* [*Lexical Characteristics of Japanese*], 2 vols. Tokyo: Sanseido.

Hanks, P. et al. (eds) (1979) *Collins Dictionary of the English Language*. London: Collins.

Ichikawa, S. (gen. ed.) (1995) *Eiwa Katsuyou Daijiten* [*The Kenkyusha Dictionary of English Collocations*]. Tokyo: Kenkyusha.

Ikehara, S. et al. (eds) (1997) *Nihongo Goi Taikei* [*Large-Scale Japanese Thesaurus*], Vol. 1. *Imi Taikei* [*Semantic System*]. Tokyo: Iwanami Shoten.

Katsumata, S. (1958) *New Dictionary of English Collocation*. Tokyo: Kenkyusha.

Konishi, T. (ed.) (1980) *Eigo Kihon Doushi Jiten* [*A Dictionary of English Word Grammar on Verbs*]. Tokyo: Kenkyusha.

Muthmann, G. (1999) *Reverse English Dictionary: Based on Phonological and Morphological Principles*. Kortmann, B and Traugott, E.C. (eds) *Topics in English Linguistics* 29. Berlin: Mouton de Gruyter.

Otsuka, T. and Nakajima, F. (eds) (1982) *Shin Eigogaku Jiten* [*The Kenkyusha Dictionary of English Linguistics and Philology*]. Tokyo: Kenkyusha.

Roget's International Thesaurus. (1974) New York: Thomas Y. Crowell Company.

Roget's International Thesaurus (4th edn). (1977) New York: Thomas Y. Crowell Company.

Tutin, J.R. (1891) *The Wordsworth Dictionary of Persons and Places: With the Familiar Quotations from His Works (Including Full Index) and a Chronologically-Arranged List of His Best Poems*. New York: Johnson Reprint Corporation.

Wales, K. (1989) *A Dictionary of Stylistics*. Toyota, M. et al. (trans.) (2000) *Eigo Buntairon Jiten* [*A Dictionary of Stylistics*]. Tokyo: Sanseido.

Appendix

List 1.1: Alphabetical frequency list for *The Prelude*

Word	Freq.
a	1420
abandon'd	2
abasement	1
abash'd	2
abated	3
abbey	1
abbot	1
Abel	1
abide	1
abides	1
abideth	1
abiding-place	2
ability	1
abject	3
abode	16
abodes	2
abolish'd	1
aboriginal	1
abound	1
about	47
above	34
Abraham	1
abridg'd	1
abroad	17
abrupt	2
abruptly	5
absence	7
absolute	8
absorb'd	1
abstemiousness	1
abstract	2
abstraction	2
abstractions	1
abstracts	1
abstruse	2
abstruser	1
abundantly	1
abyss	2
Abyssinian	1
academic	6
accents	1
accepted	1
access	3
accidental	1
accidents	9
accompanied	1
accomplish	2
accomplish'd	4
accomplishment	1
accord	1
according	2
accordingly	2
account	2
accoutred	1
accusation	1
accuse	1
accustom'd	1
accustomed	1
ace	1
aching	1
acknowledg'd	1
acknowledge	1
acknowledgements	1
acknowledging	1
acorn	1
acquaintance	1
acquaintances	3
acquisitions	1
across	6
act	1
acting	3
action	5
actions	2
active	5
activities	1
activity	1
acts	3
actual	2
Adam	1
adamantine	1
add	15
added	4
address'd	1
adhere	1
adieu	1
administer	2
admirals	1
admiration	7
admir'd	1
admired	1
admittance	1
admitted	1
admitting	1
admonish	1
admonish'd	2
admonishment	1
admonishments	1
admonition	3
admonitions	1
admonitory	1
adopted	1
adopts	1
adore	1
adorn'd	3
Adria's	1
adroit	1
adulterate	1
advance	1
advanc'd	4
advanced	6
advancing	2
advantage	1
adventure	1
adventurer	1
adventurers	1
adventures	1
adverse	1
advertisements	1
advice	1
advocate	1
advocates	2
aerial	2
aestuary	1
afar	1
affairs	1
affect	1
affecting	4
affectingly	1
affection	1
affectionate	1
affections	12
affinities	2
affliction	1
afford	1
afloat	1
afraid	1
afresh	3
after	44
after-meditation	1
afternoon	2
afternoons	4
afterwards	21
again	49
against	17
age	26
aged	4
agencies	1
agency	2
agent	2
agents	1
ages	7
aggravated	1
agitated	2
agitation	1
agitations	1
agony	1
ah	6
aid	3
aids	1
aim	6
aim'd	1
aiming	1
aims	3
air	25
airs	4
airy	5
akin	4
alas	7
albeit	5
albinos	1
Alcairo	1
alder	1
alder-fringed	1
alert	1
alien	3
alienation	1
alike	12
alive	9
all	352
allegiance	1
allegoric	1
alley	1
alliance	3
allied	2
allotted	1
allow	1
allowance	2
alloy	1
allude	2
allurement	1
alluring	1
almost	31
alms	2
aloft	2
alone	38
along	45
aloud	6
Alpine	2
Alps	6
already	12
also	24
altar	1
alternate	1
alternately	1
alternative	1
although	5
always	3
am	15
amain	3
amass'd	1
ambiguously	1
ambition	6
ambitious	1
ambitiously	1
amends	1
America	1
amid	12
amiss	2
amity	1
among	121
amorous	1
amphibious	1
ample	3
ampler	2
amplest	1
amplitude	2
amused	1
amusement	2
amusements	1
an	167
analogies	1
analogous	1
analogy	1
analyse	1
analysis	1
analytic	1
anarchy	1
anchor	1
ancient	21
and	2715
angel	1
Angelica	1
angelical	1
angels	3
anger	2
angled	1
angry	2
animal	3
animate	1
animated	1
animates	1
animating	1
animation	2
announce	1
announced	1
annual	2
annually	1
annull'd	1
anon	3
another	18
another's	5
answer	5
answer'd	1
answers	2
antechapel	1
Anthony	1
antic	1
antics	1
Antiparos	1
antiquarian's	1
antique	1
antiquity	2
ant-like	1
anxiety	3
anxious	3
anxiousness	1
any	26
anything	3
anywhere	1
apart	4
apartments	1
apathy	1
ape	2
apocalypse	1
apology	1
apostacy	1
appanage	1
apparition	1
appeal	1
appear	2
appearance	3
appearances	5
appear'd	19
appeared	1
appears	6
appertain'd	2
appetite	1
appetites	4
apples	1
application	2
applied	1
appointed	1
apprehend	1
apprehension	1
apprehensive	1
apprise	1
approach	6
approachable	1
approach'd	4
approaching	2
appropriate	1
apt	2
aptest	1
aptly	2
Arab	5
Arabian	3
Araby	1
arbitrement	1
arbours	2
arcades	1
Arcadia	1
Arcadian	1
arch	3
Archimedes	1
arcs	1
Arden	1
ardent	3
arduous	1
are	126
area	1
Arethuse	1
argument	9
arguments	2
Aristogiton	1
arm	6
arm'd	1
armed	1
armies	1
armoury	1
arms	14
arm's	1
army	1
aromatic	1
around	5
arranged	1
Arras	2
array	4
array'd	1
arrest	1
arrive	1
arrived	1
arrow's	1
art	20
artful	1
Arthur's	1
articulate	3
artificer	1
artificial	2
artist	1
artless	1
arts	4
as	477
ascend	1
ascending	7
ascent	3
ascents	1
ascertain	1
ascribed	1
ash	2
ashamed	2
aside	4
ask	3
ask'd	3
asleep	7
aspect	4
aspiration	3
aspirations	1
aspire	1
aspires	1
aspiring	1
assemblage	1
assembled	1
assembly	1
assembly-room	1
assert	2
assiduous	1
assign'd	1
assist	3
assisted	1
associate	2
associates	2
assumed	1
assumes	1
assurance	1
assurances	1
assur'd	1
assured	2
astir	1
astonish'd	1
astonishment	5
astray	1
at	334
atchiev'd	1
atchieves	1
ate	2
atheist	1
athwart	1
atrocities	1
attach'd	2
attack	1
attain'd	1
attaining	1
attemper'd	1
attempt	2
attempts	1
attend	4
attendant	5
attendants	1
attended	4
attending	1
attends	2
attention	3
attest	3
Attic	1
attir'd	1
attire	2
attracted	1
attraction	1
attractive	1
attribute	1
attributes	1
attun'd	1
attuned	1
audible	6
audibly	1
audience	1
Augean	1
aught	14
augment	1
augmented	1
augurs	1
Aurora	1
authentic	2
authority	7
authorship	1
autumn	6
autumnal	1
auxiliar	1
auxiliars	1
avail	1
avail'd	1
avenue	1
avenues	1
avoid	1
avow	1
await	1
awaits	2
awak'd	1
awake	1
awaked	1
awaken'd	1
awakening	1
away	34
aw'd	1
awe	7
awed	1
awful	14
awhile	6
awry	1
azure	1
babe	16
Babel	1
Babel-like	1
babes	3
Babylon	1
bachelor	2
back	39
backs	1
backward	1
backwards	2
bad	3
bade	5
badge	1
badger	1
baffled	4
baffling	1
balance	4
balanced	3
bald	1
ballad	1
ballads	1
ballad-singer	1
ballast	1
balmy	2
band	11
banded	1
bandied	1
banishment	1
bank	2
bank'd	1
banks	7
banners	3
bar	1
barbarian	1
barbaric	1
bard	7
bare	9

155

156   Wordsworth's Vocabulary in *The Prelude*

word	n	word	n	word	n	word	n	word	n	word	n
barely	2	bellowing	1	blest	3	brawny	1	butterflies	1	caution	1
bark	3	bells	4	blew	3	breach	1	Buttermere	2	cautious	1
barking	1	belong	1	blighted	1	break	8	buy	1	cavaliers	1
barren	4	belong'd	4	blind	11	breakfasts	1	by	447	cave	5
barrier	1	belonging	1	bliss	7	breaking	2	bye-spots	1	cavern	5
barrows	1	belov'd	4	blithe	1	breast	11	bye-tracts	1	caverns	2
bars	2	beloved	1	block	2	breasts	1	cabin	1	caves	2
barter	1	beloved	12	Blois	1	breath	10	cabinet	1	cavities	1
Bartholomew	1	below	4	blood	7	breath'd	7	cabins	1	ceas'd	3
base	4	belt	2	blood-red	1	breathe	12	cadence	1	cease	1
basest	1	belying	1	bloody	1	breathed	1	caged	1	ceaseless	1
basis	3	bench	2	bloom	1	breathes	2	Calais	1	celestial	1
bask'd	2	bend	4	blossoms	1	breathing	4	calamity	1	cell	1
basket	1	bending	3	blots	1	breathing-place	1	calendars	1	cells	1
bastard	1	beneath	45	blotted	1	breathings	2	call	15	centre	4
bastile	1	benediction	2	blow	6	breathless	3	call'd	22	centring	1
bathing	2	beneficent	1	blowing	6	breath-like	1	called	2	certain	6
batten'd	1	benefit	1	blown	3	bred	6	calling	5	Cervantes	2
battle	2	benefits	1	blows	2	breeds	1	calls	2	chace	5
bawling	1	benevolence	2	blue	6	breeze	10	call'st	1	chaced	1
bay	3	benevolent	1	blue-breech'd	1	breezes	5	calm	22	chafed	1
bays	1	benighted	1	blue-frosted	1	breezy	1	calmer	4	chaffering	1
be	236	benign	1	blunt	1	brethren	2	calmly	2	chain	2
beach	2	benignant	1	blushing	1	bribe	1	calmness	3	chains	2
beacon	4	benignity	1	board	6	bridge	1	Calvert	1	chair	4
bead	1	bent	7	boards	1	bridged	1	Cam	3	chairs	1
beads	1	bequest	1	boast	3	bridges	1	Cambridge	1	chaise	1
beams	1	bereft	1	boat	7	bridle	1	came	42	chaises	1
bear	6	beseem'd	1	boats	1	brief	2	campaign	1	chalk	1
beard	1	beset	4	bodied	1	briefly	2	cam'st	1	chamber	2
bearded	1	beside	6	bodies	1	bright	12	can	42	chambers	2
bearing	2	besides	1	bodily	5	brighten	1	candidates	1	chamber-window	1
bearings	1	bespeak	1	body	13	brighter	2	cane	1	Chambord	1
bears	2	best	27	boisterous	3	bright-eyed	1	cannon	1	chamois'	1
beast	3	bestow'd	2	boisterously	1	brightness	1	cannot	18	Chamouny	1
beasts	4	bestows	1	bold	5	brim	1	canon	1	champion	1
beat	10	bestud	1	bolder	1	bring	14	canons	1	chanc'd	2
beaten	2	bethinking	1	boldly	3	bringing	3	canopy	2	chance	16
beating	4	Bethkelet's	1	bolt	1	brings	2	canst	1	chance-comer	1
beatings	1	betimes	2	bolted	1	brink	3	canvas-cover'd	1	chanced	7
beatitude	1	betook	2	bond	5	Britain	4	cap	1	chancing	1
beats	3	betray	1	bondage	3	British	1	capability	1	chang'd	6
Beaupuis	1	betray'd	1	bonds	3	Briton	2	capable	2	change	24
beauteous	14	better	26	bond-slave	1	broad	7	capacious	1	changed	4
beautified	1	between	11	bone	1	broadening	1	capaciousness	1	changeful	2
beautiful	10	betwixt	7	bones	2	broke	2	capacity	1	changes	3
beauty	29	bewail	1	bonnet	1	broken	2	capital	2	changing	1
became	5	bewilder'd	6	book	11	bronz'd	1	captivated	1	channel	3
because	3	bewitch	1	book-mindedness	1	brood	3	captive	5	channels	1
become	10	beyond	21	books	34	brooding	2	captivity	2	chaos	1
becomes	2	Bible	1	book-stalls	1	brook	9	car	1	chapel	4
becoming	1	bidding	2	boon	2	brooks	6	caravan	1	chaplet	1
bed	10	bids	1	Booths	2	brook-side	1	car'd	1	character	8
bedded	3	bigot	1	border	1	brothel	1	cards	2	characters	6
Bedfords	1	bigotry	1	borders	4	brother	8	card-tables	1	charcoal	1
bedlam	1	bind	2	bore	8	brotherhood	4	care	4	charg'd	1
bedlamites	1	binds	1	born	10	brothers	4	careless	5	charge	6
Bedouin	1	biographic	1	borne	3	brothers-water	1	carelessly	2	chariots	1
bedroom	1	bird	6	borrowing	1	brought	25	carelessness	1	charitable	1
beds	4	birds	17	bosom	8	brow	1	cares	9	charity	1
bee	1	birth	17	bosom'd	1	brows	1	caress'd	1	charm	11
beechen	1	birthplace	2	both	33	brute	1	caressing	1	charm'd	2
been	162	birth-place	1	Bothnic	1	Brutus	1	caring	1	charms	1
bees	4	birth-right	3	bottom	4	bubbles	1	carnage	1	charnel-house	1
befal	1	birtly	1	bottom'd	1	Bucer	1	carousel	1	charter	1
befel	2	bishop	1	bough	1	budding	2	Carra	1	chartered	1
befit	1	bitter	1	boughs	1	budding-time	1	carriage	2	Chartreuse	2
before	80	bitterest	1	bounced	1	buffoonery	1	carried	9	chas'd	1
beg	1	bitterly	1	bound	11	buffoons	1	carries	2	chase	1
began	17	black	4	boundaries	1	build	8	carry	1	chasm	2
beggar	1	blackbird's	1	bounded	1	builder	1	carrying	1	chasten'd	1
beggars	1	blades	1	bounded	1	builders	1	Cartmell's	1	chastening	1
begg'd	3	blame	6	boundless	1	building	3	carve	1	chastisement	3
begin	6	blameless	1	boundless	1	buildings	1	carved	1	chat	1
beginning	6	Blanc	1	bounds	5	builds	1	carving	2	chattering	2
beginnings	1	bland	1	bounties	1	built	8	cascades	1	Chaucer	1
begirt	1	blank	5	bourne	2	burden	1	case	1	chaunt	1
begs	1	blasphemy	1	bow'd	1	burghers	1	casement	1	chaunted	1
beguile	3	blast	3	bowels	2	Burgundy	1	casket	1	chauntry	1
beguiled	1	blasted	3	bower	2	burial-place	1	Cassandra	1	cheap	1
begun	7	blasts	4	bowers	6	buried	2	cast	4	chear	4
behalf	1	blaz'd	1	bowl	1	burning	1	castle	3	chear'd	3
beheld	24	blaze	1	bowling-green	1	burnish'd	1	casual	4	chearful	4
behind	20	blazon	1	box'd	1	burnished	1	catacombs	1	chearfully	1
behold	22	blazon'd	1	boy	19	burst	4	catalogu'd	1	chearfulness	2
beholding	2	bleak	2	boyish	4	bursting	1	cataracts	3	chearing	1
beholds	3	bleat	1	Boyle	1	bursts	1	catastrophe	1	check'd	3
being	40	Blencathra's	1	boys	5	burthen	3	catch	1	cheek	5
beings	4	blend	1	Brabant	1	bury	1	caterpillars	1	cheeks	2
belfry	1	blended	1	brace	1	bush	1	cattle	1	cherish	1
belief	6	bless	3	brain	7	busier	1	caught	4	cherish'd	1
believe	4	bless'd	4	branch	2	business	13	caus'd	1	cherishes	1
believed	2	blessed	9	branches	1	bust	1	cause	20	cherry	1
believing	1	blessedness	5	brave	1	bustle	1	caused	1	chest	3
belike	1	blessing	6	bravest	1	busy	13	causes	2	chestnut	1
bell	3	blessings	3	brawls	1	but	322	causeway	1	chief	8

Appendix 157

word	count	word	count	word	count	word	count	word	count
chiefly	17	clung	1	composure	6	contagious	1	courting	1	cut	7
child	36	cluster'd	1	comprehension	1	contamination	1	courts	5	cyphers	1
child-bed	1	clusters	1	comprehensive	1	contemplated	2	cove	1	cypress	1
childhood	16	coaches	3	comprehensiveness	1	contemplation	5	covenant	1	daffodils	1
childless	1	coalesce	1	compunction	1	contemplations	1	cover	1	daily	25
child-like	4	coarse	1	comrade	2	contemplative	1	cover'd	5	daisies	1
children	15	coarser	1	comrades	2	contempt	3	covert	3	dales	1
child's	2	coasted	1	concave	1	contempts	1	covertly	1	dame	9
chimney-nook	1	coasting	1	conceal	1	content	6	coverts	1	damp	1
China's	1	coasts	1	conceal'd	2	contented	2	coves	2	damp'd	2
Chinese	1	coat	3	conceit	4	contentedness	2	coward	1	damps	1
chivalrous	1	cock	1	conceited	1	contention	1	cowardice	1	danc'd	1
chivalry	2	Cockermouth	1	conceits	2	contentious	1	cowardise	1	dance	8
choice	10	coercing	1	conceiv'd	1	contents	1	coy	1	danced	2
chok'd	1	coffins	1	conception	2	contest	2	crack	1	dances	2
choristers	1	Coker's	1	concern	4	continence	1	cradle	5	dancing	2
chose	1	cold	3	concerns	3	continent	1	cradles	1	danger	7
chosen	8	Coleridge	2	concise	1	continually	1	craft	5	dangerous	5
Christabel	1	collar'd	1	conclude	1	continu'd	1	crag	6	danger's	1
Christian	1	collateral	2	conclusions	1	continue	2	craggy	3	dangle	1
Christmas-time	1	collaterally	2	concourse	1	continued	5	crags	13	dangling	1
chronicle	3	collected	1	concussions	1	continues	1	craved	3	dare	1
chronicles	1	college	5	condemnation	1	continuing	2	craven's	1	dared	2
church	7	collegiate	1	condescension	1	contracted	1	craves	1	daring	3
churches	2	collisions	1	condition	4	contrarieties	1	craving	1	dark	13
churchyard	2	colloquies	1	conditions	2	contrast	1	cravings	2	darker	1
churlish	1	colour	2	conduct	1	contrastive	1	crawl	1	dark-eyed	1
chuse	5	colour'd	1	conducted	5	control'd	1	craz'd	2	darkly	1
chuses	2	colouring	1	conductor	1	controul	4	cream	1	darkness	16
circle	2	colours	13	confederate	1	conven'd	1	create	2	darling	4
circles	2	colt	1	confederated	1	convent	4	created	2	dart	1
circuit	4	comates	1	confess	3	conventicle	1	creates	2	dash'd	1
circuitous	1	combat	2	confess'd	2	convention	1	creation	2	dashing	1
circumambient	2	combatants	2	confession	1	conversant	1	creative	6	date	2
circumfus'd	1	combination	1	confidence	8	conversation	3	creator	1	daughter	2
circumfuse	1	combinations	1	confident	1	convers'd	2	creature	13	daunt	1
circumscribed	1	combine	1	confiding	1	converse	2	creatures	11	dawn	10
circumspection	2	combines	1	confine	1	conversed	1	credit	1	dawning	2
circumstance	7	combs	1	confined	1	conversion	1	creed	5	day	118
circumstances	3	come	50	confirmation	1	convey	1	creek	2	day-dream	1
cistern	1	comedy	1	confirm'd	1	conviction	2	creeks	1	daylight	1
cities	5	comely	1	confirmed	1	convictions	1	creeping	3	day-light	1
city	25	comers	1	conflict	1	convinced	1	crept	1	days	45
city's	2	comes	18	conflicting	1	convocation	1	crescent	1	day's	4
civic	1	comfort	6	conflicts	1	convoked	1	cressets	1	day-spring	1
civil	4	comfortless	1	confluence	1	cool	2	crest	1	day-thoughts	1
clad	3	comforts	2	conform	1	coombs	1	crested	1	day-time	1
claim	1	coming	8	conformity	1	coop'd	1	crests	1	dazzle	1
claims	2	command	5	confounded	4	coppice	1	crevices	1	dazzled	3
clamorous	2	commanding	1	confronting	1	copse	1	crew	4	dazzling	2
clandestine	1	commendable	1	confusion	4	copying	1	cried	1	dead	17
class	1	commendation	1	confusion-stricken	1	cord	1	cries	2	deadening	1
class-fellow	1	comments	1	congenial	1	cordial	2	crimes	4	deadly	1
classic	1	commerce	2	congratulation	1	Corin	1	criminal	1	deaf	2
claws	1	commingled	1	congregated	1	corn	1	cripple	2	deafen'd	1
clay	3	commiseration	1	congregating	1	corner	2	critic	1	deal	6
cleanse	1	commission'd	1	congregation	3	corners	2	crocodiles	1	dealing	1
clear	8	committed	1	congress	1	coronal	1	crocus	1	deals	1
clear'd	3	commix'd	1	conjectures	1	corporeal	1	crook	2	dealt	4
clearer	3	common	34	conjecturing	1	corps	1	cross	7	deans	1
clearest	1	commonly	1	conjured	1	corrected	2	cross'd	9	dear	27
clear-shining	1	common-place	1	conjurors	1	correction	1	crossed	2	dearest	7
cleave	2	commonplaces	1	connect	1	correspondence	1	crosses	1	dearly	1
cliff	3	commonwealth	1	connected	2	corresponding	2	cross-legg'd	1	death	17
cliffs	3	commotion	2	connection	1	corrupted	1	crouches	1	deathless	1
climate	1	commotions	1	conning	1	cost	1	crowd	12	deharr'd	1
climb'd	2	commun'd	1	conquer'd	1	costly	1	crow'd	1	debase	1
climbs	1	commune	1	conqueror	1	cotes	1	crowded	5	debasement	1
clime	2	communed	1	conquerors	1	cottage	16	crowds	1	debts	1
climes	1	communing	1	conquest	1	cottagers	4	crown	5	decanters	1
clinging	1	communion	5	conscience	4	cottages	4	crucibles	1	decay	5
Clitumnus	1	community	1	conscious	8	couch'd	1	crude	2	decay'd	2
cloak	2	Como	1	consciousness	3	couching-time	1	crudest	1	decaying	1
cloath'd	1	Como's	1	consciousnesses	2	could	103	cruel	4	deceit	1
clock	3	companion	3	consecrate	1	counsel	2	crush'd	1	deceive	1
clocks	1	companionless	1	consecrated	1	countenance	11	cry	1	deceived	2
clock-work	1	companions	2	consecrates	1	countenances	1	crying	3	decency	3
clog	1	companionships	1	consent	2	counteract	1	cull'd	2	decision	1
cloisters	2	company	5	consequence	1	countermarch'd	1	culling	1	decisive	1
cloistral	1	comparative	1	consequence	1	counterpart	2	culprits	1	deck	1
clomb	2	compar'd	3	consisted	1	counterpoise	1	culture	1	deck'd	1
close	11	compared	1	consistency	1	counter-turns	1	Cumberland	1	declared	1
closed	1	comparing	1	consolation	3	counterview	1	Cumbria's	1	declin'd	1
closelier	1	comparison	1	consolations	2	counter-winds	1	cunning	1	declining	1
closely	2	compeer	1	consoled	1	country	11	cups	2	decoration	1
cloth'd	2	compeers	1	consoling	1	country-playhouse	1	cur	1	decoy'd	1
clothes	1	compell'd	4	consorted	1	country's	3	cure	1	dedicate	2
clothing	1	complacency	2	consorting	1	coupled	1	curfew-time	1	dedicated	1
cloud	6	complacently	1	conspicuous	4	courage	3	curious	2	deduced	1
clouded	3	complaint	1	constancy	1	courageous	1	curling	1	deed	5
cloud-loving	1	complete	7	constant	2	cours'd	1	current	1	deeds	5
clouds	25	complex	1	constellations	1	course	23	currents	1	deem	6
clove	1	compos'd	1	constitute	2	courser	1	cushion	1	deem'd	3
clowns	1	compose	1	constitution	1	court	3	custody	1	deep	40
clubs	2	composed	6	constrain'd	3	courteous	2	custom	12	deep-dale	1
clumsy	1	composition	2	consummate	1	courtesy	1	customs	1	deeper	11

158 Wordsworth's Vocabulary in *The Prelude*

word	count	word	count	word	count	word	count	word	count
deepest	6	destitute	4	dislike	2	drank	2	eat	1	enclosures	1
deeply	10	destroyer	1	disliking	1	draw	2	eating	1	encourag'd	2
deeps	1	destruction	1	dislocated	1	drawing	3	ebb	2	encouragement	1
deer	1	detach'd	1	dislodg'd	1	drawn	5	ebbs	1	encourager	1
defeated	1	detached	1	dismal	5	drayman's	1	echo	2	encreas'd	1
defence	2	detail	1	dismally	1	dread	5	echoed	1	increased	1
defenceless	1	detain	1	dismantled	3	dream	18	echoes	4	end	28
defenders	1	detain'd	3	dismay	4	dreamer	1	eclips'd	1	endear'd	2
deferr'd	1	detains	1	dismay'd	1	dreamers	1	eclipse	3	endeavour	1
definite	1	detect	1	dismiss'd	3	dreaming	2	ecstasy	1	endeavour'd	2
deformities	1	detects	1	dismounting	1	dreamless	1	eddy's	1	endeavoured	1
defrauded	1	determin'd	1	disobedience	1	dreams	15	edge	4	endeavours	2
defrauding	1	determined	1	disown'd	1	dreamt	1	edged	1	ended	5
degeneracy	2	devilish	1	dispers'd	3	dreariness	1	edges	1	endless	11
degradation	1	devious	4	display	1	dreary	6	edict	1	endlessly	2
degree	7	devis'd	2	dispos'd	1	drench'd	1	edifice	2	endow'd	1
degrees	3	devoted	2	disposes	1	dress	5	edifices	1	endowment	1
deity	2	devotion	4	dispositions	1	dressing-gown	1	Edinburgh	1	endowments	4
dejected	1	devour'd	1	disquiet	1	drew	3	education	1	ends	8
dejection	4	devouring	3	disquietude	1	dried	1	e'er	2	endues	1
delay	2	devout	1	dissolute	3	drift	1	effect	8	endurance	1
Delecarlia's	1	devoutest	1	dissolves	1	drifted	1	effeminately	1	endur'd	1
delegates	1	devoutly	1	distance	11	drink	4	efficacious	1	endure	7
deliberate	1	dew	3	distant	23	drinking	2	effort	4	endures	1
delicacy	1	dews	1	distinct	4	drinks	1	efforts	1	enduring	8
delicate	3	diadem	1	distinction	2	dripp'd	1	effulgence	1	endur'st	1
delicious	5	diagrams	1	distinctions	3	dripping	1	eglantine	1	enemies	1
delight	48	dialogues	2	distinctly	2	drive	4	eight	2	enemy	4
delighted	4	diamond	1	distinctness	1	drivellers	1	eight-days'	1	energy	4
delightful	11	diamonds	2	distinguishable	2	driven	2	eighty	2	enflam'd	3
delights	9	dictates	1	distinguish'd	1	drives	1	either	9	enflame	1
delirious	1	dictators	1	distracted	1	drizzling	1	elaborate	5	enflamed	1
deliver'd	1	did	152	distraction	1	dromedary	3	elaborately	1	enfold	1
deliverer's	1	didst	12	distress	7	droop	1	elate	1	enfranchis'd	1
dells	2	die	4	distress'd	1	drooping	2	elbow	1	engender'd	1
deluded	1	died	1	district	2	drop	1	elbowing	1	engines	1
deluge	1	diet	1	districts	1	dropp'd	3	elders	1	England	6
delusion	3	differ'd	1	disturb	1	drops	2	elder-tree	1	English	4
delusions	1	difference	3	disturbance	1	drove	1	eldest	1	Englishman	2
demand	3	differences	2	disturb'd	2	drown'd	1	elegance	3	Englishmen	3
demanded	1	different	20	diurnal	1	drowning	1	elegances	1	engrafted	2
demanding	1	differing	1	divers	2	Druids	1	elegy	1	engraven	1
demeanor	1	difficult	1	diversity	2	dry	3	element	6	engross'd	1
demure	1	difficulty	1	divide	2	dubious	1	elements	14	engulph'd	1
den	1	diffidence	1	divided	2	due	5	elevate	1	enhanced	1
denied	1	diffus'd	3	dividually	1	dukes	1	elevated	3	enjoy'd	1
denounced	1	diffused	2	divin'd	1	dull	4	elevating	1	enjoyment	3
dens	1	diffusing	2	divine	18	dulness	1	elevation	2	enjoyments	3
denunciation	1	diffusive	1	divined	1	duly	2	elfin	1	enlarged	4
depart	1	dignified	1	divinely	1	dumb	4	elms	2	enmities	1
departed	2	dignity	13	diviner	1	dunces	1	eloquence	3	enmity	2
departure	2	dilatory	1	divinity	1	dupe	1	eloquent	1	Enna	1
depended	1	dim	7	divisions	2	dupes	1	else	30	ennobled	1
dependency	1	dimm'd	1	divorced	1	during	1	elsewhere	8	ennobling	3
depicted	1	dimple	1	do	45	dusky	5	emanations	1	enormities	1
depravation	1	dimpling	2	doctor	2	dust	3	emancipated	1	enough	19
deprav'd	1	din	6	doctors	2	duteous	1	embalm'd	1	enow	2
depress'd	4	dinners	1	does	10	duty	7	embark'd	1	enquiring	1
depth	9	Dion	1	dog	7	dwarf	2	emblazonry	1	enrich'd	2
depths	3	dipp'd	2	dog-day	1	dwarfs	1	emblem	2	enshrine	1
dereliction	1	dire	1	dogs	1	dwell	6	embodied	3	ensigns	1
deriv'd	1	direct	3	doing	4	dweller	1	embody	1	enslave	1
Derwent	3	directing	1	doings	2	dwelling	5	embodying	1	ensu'd	1
desart	7	directions	1	domain	6	dwelling-place	2	embosom	1	ensue	2
desarts	1	directly	2	dome	2	dwellings	2	emboss'd	2	ensued	5
descend	3	disappear	4	domes	1	dwells	2	embraced	1	ensues	1
descended	1	disappear'd	1	domestic	10	dwelt	4	embracing	1	ensuing	2
descending	3	disappearing	1	domination	2	dwindle	2	emerging	1	entail	1
describe	1	disappointed	1	dominion	2	dying	1	emigrants	1	entangle	1
described	2	disappointment	4	done	14	dynasty	1	eminence	6	entangled	1
descried	2	disapproved	1	dons	1	dythrambic	1	Emont	1	enter	6
desert	1	disarm'd	1	doom	2	each	45	emotion	4	enter'd	3
deserted	1	disasters	1	doom'd	2	eager	9	emotions	1	entering	4
desertion	2	disastrous	2	door	15	eagerly	5	empedocles	1	enterprize	1
deserv'd	1	disbelieving	1	doors	7	eagerness	1	emperor	1	entertain'd	1
deserve	1	discharg'd	1	dost	9	eagle	1	emphatically	1	entertainments	1
deserves	1	discipline	8	dotards	1	eagle's	1	empire	6	enthrall'd	1
design	3	discomfiture	1	doth	23	ear	7	employ	2	enthralment	1
design'd	1	disconsolate	2	doubly	1	earlier	2	employ'd	6	enthusiast	2
desir'd	1	discordant	1	doubt	8	earliest	6	employment	3	enthusiastic	3
desire	12	discountenance	1	doubted	3	early	29	employments	2	enticing	2
desireable	1	discouraged	1	doubting	1	earnest	3	employs	1	entire	7
desires	9	discourse	6	doubtless	6	ears	11	emporium	1	entirely	3
desolate	1	discover'd	1	doubts	2	earth	62	empress	1	entomb'd	1
desolated	1	discoveries	1	dove	2	earthly	4	emptied	1	entrance	2
desolation	2	discretion	1	dovedale	1	earthquake	1	emptiness	3	entrancement	1
despair	5	discriminate	1	dower	1	earthquakes	1	empty	7	entreated	1
desperate	5	discursive	1	down	60	earth's	1	empyrean	1	entrust	1
desperation	1	disdain	1	down-bending	1	earthward	1	emulation	1	entrusted	2
despis'd	1	disease	2	downs	1	ease	2	enable	1	entwine	1
despised	1	disgrace	1	downwards	3	easier	3	enabled	2	envied	1
despite	5	disguis'd	1	downy	1	easily	8	enables	2	environ	1
despondency	1	dish	1	doze	1	east	6	enchanter	1	environ'd	2
despotic	1	disjoin'd	1	dragging	1	eastern	3	enchanting	3	envy	1
destined	4	disjoining	1	dramas	1	eastward	1	enchantment	2	enwrought	1
destiny	4	disjointed	1	dramatic	1	easy	5	enclosure	2	eolian	1

Appendix

word	count	word	count	word	count	word	count	word	count
ephemeral	1	excursion	1	falsely	5	fetters	1	flourish'd	1	four	4
equal	2	excursions	2	false-seeming	1	feuds	1	flourishing	1	fourteen	1
equality	1	excursively	1	falsest	1	fever	1	flow	2	fowl	1
equally	1	excuse	1	falsly	1	feverish	2	flow'd	7	fowler's	1
equestrians	1	executions	1	faltering	1	few	31	flower	8	fox	1
equipages	1	exempt	1	fame	5	fiction	2	flowers	17	foxglove	1
equipment	1	exercise	6	famed	1	fictions	4	flowery	2	fractur'd	1
equipp'd	2	exercised	1	familiar	9	fiddle	2	flowing	3	fracture	1
equity	2	exerts	1	familiarly	5	field	17	flown	1	fractured	1
Erasmus	1	exhalations	1	family	10	fields	29	flute	2	fragment	2
ere	25	exhausted	1	famous	8	field-ward	1	flying	2	fragments	1
erect	2	exhibited	1	fan	1	fierce	3	foes	4	fragrance	3
erelong	6	exhibition	1	fancied	6	fiercest	1	fog	2	frail	1
erewhile	5	exhibitions	1	fancies	5	fiery	1	fogs	1	frailties	1
ermined	1	exhortations	1	fancy	17	fife	1	foil	1	fram'd	6
Erminia	1	exile	2	fane	1	fifteen	1	foil'd	1	frame	22
err	1	exist	1	fann'd	1	fifth	1	fold	1	framed	4
errand	7	existed	1	far	93	fight	2	foliage	1	frames	1
errant	2	existence	4	fare	4	fighting	2	folios	1	France	18
erring	2	existing	1	fared	4	figure	2	follies	2	Francis	1
error	6	exists	5	farewell	3	figures	3	follow	7	frank	1
errors	3	expanse	1	farewells	1	figuring	1	follow'd	6	frank-hearted	1
escape	1	expectancy	1	far-fetch'd	1	filch'd	1	followed	3	frankly	1
escaped	2	expectation	2	farm	1	files	3	follower	1	fraternal	2
escapes	1	expectations	1	farms	1	filial	2	followers	1	fraught	1
espied	2	expected	2	far-secluded	1	fill	10	following	3	fray	1
espy	2	expense	1	farther	3	fill'd	10	follows	2	freaks	1
essay'd	1	experienc'd	1	far-travell'd	1	filled	1	folly	5	free	18
essences	1	experience	6	fascination	1	filling	1	fond	7	freedom	10
essential	1	experiments	1	fashion	4	fills	1	fondly	2	freely	2
establish	1	explain	1	fashion'd	3	final	2	fondness	2	freeman	2
establish'd	1	explain'd	1	fashioning	1	finally	5	food	11	freer	1
estate	1	expos'd	1	fast	12	find	30	foolish	2	freight	4
esteem	4	exposed	1	fasten	1	finding	1	foolishness	2	Frenchman	2
esteem'd	1	express	1	fasten'd	1	finds	8	foot	9	Frenchmen	1
Esthwaite's	2	express'd	3	fastening	1	fine	2	foot-bound	1	frequent	9
estimate	2	expressing	2	faster	1	finely	1	footing	1	frequented	1
estimates	1	exquisite	2	fastnesses	1	finer	2	for	399	frequently	5
etcetera	1	exquisitely	4	fate	8	fingers	1	foraging	1	fresh	12
eternal	2	exterior	1	father	13	finish'd	1	forbade	1	fresher	2
eternity	3	external	8	father'd	1	fire	5	forbearance	1	freshness	2
etesian	1	extinguish'd	2	father's	17	fire-like	1	forbearing	1	fret	1
ethereal	1	extraordinary	1	fatter	1	fires	1	forbidding	2	fretful	1
etherial	1	extravagance	1	favor'd	4	fireside	1	force	9	friend	72
Etna	1	extravagate	1	favorite	4	fireworks	1	forced	4	friendlessness	1
Etna's	2	extremes	1	favour'd	1	firm	3	forcibly	1	friendly	2
Euclid's	1	extrinsic	2	favourite	3	firmament	1	fords	1	friends	9
Eudemus	1	exultation	8	fear	39	firmer	3	fore	1	friendship	2
Europe	1	exultations	1	fearless	3	firmest	1	forego	1	friendships	2
European	1	exulted	1	fears	5	firmly	4	forehead	1	fro	2
evangelist	1	exulting	3	feast	3	firmness	2	foreign	4	from	447
evangelists	1	eye	33	feast-days	1	first	104	foremost	3	front	4
eve	2	eyed	1	feather'd	1	first-born	1	forerunners	1	fronted	1
even	108	eyelet	2	feats	2	firth	1	foresight	2	frontier	1
evening	20	eyes	46	features	1	fish	2	forest	6	fronts	1
evenings	2	eyesight	1	fed	9	fishermen	1	forests	5	frost	4
event	2	fabled	1	federal	1	fishes	2	foretasted	1	frosty	3
eventide	1	fabric	2	feeble	4	fissures	1	foretold	1	froward	2
events	10	fabulous	1	feebler	2	fit	10	forgers	1	froze	1
ever	46	face	40	feed	5	fitness	1	forget	8	frugal	2
ever-flowing	1	faces	3	feeding	1	fits	5	forgetful	2	fruit	5
evergrowing	1	fact	1	feeds	4	fitted	3	forgets	1	fruitfulness	1
everlasting	1	factionists	1	feel	29	fitting	1	forgive	3	fruitless	1
ever-living	1	factions	2	feeling	34	five	5	forgiven	1	fruits	3
evermore	3	facts	1	feelingly	1	fix'd	4	forgot	5	fuel	1
ever-varying	1	faculties	14	feelings	18	fix'd	6	forgotten	9	fugitive	1
every	77	faculty	5	feels	4	fixed	1	forlorn	6	fugitives	1
every-day	1	fade	1	feet	9	fixedly	1	form	13	fulgent	1
everyone	1	faded	1	feign'd	2	flagelet	1	formal	1	full	30
everything	5	fading	1	fell	14	flagg'd	1	form'd	4	full-blown	1
everywhere	12	fail	6	fellow	3	flame	1	former	7	full-form'd	2
evidence	4	fail'd	7	fellow-beings	1	flames	2	forming	1	fulness	2
evil	14	fails	2	fellow-countrymen	1	flar'd	1	forms	37	furnes	1
evil-minded	1	faint	2	fellow-labourer	1	flash	5	forsaken	1	function	4
exact	2	fainted	1	fellows	1	flash'd	2	forsook	1	functions	5
exactness	1	fainting	1	fellowship	4	flashes	3	forsworn	1	funds	3
exalt	4	faintly	2	fellow-travellers	1	flashing	1	forth	54	funereal	1
exalted	4	fair	23	fells	1	flat	3	forth-breathing	1	furnace	1
exalts	1	fairer	1	felt	49	flatter	1	forthwith	4	Furness	1
examinations	1	fairest	2	female	7	flattered	1	fortitude	3	furnish'd	2
example	1	Fairfield's	1	fenc'd	1	flatteries	1	fortunate	4	further	14
examples	1	fairies	1	fenced	1	flattering	2	fortunatus	1	furtherance	1
exceeding	1	fairly	1	ferment	2	fled	3	fortune	2	furthermore	1
excellence	2	fairy	5	fermentation	1	fledged	1	fortune's	1	future	9
excellent	2	fairy's	1	fern	1	fleecy	1	forward	10	futurity	2
except	2	faith	20	ferryman	1	fleet	2	forwards	3	gaiety	3
excess	6	faithful	4	fervent	3	fleeting	1	foster'd	2	gain	3
excessive	3	faithfully	2	fervently	1	fleshly	1	fought	2	gain'd	9
exchange	1	fall	11	fervour	4	flew	3	foul	1	gains	2
excitation	1	fallacious	1	festal	1	flight	6	found	51	gait	2
excite	1	fallen	7	festival	4	floating	4	foundation	1	galaxy	1
exclaim	1	falling	4	festivals	1	flock	11	foundations	3	gale	1
exclude	2	falling-off	1	festive	3	flocks	4	founded	1	gales	1
exclusion	1	falls	6	festoons	1	flood	1	fountain	7	Galesus	1
exclusive	1	false	18	fetch	1	floor	1	fountains	1	gallant	2
exclusively	1	falsehood	2	fetching	1	Florizel	1	fountain-side	1	gallantry	1

159

Wordsworth's Vocabulary in *The Prelude*

word	count	word	count	word	count	word	count	word	count
gallery	1	glean'd	1	gratulatest	1	half-absence	1	head	26	highways	2
gallop	1	glee	2	grave	13	half-and-half	1	headlands	1	high-wrought	1
galloping	1	glen	3	Gravedona	1	half-frequented	1	headlong	2	hill	14
game	1	glided	2	graven	1	half-hour	1	heads	5	hillocks	1
games	3	glides	2	graves	4	half-hour's	1	heady	1	hills	37
gaming-house	1	glimmering	2	gravest	1	half-inch	1	healing	1	hill-top	1
Ganymede	1	glimpse	4	gravitation	1	half-infant	1	health	7	hill-tops	1
garb	5	glimpses	1	gray	1	half-insensate	1	healthful	2	him	130
garden	6	glistens	1	grazed	1	half-insight	1	healthy	1	himself	29
garden-gate	1	glister'd	1	great	70	half-learn'd	1	heap	2	hindrance	2
gardens	6	glitter	2	greater	2	half-mile	1	heap'd	1	hindrances	1
garish	1	glitter'd	1	greatest	4	half-possess'd	1	hear	18	hinge	1
garland	1	glittering	7	greatly	3	half-rural	1	heard	42	hint	2
garlands	2	globe	2	greatness	6	half-shelter'd	1	hearing	5	hinted	3
garments	5	Glocesters	1	Grecian	1	half-sitting	1	heart	113	his	354
garnish'd	1	gloom	4	Greece	1	half-standing	1	heart-bracing	1	hiss'd	1
gates	2	gloomier	1	greedily	1	half-yearly	1	heart-depressing	1	hissing	1
gateways	2	gloomy	7	greedy	2	half-years	1	heart-experience	1	historian's	2
gather	5	gloried	1	green	24	hall	2	hearth	1	history	16
gather'd	5	glorified	2	green-house	1	hallelujah	1	heartless	4	hit	1
gathering	4	glorious	14	greenland	1	halloos	1	hearts	14	hither	3
gaudy	5	glory	23	greeted	3	hallow	1	heart's	1	hitherto	10
gave	16	glorying	1	greeting	3	hallow'd	1	hearts'	1	hoard	1
gawds	1	gloss	1	greetings	3	hallowed	1	heartsome	1	hoarded	2
gay	10	glossy	1	greets	1	hallowing	1	heart-stricken	1	hoary	2
gaz'd	2	glow-worm	1	Greta	1	halls	1	heat	7	hobbled	1
gaze	1	gluttony	1	grew	8	halted	2	heaven	31	hold	14
gazed	1	go	6	grey	5	halting	1	heavenly	1	holden	2
Gehol's	1	goaded	2	grey-hair'd	1	halts	2	heavens	8	holds	5
gems	1	goadings	1	grief	12	hamlets	1	heaven's	2	holiday	5
general	9	goathered	1	griefs	2	hand	38	heavier	1	holidays	4
generations	1	goat-herd	1	griev'd	5	handed	2	heaviest	1	holiest	2
generous	4	God	30	grieve	3	handle	1	heaving	1	hollow	5
Genevière	1	godhead	2	grieved	1	handmaid	1	heavy	7	hollowness	1
genial	6	godhead's	1	grieves	2	hands	9	hedge	1	hollows	2
genii	1	godlike	1	grimace	1	hang	4	hedgehog	1	holy	11
genius	5	god-like	1	grimacing	1	hangs	2	hedge-row	1	homage	1
gentle	21	gods	1	grin	1	hap	1	hedges	1	home	39
gentleman's	1	god's	2	grinds	1	haply	14	heeded	2	homeless	1
gentlemen	1	goers	1	Grisdale	1	happen'd	1	heedeth	1	homeliness	1
gentleness	3	goes	2	Grisdale's	1	happier	3	heedling	1	homely	6
gentler	5	goggling	1	groan'd	1	happiest	2	heedless	1	homely-featured	1
gentlest	3	going	7	groans	2	happily	1	heels	2	homer	1
gently	7	goings	1	grooms	1	happiness	21	heifer	2	homes	2
genuine	9	goings-on	2	gross	2	happy	24	heifer's	1	homeward	5
geometric	3	gold	5	grosser	1	haranguers	1	height	10	honest	3
geometry	1	golden	11	grossest	1	harbinger	1	heighten	2	honey	2
George	1	gondolas	1	grossly	1	harbour	4	heights	6	honorable	4
gesture	1	gone	28	grotesque	1	harbour'd	2	heinous	1	honor'd	7
gestures	2	good	38	grots	1	harbours	1	heirs	1	honour	13
gewgaw	1	good-natured	1	ground	24	hard	14	held	12	honour'd	3
ghastly	5	goodness	3	grounds	2	harder	2	hell	2	honours	7
ghost	2	gorgeous	4	grove	8	hardhood	1	help	117	hoofs	1
ghostly	1	Gorsas	1	groves	19	hardly	3	help'd	2	hoop	1
ghosts	1	Goslar	2	grow	5	hardship	1	helper	3	hootings	1
giant	2	gossamer	1	growing	9	hardships	1	helpers	4	hope	59
giant-killer	2	government	6	grown	4	hardy	2	Helvellyn	6	hopes	28
giants	1	gown	2	grows	2	hare	1	hemisphere	1	horizon	5
giant-size	1	gown'd	1	growth	10	harlequins	1	hemm'd	1	horn	3
gibbet-mast	1	gowns	2	grunsel	1	harm	1	hen	1	horns	1
giddy	4	grace	16	guard	1	Harmodius	1	hence	31	horse	6
gift	14	graced	2	guardian	2	harmonious	2	henceforth	3	horseman	1
gifted	1	graceful	1	guards	1	harmonising	1	her	203	horsemanship	1
gifts	6	gracefully	1	guess	2	harmony	5	herbs	1	horsemen	1
gigantic	1	graces	2	guesses	1	harp	1	Herculean	1	horses	2
gilded	1	gracious	5	guest	1	Harry	1	Hercynian	1	hose	1
gilding	1	graciously	1	guests	1	harsh	3	herd	1	hospitably	1
girl	5	graciousness	1	guide	16	harvest	1	herded	1	hospital	1
girlish	1	gradation	1	guided	2	has	14	herds	2	host	6
girls	2	gradations	1	guides	2	hast	10	herdsman	1	hot	2
girt	1	gradual	1	guildhall	1	haste	2	here	82	hotel	1
give	33	gradually	3	guile	1	hasten	2	hereafter	2	hour	38
given	34	grafted	1	guilt	6	hastening	1	hereby	1	hourly	1
giver	1	grain-tinctured	1	guise	1	hastily	1	herein	3	hours	26
gives	11	grammars	1	gulph	1	hat	2	heretofore	9	hour's	1
giving	4	grand	4	gushes	1	hate	4	hermitage	1	hours'	1
giv'n	1	grandame	1	gust	1	hater	1	hermits	2	house	33
giv'st	1	grandest	1	Gustavus	1	hath	79	hermit's	2	household	5
glad	9	grandeur	10	gusty	1	hatred	1	hero	2	housekeeping	1
gladden'd	1	grandsire's	1	ha	1	haunt	4	heroes	3	houseless	1
glade	1	grant	1	habiliments	2	haunted	2	heroic	2	houses	3
gladly	3	Granta's	1	habit	9	haunting	2	heron	1	housewife	1
gladness	3	grapple	1	habitation	2	hauntings	1	hers	1	how	88
gladsome	6	grappling	1	habitations	2	haunts	7	herself	11	howe'er	1
glance	2	grasp	1	habits	9	have	248	hew	1	however	2
glanced	3	grasping	2	habitual	3	haven	1	hid	3	howl'd	1
glancing	1	grasps	1	habitually	3	having	39	hidden	6	howling	1
glare	1	grass	13	habitude	1	hawkers	2	hides	1	howsoe'er	3
glaring	2	grass-plot	1	hackney	1	hawker's	1	hiding-places	1	howsoever	1
glassed	1	grassy	2	had	349	hawthorn	3	hie	1	hubbub	2
glasses	2	grateful	2	hail	3	haycock	1	high	27	huckster's	1
glassy	1	gratify	1	hail'd	3	hay-grounds	1	higher	17	huddled	1
gleam	4	gratitude	8	hair	2	hazard	2	highest	13	hues	3
gleam'd	1	gratuitous	1	hair-breadth	1	hazards	1	high-seated	1	huge	13
gleaming	3	gratulant	1	half	15	hazel	2	highway	1	human	63
gleams	9					he	276	high-way	2	human-heartedness	1

Appendix

word	count	word	count	word	count	word	count	word	count	word	count
humanity	4	imperishable	2	infinite	3	interest	3	jealousy	4	lac'd	1
humble	3	impersonated	1	infinitude	1	interests	5	Jew	1	lack	5
humbled	2	impervious	1	infinity	2	interfere	1	Jewish	1	lacking	1
humbleness	2	impiety	1	infirmity	2	interference	1	jingling	2	lad	1
humbler	5	impious	1	influence	12	interfus'd	2	job	1	ladder	1
humblest	5	impiously	1	influx	1	interlunar	1	jocund	2	ladder's	2
humility	2	implements	2	influxes	1	intermeddlers	1	jog	1	laden	2
humming	1	implore	1	informs	1	intermeddling	1	John	1	ladies	3
humour	3	imply	1	infus'd	1	intermediate	2	join	2	lady	5
humourists	1	importance	4	infused	1	interminable	1	join'd	1	lady's	1
humours	1	important	2	ingender'd	1	intermingled	2	joining	1	laggards	1
hundred	8	importunate	1	ingenuous	3	intermingles	1	joint	1	laid	11
hung	12	impose	1	inglorious	3	intermitting	1	joint-labourers	1	lain	4
hunger	1	imposed	1	ingrate's	1	intermittingly	1	joints	1	lair	1
hunger-bitten	1	imposing	1	ingress	1	intermix'd	1	jostling	1	lake	16
hunger-press'd	1	impossible	1	inhabitant	1	intermixture	1	journey	13	lakes	6
hungry	1	impostors	1	inhabitants	3	internal	7	journey'd	3	lamb	3
hunt	2	impotence	1	inherent	1	internally	1	journeyed	1	lambs	1
hunted	1	impotent	1	inheritance	2	interpose	1	joust	1	lamb's	1
hunter-Indian	1	impregnate	1	inhuman	1	interposition	1	joy	69	lame	1
hunters	2	impregnated	1	injuries	2	interregnum's	1	joyous	5	lamentable	2
Huntingdon	1	impregnations	1	injury	2	interrupt	1	joys	5	lamps	3
hurdy-gurdy	1	impress	2	injustice	1	interrupted	2	judge	6	lance	2
hurried	2	impress'd	2	inland	2	interrupting	1	judgements	2	land	23
hurry	1	impresses	1	inlets	1	interspers'd	2	judging	2	landed	3
hurrying	3	impression	1	inly	2	intertwine	1	judgment	6	landing	1
husband	1	impressions	3	intervals	3	intervene	1	judgments	2	lands	2
husbanded	1	impressive	1	inmates	1	intervention	2	judicious	1	landscape	2
hush	1	imprison'd	1	inn	7	intervening	1	Julia	12	land-warriors	1
hush'd	2	impulse	6	inner	12	interventions	1	Julia's	1	lane	1
hut	3	in	1269	inn-keeper	1	interview	1	Juliet	1	lanes	3
huts	5	inaptitude	1	innocence	4	interwoven	1	jumbled	1	language	14
hymn	1	inasmuch	1	innocent	14	intimate	4	June	1	languages	1
hyperboles	1	inaudible	1	innocuously	1	intimation	1	Jupiter	1	languid	1
I	937	inborn	1	innumerable	1	into	79	just	18	languidly	3
ice	4	incapable	1	inobtrusive	1	intolerant	2	justice	5	languish	2
icy	1	incarnation	1	inordinate	1	intoxicate	1	justifies	1	languish'd	1
idea	1	incense	1	inquire	2	intricate	3	justify	2	languor	1
ideal	2	incensed	1	inquired	1	intrigue	1	justly	1	lank	1
identity	1	incident	2	inquiries	2	introduc'd	1	jutting	1	lap	1
idle	2	incidental	1	inquisition	2	intruded	1	juvenile	1	lapse	5
idleness	4	incidents	2	inroads	1	intruder	1	keen	9	large	15
idler	4	incited	1	insane	1	intrusion	1	keep	2	largely	3
idlers	1	inclination	3	insatiably	1	intuition	1	keepest	1	larger	1
idly	2	incline	1	inscrib'd	1	intuitive	2	keeping	1	lark	1
idol	2	inclines	1	inscribed	4	invaders	1	Kendal	1	lark's	1
idolater	1	incommunicable	1	insects	2	invest	1	kept	5	lascars	1
idolatry	2	inconsiderate	1	insensible	1	invested	1	kettle-drum	1	lass	1
idols	1	incumbences	2	insensibly	3	invests	1	kind	19	lassitudes	1
if	126	incumbent	1	inseparable	1	invigorate	1	kinder	1	last	36
ignoble	2	incumbrances	1	inside	1	invigorating	1	kindled	1	lasting	2
ignominy	1	indecent	1	insidious	1	inviolable	1	kindles	1	lastly	7
ignorance	7	indecision	1	insight	4	inviolate	2	kindliness	1	lasts	2
ignorant	3	indecisive	1	insignificant	2	invisible	14	kindlings	1	latch	1
ill	9	indeed	17	insinuated	1	invisibly	2	kindness	3	late	9
ill-fated	1	indefinite	1	insisted	1	invitations	1	kindred	13	lately	3
illimitable	1	independence	3	insolent	1	inviting	2	king	6	latent	1
ill-sorted	1	independent	8	inspiration	2	involuntary	1	kingdom	1	later	15
ill-suppress'd	1	index	1	inspir'd	1	inward	3	kings	4	latter	3
illustrated	1	Indian	5	inspire	2	inwardly	3	king's	2	laugh	4
illustration	1	Indians	1	inspired	3	inwoven	1	kirk-pillars	1	laugh'd	2
illustrious	4	Indian-wise	1	inspiréd	1	irksomeness	1	kiss'd	1	laughing	2
image	25	indications	1	instance	2	iron	4	kissed	1	laughter	2
imaged	1	indifference	5	instant	3	ironic	1	kitchens	1	laughters	1
imagery	1	indifferent	4	instantaneous	2	irons	5	kite	1	lavish	1
images	17	indigenous	1	instantaneously	1	irradiates	1	kitten	1	law	12
imagination	16	indigent	1	instantly	3	irradiation	1	knapsack	1	lawgivers	1
imaginations	2	indignation	3	instead	1	irreconcilable	1	knaves	1	lawless	1
imaginative	3	indirect	1	instil	1	irregular	1	knee	2	lawn	1
imbecile	1	indiscreet	1	instinct	5	irresistible	1	knees	1	lawns	1
imbibed	1	indiscretion	1	instinctive	1	irresolute	1	knew	15	laws	11
imitate	1	indisposed	1	instinctively	1	irreverence	2	knife	1	lawyers	2
imitations	1	indisputable	1	instincts	2	is	292	knight	5	lay	35
imitative	2	individual	16	institutes	2	Isaiah	1	knights	2	lays	1
immaturity	1	indolence	3	institutions	1	island	14	knight's	1	lazily	1
immeasurable	1	indolent	1	instruct	2	islanded	1	knitting	1	lazy	1
immediate	2	in-door	1	instructed	1	islands	3	knock'd	1	Le Brun	1
immediately	4	induce	1	instruction	1	isle	3	knocking	1	lead	5
immense	3	induced	1	instructor	1	isles	2	knot	1	leaded	1
immensity	1	indulgence	1	instrument	1	issue	2	knots	2	leads	9
immortal	1	indulgent	1	instruments	2	issued	4	know	19	leaf	3
immunities	1	industrious	3	insuperable	1	issues	1	knoweth	1	leafless	1
immured	2	industry	3	integrity	1	issuing	1	knowing	9	leafy	1
impair'd	3	ineffable	1	intellect	9	isthmus	1	knowingly	1	leagu'd	1
impart	1	inert	1	intellects	1	it	285	knowledge	35	league	8
imparted	1	inevitable	2	intellectual	9	Italian	2	known	22	leagued	1
impassion'd	3	inexorable	1	intelligence	2	Italy	1	knows	8	leagues	1
impatience	2	inexperience	1	intended	2	itinerant	1	label	1	league's	1
impatient	3	infancy	5	intense	9	its	142	labors	1	lean	3
impeach'd	1	infant	15	intensely	1	itself	58	labour	17	lean'd	1
impediments	2	infantine	2	intent	7	ivy	2	labourers	2	leap	3
impell'd	2	infants	1	interchang'd	2	Jack	2	labouring	3	leap'd	3
imperceptibly	1	infection	1	interchange	6	Jacobins	1	labours	4	leaping	1
imperfect	4	inference	1	interchanged	1	James	1	labyrinth	1	leaps	1
imperfection	1	inferior	3	intercourse	13	jealousies	1	labyrinths	1	leapt	2
imperial	4	infernal	1	interdict	1						

Wordsworth's Vocabulary in *The Prelude*

word	n	word	n	word	n	word	n	word	n	word	n
lear	1	liveliness	1	lowly	4	masquerade	1	methought	4	modest	6
learn	5	lively	4	lows	1	mass	3	metropolis	3	modesty	5
learn'd	11	liveried	1	low-standing	1	massacre	1	mettlesome	1	modified	1
learned	3	liveries	1	loyal	3	massacres	1	microscopic	2	mold	2
learning	4	livery	1	Lu	1	masses	1	mid	3	Moloch	1
learnings	1	lives	7	Lucretilis	1	massy	1	' mid	11	moment	14
learns	1	liveth	1	lull	1	master	10	middle	1	moments	8
least	37	living	39	lull'd	3	master'd	1	midnight	3	moment's	3
leave	12	lo	5	lump	1	masters	1	midst	10	monarch	1
leaves	9	loath'd	1	lure	1	mastery	1	midway	6	monarchs	1
leaving	11	loathing	1	lurking	6	match'd	1	mien	2	monasteries	1
lecturer's	1	loathsome	1	lurking-place	1	materials	1	might	100	monastery	1
lectures	1	local	4	lurks	1	maternal	1	mighty	23	monastic	1
led	23	Locarno	1	lusters	1	mates	1	migration	1	' mong	1
left	65	Locarno's	1	lustily	1	mathematics	1	mild	7	monies	2
legalized	1	lock	2	lustre	1	matin	1	milder	5	monitory	2
legends	1	lock'd	7	lusty	2	matins	1	mildest	1	monk	1
leisure	3	locks	1	lute	1	matron	2	mildness	1	monkeys	1
lend	2	locusts	1	luxurious	1	matrons	1	mile	3	monkies	1
length	27	lodg'd	6	lyre	1	matron's	1	miles	5	monkish	1
lengthen'd	2	lodge	5	machine	1	matter	9	milestone	1	monster	1
lengthening	1	lodged	4	mad	3	matters	2	militant	1	monsters	2
lent	1	lodger	1	madding	1	matur'd	3	military	4	monstrous	1
less	80	lodges	1	made	62	mature	3	milk	1	Mont Blanc	1
lesser	2	lodging	3	madness	10	matured	2	milk-white	1	Mont Martyr	1
lesson	1	loftier	2	Magdalene	2	maturer	3	mill	7	month	12
let	27	loftiest	3	magic	3	matures	1	millions	2	months	10
letter	2	lofty	11	magician's	1	maugre	1	mill-race	1	months'	1
letters	4	logic	4	magisterially	2	Maximilian	1	mills	1	monument	3
level	7	Loire	4	magistrate	1	may	68	Milton	3	monumental	3
level'd	1	loiter'd	1	magnanimity	1	may-bush	1	Milton's	1	monuments	1
Leven's	1	loiterer	1	magnanimous	1	mayor	1	mimic	4	mood	15
libations	1	loitering	1	magnificent	3	may-pole	1	mind	161	moods	5
liberal	1	London	7	magnified	1	maze	1	minds	24	moody	1
liberties	1	loneliness	2	magnitude	1	mazes	1	mind's	3	moon	18
liberty	25	lonely	14	maid	12	me	295	mine	40	moonlight	5
licence	1	lonesome	6	maiden	4	meadow	1	mines	1	moon's	2
licens'd	1	long	78	maiden's	1	meadow-ground	1	mingled	5	moonshine	3
license	1	long-back'd	1	maids	5	meadows	5	mingling	4	moor	2
lie	13	long-continued	1	maid's	1	meagre	6	miniature	1	mooring-place	1
liege	1	long'd	1	mail	1	meal	1	minister	2	moors	2
lies	13	longer	10	maim'd	1	meals	1	ministers	1	moral	15
liest	1	longing	2	main	7	mean	25	ministration	1	morality	1
lieu	1	longings	1	mainly	2	meanest	3	more	223
life	128	look	34	maintain	2	meaning	4	ministry	5	moreover	2
lifeless	3	look'd	30	maintain'd	3	meanings	1	minstrel	2	mom	2
life-like	1	looked	5	maintains	2	meanness	2	minstrels	1	morning	23
life's	5	lookers-on	1	maintenance	2	means	11	minstrelsies	1	mortal	6
lift	1	looketh	1	majestic	7	meantime	2	minuet	1	mortality	1
lifted	2	looking	10	majesty	6	meanwhile	24	minute	5	Morven	1
lifting	1	looks	11	make	41	measur'd	3	minuter	2	Moses	1
lifts	2	loop-holes	1	makes	11	measure	6	miracles	1	moss	1
light	48	loose	13	making	9	measured	1	miraculous	1	most	64
lighted	2	loosely	1	Malays	1	measures	1	mirror	2	mother	9
lighter	1	loquacious	1	male	2	mechanic	1	mirth	3	motherly	1
lightly	7	lord	8	man	141	meditate	1	miscellaneous	1	mother's	13
lightning	1	lorded	1	manacles	1	meditated	1	mischance	1	motion	15
lights	5	lordly	1	manage	2	meditation	5	misdeem	1	motionless	2
lightsome	2	lords	1	management	1	meditations	6	miserable	5	motions	10
like	147	lore	1	mandate	3	meditative	4	miseries	2	motive	1
likewise	4	lorn	1	manhood	5	medley	1	misery	4	motley	2
liking	2	lose	1	maniac's	1	meek	6	misfortunes	1	moulder'd	3
likings	2	loses	1	manifest	3	meeker	1	misguided	2	mouldering	3
lillies	1	losing	2	manifested	1	meekness	1	misguiding	1	moulds	2
limbs	2	loss	4	manifold	2	meet	6	mishap	2	mound	1
limited	1	losses	1	mankind	14	meeting-point	1	mislead	2	mounds	1
limits	3	lost	16	manliness	1	meets	1	misled	4	mount	2
line	8	lot	4	manly	2	melancholy	15	misplaced	1	mountain	22
lineaments	2	loth	3	manner	2	Melancthon	1	misrule	1	mountain-chapel	2
lines	4	loud	11	manners	11	mellow	1	miss	1	mountain-echoes	1
linger	5	louder	1	man's	10	mellower	2	miss'd	1	mountaineer	1
linger'd	3	loudly	1	mansion	6	melodies	1	misses	1	mountain-ground	1
lingerer	1	lounging	1	mantle	2	melodious	2	mission	1	mountainous	1
lingering	3	Louvet	2	many	48	melody	1	mist	6	mountains	24
link	1	lov'd	25	many-headed	1	melt	2	mistake	1	mountain's	2
link'd	4	love	132	map	1	melted	2	mistaken	1	mountebank	1
linking	1	love-beacons	1	maple	1	memorable	2	mistakes	2	mounted	6
links	1	loved	8	maps	1	memorial	3	mistaking	2	mountings	1
lion	2	love-knot	1	march	4	memory	19	mistress	1	mounts	1
lips	2	lovelier	1	march'd	2	men	79	mistrust	2	mourn'd	1
liquid	1	loveliest	1	margin	4	men's	1	mists	4	mournful	1
lisping	1	love-liking	1	mariner	3	mention	4	misty	1	mouth	3
listen'd	5	loveliness	2	mark	4	mention'd	4	misus'd	1	mouths	1
listening	7	lovely	9	mark'd	1	mercies	1	mithridates	1	mov'd	14
listless	1	lover	6	market	1	mercy	1	mitigate	2	move	11
listlessly	1	lovers	4	marks	2	mere	3	mitred	1	moveables	1
listlessness	1	lover's	1	mark'st	1	merely	6	mix'd	3	moved	6
literature	1	loves	10	marriage	1	merit	1	mobs	1	movement	2
litter	1	lovest	1	Mars	1	merits	1	mock	5	moves	5
little	58	loveth	1	martial	1	merlins	1	mock'd	1	moving	9
little-ones	1	loving	2	martyrs	1	merriment	1	mockery	6	mov'st	1
liv'd	15	low	13	martyr's	1	merry	1	mocks	1	mower's	1
live	26	lower	4	marvel	1	messenger	1	model	1	much	32
lived	7	lowest	2	marvellous	5	met	11	moderated	3	multifarious	1
livelier	1	low-hung	1	Mary	2	metal	1	modern	3	multitude	6
liveliest	1	lowliness	1	Mary's	2	methinks	3	modes	2	multitudes	4

Appendix 163

word	count	word	count	word	count	word	count	word	count
mumbling	1	night	46	obviously	1	ostrich-like	1	palms	1	pebbles	1
murder	1	nights	7	occasion	3	other	79	palpable	3	peculiar	4
murderer	2	night's	1	occasional	1	others	16	pamper'd	1	pedestal	1
murderer's	1	nightshade	2	occasions	1	other's	5	pampering	1	peep'd	1
murmur	2	night-wanderings	1	occupation	2	others'	1	pamphlets	1	peeping	1
murmur'd	1	Nile	1	occupations	4	otherwise	8	Pan	1	pelican	1
murmuring	7	nine	4	occupied	2	ought	7	pang	1	pen	1
murmurs	1	no	158	ocean	4	our	170	pangs	1	pencil	2
muse	1	nobility	2	ode	1	ours	8	panoply	1	pendant	1
mused	2	noble	10	Odin	1	ourselves	9	panted	1	penetrate	1
muses	2	nobler	3	odious	1	out	86	panting	1	penetrates	1
Muse's	2	noise	10	o'er	26	outbreak	1	pantomimic	1	peninsulas	1
museum	1	noiseless	1	o'ercome	2	outcast	1	paper	1	penn'd	3
music	18	noisier	1	o'erhanging	1	outcry	1	parade	2	penny	1
musical	1	noisy	1	o'erpower'd	1	outer	1	parading	2	pennyless	1
music's	1	none	5	o'erthrown	3	outlandish	2	paradise	8	pension'd	1
musing	2	nook	11	of	2378	outlast	1	paramount	6	pensioner	1
musings	2	nooks	3	off	25	outline	2	parcel	1	pensive	2
muslin	1	noon	6	off-and-on	1	out-o'-th'-way	1	parcell'd	1	pensively	1
must	51	noon-day	1	offences	1	outrage	1	parent	3	penury	1
mustered	1	noon's	1	offensive	1	outrun	1	parents	6	people	11
mute	6	noontide	2	offer'd	3	outset	1	parent's	1	peopled	1
mutter	1	noos'd	1	offering	2	outside	6	Paris	2	peradventure	1
mutter'd	1	nor	121	office	8	outward	23	park	1	perceiv'd	1
muttering	2	north	1	officers	2	outwardly	2	parliament	1	perceive	2
mutual	1	northern	2	officious	1	over	31	parlour	1	perceived	1
my	538	northward	2	oft	24	over-anxious	1	parrot's	1	perch	1
myriads	1	northwards	1	often	35	over-arch'd	1	part	30	perchance	3
myrtle	1	not	364	oftener	1	overbless'd	1	partake	3	Perdita	1
myself	53	note	16	oftentimes	12	overblown	1	parted	7	perennial	2
mysteries	2	notes	3	oft-times	3	overborn	1	participate	1	perfect	13
mysterious	1	nothing	27	oh	36	overbridged	1	particular	2	perfection	1
mystery	4	notic'd	1	old	59	overcame	1	parties	1	perfectly	1
mystical	1	notice	8	omen	2	overcast	2	parting	1	perfidious	1
naked	20	noticeable	1	omit	1	overcome	1	partisan	1	perfidiously	1
nam'd	4	notices	3	omitted	1	overflow	2	partly	2	perforce	2
name	42	notions	6	on	316	overflow'd	1	partner	1	perform	5
named	5	notwithstanding	1	once	58	overflowing	3	parts	7	perform'd	5
nameless	3	nought	2	one	188	over-fondly	1	party-colour'd	1	perhaps	27
names	14	nourished	1	ones	9	over-great	1	pass	16	perilous	2
narrative	1	nourishment	1	only	49	overhead	2	passage	3	perils	2
narratives	1	novel	3	onward	4	overhung	1	passages	2	period	3
narrow	8	novelties	3	open	38	overloaded	1	pass'd	39	perish	2
narrowing	1	novelty	4	open'd	4	overlook	3	passed	1	perishable	1
nation	1	November	1	opened	1	overlook'd	3	passenger	1	perish'd	5
national	1	novice	1	opening	4	overlove	1	passes	2	perk'd	1
nations	10	noviciate	1	openly	2	overmuch	1	passing	11	permanence	1
native	18	now	165	openness	2	over-near	1	passion	38	permanent	5
natural	13	nowhere	5	opera	1	overpass'd	1	passionate	3	permit	2
naturally	2	nowise	1	opinion	3	over-pressure	1	passionately	2	permitted	2
nature	117	number	1	opinions	6	overpriz'd	1	passions	19	perpetual	2
natures	6	numberless	1	opportune	1	overruns	1	passive	1	perpetually	1
nature's	29	numbers	1	oppose	2	overspread	3	past	22	perplex	1
nave	1	numerous	5	opposed	3	overstepp'd	1	pastime	2	perplex'd	5
nay	9	nun	1	opposite	5	over-sternness	1	pastimes	1	perplexity	1
near	31	nuptials	1	opposites	1	overtake	1	pastime's	1	Persepolis	1
nearer	5	nurs'd	2	opposition	7	overthrow	4	pastoral	7	persisted	1
necessary	1	nurse	4	oppress	1	over-toil	1	pasture	4	person	4
necessities	1	nursed	1	oppress'd	4	overweeningly	1	pastures	2	personal	10
neck	2	nurse's	1	oppressed	1	overwhelm'd	1	patch	1	persons	4
nectar	1	nursing	1	oppression	5	overwrought	1	patch'd	1	persuasion	2
need	24	nurslings	1	oppressor	1	owe	1	path	9	pertain'd	1
needed	3	O	42	oppressors	1	owed	4	pathetic	2	pertains	1
needful	7	oaken	1	opprobrious	1	owls	1	pathless	2	perturb'd	1
needless	1	oaks	1	opprobrium	1	own	104	paths	3	perusal	1
needs	11	oaks'	1	or	365	own'd	3	pathway	1	perus'd	3
ne'er	2	oars	3	oracular	1	ox	1	pathways	2	peruse	1
neglect	1	oaths	2	orange	1	pace	6	patience	2	perused	1
neglected	4	obduracy	1	orations	1	paced	2	patient	2	perusing	2
neglectful	1	obedience	1	orator	1	pacing	1	patriarchal	1	pervade	1
negligence	1	obedient	2	oratory	1	pack	1	patrimonial	1	pervades	3
Negro	3	obeisance	2	orb	2	page	5	patrimony	2	pervading	2
neighbour	2	obeisances	1	orchard	2	pageant	5	patriot	5	perverse	1
neighbourhood	10	obey'd	1	orchards	1	pageantry	1	patriotic	3	perverseness	1
neighbouring	1	object	16	order	5	pages	1	patriot's	1	perverted	1
neighbours	3	objects	35	orders	1	paid	2	patron	2	pervious	1
neither	15	obligation	1	ordinary	7	pain	18	Patterdale	1	pest	1
nest	5	obliquities	1	organ	2	painful	3	pattern	1	pestilence	2
nests	1	obolus	1	organic	1	painfully	1	Paul's	1	Peter's	1
net	1	obscure	7	organs	3	pains	8	pause	9	petty	3
never	51	obscurely	2	orient	1	paint	4	paused	1	phantom	2
never-ending	3	obscurities	1	oriental	1	painted	2	pauses	1	phantoms	2
never-failing	1	obscurity	2	orifice	1	painter	1	pavèd	1	Phillis	1
nevertheless	5	obsequious	3	origin	3	painter's	1	pavement	1	philosopher	1
new	33	observance	1	original	1	painting	1	paw'd	1	philosophers	2
new-born	3	observation	1	originate	1	pair	11	pay	2	philosophic	3
newcomer	1	observations	1	originates	1	pairs	2	pay'd	1	philosophy	4
new-fallen	1	observ'd	3	Orion	1	palace	7	peace	28	phoebe	1
newly	2	observes	1	Orleans	1	palaces	2	peaceful	5	phrase	3
news	4	obstacle	1	ornament	2	palate	1	peacefully	1	phrases	1
Newton	7	obstacles	2	ornaments	3	pale	2	peaks	2	physiognomies	1
Newton's	1	obstinate	2	orphan	1	pale-fac'd	1	pealing	2	picking	1
next	6	obstruct	1	orphans	1	pales	1	peals	1	picture	4
next-door	1	obtain	1	Orphean	1	palfrey	1	pears	1	pictured	1
nice	3	obtain'd	1	Ossian	1	paling	1	peasant	4	pictures	4
niceties	1	obvious	4	ostentatious	1	palm	2	peat-fire	1	piety	3

Wordsworth's Vocabulary in *The Prelude*

word	n	word	n	word	n	word	n	word	n
pig	1	plying	1	prepares	1	promoted	1	quarter'd	1	rear	2
pike	1	pocketed	1	prepossession	1	prompt	5	quarters	3	rear'd	11
pil'd	1	poem	2	presage	1	prompter's	1	queen	1	reascend	1
pile	5	poems	1	prescience	1	promptest	1	queens	1	reascending	1
piled	2	poesy	4	prescrib'd	1	promptings	1	quell'd	1	reason	28
pilfer'd	1	poet	9	prescriptive	1	pronounc'd	1	quest	1	reasonable	1
pilgrim	3	poetic	4	presence	27	pronounce	1	question	4	reasoning	1
pilgrimage	1	poetry	1	presences	2	pronounced	2	question'd	2	reason's	1
pilgrim-friars	1	poets	11	present	28	proof	4	questioning	1	rebellion	1
pilgrims	1	poet's	11	presented	1	prop	1	questions	3	rebellious	1
pillow	3	point	4	presenting	1	propagate	1	quick	4	rebound	1
pillowy	1	pointed	3	presents	1	proper	3	quicken'd	2	rebuild	1
pilot	1	pointing	2	preserv'd	3	properties	1	quickening	3	recall'd	1
pine	2	points	1	preserve	2	prophecy	1	quickens	1	recedes	1
pinfold	1	polar	1	preserved	1	prophesy	1	quicker	1	receiv'd	3
pining	2	pole	1	presidents	1	prophet	1	quickly	1	receive	9
pink-vested	1	poles	2	presides	1	prophetic	1	quiescent	1	received	7
pinnace	2	policies	1	presiding	1	prophets	3	quiet	22	receiver	1
pinnacle	2	polish'd	1	press	4	prophet's	1	quietly	1	receives	4
pinnacles	1	polity	2	press'd	6	proportion	3	quietness	6	receiving	2
pins	1	pomp	10	presses	1	proportions	3	quire	2	recent	4
pious	2	pompous	1	pressure	1	propositions	1	quit	6	recently	1
pipe	2	ponderous	2	presumption	2	propp'd	2	quite	1	receptacle	1
piping	1	pool	4	presumptuously	1	propping	1	quits	1	recess	6
pitch	1	pools	2	prettiest	1	props	3	quitted	4	recesses	4
pitch'd	1	poor	12	pretty	2	prose	1	quitting	1	recipient	1
pitcher	1	pope	1	prevail'd	1	prospect	14	quivering	1	reckless	1
piteous	1	popinjays	1	prevails	2	prosper'd	1	quoth	1	reckoning	1
piteously	1	popular	2	prey	3	prostrate	1	rabblement	1	reclining	1
pitiably	1	populous	1	price	1	prostrated	1	race	16	recognis'd	2
pitied	1	pored	1	pride	19	protecting	1	radiance	4	recognise	2
pity	2	port	1	priestly	1	protection	2	radiant	2	recognised	1
placable	1	portals	1	primaeval	1	protects	1	rage	4	recognize	1
plac'd	3	porters	1	prime	8	protracted	2	raged	1	recoil	1
place	66	porter's	1	primitive	2	proud	11	ragged	1	recoil'd	1
placed	2	portion	8	primrose	1	prouder	2	rain	7	recollected	1
places	6	portions	2	primrose-time	1	proudest	1	rainbow	1	recollection	2
placid	4	posies	1	princes	1	proudly	2	rains	2	recollections	2
plain	30	possess'd	8	principle	3	prov'd	1	rainy	1	recompense	3
plain-living	1	possessed	1	principles	4	prove	2	rais'd	6	reconcil'd	1
plainly	1	possession	3	print	1	proved	2	raise	1	reconcilement	1
plainness	2	possible	2	printed	1	proves	1	raised	2	reconciles	1
plains	5	possibly	1	prism	1	provide	1	rake	1	record	11
plaintive	2	posting	1	prison	5	providence	2	rambled	1	recorded	4
plan	2	posts	1	prisoner	3	province	4	rambling	3	records	1
planet	1	posture-masters	1	privacy	3	proving	1	rampart's	1	recovering	1
planning	1	potent	2	private	12	provokes	1	ran	7	recreant	2
plans	2	potentates	1	privation	1	prowess	4	random	2	rectified	1
plant	4	potter's	1	privileg'd	2	prudence	1	Ranelagh	1	recusants	1
planted	1	pound	1	privilege	9	prying	1	rang	2	red	7
planting	1	pour	7	priz'd	2	public	20	rang'd	3	redbreasts	1
plants	1	pour'd	3	prize	4	puff'd	1	range	6	redeem'd	1
plastic	2	pourtray'd	1	prized	2	puffs	3	ranged	3	redemption	1
platform	2	poverty	3	prizing	1	puissant	1	ranging	3	redoubled	2
Plato	1	powder	1	probation	1	pull	1	rank	4	redounding	1
Platonic	1	power	83	probe	1	pulpit	1	rank'd	1	redounds	1
play	6	powerful	2	proceed	4	pulse	2	ranks	1	reduce	1
play'd	7	powers	16	proceeding	2	punctilios	1	ransacks	1	reduced	1
play-fellows	1	practice	1	proceeds	1	punctual	7	rapid	2	redundancy	1
playful	1	practis'd	1	process	4	punishment	2	rapt	6	redundant	2
playmate	1	praise	8	processes	1	puny	1	rapture	4	reel'd	1
playmates	2	praises	3	procession	3	pupil	2	raptures	1	re-establish'd	1
playmate's	1	prancing	1	processions	1	puppet-shows	1	rare	2	reference	1
plaything	3	prate	1	proclaim'd	1	purchas'd	1	raree-show	1	refin'd	1
playthings	1	prattle	2	proclaims	1	pure	23	rarely	2	refine	1
playtime	1	prattlers	1	proclamation	1	purer	4	rarities	2	refined	1
pleaded	1	prattling	1	proclamations	1	purest	6	rarity	1	reflect	2
pleas	1	pray	1	procured	1	purified	3	rash	1	reflected	2
pleasant	17	pray'd	2	prodigal	1	purifying	1	rashly	1	reflecting	1
pleas'd	17	prayer	2	prodigies	2	purity	3	rather	14	reflections	1
please	1	prayers	2	prodigy	1	purple	1	rational	2	refresh	1
pleased	10	preach'd	1	produc'd	1	purpose	4	rattles	1	refresh'd	1
pleases	2	preamble	1	produce	7	purposes	3	rattling	1	refreshment	2
pleasing	3	preceding	1	producing	1	purses	1	ravage	2	refreshments	1
pleasingly	1	preceptress	1	profane	1	pursu'd	4	raven's	1	refuge	1
pleasure	37	precincts	2	profess'd	1	pursue	4	raving	1	regain'd	1
pleasure-ground	1	precious	4	professedly	1	pursued	9	raw	1	regal	1
pleasures	10	precipices	2	profit	1	pursues	2	reach	14	regard	7
pleasure's	1	precipitate	1	profitable	1	pursuing	1	reach'd	6	regards	4
plebeian	1	precipitated	1	profitless	2	pursuit	1	reached	1	regenerated	1
pledge	1	preconceptions	1	profound	5	pursuits	5	reaching	1	regent	1
pledges	1	precursor	1	profusely	3	push'd	2	read	23	regiment	1
plenteous	1	predestin'd	1	profusion	1	put	19	readiest	1	region	17
plied	1	predominant	2	progress	13	putting	1	readily	1	regions	6
plight	1	pre-eminence	1	projections	1	puzzle	1	reading	5	register	1
plot	3	pre-eminent	2	projects	1	puzzled	1	ready	3	register'd	1
plots	1	pregnant	1	prolong'd	2	quaint	1	real	11	regret	4
plough	1	prejudice	3	Promethean	1	qualities	2	realities	2	regrets	1
ploughman	1	prelibation	1	prominent	1	quality	3	reality	2	regretted	1
pluck	1	prelude	1	promiscuous	1	Quantock's	1	realiz'd	1	regular	4
pluck'd	2	pre-occupy	1	promise	13	quarrel'd	1	really	3	regulate	1
plumage	1	pre-ordain'd	1	promised	2	quarrels	1	realms	2	regulation	1
plumes	2	preparation	2	promises	8	quarrelsome	1	reap	3	regulations	1
plunderer	1	prepar'd	1	promising	1	quarry	1	reaper	1	rein	1
plunged	1	prepare	1	promontory	3	quarry-man	1	reappear	1	rejected	2
ply	1	prepared	6	promote	1	quarter	1	reaps	1	rejoic'd	1

Appendix

rejoice	3	resign'd	2	right	30	rubbish	1	Savoyards	1	seed-time	1
rejoiced	6	resistance	1	righteous	1	ruddy	1	saw	58	seeing	10
rejoicing	1	resolute	1	righteousness	1	rude	1	say	24	seek	9
rejoicings	1	resolution	1	rightly	3	rudely	1	saying	3	seeking	7
relate	4	resolutions	1	rights	11	rudest	2	Scafell	1	seeks	2
related	1	resolve	3	rigorous	3	rudiments	1	scale	3	seem	24
relating	2	resort	1	rill	3	rueful	2	scamper'd	1	seem'd	64
relation	1	resorted	1	rimy	1	ruffian	1	scandal	1	seemeth	2
relations	2	resound	1	ring	6	rugged	1	scann'd	2	seeming	5
relationship	1	resounded	1	rioted	1	ruin	1	scanty	1	seemliness	1
relaxing	1	resounding	3	riots	1	rul'd	1	scarce	3	seemly	2
relent	1	respect	3	ripe	1	rule	3	scarcely	26	seems	11
relick	1	respiration	1	ripen'd	2	ruled	2	scar'd	1	seen	44
relief	1	respirations	1	ripens	1	rulers	2	scare-crow	1	sees	10
religion	1	respired	1	riper	3	rules	3	scared	1	seest	1
religious	6	respite	1	rippling	1	ruling	2	scatter'd	14	seiz'd	2
religiously	2	respites	1	rise	4	ruminate	1	scatterings	1	seize	2
reliques	1	resplendent	1	risen	3	ruminating	1	scavenger	1	seizing	1
relish	1	responsive	1	rises	1	rumour	1	scene	20	seldom	12
reluctance	1	rest	26	rising	4	rumours	1	scenery	1	select	1
reluctant	2	rested	3	risings	2	run	5	scenes	12	selected	1
reluctantly	2	resting	2	rites	2	running	2	sceptre	3	self	14
remain	7	resting-place	3	ritual	1	runs	2	scheme	4	self-applauding	1
remain'd	9	restless	3	rival	1	rural	11	schemed	1	self-blame	1
remained	2	restlessly	1	rivalship	1	rush'd	1	schemers	1	self-command	1
remains	2	restoration	3	river	13	russet	1	schemes	2	self-conceit	1
remedies	1	restorative	1	rivers	9	Russian	1	scholar	1	self-congratulation	1
remember	8	restor'd	1	river's	1	rustic	2	scholars	1	self-created	1
rememberable	1	restored	5	river-sides	1	rustic's	1	scholar's	1	self-defence	1
remember'd	4	restraint	2	rivet	1	rusted	1	scholastic	2	self-destroying	1
remembering	4	restraints	1	rivulet's	1	rustling	2	school	12	self-devotion	1
remembrance	5	rests	3	road	18	Sabbath	3	schoolboy	1	self-forgetfulness	1
remembrances	10	result	2	roads	11	Sabine	1	school-boy	2	selfish	4
remiss	1	resum'd	1	road's	1	sabra	1	school-boys	2	selfishness	3
remissly	1	resume	1	roam	4	sacred	1	school-boys	1	self-knowledge	1
remissness	1	retain	2	roam'd	5	sacrificed	1	schoolboy's	1	self-pleasing	1
remonstrances	1	retain'd	4	roaming	1	sacrificial	2	school-day	2	self-possession	1
remorse	2	retainers	1	roar	4	sad	3	schoolfellows	1	self-presence	1
remote	6	retaineth	1	roaring	6	Sadler's Wells	1	schoolmen	1	self-presented	1
remotest	2	retains	1	roars	1	sadness	4	schools	4	self-respect	1
remoulds	1	retir'd	2	robe	1	safe	7	science	5	self-restraint	1
remounted	1	retire	1	Robespierre	5	safeguard	3	scoff	1	self-rule	1
removal	1	retired	6	Robin Hood	1	safer	1	scoffers	1	self-sacrifice	1
remov'd	3	retiredness	1	rock	17	safety	4	scoffs	1	self-same	6
render'd	1	retirement	4	rock'd	2	sagacious	1	scolding	1	self-slaughter	1
renders	1	retiring	2	rock-like	1	sage	2	scope	1	self-submission	1
rendezvous	2	retrac'd	1	rocks	19	sages	1	scorn	3	self-sufficing	1
renew'd	5	retrace	3	rocky	7	said	31	Scotch	1	self-taught	1
renovated	1	retreat	2	rod	2	sail	1	Scotland	1	self-transmuted	1
renovation	1	retreating	1	rode	2	sail'd	3	scratch	1	self-will'd	1
renown'd	3	retrograde	1	Roland	1	sailor's	1	scratches	1	selves	2
rent	2	retrospect	1	roll'd	4	sails	1	scream	2	semi-Quixote	1
repair	1	return	12	rolling	2	saint	1	screaming	1	senate	2
repair'd	6	return'd	18	Roman	2	sainted	1	screams	1	senators	1
repass'd	1	returned	1	romance	6	saints	1	scribbled	1	send	3
repast	1	returning	8	romances	1	sake	8	scrolls	1	sending	1
repasts	1	returns	2	romantic	2	sakes	1	scruple	1	send'st	1
repeat	1	reunite	1	Rome	3	Salisburys	1	scrupulous	1	sensation	1
repeated	6	reveal'd	2	Romeo	1	sallied	2	scrupulously	1	sensations	6
repeating	1	revelation	1	Romish	1	sallying	1	scudding	1	sense	50
repetition	1	revelation's	1	Romorentin	1	salt-box	1	scythe	1	senseless	4
repining	1	revelry	3	romping	1	salutation	4	sea	31	senses	5
replied	1	reverberated	1	roof	7	saluted	2	sea-fight	1	sensibility	2
reply	1	revered	1	roof'd	1	salutes	1	seal	1	sensible	2
report	5	reverenc'd	1	roofless	2	same	40	seams	1	sensibly	1
reportest	1	reverence	7	roofs	2	samples	2	search	7	sensitive	1
repos'd	1	reverenced	4	room	4	sanative	1	search'd	1	sensual	1
repose	8	reverential	1	rooms	2	sanctified	3	sea-shells	1	sensuous	2
reposed	1	reverentially	1	rooted	1	sanctifying	1	sea-shore	1	sent	13
reposing	2	reverie	1	roots	4	sanction	5	sea-side	1	sentence	2
represent	2	reverse	1	rope-dancers	1	sanction'd	1	season	19	sentiment	5
representative	1	reverted	1	rose	27	sanctity	5	seasonable	1	sentiments	7
reproach	3	reviewing	1	rosy	4	sanctuaries	1	seasoned	1	separate	2
reproach'd	1	revived	2	Rotha's	1	sanctuary	2	seasons	9	separation	3
reproaches	1	reviving	1	rotted	1	sanctuary's	1	seat	9	September	1
reproof	5	revolution	1	rotten	1	sand	3	seated	1	sequel	1
republic	3	revolutionary	1	rough	5	sandal	1	secluded	1	sequester'd	7
republican	1	revolutions	1	rough-cast	1	sands	7	seclusion	1	seraphic	1
repute	1	revolv'd	2	roughest	1	sandy	2	seclusions	1	seraphs	1
reputed	1	revolve	1	round	44	sang	6	second	6	serene	2
request	2	revolved	1	roundabouts	1	sanguine	1	secondary	5	serious	2
requesting	1	revolving	1	roundly	1	sank	4	second-sight	1	Sertorius	1
requiem	1	reward	3	rounds	1	sapp'd	1	seeresy	1	servant	1
requir'd	1	Rhine	1	rous'd	1	Sarum	1	secret	3	serv'd	4
require	1	Rhone	1	rout	2	sate	24	secreted	1	serve	5
required	2	rhymes	2	routs	1	satire	1	sects	1	service	14
requires	2	ribaldry	1	rouz'd	5	satisfi'd	1	secure	4	services	1
rescue	1	rich	13	rouze	2	satisfied	6	security	2	servile	1
research	1	richly	2	rouzed	2	satyrs	1	sedan	1	serving	1
resemblance	1	ride	4	rov'd	2	saucy	1	sedate	1	servitude	2
resembled	1	ridge	3	roving	1	saunter'd	2	sedentary	1	set	21
resembling	1	ridges	1	row	1	sauntering	1	seduce	2	sets	3
reserv'd	2	ridicule	1	row'd	2	savage	1	sedulous	2	setting	6
reserve	3	ridiculous	1	royal	3	save	7	see	44	settle	1
reservoir	1	riding	1	royalists	1	saving	2	seed	2	settled	2
residence	4	rife	1	royalties	1	savings	1	seeds	1	settler	1

166 Wordsworth's Vocabulary in *The Prelude*

word	n	word	n	word	n	word	n	word	n
settling	2	showing	1	slack	1	some	130	splitting	2	steep'd	1
settling-time	1	showman	1	slacken'd	1	something	28	spoil'd	1	steeple	1
seven	1	showman's	1	slackening	3	sometimes	23	spoiler	1	steeples	1
seventeenth	1	shows	4	slackens	1	somewhat	5	spoils	1	steps	1
sever	1	shrewd	1	slackness	1	somewhere	2	spoken	5	steer'd	1
several	8	shrill	1	slate	1	son	7	spontaneously	1	stem	1
sever'd	1	shrillest	1	slaughter	1	song	16	sport	5	stemm'd	1
severe	4	shrine	1	slave	1	songs	4	sported	1	step	17
severer	1	shrines	1	slaves	1	soon	26	sporting	1	stepp'd	1
severest	1	shrink	1	sleep	19	sooner	5	sportive	1	steps	17
severing	1	shrouded	1	sleeping	2	sooth'd	3	sportively	1	stern	4
severings	1	shrub	1	sleeps	4	soothe	1	sports	3	sterner	1
shade	10	shrubs	1	sleety	1	soothed	2	spot	15	sternly	1
shades	13	shrunk	2	slender	6	soothes	1	spots	9	sternness	1
shading	1	shudder'd	1	slept	6	sooty	1	spotted	1	steward	1
shadings	1	shuddering	1	slight	4	sore	1	spousals	1	stewards	1
shadow	7	shuffling	1	slighted	3	sorrow	21	sprang	2	stick	1
shadow'd	1	shun	1	slip	2	sorrows	2	spray	1	sticks	1
shadows	1	shunn'd	2	slipp'd	3	sort	7	spread	19	stiff	1
shadowy	4	shunning	1	slippers	1	sought	13	spreading	4	still	78
shady	6	shut	5	slippery	1	soul	69	spreads	5	still'd	1
shake	3	shy	3	slipping	1	soulless	1	spring	14	stillness	6
shaken	3	sibyl	1	slips	2	souls	12	springes	1	stings	2
shakespear	2	Sicilian	1	slope	3	soul's	1	springs	5	stinted	2
shakespeare	1	Sicily	1	slow	8	sound	22	spring-tide	1	stipend	1
shaking	2	sick	7	slowly	9	sounded	1	springtime	1	stir	11
shall	53	sickliness	1	slow-moving	1	sounder	1	spring-time	1	stirr'd	11
shallow	3	sickly	2	slumber'd	1	sounding	2	sprinklings	1	stirring	5
shallows	1	sickness	2	slumbering	1	sounds	17	sprung	4	stole	1
shalt	1	side	41	slumbers	1	source	3	spun	2	stolen	2
shame	15	sides	11	slung	1	sources	1	spungy	1	stone	16
shameful	2	sideway	1	sly	1	sour'd	1	spur	2	stone-abbot	1
shameless	1	Sidney	1	small	23	south	1	spurious	1	stone-axe	1
shap'd	6	sifts	1	smart	2	southern	1	spurn'd	2	stone-eater	1
shape	17	sigh'd	1	smil'd	2	southward	4	spurring	1	stones	4
shaped	3	sight	44	smile	3	sovereign	4	square	1	stony	2
shapeless	1	sightless	1	smiles	1	sovereignty	2	squares	1	stood	35
shapes	19	sights	13	smites	1	sow	1	squires	1	stoop	2
shaping	1	sign	2	smitten	3	sown	8	St.	8	stoop'd	1
share	3	signal	2	smoke	1	space	21	stable	2	stooping	2
shared	1	signboard	1	smooth	13	spacious	2	staff	7	stop	1
sharp	2	signet	1	smoothly	1	spades	1	stage	8	stopp'd	8
she	71	signs	3	smoothness	1	Spain	1	staggering	1	stopping	1
sheaf	1	silence	21	smote	1	spake	7	staid	1	store	7
shed	3	silent	30	snake	1	span	1	stale	1	stores	1
sheds	1	silently	1	snakes	1	spangled	2	stalking	1	storm	14
sheep	6	silk	1	snaky	1	Spaniard	1	stall	1	storm'd	1
shell	5	silver	2	snapp'd	2	Spanish	1	stalled	1	storms	6
shells	1	silvery	1	snare	1	spann'd	1	stalls	1	stormy	5
shelter	4	simple	17	snatch	1	spar'd	1	stammerer	1	story	13
shelter'd	5	simple-mindedness	1	snatches	1	spare	3	stamp	1	straggle	1
sheltering	1	simpleness	1	sneers	1	spared	2	stamp'd	1	straggler	2
shepherd	13	simplicity	13	snow	17	sparkling	3	stand	17	straggling	4
shepherds	7	simplified	1	Snowdon	38	speak	38	standard	1	straightforward	1
shepherd's	4	simply	2	snowdrops	1	speaking	9	standers-by	1	strain	5
shew	11	since	13	snows	3	speaks	1	standing	8	strained	1
shew'd	3	sincere	1	snow-white	3	spear	1	stands	4	straining	1
shewn	1	sincerely	1	snowy	1	spears	1	star	7	strains	4
shewy	1	sinews	1	so	135	special	1	star'd	1	strait	2
shield	4	sing	1	Soane	1	specially	1	stare	1	straitway	2
shields	1	sing'd	1	soareth	1	specimens	1	staring	1	strand	1
shift	1	singers	1	sobbings	1	specious	1	star-light	1	strange	10
shifting	1	singing	1	sober	6	spectacle	13	starry	2	strangely	1
shines	1	single	28	soberly	1	spectacles	4	stars	14	strangeness	1
shining	9	singled	5	sobs	2	spectators	3	start	3	stranger	9
ship	1	singleness	1	social	8	spectre	1	starting	2	strangers	4
shipp'd	1	singly	2	societies	3	spectres	1	startling	1	stranger's	2
ships	2	sings	1	society	11	speculations	3	starved	1	strawberries	1
shipwreck	1	singular	2	sod	1	speech	7	starving	1	stray	2
shoal	1	singularity	1	sod-built	1	speed	5	state	21	stray'd	2
shock	6	sink	2	sodden	1	speedily	1	stately	7	strays	1
shock'd	1	sinning	1	soe'er	1	spell	1	station	7	streaks	1
shocks	2	sinuous	1	soft	9	spells	2	stationary	1	stream	29
shod	1	sire	1	soften	3	Spenser	1	station'd	3	streaming	1
shone	2	Sirius	1	soften'd	1	Spenser's	1	stationed	1	streams	9
shook	2	sirocco	1	softening	1	spent	1	statists	1	streamy	1
shooting	1	sister	7	softness	2	sphered	1	statue	1	street	8
shop	6	sisters	1	soil	5	spied	1	statues	1	streets	11
shore	10	sit	10	sojourn	2	spin	2	stature	2	strength	38
shores	4	site	1	sojourn'd	1	spinners	1	statute	1	strengthen'd	1
short	21	sits	3	sojourner	2	spinning	1	stay'd	2	strengthened	1
shortening	1	sitting	6	solace	2	spire	2	stays	1	strengtheners	1
short-flighted	1	six	2	solacing	1	spirit	55	stead	2	stretch	4
short-liv'd	2	sixty	1	soldier	2	spiritless	1	steadfast	3	stretch'd	4
short-lived	1	size	2	soldier's	1	spirits	9	steadied	1	strew	1
short-sighted	1	skeletons	1	soldiership	1	spirit-stirring	1	steadiest	1	strew'd	1
shot	1	Skiddaw's	1	sole	3	spiritual	7	steadily	1	stricken	1
should	64	skies	1	solemn	2	spiry	1	steadiness	1	strictly	1
shoulder	1	skiff	2	solemnity	2	spite	7	steady	13	stride	1
shouldering	1	skilful	1	solemniz'd	1	splendid	2	stealth	3	striding-edge	1
shout	2	skill	14	solemnized	1	splendor	1	steal	1	strife	10
shouting	1	skill'd	1	solicitude	1	sp[l]endid	1	stealth	1	strike	1
shouts	1	skimm'd	2	solid	9	splendour	3	steam-like	1	strikes	1
show	7	skirts	1	solitary	9	splendour's	1	steeds	3	striking	2
shower	3	sky	22	solitude	22	steel	1	string	2
showers	2	sky's	1	solitudes	5	split	1	steep	10	string'd	1

Appendix

word	n	word	n	word	n	word	n	word	n	word	n	word	n
strip	1	suiting	1	sword	2	tenderest	1	thoughtless	2	tongue-favor'd	1
stripling	3	suits	2	swords	2	tenderness	12	thoughts	73	tongues	3
stripling's	1	sullen	1	sycamore	1	tending	1	thousand	15	too	54
stripp'd	1	sultry	1	syllogistic	1	tenets	1	thousands	1	took	31
stript	1	sum	2	sylvan	1	tenor	2	thraldom	1	tool	1
strode	1	summer	27	symbol	1	tens	1	thrall	1	tooth	1
stroke	3	summers	3	symbols	3	tenth	1	thread	1	top	9
stroll'd	1	summer's	5	sympathies	8	tents	2	threaten'd	1	topmost	1
strolling	1	summer-time	1	sympathy	12	tepid	1	threatening	1	tops	3
strong	34	summit	6	synod	1	term	2	threats	1	torches	1
stronger	4	summon	3	synthesis	1	termination	1	three	13	torpid	1
strongest	3	summon'd	7	Syracuse	1	terms	2	three-years'	1	torrent	2
strongly	1	summons	6	system	1	terrace	1	threshold	5	torrents	4
struck	5	sun	37	table	5	terrestrial	1	threw	8	toss	1
structure	1	sunbeam	2	tailors	1	terrible	1	thrice	2	toss'd	2
structures	1	Sunday	1	taint	2	terrify	1	thridded	2	tossing	2
struggle	1	Sunday's	1	take	29	terrifying	1	throng	9	tottering	1
struggled	2	sundry	5	taken	9	tenor	1	throng'd	1	touch	15
struggles	1	sunny	2	takes	3	terror	8	thrilling	1	touch'd	13
struggling	1	sunrise	2	taking	5	terrors	1	thrills	1	touches	3
stuck	1	sun-rise	1	tak'st	1	test	3	thrive	1	touching	4
studded	1	sun's	1	tale	17	tether	1	thriven	1	tournament	1
student	3	sunset	2	talents	1	texture	2	thrives	1	toward	1
students	3	sunshine	5	tales	10	th'	4	thro'	4	towards	28
student's	1	superadded	1	talk	6	Thames	1	throes	2	tower	3
studied	1	superficial	4	talk'd	2	than	124	throne	2	towering	1
studies	3	superfluous	1	talking	2	thank'd	2	throned	3	towers	4
studious	5	superhuman	2	talks	1	thankfulness	1	throned	1	town	16
studiously	2	superior	3	tall	5	thanks	3	throng'd	4	towns	4
study	5	supernatural	1	tam'd	1	thanksgivings	1	throttled	1	toy	2
stuff	1	superstition	1	tame	1	that	909	through	203	trace	4
stumbling	1	super-tragic	1	tamed	1	that's	1	throughout	7	traced	1
stumping	2	supper	1	tamer	1	thaws	1	throw	1	traces	1
stung	1	suppers	1	tamper	1	the	3221	throwing	1	tracing	1
stunn'd	1	supplanted	1	taper	6	theatre	5	thrown	5	track	9
stupefied	1	supplied	4	tapers	1	theatres	1	thrush	1	track'd	3
stupendous	1	support	5	tam	1	thee	53	thrust	3	tract	4
sturdy	1	supporters	1	tarried	1	their	237	thrusts	2	tracts	2
style	1	suppos'd	3	tarrying	1	theirs	10	thumps	1	trade	2
subdu'd	1	suppose	2	Tartar	1	there's	1	thunder	1	tradesman's	1
subdued	2	suppress'd	1	Tartarian	2	them	92	thunderer	1	tradition	1
subduing	1	supreme	2	task	10	theme	22	thundering	3	traditions	1
subjected	1	sure	8	tasks	3	themes	4	thunderstricken	1	traffic	2
subjoin'd	1	surely	11	tassell'd	1	themselves	34	thus	100	traffickers	1
sublime	13	surety	1	tassels	1	then	155	thwart	2	tragedies	1
sublimer	1	surf	1	taste	4	thence	23	thwarting	1	tragic	4
sublimest	1	surface	5	tasted	1	thenceforth	1	thy	65	train	3
sublimity	1	surfaces	1	tatters	1	thenceforward	1	thyself	6	train'd	4
submission	1	surly	2	taught	10	Theocritus	1	tide	1	trampling	1
submissive	1	surmise	1	taunt	1	theories	1	tidings	4	trances	1
submissively	1	surmounted	1	taunting	1	there	159	tie	1	tranquil	8
submit	1	surpass	1	taunts	1	thereafter	3	tied	2	tranquillised	1
subordinate	2	surpassing	2	tavern	1	threat	1	tigers	1	tranquillity	1
subservience	1	surplice	1	tax	2	thereby	5	tight	1	tranquillizing	1
subservient	2	surprise	1	teach	6	therefore	6	till	28	transcendent	3
subsist	1	surpriz'd	1	teacher	1	therefrom	1	tillers	1	transfer'd	1
substance	7	surprize	2	teachers	2	therein	2	tilth	1	transformation	3
substances	1	surrounded	2	teaches	1	thereof	1	timbrel	1	transient	4
substantial	7	surrounding	1	teaching	3	thereon	1	time	169	transit	1
substantially	1	surviv'd	3	team	2	there's	3	timely	5	transition	3
substitute	1	survive	2	tear	3	thereto	2	times	52	transitory	6
subterfuge	1	survived	1	tears	11	therewith	1	timid	1	translated	1
subterraneous	1	suspected	1	tedious	3	these	137	timidly	1	transmigration	1
subtile	1	suspended	2	teeming	1	Thespian	1	Timoleon	1	transmigrations	2
subtle	4	suspicion	1	teems	1	they	162	Timonides	1	transmitted	1
subtler	1	suspicions	1	teeth	1	thick	5	timorous	1	transparent	1
subtlest	1	suspicious	1	telescopes	1	thickening	1	tingled	1	transplanted	1
subtleties	2	suspiciously	1	tell	13	thick-entangled	1	tinkled	1	transport	4
subtlety	1	sustain'd	7	telling	2	thick-ribbed	1	tints	1	transported	2
suburban	2	sustenance	2	tells	4	thin	2	tipp'd	2	transports	1
suburbs	1	swains	1	temper	8	thine	11	tired	3	trappings	1
subversion	1	swallow	1	temperament	1	thing	15	tiresome	1	travail	1
subverters	1	swallowing	1	temperance	2	things	108	'tis	26	travel	6
succedaneum	1	swallows	1	temperate	3	think	21	titled	1	travell'd	5
succeed	3	swan	1	temperately	1	thinking	5	title-page	1	traveller	15
succeeded	1	swarm	3	temperature	1	thinks	2	titles	2	travellers	6
succeeding	1	swarm'd	1	temper'd	1	third	3	Tivoli	1	traveller's	2
success	2	swarming	2	tempering	1	thirst	3	to	1322	travellers'	1
successful	1	swarms	1	tempers	3	thirsted	1	to-day	1	travelling	9
successively	1	sway	6	tempest	3	thirsty	2	toe	1	travels	1
such	186	sway'd	1	tempests	1	thirteen	1	together	22	travers'd	1
suck'd	1	Swede	1	tempestuous	2	thirty	2	toil	10	traversed	2
sudden	4	sweeping	1	temple	4	this	343	toilette	1	treacherous	1
suddenly	3	sweet	34	temples	2	thither	12	toils	3	treachery	2
suffer	1	sweeten	1	temple's	1	thitherward	1	toilsome	4	tread	8
suffer'd	8	sweeter	1	temporal	1	tho'	1	told	21	treads	2
sufferers	1	sweetest	3	tempt	1	Thorn	1	tolerant	1	treasonable	1
suffering	7	sweetly	5	temptation	1	thoroughfare	1	tolerated	1	treasur'd	1
sufferings	2	sweetness	4	tempting	1	thoroughly	2	toll'd	1	treasure	4
suffers	2	sweets	1	ten	10	those	159	tomb	1	treasures	1
suffic'd	1	swell	1	tenacious	1	thou	58	tombs	2	treat	2
suffice	3	swellings	1	tenanted	1	though	73	tombstone	1	treated	3
sufficient	1	swept	2	tended	1	thought	81	to-morrow	1	treatise	1
suggestions	1	swift	1	tendencies	1	thoughtful	1	tone	3	tree	15
suit	2	swiftness	2	tendency	1	thoughtfully	1	tones	1	trees	21
suited	3	Swiss	2	tender	16	thoughtfulness	1	tongue	7	tree-tops	1

167

Wordsworth's Vocabulary in *The Prelude*

word	n	word	n	word	n	word	n	word	n	word	n
tremble	1	ultimate	1	ungenial	1	unthinking	2	vapours	5	voluptuous	1
trembled	1	umbrage	1	ungovernable	1	unthought	4	varied	2	voluptuously	1
trembling	2	umbrageous	1	ungracious	1	unthought-of	1	variegated	4	vomit	1
tremblings	2	unabated	1	ungratefully	1	unthwarted	2	varieties	1	vomiting	1
tremendously	1	unaccustom'd	1	ungreeted	1	until	14	variety	1	votary	1
trial	6	unacknowledg'd	1	unhabitual	1	until'd	1	various	3	vouchsaf'd	1
trials	2	unadmon'd	1	unhappiness	1	untired	2	vassalage	1	vouchsafe	1
tribe	1	unadulterated	1	unhappy	8	unto	24	vast	12	vouchsafed	3
tribes	2	unaffecting	1	unhealthy	1	untokl	2	Vaudracour	11	vow	1
tribunals	1	unaim'd	1	unheard	4	untouch'd	3	vault	2	vow'd	1
tribune	1	unalarm'd	1	unhonour'd	1	untoward	1	Vauxhall	1	vows	2
tributary	1	unambitious	1	unhous'd	1	untrain'd	1	veer	1	voyage	1
trick	1	unamusing	1	uniform	1	untrod	1	veering	1	voyager	1
trick'd	1	unapprehensive	1	unimpair'd	1	untroubled	2	vehement	2	Vulcan	1
trickling	1	unassuming	1	unimportant	1	untun'd	1	vehicle	1	vulgar	14
tried	2	unawares	3	uninform'd	1	untutor'd	1	veil	3	wading	1
trifler	3	unaw'd	1	uninformed	1	unused	1	vein	1	wafted	2
trifling	2	unbaffled	1	uninhabited	1	unusual	2	veins	3	wain	1
trim	1	unbewilder'd	1	unintelligible	2	unutterable	1	velvet	1	wains	1
trimm'd	1	unbiass'd	1	uninvited	1	unvisited	2	vender's	1	waist	1
Trinity's	1	unblinded	1	union	1	unwearied	1	venerable	4	wait	3
trite	3	unborn	1	unions	1	unwelcome	1	vengeance	5	waiting	1
triumph	4	unburthen'd	1	unison	1	unwholesome	1	vent	2	waits	2
triumphal	2	unceremonious	2	united	2	unwilling	3	ventriloquists	1	wak'd	2
triumphant	3	uncertain	5	unites	1	unwillingly	3	venturous	1	wake	3
triumph'd	1	uncertainty	1	unity	3	unwithered	1	Venus	1	wakeful	2
triumphs	4	unchanged	1	universal	12	unwoo'd	1	verge	1	waking	3
trivial	5	unchasten'd	1	universe	11	unworldly-minded	1	verified	1	Wales	1
trod	7	uncheck'd	2	unjust	2	unworthily	1	verily	2	walk	17
Trompington	1	unclaimed	1	unkind	1	unworthy	5	verity	2	walk'd	9
troop	1	uncomplaining	1	unkindness	1	up	133	vermin	1	walked	5
trooping	2	unconcerned	2	unknown	19	upbraiding	1	vernal	4	walking	4
troops	2	unconquerable	1	unlaborious	1	upbraids	1	vers'd	1	walks	20
trophies	1	unconscious	2	unless	2	upheaved	1	verse	23	wall	6
tropic	2	unconsciously	1	unlike	1	upheld	2	verses	3	Wallace	3
trouble	4	uncontrol'd	1	unlock'd	1	uphold	3	very	45	wallowing	1
troubled	1	uncouth	4	unloos'd	1	upholder	1	vessels	2	walls	10
truant	1	undecaying	1	unlovely	1	upholders	1	vest	1	wan	1
true	22	undelighted	1	unluxuriant	1	upholds	1	vested	1	wand	2
truly	1	undepress'd	1	unmanageable	1	upholstery	1	vestiges	1	wander	2
trumpet	2	under	15	unmerited	1	up-leaping	1	vexation	1	wander'd	5
trumpets	1	under-agents	1	unmov'd	4	uplifted	5	vexations	1	wanderer	4
trumpet-tones	1	under-countenance	1	unmoving	1	uplooking	1	vexatious	1	wanderers	1
trunk	4	under-coverts	1	unnam'd	1	upon	203	vex'd	3	wanderer's	1
trunks	1	undergone	1	unnatural	4	uppermost	2	vexing	2	wandering	6
trust	16	undermine	1	unnecessary	1	uprear'd	1	viands	1	wanderings	6
truth	75	underneath	10	unneighbourly	1	upright	5	vice	9	wands	1
truths	8	under-powers	1	unnoticed	1	upris'n	1	vices	1	waning	1
tuft	1	under-presence	1	unnumber'd	1	uproar	5	victims	1	want	14
tumblers	1	under-sense	1	unobserv'd	1	uprose	1	victories	1	wanted	5
tumbling	1	understand	2	unorganic	1	up-shouldering	1	victorious	1	wanting	10
tumult	7	understanding	6	unpaid	1	upturning	1	victory	2	wanton	1
tumultuous	1	understanding's	1	unpeaceful	1	upwards	6	view	20	wanton'd	1
tuneable	1	understood	8	unpractis'd	3	us	67	view'd	2	wantonness	4
tuneful	1	under-thirst	1	unprepared	1	usages	2	viewless	2	wants	3
tunes	2	underwent	1	unproclaim'd	1	use	3	views	2	war	8
turbulent	1	undetermin'd	1	unprofan'd	1	used	9	vigorous	2	warble	2
turf	10	undiminish'd	1	unprofaned	1	useful	1	vigour	2	warbled	2
Turk	1	undischarged	1	unprofitable	1	usefully	1	vile	1	warbling	1
turmoil	1	undiscipln'd	1	unprofitably	1	useless	2	village	10	warblings	1
turn	24	undisguis'd	1	unpropp'd	1	uselessly	1	villager	1	wardens	1
turn'd	16	undismay'd	1	unquenchable	1	usual	2	villages	4	warehouse	1
turned	2	undisorder'd	1	unquiet	2	usurpation	1	vine-clad	1	wares	3
turning	4	undistinguishable	2	unrais'd	1	usurp'd	3	vines	1	warfare	1
turnings	1	undisturb'd	5	unreasoning	1	usury	1	vineyard	1	warm	5
turns	6	undisturbed	1	unrecogniz'd	1	utmost	2	violating	1	warmer	1
turret's	1	undoing	1	unrecorded	1	Utopia	1	violence	4	warmest	1
tutelary	1	undomestic	1	unregarded	1	utter	10	virgin	2	warmth	2
tutor'd	4	undress	1	unrelenting	2	utterance	3	virtual	1	warrior	3
tutors	2	undulation	1	unrelentingly	1	utter'd	7	virtue	16	wars	1
twain	1	unearth	2	unreprov'd	1	uttering	2	virtues	4	was	558
'twas	36	uneasiness	2	unrespited	1	utterly	5	virtuous	2	wash	1
twelvemonth's	1	uneasy	9	unrestrain'd	1	vacancy	1	visages	1	wast	1
twenty	4	unencroach'd	1	unripe	3	vacant	2	visible	23	waste	10
'twere	4	unexalted	1	unruliness	1	vacation	1	visibly	2	wasted	6
twice	4	unexampled	1	unruly	3	vagaries	1	vision	3	watch	10
twig	1	unexpected	1	unsaluted	1	vagrant	3	visionary	6	watch'd	9
twigs	1	unexpectedly	1	unscour'd	1	vagrants	1	visions	3	watchful	1
twilight	5	unextinguish'd	1	unseen	2	vague	4	visit	1	watching	2
'twill	1	unfading	1	unsettled	2	vain	16	visitant	8	water	13
twin	1	unfaithful	1	unsettles	1	vain-glory	1	visitation	1	waterfall	1
twinkle	1	unfamiliarly	1	unshar'd	1	vainly	2	visitations	3	waterfalls	1
twinkles	1	unfather'd	1	unsheltered	1	Valais	1	visited	3	water-falls	1
twinkling	1	unfeeling	1	unshrouded	1	vale	20	visitings	3	waters	17
twins	2	unfelt	3	unsightly	1	vales	6	visitor	1	water's	1
'twixt	2	unfenc'd	1	unsinged	1	valley	9	vistos	1	waterspout	1
two	38	unfenced	1	unsleeping	1	valleys	2	vital	7	water-weeds	1
twofold	4	unfetter'd	1	unsoil'd	1	vallies	1	vivid	2	watry	2
'twould	2	unfilial	1	unsought	2	vane	1	vivifying	1	wave	2
type	4	unfit	2	unsoul	1	vanish	2	voice	51	waved	1
types	1	unfold	1	unsound	1	vanish'd	2	voiceless	1	wavering	1
tyrannic	1	unfolded	1	unsubdu'd	2	vanities	1	voices	2	waves	3
tyranny	2	unforewarn'd	1	unsubstantial	1	vanity	4	voluble	1	waving	1
tyrant	1	unfrequent	1	unsuccessful	1	vanquish'd	1	volume	4	wax'd	1
tyrants	1	unfrequented	2	unsung	1	vapour	2	volumes	1	waxen	1
tyrant's	1	unfruitful	1	untaught	5	vapour'd	1	voluntary	1	wax-work	1

Appendix

word	count	word	count	word	count	word	count	word	count	word	count
way	57	Westmoreland	1	whole	29	winter	12	woody	2	yards	2
ways	10	westward	1	wholesome	1	winters	3	wooed	2	ye	42
wayside	1	wet	2	wholly	6	wisdom	4	word	17	yea	16
way-side	1	wetting	1	whom	32	wise	9	words	35	year	21
waywardness	1	what	172	whose	32	wiser	4	wore	6	yearn	1
we	272	whate'er	5	whoso	1	wisest	2	work	41	yearning	1
weak	12	whatever	9	why	14	wish	17	work'd	1	yearnings	3
weaker	1	whatsoe'er	4	wicked	1	wish'd	9	working	6	years	39
weakest	1	whatsoever	7	wicker	1	wished-for	1	workings	5	year's	1
weakness	9	wheel	1	wide	14	wishes	2	workmanship	1	years'	1
wealth	7	wheel'd	1	widely	3	wishing	2	workmen	1	yellings	1
wealthy	1	wheeled	1	widely-parted	1	wishing-cap	1	works	25	yellow	7
weapons	1	wheels	1	widening	1	wit	2	world	69	yellowing	1
wear	6	when	251	wider	5	with	779	worldly	3	yes	4
wearied	2	whence	16	wide-scatter'd	1	withal	8	worlds	2	yester	1
weariness	1	whencesoe'er	1	wide-spreading	1	withdrawing	2	world's	1	yesterday	1
wearing	1	whencesoever	2	widest	1	withdrew	3	worm	1	yet	174
wearisome	2	whene'er	2	widow	1	wither	4	worm-like	1	yew-tree	1
weary	12	whenever	2	width	2	wither'd	4	worn	3	yield	5
weather	2	whensoe'er	1	wield	1	withering	1	worse	5	yielded	6
weaves	1	whensoever	1	yielded	1	within	45	worship	5	yielding	3
wedded	3	where	123	wife	4	without	70	worshipp'd	1	yoke	2
wedlock	1	whereabout	1	wild	26	withstood	3	worshipper	1	yoked	3
weeds	3	whereat	3	wilderness	4	witless	2	worshippers	3	yoke-fellows	1
week	6	whereby	1	wilds	2	witness	4	worst	8	yon	4
weekday	1	where'er	3	wilful	2	wives	2	worth	11	Yordas	1
weekly	1	wherefore	3	wilfully	2	wizard	1	worthiest	1	Yorkshire	1
weeks	4	wherein	2	wilfulness	1	woe	2	worthiness	1	you	23
weeks'	1	whereof	1	will	65	woeful	2	worthy	10	young	21
weep	3	whereunto	1	willing	4	woes	3	would	86	Young	1
weigh'd	4	wherever	4	willingly	7	wold	1	wound	2	your	26
weighs	1	wherewith	2	willow	4	wolf-skin	1	woven	1	yours	4
weight	14	whether	18	wilt	6	wolves	1	wrap	1	yourselves	1
welcom'd	1	which	441	wily	1	woman	10	wrath	2	youth	67
welcome	12	while	60	Winander	1	woman's	1	wreath	1	youthful	14
welcomed	2	whip	1	wind	25	women	4	wreath'd	1	youths	4
welfare	3	whirl	1	Windermere	3	won	8	wreck	1	youth's	5
well	37	whirl'd	1	winding	5	wonder	6	wren	1	Zacynthus	1
well-born	1	whirling	1	windings	2	wonder'd	1	wrench'd	1	zeal	11
well-known	2	whirlwinds	1	wind-mill	1	wonders	4	wren-like	1	zealously	1
well-match'd	1	whispered	1	window	3	wondrous	4	wretched	3	zephyrs	1
well-spring	1	whispering	1	window-garlands	1	wond'rous	1	wretchedness	5	zest	1
welterings	1	whispers	1	windows	3	wood	12	wrinkles	1		
went	30	whist	1	window's	1	wood-built	1	writhing	1		
wept	3	whistle	1	winds	20	woodcocks	1	writing	1		
were	200	whistling	3	wine	4	wooden	1	written	10		
wert	4	white	5	wing	1	wood-honey	1	wrong	7		
west	4	whither	3	wings	5	woodland	2	wrongs	3		
western	2	Whittington	1	winning	2	woodman	2	wrote	1		
Westminster	1	who	166	wins	1	woods	28	wrought	18		

169

List 1.2: Rank frequency list for *The Prelude*

Rank	Word	Freq.
1	the	3221
2	and	2715
3	of	2378
4	a	1420
5	to	1322
6	in	1269
7	I	937
8	that	909
9	with	779
10	was	558
11	my	538
12	as	477
13	by	447
13	from	447
15	which	441
16	for	399
17	or	365
18	not	364
19	his	354
20	all	352
21	had	349
22	this	343
23	at	334
24	but	322
25	on	316
26	me	295
27	is	292
28	it	285
29	he	276
30	we	272
31	when	251
32	have	248
33	their	237
34	be	236
35	more	223
36	her	203
36	through	203
36	upon	203
39	were	200
40	one	188
41	such	186
42	yet	174
43	what	172
44	our	170
45	time	169
46	an	167
47	who	166
48	now	165
49	been	162
49	they	162
51	mind	161
52	there	159
52	those	159
54	no	158
55	then	155
56	did	152
57	like	147
58	its	142
59	man	141
60	these	137
61	so	135
62	up	133
63	love	132
64	him	130
64	some	130
66	life	128
67	are	126
68	if	126
69	than	124
70	where	123
71	among	121
71	nor	121
73	day	118
74	nature	117
75	heart	113
76	even	108
76	things	108
78	first	104
78	own	104
80	could	103
81	might	100
81	thus	100
83	far	93
84	them	92
85	how	88
86	out	86
86	would	86
88	power	83
89	here	82
90	thought	81
91	before	80
91	less	80
93	hath	79
93	into	79
93	men	79
93	other	79
97	long	78
97	still	78
99	every	77
100	truth	75
101	though	73
101	thoughts	73
103	friend	72
104	she	71
105	great	70
105	without	70
107	joy	69
107	soul	69
107	world	69
110	may	68
111	us	67
111	youth	67
113	place	66
114	left	65
114	thy	65
114	will	65
117	most	64
117	seem'd	64
117	should	64
120	human	63
121	earth	62
121	made	62
123	down	60
123	while	60
125	hope	59
125	old	59
127	itself	58
127	little	58
127	once	58
127	saw	58
127	thou	58
132	way	57
133	spirit	55
134	forth	54
134	too	54
136	myself	53
136	shall	53
136	thee	53
139	times	52
140	found	51
140	must	51
140	never	51
140	voice	51
144	come	50
144	sense	50
146	again	49
146	felt	49
146	only	49
149	delight	48
149	light	48
149	many	48
152	about	47
153	ever	46
153	eyes	46
153	night	46
156	along	45
156	beneath	45
156	days	45
156	do	45
156	each	45
156	very	45
156	within	45
163	after	44
163	round	44
163	see	44
163	seen	44
163	sight	44
168	came	42
168	can	42
168	heard	42
168	name	42
168	O	42
168	ye	42
174	make	41
174	side	41
174	work	41
177	being	40
177	deep	40
177	face	40
177	mine	40
177	same	40
182	back	39
182	fear	39
182	having	39
182	home	39
182	living	39
182	pass'd	39
182	years	39
189	alone	38
189	good	38
189	hand	38
189	hour	38
189	open	38
189	passion	38
189	speak	38
189	strength	38
189	two	38
198	forms	37
198	hills	37
198	joy	37
198	least	37
198	pleasure	37
198	sun	37
198	well	37
204	'twas	36
204	child	36
204	last	36
204	oh	36
208	knowledge	35
208	lay	35
208	objects	35
208	often	35
208	stood	35
208	words	35
214	above	34
214	away	34
214	books	34
214	common	34
214	feeling	34
214	given	34
214	look	34
214	strong	34
214	sweet	34
214	themselves	34
224	both	33
224	eye	33
224	give	33
224	house	33
224	new	33
229	much	32
229	whom	32
229	whose	32
232	almost	31
232	few	31
232	heaven	31
232	hence	31
232	near	31
232	over	31
232	said	31
232	sea	31
232	took	31
241	else	30
241	find	30
241	full	30
241	God	30
241	look'd	30
241	part	30
241	plain	30
241	right	30
241	silent	30
241	went	30
251	beauty	29
251	early	29
251	feel	29
251	fields	29
251	himself	29
251	nature's	29
251	stream	29
251	take	29
251	whole	29
260	end	28
260	gone	28
260	hopes	28
260	peace	28
260	present	28
260	reason	28
260	single	28
260	something	28
260	till	28
260	towards	28
260	woods	28
271	best	27
271	dear	27
271	high	27
271	length	27
271	let	27
271	nothing	27
271	perhaps	27
271	presence	27
271	rose	27
271	summer	27
281	'tis	26
281	age	26
281	any	26
281	better	26
281	head	26
281	hours	26
281	live	26
281	o'er	26
281	rest	26
281	scarcely	26
281	soon	26
281	wild	26
281	your	26
294	air	25
294	brought	25
294	city	25
294	clouds	25
294	daily	25
294	ere	25
294	image	25
294	liberty	25
294	lov'd	25
294	mean	25
294	off	25
294	wind	25
294	works	25
307	also	24
307	beheld	24
307	change	24
307	green	24
307	ground	24
307	happy	24
307	meanwhile	24
307	minds	24
307	mountains	24
307	need	24
307	oft	24
307	sate	24
307	say	24
307	seem	24
307	turn	24
307	unto	24
323	course	23
323	distant	23
323	doth	23
323	fair	23
323	glory	23
323	land	23
323	led	23
323	mighty	23
323	morning	23
323	outward	23
323	pure	23
323	read	23
323	small	23
323	sometimes	23
323	thence	23
323	verse	23
323	visible	23
323	you	23
341	behold	22
341	call'd	22
341	calm	22
341	frame	22
341	known	22
341	mountain	22
341	past	22
341	quiet	22
341	sky	22
341	solitude	22
341	sound	22
341	theme	22
341	together	22
341	true	22
355	afterwards	21
355	ancient	21
355	beyond	21
355	gentle	21
355	happiness	21
355	set	21
355	short	21
355	silence	21
355	sorrow	21
355	space	21
355	state	21
355	think	21

Appendix

355	told	21	451	lake	16	551	father	13	638	fall	11
355	trees	21	451	lost	16	551	form	13	638	flock	11
355	year	21	451	note	16	551	grass	13	638	food	11
355	young	21	451	object	16	551	grave	13	638	gives	11
371	art	20	451	others	16	551	highest	13	638	golden	11
371	behind	20	451	pass	16	551	honour	13	638	herself	11
371	cause	20	451	powers	16	551	huge	13	638	holy	11
371	different	20	451	race	16	551	intercourse	13	638	laid	11
371	evening	20	451	song	16	551	journey	13	638	laws	11
371	faith	20	451	stone	16	551	kindred	13	638	learn'd	11
371	naked	20	451	tender	16	551	lie	13	638	leaving	11
371	public	20	451	town	16	551	lies	13	638	lofty	11
371	scene	20	451	trust	16	551	loose	13	638	looks	11
371	vale	20	451	turn'd	16	551	low	13	638	loud	11
371	view	20	451	vain	16	551	mother's	13	638	makes	11
371	walks	20	451	virtue	16	551	natural	13	638	manners	11
371	winds	20	451	whence	16	551	perfect	13	638	means	11
384	appear'd	19	451	yea	16	551	progress	13	638	met	11
384	boy	19	481	add	15	551	promise	13	638	move	11
384	enough	19	481	am	15	551	rich	13	638	needs	11
384	groves	19	481	call	15	551	river	13	638	nook	11
384	kind	19	481	children	15	551	sent	13	638	pair	11
384	know	19	481	door	15	551	shades	13	638	passing	11
384	memory	19	481	dreams	15	551	shepherd	13	638	people	11
384	passions	19	481	half	15	551	sights	13	638	poet's	11
384	pride	19	481	infant	15	551	simplicity	13	638	poets	11
384	put	19	481	knew	15	551	since	13	638	proud	11
384	rocks	19	481	large	15	551	smooth	13	638	real	11
384	season	19	481	later	15	551	sought	13	638	rear'd	11
384	shapes	19	481	liv'd	15	551	spectacle	13	638	record	11
384	sleep	19	481	melancholy	15	551	steady	13	638	rights	11
384	spread	19	481	mood	15	551	story	13	638	roads	11
384	unknown	19	481	moral	15	551	sublime	13	638	rural	11
400	another	18	481	motion	15	551	tell	13	638	seems	11
400	cannot	18	481	neither	15	551	three	13	638	shew	11
400	comes	18	481	shame	15	551	touch'd	13	638	sides	11
400	divine	18	481	spot	15	557	water	13	638	society	11
400	dream	18	481	thing	15	596	affections	12	638	stir	11
400	false	18	481	thousand	15	596	alike	12	638	stir'd	11
400	feelings	18	481	touch	15	596	already	12	638	streets	11
400	France	18	481	traveller	15	596	amid	12	638	surely	11
400	free	18	481	tree	15	596	beloved	12	638	tears	11
400	hear	18	481	under	15	596	breathe	12	638	thine	11
400	just	18	506	arms	14	596	bright	12	638	universe	11
400	moon	18	506	aught	14	596	crowd	12	638	Vaudracour	11
400	music	18	506	awful	14	596	custom	12	638	worth	11
400	native	18	506	beauteous	14	596	desire	12	638	zeal	11
400	pain	18	506	bring	14	596	didst	12	702	beat	10
400	return'd	18	506	done	14	596	everywhere	12	702	beautiful	10
400	road	18	506	elements	14	596	fast	12	702	become	10
400	whether	18	506	evil	14	596	fresh	12	702	bed	10
400	wrought	18	506	faculties	14	596	grief	12	702	born	10
419	abroad	17	506	fell	14	596	held	12	702	breath	10
419	against	17	506	further	14	596	hung	12	702	breeze	10
419	began	17	506	gift	14	596	influence	12	702	choice	10
419	birds	17	506	glorious	14	596	inner	12	702	dawn	10
419	birth	17	506	haply	14	596	Julia	12	702	deeply	10
419	chiefly	17	506	hard	14	596	law	12	702	does	10
419	dead	17	506	has	14	596	leave	12	702	domestic	10
419	death	17	506	hearts	14	596	maid	12	702	events	10
419	fancy	17	506	hill	14	596	month	12	702	family	10
419	field	17	506	hold	14	596	oftentimes	12	702	fill'd	10
419	father's	17	506	innocent	14	596	poor	12	702	fit	10
419	flowers	17	506	invisible	14	596	private	12	702	forward	10
419	help	17	506	island	14	596	return	12	702	freedom	10
419	higher	17	506	language	14	596	scenes	12	702	gay	10
419	images	17	506	lonely	14	596	school	12	702	grandeur	10
419	indeed	17	506	mankind	14	596	seldom	12	702	growth	10
419	labour	17	506	moment	14	596	souls	12	702	hast	10
419	pleas'd	17	506	mov'd	14	596	sympathy	12	702	height	10
419	pleasant	17	506	names	14	596	tenderness	12	702	hitherto	10
419	region	17	506	prospect	14	596	thither	12	702	longer	10
419	rock	17	506	rather	14	596	universal	12	702	looking	10
419	shape	17	506	reach	14	596	vast	12	702	loves	10
419	simple	17	506	scatter'd	14	596	weak	12	702	madness	10
419	sounds	17	506	self	14	596	weary	12	702	man's	10
419	stand	17	506	service	14	596	welcome	12	702	master	10
419	step	17	506	skill	14	596	winter	12	702	midst	10
419	steps	17	506	spring	14	596	wood	12	702	months	10
419	tale	17	506	stars	14	638	'mid	11	702	motions	10
419	walk	17	506	storm	14	638	band	11	702	nations	10
419	waters	17	506	until	14	638	between	11	702	neighbourhood	10
419	wish	17	506	vulgar	14	638	blind	11	702	noble	10
419	word	17	506	want	14	638	book	11	702	noise	10
451	abode	16	506	weight	14	638	bound	11	702	personal	10
451	babe	16	506	why	14	638	breast	11	702	pleased	10
451	chance	16	506	wide	14	638	charm	11	702	pleasures	10
451	childhood	16	506	youthful	14	638	close	11	702	pomp	10
451	cottage	16	551	body	13	638	countenance	11	702	remembrances	10
451	darkness	16	551	business	13	638	country	11	702	seeing	10
451	gave	16	551	busy	13	638	creatures	11	702	sees	10
451	grace	16	551	colours	13	638	deeper	11	702	shade	10
451	guide	16	551	crags	13	638	delightful	11	702	shore	10
451	history	16	551	creature	13	638	distance	11	702	sit	10
451	imagination	16	551	dark	13	638	ears	11	702	steep	10
451	individual	16	551	dignity	13	638	endless	11	702	strange	10

Wordsworth's Vocabulary in *The Prelude*

702	strife	10	770	uneasy	9	938	asleep	7	938	sentiments	7
702	tales	10	770	used	9	938	authority	7	938	sequester'd	7
702	task	10	770	valley	9	938	awe	7	938	shadow	7
702	taught	10	770	vice	9	938	banks	7	938	shepherds	7
702	ten	10	770	walk'd	9	938	bard	7	938	show	7
702	theirs	10	770	watch'd	9	938	begun	7	938	sick	7
702	toil	10	770	weakness	9	938	bent	7	938	sister	7
702	turf	10	770	whatever	9	938	betwixt	7	938	solemn	7
702	underneath	10	770	wise	9	938	bliss	7	938	son	7
702	utter	10	770	wish'd	9	938	blood	7	938	sort	7
702	village	10	857	absolute	8	938	boat	7	938	spake	7
702	walls	10	857	bore	8	938	brain	7	938	speech	7
702	wanting	10	857	bosom	8	938	breath'd	7	938	spite	7
702	waste	10	857	break	8	938	broad	7	938	staff	7
702	watch	10	857	brother	8	938	chanced	7	938	star	7
702	ways	10	857	build	8	938	church	7	938	stately	7
702	woman	10	857	built	8	938	circumstance	7	938	station	7
702	worthy	10	857	character	8	938	complete	7	938	store	7
702	written	10	857	chief	8	938	cross	7	938	substance	7
770	accidents	9	857	chosen	8	938	cut	7	938	substantial	7
770	alive	9	857	clear	8	938	danger	7	938	suffering	7
770	argument	9	857	coming	8	938	dearest	7	938	summon'd	7
770	bare	9	857	confidence	8	938	degree	7	938	sustain'd	7
770	blessed	9	857	conscious	8	938	delicate	7	938	throughout	7
770	brook	9	857	dance	8	938	desart	7	938	tongue	7
770	cares	9	857	discipline	8	938	died	7	938	tumult	7
770	carried	9	857	doubt	8	938	dim	7	938	utter'd	7
770	cross'd	9	857	easily	8	938	distress	7	938	vital	7
770	dame	9	857	effect	8	938	dog	7	938	wealth	7
770	delights	9	857	elsewhere	8	938	doors	7	938	whatsoever	7
770	depth	9	857	ends	8	938	ear	7	938	willingly	7
770	desires	9	857	enduring	8	938	empty	7	938	wrong	7
770	eager	9	857	external	8	938	endure	7	938	yellow	7
770	either	9	857	exultation	8	938	entire	7	1072	academic	6
770	familiar	9	857	famous	8	938	errand	7	1072	across	6
770	fed	9	857	fate	8	938	fail'd	7	1072	act	6
770	feet	9	857	finds	8	938	fallen	7	1072	advanced	6
770	foot	9	857	flower	8	938	female	7	1072	ah	6
770	force	9	857	forget	8	938	flow'd	7	1072	aim	6
770	forgotten	9	857	gratitude	8	938	follow	7	1072	aloud	6
770	frequent	9	857	grew	8	938	fond	7	1072	Alps	6
770	friends	9	857	grove	8	938	former	7	1072	ambition	6
770	future	9	857	heavens	8	938	fountain	7	1072	appears	6
770	gain'd	9	857	hundred	8	938	gently	7	1072	approach	6
770	general	9	857	independent	8	938	glittering	7	1072	arm	6
770	genuine	9	857	knows	8	938	gloomy	7	1072	audible	6
770	glad	9	857	league	8	938	going	7	1072	autumn	6
770	gleams	9	857	line	8	938	haunts	7	1072	awhile	6
770	growing	9	857	lord	8	938	health	7	1072	bear	6
770	habit	9	857	loved	8	938	heat	7	1072	begin	6
770	habits	9	857	moments	8	938	heavy	7	1072	beginning	6
770	hands	9	857	narrow	8	938	honor'd	7	1072	belief	6
770	heretofore	9	857	notice	8	938	honours	7	1072	beside	6
770	ill	9	857	office	8	938	ignorance	7	1072	bewilder'd	6
770	intellect	9	857	otherwise	8	938	inn	7	1072	bird	6
770	intellectual	9	857	ours	8	938	intent	7	1072	blame	6
770	intense	9	857	pains	8	938	internal	7	1072	blessing	6
770	keen	9	857	paradise	8	938	lastly	7	1072	blow	6
770	knowing	9	857	portion	8	938	level	7	1072	blowing	6
770	late	9	857	possess'd	8	938	lightly	7	1072	blue	6
770	leads	9	857	praise	8	938	listening	7	1072	board	6
770	leaves	9	857	prime	8	938	lived	7	1072	bowers	6
770	lovely	9	857	promises	8	938	lives	7	1072	bred	6
770	making	9	857	remember	8	938	lock'd	7	1072	brooks	6
770	matter	9	857	repose	8	938	London	7	1072	certain	6
770	mother	9	857	returning	8	938	main	7	1072	chang'd	6
770	moving	9	857	sake	8	938	majestic	7	1072	characters	6
770	nay	9	857	several	8	938	mild	7	1072	charge	6
770	ones	9	857	slow	8	938	murmuring	7	1072	cloud	6
770	ourselves	9	857	social	8	938	needful	7	1072	comfort	6
770	path	9	857	sown	8	938	nights	7	1072	composed	6
770	pause	9	857	St.	8	938	obscure	7	1072	composure	6
770	poet	9	857	stage	8	938	opposition	7	1072	content	6
770	privilege	9	857	standing	8	938	ordinary	7	1072	crag	6
770	pursued	9	857	stopp'd	8	938	ought	7	1072	creative	6
770	receive	9	857	street	8	938	palace	7	1072	deal	6
770	remain'd	9	857	suffer'd	8	938	parted	7	1072	deem	6
770	rivers	9	857	sure	8	938	parts	7	1072	deepest	6
770	seasons	9	857	sympathies	8	938	pastoral	7	1072	din	6
770	seat	9	857	temper	8	938	play'd	7	1072	discourse	6
770	seek	9	857	terror	8	938	produce	7	1072	domain	6
770	shining	9	857	tranquil	8	938	punctual	7	1072	doubtless	6
770	slowly	9	857	tread	8	938	quest	7	1072	dreary	6
770	soft	9	857	truths	8	938	rain	7	1072	dwell	6
770	solid	9	857	understood	8	938	ran	7	1072	earliest	6
770	solitary	9	857	unhappy	8	938	received	7	1072	east	6
770	speaking	9	857	visitant	8	938	regard	7	1072	element	6
770	spirits	9	857	war	8	938	remain	7	1072	eminence	6
770	spots	9	857	withal	8	938	reverence	7	1072	empire	6
770	stranger	9	857	won	8	938	rocky	7	1072	employ'd	6
770	streams	9	857	worst	8	938	roof	7	1072	England	6
770	taken	9	938	absence	7	938	safe	7	1072	enter	6
770	throng	9	938	admiration	7	938	sands	7	1072	erelong	6
770	top	9	938	ages	7	938	save	7	1072	error	6
770	track	9	938	alas	7	938	search	7	1072	excess	6
770	travelling	9	938	ascending	7	938	seeking	7	1072	exercise	6

Appendix 173

1072	experience	6	1072	sitting	6	1268	dwelling	5	1268	nest	5
1072	fail	6	1072	slender	6	1268	eagerly	5	1268	nevertheless	5
1072	falls	6	1072	slept	6	1268	eagerness	5	1268	none	5
1072	fancied	6	1072	sober	6	1268	easy	5	1268	nowhere	5
1072	fix'd	6	1072	stillness	6	1268	elaborate	5	1268	numerous	5
1072	flight	6	1072	storms	6	1268	ended	5	1268	opposite	5
1072	follow'd	6	1072	summit	6	1268	ensued	5	1268	oppression	5
1072	forest	6	1072	summons	6	1268	erewhile	5	1268	order	5
1072	forlorn	6	1072	sway	6	1268	everything	5	1268	other's	5
1072	fram'd	6	1072	talk	6	1268	exists	5	1268	page	5
1072	garden	6	1072	taper	6	1268	faculty	5	1268	pageant	5
1072	gardens	6	1072	teach	6	1268	fairy	5	1268	patriot	5
1072	genial	6	1072	therefore	6	1268	falsely	5	1268	peaceful	5
1072	gifts	6	1072	thyself	6	1268	fame	5	1268	perform	5
1072	gladsome	6	1072	tide	6	1268	familiarly	5	1268	perform'd	5
1072	go	6	1072	transitory	6	1268	fancies	5	1268	perish'd	5
1072	government	6	1072	travel	6	1268	fears	5	1268	permanent	5
1072	grand	6	1072	travellers	6	1268	feed	5	1268	perplex'd	5
1072	greatness	6	1072	trial	6	1268	finally	5	1268	pile	5
1072	guilt	6	1072	turns	6	1268	fire	5	1268	plains	5
1072	heights	6	1072	understanding	6	1268	fits	5	1268	prison	5
1072	Helvellyn	6	1072	upwards	6	1268	five	5	1268	profound	5
1072	hidden	6	1072	vales	6	1268	flash	5	1268	prompt	5
1072	homely	6	1072	visionary	6	1268	folly	5	1268	pursuits	5
1072	horse	6	1072	wall	6	1268	forests	5	1268	reading	5
1072	host	6	1072	wandering	6	1268	forgot	5	1268	remembrance	5
1072	impulse	6	1072	wanderings	6	1268	frequently	5	1268	renew'd	5
1072	interchange	6	1072	wasted	6	1268	fruit	5	1268	report	5
1072	judge	6	1072	watchful	6	1268	functions	5	1268	reproof	5
1072	judgment	6	1072	wear	6	1268	garb	5	1268	restored	5
1072	judgments	6	1072	week	6	1268	garments	5	1268	roam'd	5
1072	king	6	1072	wholly	6	1268	gather	5	1268	Robespierre	5
1072	lakes	6	1072	wilt	6	1268	gather'd	5	1268	rough	5
1072	lodg'd	6	1072	wonder	6	1268	gaudy	5	1268	rouz'd	5
1072	lonesome	6	1072	wore	6	1268	genius	5	1268	run	5
1072	lover	6	1072	working	6	1268	gentler	5	1268	sanction	5
1072	lurking	6	1072	yielded	6	1268	ghastly	5	1268	sanctity	5
1072	majesty	6	1268	abruptly	5	1268	girl	5	1268	science	5
1072	mansion	6	1268	action	5	1268	gold	5	1268	secondary	5
1072	meagre	6	1268	active	5	1268	gracious	5	1268	seeming	5
1072	measure	6	1268	airy	5	1268	grey	5	1268	senses	5
1072	meditations	6	1268	albeit	5	1268	griev'd	5	1268	sentiment	5
1072	meek	6	1268	although	5	1268	grow	5	1268	serve	5
1072	meet	6	1268	answer	5	1268	harmony	5	1268	shell	5
1072	merely	6	1268	appearances	5	1268	heads	5	1268	shelter'd	5
1072	midway	6	1268	Arab	5	1268	hearing	5	1268	shut	5
1072	mist	6	1268	around	5	1268	holds	5	1268	singled	5
1072	mockery	6	1268	attendant	5	1268	holiday	5	1268	soil	5
1072	modest	6	1268	bade	5	1268	hollow	5	1268	solitudes	5
1072	mortal	6	1268	became	5	1268	homeward	5	1268	somewhat	5
1072	mounted	6	1268	blank	5	1268	horizon	5	1268	sooner	5
1072	moved	6	1268	blessedness	5	1268	household	5	1268	speed	5
1072	multitude	6	1268	bodily	5	1268	humbler	5	1268	spoken	5
1072	mute	6	1268	bold	5	1268	humblest	5	1268	sport	5
1072	natures	6	1268	bond	5	1268	huts	5	1268	spreads	5
1072	next	6	1268	bounds	5	1268	imagery	5	1268	springs	5
1072	noon	6	1268	boys	5	1268	Indian	5	1268	square	5
1072	notions	6	1268	breezes	5	1268	indifference	5	1268	stormy	5
1072	opinions	6	1268	calling	5	1268	infancy	5	1268	strain	5
1072	outside	6	1268	captive	5	1268	instinct	5	1268	struck	5
1072	pace	6	1268	careless	5	1268	interests	5	1268	studious	5
1072	paramount	6	1268	cave	5	1268	joyous	5	1268	study	5
1072	parents	6	1268	cavern	5	1268	joys	5	1268	summer's	5
1072	places	6	1268	chace	5	1268	justice	5	1268	sundry	5
1072	play	6	1268	cheek	5	1268	kept	5	1268	sunshine	5
1072	prepared	6	1268	chuse	5	1268	knight	5	1268	support	5
1072	press'd	6	1268	cities	5	1268	lack	5	1268	surface	5
1072	purest	6	1268	college	5	1268	lady	5	1268	sweetly	5
1072	quietness	6	1268	command	5	1268	lapse	5	1268	table	5
1072	quit	6	1268	communion	5	1268	lead	5	1268	taking	5
1072	rais'd	6	1268	company	5	1268	learn	5	1268	tall	5
1072	range	6	1268	conducted	5	1268	life's	5	1268	theatre	5
1072	rapt	6	1268	contemplation	5	1268	lights	5	1268	thereby	5
1072	reach'd	6	1268	continued	5	1268	linger	5	1268	thick	5
1072	recess	6	1268	courts	5	1268	listen'd	5	1268	thinking	5
1072	regions	6	1268	cover'd	5	1268	lo	5	1268	threshold	5
1072	rejoiced	6	1268	cradle	5	1268	lodge	5	1268	thrown	5
1072	religious	6	1268	craft	5	1268	looked	5	1268	timely	5
1072	remote	6	1268	creed	5	1268	maids	5	1268	tired	5
1072	repair'd	6	1268	crowded	5	1268	manhood	5	1268	travell'd	5
1072	repeated	6	1268	crown	5	1268	marvellous	5	1268	trivial	5
1072	retired	6	1268	dangerous	5	1268	meadows	5	1268	twilight	5
1072	ring	6	1268	decay	5	1268	meditation	5	1268	uncertain	5
1072	roaring	6	1268	deed	5	1268	milder	5	1268	undisturb'd	5
1072	romance	6	1268	deeds	5	1268	miles	5	1268	untaught	5
1072	sang	6	1268	delicious	5	1268	mingled	5	1268	unworthy	5
1072	satisfied	6	1268	despair	5	1268	ministry	5	1268	uplifted	5
1072	second	6	1268	desperate	5	1268	minute	5	1268	upright	5
1072	self-same	6	1268	despite	5	1268	miserable	5	1268	uproar	5
1072	sensations	6	1268	dismal	5	1268	mock	5	1268	utterly	5
1072	setting	6	1268	drawn	5	1268	modesty	5	1268	vapours	5
1072	shady	6	1268	dread	5	1268	moods	5	1268	vengeance	5
1072	shap'd	6	1268	dress	5	1268	moonlight	5	1268	walked	5
1072	sheep	6	1268	due	5	1268	moves	5	1268	wander'd	5
1072	shock	6	1268	dusky	5	1268	named	5	1268	wanted	5
1072	shop	6	1268	duty	5	1268	nearer	5	1268	warm	5

174 Wordsworth's Vocabulary in *The Prelude*

1268	whate'er	5	1530	die	4	1530	iron	4	1530	regret	4
1268	white	5	1530	disappear	4	1530	issued	4	1530	regrets	4
1268	wider	5	1530	disappointment	4	1530	jealousy	4	1530	regular	4
1268	winding	5	1530	dismay	4	1530	Julia's	4	1530	relate	4
1268	wings	5	1530	distinct	4	1530	kings	4	1530	remember'd	4
1268	workings	5	1530	divided	4	1530	labouring	4	1530	remembering	4
1268	worse	5	1530	doing	4	1530	lain	4	1530	residence	4
1268	worship	5	1530	drink	4	1530	learning	4	1530	retain'd	4
1268	wretchedness	5	1530	drive	4	1530	letters	4	1530	retirement	4
1268	yield	5	1530	dull	4	1530	likewise	4	1530	rise	4
1268	youth's	5	1530	dumb	4	1530	lines	4	1530	rising	4
1530	accomplish'd	4	1530	dwelt	4	1530	link'd	4	1530	roam	4
1530	added	4	1530	earthly	4	1530	lively	4	1530	roar	4
1530	advance	4	1530	echoes	4	1530	local	4	1530	roll'd	4
1530	affecting	4	1530	edge	4	1530	lodged	4	1530	room	4
1530	afternoons	4	1530	effort	4	1530	logic	4	1530	roots	4
1530	aged	4	1530	emotion	4	1530	Loire	4	1530	rosy	4
1530	airs	4	1530	endowments	4	1530	lordly	4	1530	sadness	4
1530	akin	4	1530	enemy	4	1530	loss	4	1530	safety	4
1530	apart	4	1530	energy	4	1530	lot	4	1530	salutation	4
1530	appetites	4	1530	English	4	1530	lovers	4	1530	sank	4
1530	approach'd	4	1530	enlarged	4	1530	lower	4	1530	scheme	4
1530	array	4	1530	entering	4	1530	lowly	4	1530	schools	4
1530	arts	4	1530	esteem	4	1530	maiden	4	1530	secure	4
1530	aside	4	1530	evidence	4	1530	march	4	1530	selfish	4
1530	aspect	4	1530	exalt	4	1530	margin	4	1530	senseless	4
1530	attend	4	1530	exalted	4	1530	mark	4	1530	serv'd	4
1530	attended	4	1530	existence	4	1530	meaning	4	1530	severe	4
1530	baffled	4	1530	exquisitely	4	1530	meditative	4	1530	shadowy	4
1530	balance	4	1530	faithful	4	1530	mention	4	1530	shelter	4
1530	barren	4	1530	falling	4	1530	mention'd	4	1530	shepherd's	4
1530	base	4	1530	fare	4	1530	methought	4	1530	shield	4
1530	beacon	4	1530	fared	4	1530	military	4	1530	shores	4
1530	beasts	4	1530	fashion	4	1530	mimic	4	1530	shows	4
1530	beating	4	1530	favor'd	4	1530	mingling	4	1530	sleeps	4
1530	beds	4	1530	favorite	4	1530	misery	4	1530	slight	4
1530	bees	4	1530	feeble	4	1530	misled	4	1530	songs	4
1530	beings	4	1530	feeds	4	1530	mists	4	1530	southward	4
1530	believe	4	1530	feels	4	1530	multitudes	4	1530	sovereign	4
1530	bells	4	1530	fellowship	4	1530	mystery	4	1530	spectacles	4
1530	belong'd	4	1530	fervour	4	1530	nam'd	4	1530	spreading	4
1530	belov'd	4	1530	festival	4	1530	neglected	4	1530	sprung	4
1530	below	4	1530	fictions	4	1530	news	4	1530	stands	4
1530	bend	4	1530	firmly	4	1530	nine	4	1530	stern	4
1530	benign	4	1530	fix	4	1530	novelty	4	1530	stones	4
1530	beset	4	1530	floating	4	1530	nurse	4	1530	straggling	4
1530	black	4	1530	flocks	4	1530	obvious	4	1530	strains	4
1530	blasts	4	1530	foes	4	1530	occupations	4	1530	strangers	4
1530	bless'd	4	1530	forced	4	1530	ocean	4	1530	stretch	4
1530	borders	4	1530	foreign	4	1530	onward	4	1530	stretch'd	4
1530	bottom	4	1530	form'd	4	1530	open'd	4	1530	stronger	4
1530	boyish	4	1530	forthwith	4	1530	opening	4	1530	subtle	4
1530	breathing	4	1530	fortunate	4	1530	oppress'd	4	1530	sudden	4
1530	Britain	4	1530	four	4	1530	overthrow	4	1530	superficial	4
1530	brotherhood	4	1530	framed	4	1530	owed	4	1530	supplied	4
1530	brothers	4	1530	freight	4	1530	paint	4	1530	sweetness	4
1530	burst	4	1530	front	4	1530	pasture	4	1530	taste	4
1530	calmer	4	1530	frost	4	1530	pathways	4	1530	tells	4
1530	care	4	1530	function	4	1530	patient	4	1530	temple	4
1530	cast	4	1530	gathering	4	1530	peasant	4	1530	th'	4
1530	casual	4	1530	generous	4	1530	peculiar	4	1530	themes	4
1530	caught	4	1530	giants	4	1530	person	4	1530	thro'	4
1530	centre	4	1530	giddy	4	1530	persons	4	1530	throng'd	4
1530	chair	4	1530	giving	4	1530	philosophy	4	1530	tidings	4
1530	changed	4	1530	gleam	4	1530	picture	4	1530	toilsome	4
1530	chapel	4	1530	glimpse	4	1530	pictures	4	1530	torrents	4
1530	chear	4	1530	gloom	4	1530	placid	4	1530	touching	4
1530	chearful	4	1530	gorgeous	4	1530	plant	4	1530	towers	4
1530	child-like	4	1530	graves	4	1530	poesy	4	1530	towns	4
1530	circuit	4	1530	greatest	4	1530	poetic	4	1530	trace	4
1530	civil	4	1530	grown	4	1530	point	4	1530	tract	4
1530	compell'd	4	1530	hang	4	1530	pool	4	1530	tragic	4
1530	conceit	4	1530	harbour	4	1530	precious	4	1530	train'd	4
1530	concern	4	1530	hate	4	1530	press	4	1530	transient	4
1530	condition	4	1530	haunt	4	1530	principles	4	1530	transport	4
1530	confounded	4	1530	heartless	4	1530	prize	4	1530	treasure	4
1530	confusion	4	1530	helpers	4	1530	proceed	4	1530	triumph	4
1530	conspicuous	4	1530	holidays	4	1530	process	4	1530	triumphs	4
1530	controul	4	1530	honorable	4	1530	proof	4	1530	trod	4
1530	convent	4	1530	humanity	4	1530	province	4	1530	trouble	4
1530	cottages	4	1530	ice	4	1530	prowess	4	1530	trunk	4
1530	couch'd	4	1530	idleness	4	1530	purer	4	1530	turning	4
1530	crew	4	1530	idler	4	1530	purpose	4	1530	tutor'd	4
1530	crimes	4	1530	illustrious	4	1530	pursue	4	1530	twenty	4
1530	cruel	4	1530	immediately	4	1530	question	4	1530	twice	4
1530	darling	4	1530	immortal	4	1530	quick	4	1530	twofold	4
1530	day's	4	1530	imperfect	4	1530	quitted	4	1530	type	4
1530	dealt	4	1530	imperial	4	1530	radiance	4	1530	uncouth	4
1530	dejection	4	1530	importance	4	1530	rage	4	1530	unheard	4
1530	delighted	4	1530	indifferent	4	1530	rank	4	1530	unmov'd	4
1530	depress'd	4	1530	infirmity	4	1530	rapture	4	1530	unnatural	4
1530	destined	4	1530	innocence	4	1530	receives	4	1530	unthought	4
1530	destiny	4	1530	inscribed	4	1530	recess	4	1530	vague	4
1530	destitute	4	1530	insight	4	1530	recesses	4	1530	vanity	4
1530	devious	4	1530	intelligence	4	1530	recorded	4	1530	variegated	4
1530	devotion	4	1530	intimate	4	1530	regards	4	1530	venerable	4

Appendix

1530	vernal	4	1933	bringing	3	1933	enchantment	3	1933	impassion'd	3
1530	villages	4	1933	brink	3	1933	enflam'd	3	1933	impatient	3
1530	violence	4	1933	brood	3	1933	Englishmen	3	1933	impressions	3
1530	virtues	4	1933	building	3	1933	enjoyment	3	1933	inclination	3
1530	volume	4	1933	burthen	3	1933	enjoyments	3	1933	independence	3
1530	walking	4	1933	calmness	3	1933	ennobling	3	1933	indignation	3
1530	wanderer	4	1933	Cam	3	1933	enter'd	3	1933	indolence	3
1530	wantonness	4	1933	castle	3	1933	enthusiastic	3	1933	industrious	3
1530	weeks	4	1933	cataracts	3	1933	entirely	3	1933	industry	3
1530	weigh'd	4	1933	ceas'd	3	1933	errors	3	1933	inferior	3
1530	wert	4	1933	changes	3	1933	eternity	3	1933	infinite	3
1530	west	4	1933	channel	3	1933	evermore	3	1933	ingenuous	3
1530	whatsoe'er	4	1933	chastisement	3	1933	excessive	3	1933	inglorious	3
1530	wherever	4	1933	chear'd	3	1933	express'd	3	1933	inhabitants	3
1530	wife	4	1933	check'd	3	1933	exulting	3	1933	inmate	3
1530	wilderness	4	1933	chest	3	1933	faces	3	1933	insensibly	3
1530	willing	4	1933	chronicle	3	1933	farewell	3	1933	inspired	3
1530	willow	4	1933	circumstances	3	1933	farther	3	1933	instant	3
1530	wine	4	1933	clad	3	1933	fashion'd	3	1933	instantly	3
1530	wisdom	4	1933	clay	3	1933	favourite	3	1933	interest	3
1530	wiser	4	1933	clear'd	3	1933	fearless	3	1933	intervals	3
1530	wither	4	1933	clearer	3	1933	feast	3	1933	intricate	3
1530	wither'd	4	1933	cliff	3	1933	fellow	3	1933	inward	3
1530	witness	4	1933	cliffs	3	1933	fervent	3	1933	inwardly	3
1530	women	4	1933	clock	3	1933	festive	3	1933	islands	3
1530	wonders	4	1933	clouded	3	1933	fierce	3	1933	isle	3
1530	yes	4	1933	coaches	3	1933	figures	3	1933	journey'd	3
1530	yon	4	1933	coat	3	1933	files	3	1933	kindness	3
1530	yours	4	1933	cold	3	1933	firm	3	1933	labourers	3
1530	youths	4	1933	companion	3	1933	firmer	3	1933	ladies	3
1933	Abated	3	1933	compar'd	3	1933	fitted	3	1933	lamb	3
1933	abject	3	1933	concerns	3	1933	flashes	3	1933	lamps	3
1933	access	3	1933	confess	3	1933	flat	3	1933	landed	3
1933	acquaintances	3	1933	congregation	3	1933	fled	3	1933	lanes	3
1933	acting	3	1933	consciousness	3	1933	flew	3	1933	languidly	3
1933	acts	3	1933	consolation	3	1933	flowing	3	1933	largely	3
1933	adorn'd	3	1933	constrain'd	3	1933	followed	3	1933	lately	3
1933	afresh	3	1933	contempt	3	1933	following	3	1933	latter	3
1933	aid	3	1933	conversation	3	1933	foremost	3	1933	leaf	3
1933	aims	3	1933	country's	3	1933	forgive	3	1933	lean	3
1933	alien	3	1933	courage	3	1933	fortitude	3	1933	leap	3
1933	alliance	3	1933	court	3	1933	forwards	3	1933	learned	3
1933	always	3	1933	covert	3	1933	foundations	3	1933	leisure	3
1933	amain	3	1933	craggy	3	1933	fragrance	3	1933	lifeless	3
1933	ample	3	1933	craved	3	1933	frosty	3	1933	limits	3
1933	angels	3	1933	creeping	3	1933	fruits	3	1933	linger'd	3
1933	animal	3	1933	crying	3	1933	funds	3	1933	lingering	3
1933	anon	3	1933	daring	3	1933	gaiety	3	1933	lodging	3
1933	anxiety	3	1933	dazzled	3	1933	gain	3	1933	loftiest	3
1933	anxious	3	1933	decency	3	1933	games	3	1933	loth	3
1933	anything	3	1933	deem'd	3	1933	gentleness	3	1933	loyal	3
1933	appearance	3	1933	degrees	3	1933	gentlest	3	1933	lull'd	3
1933	Arabian	3	1933	deluge	3	1933	geometric	3	1933	mad	3
1933	arch	3	1933	delusion	3	1933	gladly	3	1933	magic	3
1933	ardent	3	1933	demand	3	1933	gladness	3	1933	magnificent	3
1933	area	3	1933	depths	3	1933	glanced	3	1933	maintain'd	3
1933	articulate	3	1933	Derwent	3	1933	gleaming	3	1933	mandate	3
1933	ascent	3	1933	descend	3	1933	glen	3	1933	manifest	3
1933	ask	3	1933	descending	3	1933	goodness	3	1933	mariner	3
1933	ask'd	3	1933	design	3	1933	gradually	3	1933	mass	3
1933	aspiration	3	1933	detain'd	3	1933	greatly	3	1933	matur'd	3
1933	assist	3	1933	devouring	3	1933	greeted	3	1933	mature	3
1933	attention	3	1933	dew	3	1933	greeting	3	1933	maturer	3
1933	attest	3	1933	difference	3	1933	greetings	3	1933	meanest	3
1933	babes	3	1933	difficult	3	1933	grieve	3	1933	measur'd	3
1933	bad	3	1933	diffus'd	3	1933	habitual	3	1933	melted	3
1933	balanced	3	1933	direct	3	1933	habitually	3	1933	memorial	3
1933	banners	3	1933	disgrace	3	1933	hail	3	1933	mere	3
1933	bark	3	1933	dismantled	3	1933	hail'd	3	1933	methinks	3
1933	basis	3	1933	dismiss'd	3	1933	happier	3	1933	metropolis	3
1933	basket	3	1933	dispers'd	3	1933	hardly	3	1933	mid	3
1933	bay	3	1933	dissolute	3	1933	harsh	3	1933	midnight	3
1933	beast	3	1933	distinctions	3	1933	hawthorn	3	1933	mile	3
1933	beats	3	1933	dost	3	1933	helper	3	1933	Milton	3
1933	because	3	1933	doubted	3	1933	henceforth	3	1933	mind's	3
1933	bedded	3	1933	doubting	3	1933	herein	3	1933	mirth	3
1933	begg'd	3	1933	downwards	3	1933	heroes	3	1933	mix'd	3
1933	beguile	3	1933	drawing	3	1933	hid	3	1933	modern	3
1933	beholds	3	1933	drew	3	1933	hinted	3	1933	moment's	3
1933	bell	3	1933	dromedary	3	1933	hither	3	1933	monument	3
1933	bending	3	1933	dropp'd	3	1933	honest	3	1933	monumental	3
1933	birthright	3	1933	dry	3	1933	honour'd	3	1933	moonshine	3
1933	blast	3	1933	duly	3	1933	hoofs	3	1933	moulder'd	3
1933	bless	3	1933	dust	3	1933	horn	3	1933	mouldering	3
1933	blessings	3	1933	dweller	3	1933	houses	3	1933	mouth	3
1933	blest	3	1933	earnest	3	1933	howsoe'er	3	1933	nameless	3
1933	blew	3	1933	easier	3	1933	hues	3	1933	needed	3
1933	blown	3	1933	eastern	3	1933	humble	3	1933	Negro	3
1933	boast	3	1933	eclipse	3	1933	humour	3	1933	neighbours	3
1933	boisterous	3	1933	elate	3	1933	hurrying	3	1933	never-ending	3
1933	boldly	3	1933	elegance	3	1933	husband	3	1933	new-born	3
1933	bondage	3	1933	elevated	3	1933	hut	3	1933	nice	3
1933	bonds	3	1933	eloquence	3	1933	ignorant	3	1933	nobler	3
1933	borne	3	1933	embodied	3	1933	imaginative	3	1933	nooks	3
1933	boughs	3	1933	emptiness	3	1933	immense	3	1933	notes	3
1933	breathless	3	1933	enchanting	3	1933	impair'd	3	1933	notices	3

175

Wordsworth's Vocabulary in *The Prelude*

1933	novel	3	1933	revelry	3	1933	tempest	3	2566	abstruse	2
1933	novelties	3	1933	reward	3	1933	test	3	2566	abyss	2
1933	o'erthrown	3	1933	ridge	3	1933	thanks	3	2566	accomplish	2
1933	oars	3	1933	rightly	3	1933	there's	3	2566	according	2
1933	obsequious	3	1933	rigorous	3	1933	thereafter	3	2566	accordingly	2
1933	observ'd	3	1933	rill	3	1933	third	3	2566	account	2
1933	occasion	3	1933	riper	3	1933	thirst	3	2566	actions	2
1933	offer'd	3	1933	risen	3	1933	threw	3	2566	actual	2
1933	oft-times	3	1933	Rome	3	1933	throned	3	2566	administer	2
1933	opinion	3	1933	royal	3	1933	thrust	3	2566	admonish'd	2
1933	opposed	3	1933	rule	3	1933	thundering	3	2566	advancing	2
1933	organs	3	1933	rules	3	1933	toils	3	2566	advocates	2
1933	origin	3	1933	Sabbath	3	1933	tone	3	2566	aerial	2
1933	ornaments	3	1933	sad	3	1933	tongues	3	2566	affinities	2
1933	overflowing	3	1933	safeguard	3	1933	tops	3	2566	afternoon	2
1933	overlook	3	1933	sail'd	3	1933	touches	3	2566	agency	2
1933	overlook'd	3	1933	sanctified	3	1933	tower	3	2566	agent	2
1933	overspread	3	1933	sand	3	1933	track'd	3	2566	agitated	2
1933	own'd	3	1933	saying	3	1933	train	3	2566	allied	2
1933	paid	3	1933	scale	3	1933	transcendent	3	2566	allowance	2
1933	painful	3	1933	scarce	3	1933	transferr'd	3	2566	allude	2
1933	palpable	3	1933	sceptre	3	1933	transformation	3	2566	aloft	2
1933	parent	3	1933	scorn	3	1933	transition	3	2566	Alpine	2
1933	partake	3	1933	secret	3	1933	treated	3	2566	amiss	2
1933	passage	3	1933	selfishness	3	1933	trifler	3	2566	ampler	2
1933	passionate	3	1933	send	3	1933	trite	3	2566	amplitude	2
1933	paths	3	1933	separation	3	1933	triumphant	3	2566	amusement	2
1933	patriotic	3	1933	sets	3	1933	unawares	3	2566	anger	2
1933	penn'd	3	1933	shake	3	1933	unfelt	3	2566	angry	2
1933	perchance	3	1933	shaken	3	1933	unity	3	2566	animation	2
1933	period	3	1933	shallow	3	1933	unkind	3	2566	annual	2
1933	perus'd	3	1933	shaped	3	1933	unpractis'd	3	2566	answers	2
1933	pervades	3	1933	share	3	1933	unripe	3	2566	antiquity	2
1933	petty	3	1933	shed	3	1933	unruly	3	2566	ape	2
1933	philosophic	3	1933	shew'd	3	1933	untouch'd	3	2566	appear	2
1933	phrase	3	1933	ship	3	1933	unwilling	3	2566	appertain'd	2
1933	piety	3	1933	shot	3	1933	unwillingly	3	2566	application	2
1933	pilgrim	3	1933	shower	3	1933	uphold	3	2566	approaching	2
1933	pillow	3	1933	shy	3	1933	use	3	2566	apt	2
1933	plac'd	3	1933	signs	3	1933	usurp'd	3	2566	aptly	2
1933	plaything	3	1933	sits	3	1933	utterance	3	2566	arbours	2
1933	pleasing	3	1933	slackening	3	1933	vagrant	3	2566	arguments	2
1933	plot	3	1933	slighted	3	1933	various	3	2566	arm'd	2
1933	pointed	3	1933	slipp'd	3	1933	veil	3	2566	Arras	2
1933	possession	3	1933	slope	3	1933	veins	3	2566	artificial	2
1933	pour'd	3	1933	smile	3	1933	verses	3	2566	ash	2
1933	poverty	3	1933	smitten	3	1933	vex'd	3	2566	ashamed	2
1933	praises	3	1933	snow	3	1933	vision	3	2566	assert	2
1933	prejudice	3	1933	snows	3	1933	visions	3	2566	associate	2
1933	preserv'd	3	1933	snow-white	3	1933	visitations	3	2566	associates	2
1933	prey	3	1933	societies	3	1933	visited	3	2566	assured	2
1933	principle	3	1933	soften'd	3	1933	visitings	3	2566	astonishment	2
1933	prisoner	3	1933	sole	3	1933	vouchsafed	3	2566	ate	2
1933	privacy	3	1933	sooth'd	3	1933	wait	3	2566	attach'd	2
1933	procession	3	1933	source	3	1933	wake	3	2566	attempt	2
1933	profusely	3	1933	spare	3	1933	waking	3	2566	attends	2
1933	promontory	3	1933	sparkling	3	1933	Wallace	3	2566	attire	2
1933	proper	3	1933	spectators	3	1933	wants	3	2566	authentic	2
1933	prophets	3	1933	speculations	3	1933	wares	3	2566	autumnal	2
1933	proportion	3	1933	splendour	3	1933	warrior	3	2566	awaits	2
1933	proportions	3	1933	sports	3	1933	waves	3	2566	bachelor	2
1933	props	3	1933	spring-time	3	1933	wedded	3	2566	backwards	2
1933	purified	3	1933	stamp	3	1933	weeds	3	2566	balmy	2
1933	purity	3	1933	start	3	1933	weep	3	2566	bank	2
1933	purposes	3	1933	station'd	3	1933	welfare	3	2566	barely	2
1933	pursu'd	3	1933	steadfast	3	1933	wept	3	2566	bars	2
1933	qualities	3	1933	steadiness	3	1933	where'er	3	2566	bask'd	2
1933	quality	3	1933	steal	3	1933	whereat	3	2566	bathing	2
1933	quarters	3	1933	steeds	3	1933	wherefore	3	2566	battle	2
1933	questions	3	1933	stripling	3	1933	whistling	3	2566	beach	2
1933	quickening	3	1933	stroke	3	1933	whither	3	2566	bearing	2
1933	rambling	3	1933	strongest	3	1933	widely	3	2566	bears	2
1933	rang'd	3	1933	student	3	1933	Windermere	3	2566	beaten	2
1933	ranged	3	1933	students	3	1933	window	3	2566	becomes	2
1933	ranging	3	1933	studies	3	1933	windows	3	2566	befel	2
1933	ready	3	1933	succeed	3	1933	winters	3	2566	beholding	2
1933	really	3	1933	suddenly	3	1933	withdrew	3	2566	believed	2
1933	reap	3	1933	suffice	3	1933	withstood	3	2566	belt	2
1933	receiv'd	3	1933	sufficient	3	1933	woes	3	2566	bench	2
1933	recompense	3	1933	suited	3	1933	worldly	3	2566	benediction	2
1933	rejoice	3	1933	summers	3	1933	worn	3	2566	benevolence	2
1933	remov'd	3	1933	summon	3	1933	worshippers	3	2566	bestow'd	2
1933	renown'd	3	1933	superior	3	1933	wretched	3	2566	betimes	2
1933	reproach	3	1933	suppos'd	3	1933	wrongs	3	2566	betook	2
1933	republic	3	1933	surviv'd	3	1933	yearnings	3	2566	bidding	2
1933	reserve	3	1933	swarm	3	1933	yielding	3	2566	bind	2
1933	resolve	3	1933	swarm'd	3	1933	yoked	3	2566	birthplace	2
1933	resounding	3	1933	sweetest	3	2566	'twixt	2	2566	bleak	2
1933	respect	3	1933	symbols	3	2566	'twould	2	2566	block	2
1933	rested	3	1933	takes	3	2566	abandon'd	2	2566	blows	2
1933	resting-place	3	1933	tasks	3	2566	abash'd	2	2566	bones	2
1933	restless	3	1933	teaching	3	2566	abiding-place	2	2566	boon	2
1933	restoration	3	1933	tear	3	2566	abodes	2	2566	Booths	2
1933	restraint	3	1933	tedious	3	2566	abrupt	2	2566	bourne	2
1933	rests	3	1933	temperate	3	2566	abstract	2	2566	bowels	2
1933	retrace	3	1933	tempers	3	2566	abstraction	2	2566	bower	2

Appendix

2566	branch	2	2566	contented	2	2566	doom'd	2	2566	feebler	2
2566	breaking	2	2566	contentedness	2	2566	dove	2	2566	feign'd	2
2566	breathes	2	2566	contest	2	2566	drank	2	2566	ferment	2
2566	breathings	2	2566	continue	2	2566	draw	2	2566	feverish	2
2566	brethren	2	2566	continuing	2	2566	dreaming	2	2566	fiction	2
2566	brief	2	2566	contracted	2	2566	drinking	2	2566	fiddle	2
2566	briefly	2	2566	conven'd	2	2566	driven	2	2566	fight	2
2566	brighter	2	2566	convers'd	2	2566	drooping	2	2566	fighting	2
2566	brings	2	2566	conversant	2	2566	drop	2	2566	figure	2
2566	broke	2	2566	converse	2	2566	drops	2	2566	filial	2
2566	brooding	2	2566	conviction	2	2566	dwarf	2	2566	final	2
2566	budding	2	2566	cool	2	2566	dwarfs	2	2566	fine	2
2566	buffoons	2	2566	cordial	2	2566	dwelling-place	2	2566	finer	2
2566	buried	2	2566	corner	2	2566	dwellings	2	2566	firmness	2
2566	Buttermere	2	2566	corners	2	2566	dwells	2	2566	fish	2
2566	cabinet	2	2566	corrected	2	2566	dwindle	2	2566	fishes	2
2566	cadence	2	2566	corresponding	2	2566	e'er	2	2566	flames	2
2566	called	2	2566	counsel	2	2566	earlier	2	2566	flash'd	2
2566	calls	2	2566	counterpart	2	2566	ease	2	2566	flattering	2
2566	calmly	2	2566	courteous	2	2566	ebb	2	2566	fleet	2
2566	canopy	2	2566	coves	2	2566	echo	2	2566	flow	2
2566	capable	2	2566	cravings	2	2566	edifice	2	2566	flowery	2
2566	capital	2	2566	craz'd	2	2566	education	2	2566	flute	2
2566	captivity	2	2566	create	2	2566	eight	2	2566	flying	2
2566	cards	2	2566	created	2	2566	eighty	2	2566	fog	2
2566	carelessly	2	2566	creates	2	2566	elevation	2	2566	follies	2
2566	carries	2	2566	creation	2	2566	elms	2	2566	follows	2
2566	catch	2	2566	creek	2	2566	emblem	2	2566	fondly	2
2566	causes	2	2566	cripple	2	2566	emboss'd	2	2566	fondness	2
2566	caverns	2	2566	crook	2	2566	employ	2	2566	foolish	2
2566	caves	2	2566	crossed	2	2566	employment	2	2566	foolishness	2
2566	Cervantes	2	2566	crude	2	2566	employments	2	2566	forbidding	2
2566	chain	2	2566	cull'd	2	2566	empyrean	2	2566	foresight	2
2566	chains	2	2566	cups	2	2566	enabled	2	2566	forgetful	2
2566	chamber	2	2566	cure	2	2566	enables	2	2566	formal	2
2566	chambers	2	2566	curious	2	2566	enchanter	2	2566	fortune	2
2566	chanc'd	2	2566	damp'd	2	2566	enclosure	2	2566	foster'd	2
2566	changeful	2	2566	danced	2	2566	encourag'd	2	2566	fought	2
2566	charm'd	2	2566	dances	2	2566	encouragement	2	2566	fragment	2
2566	Chartreuse	2	2566	dancing	2	2566	endear'd	2	2566	fraternal	2
2566	chasm	2	2566	dare	2	2566	endeavour'd	2	2566	freely	2
2566	chattering	2	2566	dared	2	2566	endeavours	2	2566	freeman	2
2566	chearfulness	2	2566	date	2	2566	endlessly	2	2566	Frenchman	2
2566	cheeks	2	2566	daughter	2	2566	Englishman	2	2566	fresher	2
2566	child's	2	2566	dawning	2	2566	engrafted	2	2566	freshness	2
2566	chivalry	2	2566	dazzling	2	2566	enmity	2	2566	friendly	2
2566	churches	2	2566	deaf	2	2566	enow	2	2566	friendship	2
2566	churchyard	2	2566	decay'd	2	2566	enrich'd	2	2566	friendships	2
2566	chuses	2	2566	deceived	2	2566	ensue	2	2566	fro	2
2566	circle	2	2566	dedicate	2	2566	ensuing	2	2566	froward	2
2566	circles	2	2566	defence	2	2566	enthusiast	2	2566	frugal	2
2566	circumambient	2	2566	degeneracy	2	2566	enticing	2	2566	full-form'd	2
2566	circumspection	2	2566	degradation	2	2566	entrance	2	2566	fulness	2
2566	city's	2	2566	deity	2	2566	entrusted	2	2566	furnish'd	2
2566	claims	2	2566	delay	2	2566	envied	2	2566	furthermore	2
2566	clamorous	2	2566	dells	2	2566	environ'd	2	2566	futurity	2
2566	cleave	2	2566	departed	2	2566	envy	2	2566	gains	2
2566	climb'd	2	2566	departure	2	2566	equal	2	2566	gait	2
2566	clime	2	2566	describe	2	2566	equipp'd	2	2566	gallant	2
2566	cloak	2	2566	described	2	2566	equity	2	2566	garlands	2
2566	cloisters	2	2566	descried	2	2566	erect	2	2566	gates	2
2566	clomb	2	2566	desertion	2	2566	erring	2	2566	gateways	2
2566	closely	2	2566	desolation	2	2566	errant	2	2566	gaz'd	2
2566	cloth'd	2	2566	detail	2	2566	escaped	2	2566	gesture	2
2566	Coleridge	2	2566	devis'd	2	2566	espied	2	2566	gestures	2
2566	collateral	2	2566	devoted	2	2566	espy	2	2566	ghost	2
2566	collaterally	2	2566	devour'd	2	2566	Esthwaite's	2	2566	giant	2
2566	colour	2	2566	dialogues	2	2566	estimate	2	2566	giant-killer	2
2566	combat	2	2566	diamonds	2	2566	eternal	2	2566	girls	2
2566	combatants	2	2566	differences	2	2566	Etna's	2	2566	glance	2
2566	comforts	2	2566	diffused	2	2566	eve	2	2566	glaring	2
2566	commerce	2	2566	diffusing	2	2566	evenings	2	2566	glasses	2
2566	commotion	2	2566	dimpling	2	2566	event	2	2566	glee	2
2566	commun'd	2	2566	dipp'd	2	2566	exact	2	2566	glided	2
2566	community	2	2566	directly	2	2566	excellence	2	2566	glides	2
2566	companions	2	2566	disastrous	2	2566	excellent	2	2566	glimmering	2
2566	compared	2	2566	disconsolate	2	2566	except	2	2566	glitter	2
2566	complacency	2	2566	discordant	2	2566	exclude	2	2566	glorified	2
2566	compos'd	2	2566	disease	2	2566	excursions	2	2566	goaded	2
2566	composition	2	2566	dislike	2	2566	exile	2	2566	god's	2
2566	comprehensive	2	2566	distinction	2	2566	expectation	2	2566	godhead	2
2566	comrade	2	2566	distinctly	2	2566	expected	2	2566	goes	2
2566	comrades	2	2566	distinguishable	2	2566	expressing	2	2566	goings-on	2
2566	conceal'd	2	2566	district	2	2566	exquisite	2	2566	gown	2
2566	conceits	2	2566	disturb'd	2	2566	extinguish'd	2	2566	gowns	2
2566	conception	2	2566	divers	2	2566	extrinsic	2	2566	graced	2
2566	conditions	2	2566	diversity	2	2566	eyelet	2	2566	graces	2
2566	confess'd	2	2566	divide	2	2566	fabric	2	2566	grasping	2
2566	connected	2	2566	divisions	2	2566	factions	2	2566	grateful	2
2566	consciousnesses	2	2566	doctor	2	2566	fails	2	2566	greater	2
2566	consent	2	2566	doctors	2	2566	faint	2	2566	greedy	2
2566	consolations	2	2566	doings	2	2566	faintly	2	2566	grey-hair'd	2
2566	constant	2	2566	dome	2	2566	fairest	2	2566	griefs	2
2566	constitute	2	2566	domination	2	2566	faithfully	2	2566	grieves	2
2566	consummation	2	2566	dominion	2	2566	falsehood	2	2566	groans	2
2566	contemplated	2	2566	doom	2	2566	feats	2	2566	gross	2

Wordsworth's Vocabulary in *The Prelude*

2566	grounds	2	2566	inquisition	2	2566	manifold	2	2566	outwardly	2
2566	grows	2	2566	insects	2	2566	manly	2	2566	overcast	2
2566	guardian	2	2566	inspiration	2	2566	manner	2	2566	overflow	2
2566	guess	2	2566	inspire	2	2566	mantle	2	2566	overhead	2
2566	guided	2	2566	instance	2	2566	mark'd	2	2566	paced	2
2566	guides	2	2566	instantaneous	2	2566	marks	2	2566	painted	2
2566	guile	2	2566	instinctively	2	2566	marriage	2	2566	pairs	2
2566	guise	2	2566	instincts	2	2566	Mary	2	2566	palaces	2
2566	habitation	2	2566	institutes	2	2566	Mary's	2	2566	pale	2
2566	habitations	2	2566	instruct	2	2566	matron	2	2566	palm	2
2566	hair	2	2566	instruments	2	2566	matters	2	2566	parade	2
2566	hall	2	2566	integrity	2	2566	matured	2	2566	Paris	2
2566	halted	2	2566	intended	2	2566	meanness	2	2566	participate	2
2566	handed	2	2566	interchang'd	2	2566	meantime	2	2566	particular	2
2566	hangs	2	2566	interference	2	2566	meditate	2	2566	partly	2
2566	happiest	2	2566	interfus'd	2	2566	mellower	2	2566	passages	2
2566	harbour'd	2	2566	intermediate	2	2566	melodious	2	2566	passes	2
2566	hardy	2	2566	intermingled	2	2566	melt	2	2566	passionately	2
2566	harm	2	2566	interrupted	2	2566	memorable	2	2566	pastime	2
2566	harmonious	2	2566	interspers'd	2	2566	microscopic	2	2566	pastures	2
2566	haste	2	2566	intervenient	2	2566	mien	2	2566	pathetic	2
2566	hasten	2	2566	intolerant	2	2566	minister	2	2566	pathless	2
2566	hat	2	2566	intuitive	2	2566	minstrel	2	2566	patience	2
2566	haunted	2	2566	inviolate	2	2566	minuter	2	2566	patrimony	2
2566	haunting	2	2566	invisibly	2	2566	mirror	2	2566	patron	2
2566	hawkers	2	2566	inviting	2	2566	miseries	2	2566	pay	2
2566	hazard	2	2566	irreverence	2	2566	misguided	2	2566	peaks	2
2566	hazel	2	2566	isles	2	2566	mishap	2	2566	pealing	2
2566	headlong	2	2566	issue	2	2566	mislead	2	2566	pen	2
2566	healthful	2	2566	Italian	2	2566	miss'd	2	2566	pencil	2
2566	heaven's	2	2566	itinerant	2	2566	mistakes	2	2566	pensive	2
2566	heeded	2	2566	ivy	2	2566	mistaking	2	2566	perceive	2
2566	heifer	2	2566	Jack	2	2566	mistrust	2	2566	perceived	2
2566	heighten	2	2566	jingling	2	2566	mitigate	2	2566	perennial	2
2566	hell	2	2566	jocund	2	2566	modes	2	2566	perforce	2
2566	help'd	2	2566	join	2	2566	mold	2	2566	perilous	2
2566	hereafter	2	2566	judgements	2	2566	monies	2	2566	perils	2
2566	hermit's	2	2566	judging	2	2566	monitory	2	2566	perish	2
2566	hermits	2	2566	justify	2	2566	monsters	2	2566	permit	2
2566	hero	2	2566	keep	2	2566	moon's	2	2566	permitted	2
2566	heroic	2	2566	king's	2	2566	moor	2	2566	perpetual	2
2566	high-way	2	2566	kite	2	2566	moors	2	2566	persuasion	2
2566	highways	2	2566	knee	2	2566	moreover	2	2566	peruse	2
2566	hindrance	2	2566	knights	2	2566	morn	2	2566	perusing	2
2566	hint	2	2566	knot	2	2566	motionless	2	2566	pervading	2
2566	historian's	2	2566	knots	2	2566	motley	2	2566	pestilence	2
2566	hoarded	2	2566	labourer	2	2566	moulds	2	2566	phantom	2
2566	hoary	2	2566	labyrinth	2	2566	mount	2	2566	phantoms	2
2566	holden	2	2566	ladder's	2	2566	mountain's	2	2566	philosophers	2
2566	holiest	2	2566	laden	2	2566	mountain-chapel	2	2566	phrases	2
2566	hollows	2	2566	lamentable	2	2566	movement	2	2566	picking	2
2566	homes	2	2566	lance	2	2566	murderer	2	2566	piled	2
2566	honey	2	2566	lands	2	2566	murmur	2	2566	pine	2
2566	horses	2	2566	landscape	2	2566	Muse's	2	2566	pining	2
2566	hot	2	2566	languish	2	2566	mused	2	2566	pinnace	2
2566	however	2	2566	lasting	2	2566	muses	2	2566	pinnacle	2
2566	hubbub	2	2566	lasts	2	2566	musing	2	2566	pious	2
2566	humbled	2	2566	laugh'd	2	2566	musings	2	2566	pipe	2
2566	humbleness	2	2566	laughter	2	2566	muttering	2	2566	pity	2
2566	humility	2	2566	lawyers	2	2566	mysteries	2	2566	placed	2
2566	hunt	2	2566	leafy	2	2566	naturally	2	2566	plainness	2
2566	hunters	2	2566	leapt	2	2566	ne'er	2	2566	plaintive	2
2566	hurried	2	2566	lend	2	2566	neck	2	2566	plan	2
2566	hush'd	2	2566	lengthen'd	2	2566	neighbour	2	2566	plans	2
2566	ideal	2	2566	lesser	2	2566	newly	2	2566	plastic	2
2566	idle	2	2566	letter	2	2566	Newton	2	2566	platform	2
2566	idly	2	2566	lifted	2	2566	nightshade	2	2566	playful	2
2566	idol	2	2566	lifts	2	2566	nobility	2	2566	playmates	2
2566	idolatry	2	2566	lighted	2	2566	noontide	2	2566	pleases	2
2566	ignoble	2	2566	lightsome	2	2566	northern	2	2566	pluck'd	2
2566	imaginations	2	2566	liking	2	2566	northward	2	2566	plumes	2
2566	imitative	2	2566	likings	2	2566	nought	2	2566	poem	2
2566	immediate	2	2566	limbs	2	2566	nurs'd	2	2566	pointing	2
2566	immured	2	2566	lineaments	2	2566	o'ercome	2	2566	poles	2
2566	impediments	2	2566	link	2	2566	oaths	2	2566	polity	2
2566	impell'd	2	2566	lion	2	2566	obedient	2	2566	ponderous	2
2566	imperishable	2	2566	lips	2	2566	obeisance	2	2566	pools	2
2566	impiety	2	2566	loathsome	2	2566	obscurely	2	2566	popular	2
2566	implements	2	2566	lock	2	2566	obscurity	2	2566	portions	2
2566	important	2	2566	loftier	2	2566	obstacles	2	2566	possible	2
2566	impress	2	2566	loneliness	2	2566	obstinate	2	2566	potent	2
2566	impress'd	2	2566	longing	2	2566	occupation	2	2566	pour	2
2566	incident	2	2566	losing	2	2566	occupied	2	2566	powerful	2
2566	incidents	2	2566	Louvet	2	2566	offering	2	2566	prattle	2
2566	incumbences	2	2566	loveliness	2	2566	officers	2	2566	pray'd	2
2566	inevitable	2	2566	loving	2	2566	omen	2	2566	prayer	2
2566	inexorable	2	2566	lowest	2	2566	openly	2	2566	prayers	2
2566	infantine	2	2566	lusty	2	2566	openness	2	2566	precincts	2
2566	infinity	2	2566	Magdalene	2	2566	oppose	2	2566	precipices	2
2566	inheritance	2	2566	magisterially	2	2566	orb	2	2566	predominant	2
2566	injuries	2	2566	mainly	2	2566	orchard	2	2566	pre-eminent	2
2566	injury	2	2566	maintain	2	2566	organ	2	2566	preparation	2
2566	inland	2	2566	maintains	2	2566	Orleans	2	2566	presences	2
2566	inly	2	2566	maintenance	2	2566	ornament	2	2566	preserve	2
2566	inquire	2	2566	male	2	2566	outlandish	2	2566	presumption	2
2566	inquiries	2	2566	manage	2	2566	outline	2	2566	pretty	2

Appendix

2566	prevails	2	2566	roofs	2	2566	sojourn	2	2566	tempestuous	2
2566	primitive	2	2566	rooms	2	2566	sojourner	2	2566	temples	2
2566	privileg'd	2	2566	rout	2	2566	solace	2	2566	tendency	2
2566	priz'd	2	2566	rouze	2	2566	soldier	2	2566	tenor	2
2566	prized	2	2566	rouzed	2	2566	solemnity	2	2566	tents	2
2566	proceeding	2	2566	rov'd	2	2566	somewhere	2	2566	term	2
2566	profitless	2	2566	roving	2	2566	soothed	2	2566	terms	2
2566	prolong'd	2	2566	row'd	2	2566	sorrows	2	2566	texture	2
2566	promised	2	2566	rudest	2	2566	sounding	2	2566	thank'd	2
2566	pronounced	2	2566	rueful	2	2566	southern	2	2566	therein	2
2566	propp'd	2	2566	ruled	2	2566	sovereignty	2	2566	thereto	2
2566	protracted	2	2566	rulers	2	2566	spacious	2	2566	thin	2
2566	prouder	2	2566	ruling	2	2566	spangled	2	2566	thinks	2
2566	proudly	2	2566	running	2	2566	spared	2	2566	thirsty	2
2566	prove	2	2566	runs	2	2566	speedily	2	2566	thoroughly	2
2566	proved	2	2566	rustic	2	2566	spells	2	2566	thoughtless	2
2566	providence	2	2566	rustling	2	2566	Spenser	2	2566	thrice	2
2566	pulse	2	2566	sacrificial	2	2566	spin	2	2566	thridded	2
2566	punishment	2	2566	sage	2	2566	spire	2	2566	throes	2
2566	pupil	2	2566	sallied	2	2566	spiritual	2	2566	throne	2
2566	pursues	2	2566	saluted	2	2566	splendid	2	2566	thronèd	2
2566	push'd	2	2566	samples	2	2566	split	2	2566	tied	2
2566	question'd	2	2566	sanctuary	2	2566	splitting	2	2566	tipp'd	2
2566	quicken'd	2	2566	sandy	2	2566	sprang	2	2566	titles	2
2566	quire	2	2566	saunter'd	2	2566	spun	2	2566	tombs	2
2566	radiant	2	2566	savage	2	2566	spur	2	2566	torrent	2
2566	rains	2	2566	scann'd	2	2566	spurn'd	2	2566	toss'd	2
2566	raised	2	2566	schemes	2	2566	stalls	2	2566	tossing	2
2566	random	2	2566	scholars	2	2566	star-light	2	2566	toy	2
2566	rang	2	2566	scholastic	2	2566	starry	2	2566	tracts	2
2566	rapid	2	2566	school-boy	2	2566	starting	2	2566	trade	2
2566	raptures	2	2566	schoolboys	2	2566	stature	2	2566	traffic	2
2566	rare	2	2566	school-day	2	2566	stay'd	2	2566	transmigrations	2
2566	rarely	2	2566	scream	2	2566	stead	2	2566	transported	2
2566	rarities	2	2566	security	2	2566	steed	2	2566	traveller's	2
2566	rational	2	2566	seduce	2	2566	stings	2	2566	traversed	2
2566	ravage	2	2566	sedulous	2	2566	stinted	2	2566	treachery	2
2566	raven's	2	2566	seed	2	2566	stirring	2	2566	treads	2
2566	raw	2	2566	seeks	2	2566	stolen	2	2566	treat	2
2566	realities	2	2566	seemeth	2	2566	stony	2	2566	trembling	2
2566	reality	2	2566	seemly	2	2566	stoop	2	2566	tremblings	2
2566	realms	2	2566	seiz'd	2	2566	stooping	2	2566	trials	2
2566	rear	2	2566	seize	2	2566	straggler	2	2566	tribes	2
2566	receiving	2	2566	selves	2	2566	strait	2	2566	tributary	2
2566	recognis'd	2	2566	senate	2	2566	straitway	2	2566	tried	2
2566	recognise	2	2566	sensibility	2	2566	stranger's	2	2566	triumphal	2
2566	recognize	2	2566	sensible	2	2566	stray	2	2566	trooping	2
2566	recollection	2	2566	sensitive	2	2566	stray'd	2	2566	troops	2
2566	recollections	2	2566	sensuous	2	2566	stride	2	2566	tropic	2
2566	recreant	2	2566	sentence	2	2566	striking	2	2566	truant	2
2566	red	2	2566	separate	2	2566	string	2	2566	trumpet	2
2566	redoubled	2	2566	serene	2	2566	struggled	2	2566	tunes	2
2566	redundant	2	2566	serious	2	2566	studiously	2	2566	turned	2
2566	reflected	2	2566	servitude	2	2566	stumping	2	2566	tutors	2
2566	refreshment	2	2566	settled	2	2566	subdued	2	2566	twins	2
2566	rejected	2	2566	settling	2	2566	subordinate	2	2566	tyrannic	2
2566	relating	2	2566	shakespear	2	2569	subservient	2	2566	tyranny	2
2566	relations	2	2566	shakespeare	2	2566	subtleties	2	2566	unapprehensive	2
2566	religiously	2	2566	shaking	2	2566	suburban	2	2566	unaw'd	2
2566	reluctant	2	2566	shameful	2	2566	suburbs	2	2566	unceremonious	2
2566	reluctantly	2	2566	shapeless	2	2566	success	2	2566	unchanged	2
2566	remained	2	2566	sharp	2	2566	sufferings	2	2566	uncheck'd	2
2566	remains	2	2566	ships	2	2566	suffers	2	2566	unconcerned	2
2566	remorse	2	2566	shipwreck	2	2566	suit	2	2566	unconscious	2
2566	remotest	2	2566	shocks	2	2566	suits	2	2566	understand	2
2566	rendezvous	2	2566	shone	2	2566	sum	2	2566	undetermin'd	2
2566	rent	2	2566	shook	2	2566	sunbeam	2	2566	undistinguishable	2
2566	reposing	2	2566	short-liv'd	2	2566	sunny	2	2566	unearth	2
2566	represent	2	2566	shout	2	2566	sunrise	2	2566	uneasiness	2
2566	request	2	2566	shouts	2	2566	sunset	2	2566	unfit	2
2566	required	2	2566	showers	2	2566	superhuman	2	2566	unfrequented	2
2566	requires	2	2566	shrunk	2	2566	suppose	2	2566	unintelligible	2
2566	research	2	2566	shunn'd	2	2566	supreme	2	2566	union	2
2566	reserv'd	2	2566	sickly	2	2566	surly	2	2566	united	2
2566	resign'd	2	2566	sickness	2	2566	surpassing	2	2566	unjust	2
2566	resting	2	2566	sign	2	2566	surprize	2	2566	unless	2
2566	result	2	2566	signal	2	2566	surrounded	2	2566	unmanageable	2
2566	retain	2	2566	silk	2	2566	survive	2	2566	unquiet	2
2566	retir'd	2	2566	silver	2	2566	suspended	2	2566	unrelenting	2
2566	retiring	2	2566	simply	2	2566	sustenance	2	2566	unreprov'd	2
2566	retreat	2	2566	singly	2	2566	swarming	2	2566	unruliness	2
2566	returns	2	2566	sings	2	2566	swellings	2	2566	unseen	2
2566	reveal'd	2	2566	sink	2	2566	swept	2	2566	unsettled	2
2566	revived	2	2566	six	2	2566	Swiss	2	2566	unsought	2
2566	revolv'd	2	2566	size	2	2566	sword	2	2566	unsubdu'd	2
2566	rhymes	2	2566	skiff	2	2566	swords	2	2566	unthinking	2
2566	richly	2	2566	skimm'd	2	2566	taint	2	2566	unthwarted	2
2566	ripen'd	2	2566	sleeping	2	2566	talk'd	2	2566	untired	2
2566	rites	2	2566	slip	2	2566	talking	2	2566	untold	2
2566	rock'd	2	2566	slips	2	2566	tarn'd	2	2566	unusual	2
2566	rod	2	2566	slow-moving	2	2566	Tartarian	2	2566	unvisited	2
2566	rode	2	2566	smart	2	2566	tax	2	2566	upheld	2
2566	rolling	2	2566	smil'd	2	2566	teacher	2	2566	uppermost	2
2566	Roman	2	2566	snapp'd	2	2566	teachers	2	2566	usages	2
2566	romantic	2	2566	snare	2	2566	team	2	2566	useless	2
2566	roofless	2	2566	softness	2	2566	telling	2	2566	usual	2

2566	utmost	2	3902	abstemiousness	1	3902	alms	1	3902	artless	1
2566	uttering	2	3902	abstractions	1	3902	altar	1	3902	ascend	1
2566	vacant	2	3902	abstracts	1	3902	alternate	1	3902	ascents	1
2566	vainly	2	3902	abstruser	1	3902	alternately	1	3902	ascertain	1
2566	valleys	2	3902	abundantly	1	3902	alternative	1	3902	ascribed	1
2566	vanish	2	3902	Abyssinian	1	3902	amass'd	1	3902	aspirations	1
2566	vanities	2	3902	accents	1	3902	ambiguously	1	3902	aspire	1
2566	vapour	2	3902	accepted	1	3902	ambitious	1	3902	aspires	1
2566	varied	2	3902	accidental	1	3902	ambitiously	1	3902	aspiring	1
2566	vault	2	3902	accompanied	1	3902	amends	1	3902	assemblage	1
2566	vehement	2	3902	accomplishment	1	3902	America	1	3902	assembled	1
2566	vent	2	3902	accord	1	3902	amity	1	3902	assembly	1
2566	verily	2	3902	accoutred	1	3902	amorous	1	3902	assembly-room	1
2566	verity	2	3902	accusation	1	3902	amphibious	1	3902	assiduous	1
2566	vessels	2	3902	accuse	1	3902	amplest	1	3902	assign'd	1
2566	vexing	2	3902	accustom'd	1	3902	amused	1	3902	assisted	1
2566	victory	2	3902	accustomed	1	3902	amusements	1	3902	assumed	1
2566	view'd	2	3902	ace	1	3902	analogies	1	3902	assumes	1
2566	viewless	2	3902	aching	1	3902	analogous	1	3902	assur'd	1
2566	views	2	3902	acknowledg'd	1	3902	analogy	1	3902	assurance	1
2566	vigorous	2	3902	acknowledge	1	3902	analyse	1	3902	assurances	1
2566	vigour	2	3902	acknowledgements	1	3902	analysis	1	3902	astir	1
2566	virgin	2	3902	acknowledging	1	3902	analytic	1	3902	astonish'd	1
2566	virtuous	2	3902	acorn	1	3902	anarchy	1	3902	astray	1
2566	visibly	2	3902	acquaintance	1	3902	anchor	1	3902	atchiev'd	1
2566	visitation	2	3902	acquisitions	1	3902	angel	1	3902	atchieves	1
2566	vivid	2	3902	activities	1	3902	Angelica	1	3902	atheist	1
2566	voices	2	3902	activity	1	3902	angelical	1	3902	athwart	1
2566	voluntary	2	3902	Adam	1	3902	angled	1	3902	atrocities	1
2566	vows	2	3902	adamantine	1	3902	animate	1	3902	attack	1
2566	wafted	2	3902	address'd	1	3902	animated	1	3902	attain'd	1
2566	waits	2	3902	adhere	1	3902	animates	1	3902	attaining	1
2566	wak'd	2	3902	adieu	1	3902	animating	1	3902	attemper'd	1
2566	wakeful	2	3902	admir'd	1	3902	announce	1	3902	attempts	1
2566	Wales	2	3902	admirals	1	3902	announced	1	3902	attendants	1
2566	wand	2	3902	admired	1	3902	annually	1	3902	attending	1
2566	wander	2	3902	admittance	1	3902	annull'd	1	3902	Attic	1
2566	warble	2	3902	admitted	1	3902	another's	1	3902	attir'd	1
2566	warbled	2	3902	admitting	1	3902	answer'd	1	3902	attracted	1
2566	warmth	2	3902	admonish	1	3902	antechapel	1	3902	attraction	1
2566	watching	2	3902	admonishment	1	3902	Anthony	1	3902	attractive	1
2566	watry	2	3902	admonishments	1	3902	antic	1	3902	attribute	1
2566	wave	2	3902	admonition	1	3902	antics	1	3902	attributes	1
2566	wearied	2	3902	admonitions	1	3902	Antiparos	1	3902	attun'd	1
2566	wearisome	2	3902	admonitory	1	3902	antiquarian's	1	3902	attuned	1
2566	weather	2	3902	adopted	1	3902	antique	1	3902	audibly	1
2566	welcomed	2	3902	adopts	1	3902	ant-like	1	3902	audience	1
2566	well-known	2	3902	adore	1	3902	anxiousness	1	3902	Augean	1
2566	western	2	3902	Adria's	1	3902	anywhere	1	3902	augment	1
2566	wet	2	3902	adroit	1	3902	apartments	1	3902	augmented	1
2566	whencesoever	2	3902	adulterate	1	3902	apathy	1	3902	augurs	1
2566	whene'er	2	3902	advanc'd	1	3902	apocalypse	1	3902	Aurora	1
2566	whenever	2	3902	advantage	1	3902	apology	1	3902	authorship	1
2566	wherein	2	3902	adventure	1	3902	apostacy	1	3902	auxiliar	1
2566	wherewith	2	3902	adventurer	1	3902	appanage	1	3902	auxiliars	1
2566	width	2	3902	adventurers	1	3902	apparition	1	3902	avail	1
2566	wilds	2	3902	adventures	1	3902	appeal	1	3902	avail'd	1
2566	wilful	2	3902	adverse	1	3902	appeared	1	3902	avenue	1
2566	wilfully	2	3902	advertisements	1	3902	appetite	1	3902	avenues	1
2566	windings	2	3902	advice	1	3902	apples	1	3902	avoid	1
2566	winning	2	3902	advocate	1	3902	applied	1	3902	avow	1
2566	wisest	2	3902	æstuary	1	3902	appointed	1	3902	aw'd	1
2566	wishes	2	3902	afar	1	3902	apprehend	1	3902	await	1
2566	wishing	2	3902	affairs	1	3902	apprehension	1	3902	awak'd	1
2566	wit	2	3902	affect	1	3902	apprehensive	1	3902	awake	1
2566	withdrawing	2	3902	affectingly	1	3902	apprise	1	3902	awaked	1
2566	witless	2	3902	affection	1	3902	approachable	1	3902	awaken'd	1
2566	wives	2	3902	affectionate	1	3902	appropriate	1	3902	awakening	1
2566	woe	2	3902	affliction	1	3902	aptest	1	3902	awed	1
2566	woeful	2	3902	afford	1	3902	Araby	1	3902	awry	1
2566	woodland	2	3902	afloat	1	3902	arbitrement	1	3902	azure	1
2566	woodman	2	3902	afraid	1	3902	arcades	1	3902	Babel	1
2566	woody	2	3902	after-meditation	1	3902	Arcadia	1	3902	Babel-like	1
2566	wooed	2	3902	agencies	1	3902	Arcadian	1	3902	Babylon	1
2566	worlds	2	3902	agents	1	3902	Archimedes	1	3902	backs	1
2566	wound	2	3902	aggravated	1	3902	arcs	1	3902	backward	1
2566	wrath	2	3902	agitation	1	3902	Arden	1	3902	badge	1
2566	yards	2	3902	agitations	1	3902	arduous	1	3902	badger	1
2566	yoke	2	3902	agony	1	3902	Arethuse	1	3902	baffling	1
3902	'mong	1	3902	aids	1	3902	Aristogiton	1	3902	bald	1
3902	'twere	1	3902	aim'd	1	3902	arm's	1	3902	ballad	1
3902	'twill	1	3902	aiming	1	3902	armed	1	3902	ballads	1
3902	abasement	1	3902	albinos	1	3902	armies	1	3902	ballad-singer	1
3902	abbey	1	3902	Alcairo	1	3902	armoury	1	3902	ballast	1
3902	abbot	1	3902	alder	1	3902	army	1	3902	banded	1
3902	Abel	1	3902	alder-fringed	1	3902	aromatic	1	3902	bandied	1
3902	abide	1	3902	alert	1	3902	arranged	1	3902	banishment	1
3902	abides	1	3902	alienation	1	3902	array'd	1	3902	bank'd	1
3902	abideth	1	3902	allegiance	1	3902	arrest	1	3902	bar	1
3902	ability	1	3902	allegoric	1	3902	arrive	1	3902	barbarian	1
3902	abolish'd	1	3902	alley	1	3902	arrived	1	3902	barbaric	1
3902	aboriginal	1	3902	allotted	1	3902	arrow's	1	3902	barking	1
3902	abound	1	3902	allow	1	3902	artful	1	3902	barrier	1
3902	Abraham	1	3902	alloy	1	3902	Arthur's	1	3902	barrows	1
3902	abridg'd	1	3902	allurement	1	3902	artificer	1	3902	barter	1
3902	absorb'd	1	3902	alluring	1	3902	artist	1	3902	Bartholomew	1

Appendix

3902	basest	1	3902	blots	1	3902	buy	1	3902	chase	1
3902	bastard	1	3902	blotted	1	3902	bye-spots	1	3902	chasten'd	1
3902	bastile	1	3902	blue-breech'd	1	3902	bye-tracts	1	3902	chastening	1
3902	batten'd	1	3902	blue-frosted	1	3902	cabin	1	3902	chat	1
3902	bawling	1	3902	blunt	1	3902	cabins	1	3902	Chaucer	1
3902	bays	1	3902	blushing	1	3902	cagèd	1	3902	chaunt	1
3902	bead	1	3902	boards	1	3902	Calais	1	3902	chaunted	1
3902	beads	1	3902	boats	1	3902	calamity	1	3902	chauntry	1
3902	beams	1	3902	bodied	1	3902	calendars	1	3902	cheap	1
3902	beard	1	3902	bodies	1	3902	call'st	1	3902	chearfully	1
3902	bearded	1	3902	boisterously	1	3902	Calvert	1	3902	chearing	1
3902	bearings	1	3902	bolder	1	3902	cam'st	1	3902	cherish	1
3902	beatings	1	3902	bolt	1	3902	Cambridge	1	3902	cherish'd	1
3902	beatitude	1	3902	bolted	1	3902	campaign	1	3902	cherishes	1
3902	Beaupuis	1	3902	bond-slave	1	3902	candidates	1	3902	cherry	1
3902	beautified	1	3902	bone	1	3902	cane	1	3902	chestnut	1
3902	becoming	1	3902	bonnet	1	3902	cannon	1	3902	child-bed	1
3902	Bedfords	1	3902	book-mindedness	1	3902	canon	1	3902	childless	1
3902	bedlam	1	3902	book-stalls	1	3902	canons	1	3902	chimney-nook	1
3902	bedlamites	1	3902	border	1	3902	canst	1	3902	China's	1
3902	Bedouin	1	3902	borrowing	1	3902	canvas-cover'd	1	3902	Chinese	1
3902	bedroom	1	3902	bosom'd	1	3902	cap	1	3902	chivalrous	1
3902	bee	1	3902	Bothnic	1	3902	capability	1	3902	chok'd	1
3902	beechen	1	3902	bottom'd	1	3902	capacious	1	3902	choristers	1
3902	befal	1	3902	bough	1	3902	capaciousness	1	3902	chose	1
3902	befit	1	3902	bounced	1	3902	capacity	1	3902	Christabel	1
3902	beg	1	3902	boundaries	1	3902	captivated	1	3902	Christian	1
3902	beggar	1	3902	bounded	1	3902	car	1	3902	Christmas-time	1
3902	beggars	1	3902	bounding	1	3902	car'd	1	3902	chronicles	1
3902	beginnings	1	3902	boundless	1	3902	caravan	1	3902	churlish	1
3902	begirt	1	3902	bounties	1	3902	card-tables	1	3902	circuitous	1
3902	begs	1	3902	bow'd	1	3902	carelessness	1	3902	circumfus'd	1
3902	beguiled	1	3902	bowl	1	3902	caress'd	1	3902	circumfuse	1
3902	behalf	1	3902	bowling-green	1	3902	caressing	1	3902	circumscribed	1
3902	belfry	1	3902	box'd	1	3902	caring	1	3902	cistern	1
3902	believing	1	3902	Boyle	1	3902	carnage	1	3902	civic	1
3902	belike	1	3902	Brabant	1	3902	carousel	1	3902	claim	1
3902	bellowing	1	3902	brace	1	3902	Carra	1	3902	clandestine	1
3902	belong	1	3902	branches	1	3902	carriage	1	3902	class	1
3902	belonging	1	3902	brave	1	3902	carry	1	3902	class-fellow	1
3902	beloved	1	3902	bravest	1	3902	carrying	1	3902	classic	1
3902	belying	1	3902	brawl	1	3902	Cartmell's	1	3902	claws	1
3902	beneficent	1	3902	brawls	1	3902	carve	1	3902	cleanse	1
3902	benefit	1	3902	brawny	1	3902	carved	1	3902	clearest	1
3902	benefits	1	3902	breach	1	3902	carving	1	3902	clear-shining	1
3902	benevolent	1	3902	breakfasts	1	3902	cascades	1	3902	climate	1
3902	benighted	1	3902	breasts	1	3902	case	1	3902	climbs	1
3902	benignant	1	3902	breathed	1	3902	casement	1	3902	climes	1
3902	benignity	1	3902	breathing-place	1	3902	casket	1	3902	clinging	1
3902	bequest	1	3902	breath-like	1	3902	Cassandra	1	3902	Clitumnus	1
3902	bereft	1	3902	breeds	1	3902	catacombs	1	3902	cloath'd	1
3902	beseem'd	1	3902	breezy	1	3902	catalogu'd	1	3902	clocks	1
3902	besides	1	3902	bribe	1	3902	catastrophe	1	3902	clock-work	1
3902	bespeak	1	3902	bridge	1	3902	caterpillars	1	3902	clog	1
3902	bestows	1	3902	bridged	1	3902	cattle	1	3902	cloistral	1
3902	bestud	1	3902	bridges	1	3902	caus'd	1	3902	closed	1
3902	bethinking	1	3902	bridle	1	3902	caused	1	3902	closelier	1
3902	Bethkelet's	1	3902	brighten	1	3902	causeway	1	3902	clothes	1
3902	betray	1	3902	bright-eyed	1	3902	caution	1	3902	clothing	1
3902	betray'd	1	3902	brightness	1	3902	cautious	1	3902	cloud-loving	1
3902	bewail	1	3902	brim	1	3902	cavaliers	1	3902	clove	1
3902	bewitch	1	3902	British	1	3902	cavities	1	3902	clowns	1
3902	Bible	1	3902	Briton	1	3902	cease	1	3902	clubs	1
3902	bids	1	3902	broadening	1	3902	ceaseless	1	3902	clumsy	1
3902	bigot	1	3902	broken	1	3902	celestial	1	3902	clung	1
3902	bigotry	1	3902	bronz'd	1	3902	cell	1	3902	cluster'd	1
3902	binds	1	3902	brook-side	1	3902	cells	1	3902	clusters	1
3902	biographic	1	3902	brothel	1	3902	centring	1	3902	coalesce	1
3902	birth-place	1	3902	brothers-water	1	3902	chaced	1	3902	coarse	1
3902	birth-right	1	3902	brow	1	3902	chafed	1	3902	coarser	1
3902	bishop	1	3902	brows	1	3902	chaffering	1	3902	coasted	1
3902	bitter	1	3902	brute	1	3902	chairs	1	3902	coasting	1
3902	bitterest	1	3902	Brutus	1	3902	chaise	1	3902	coasts	1
3902	bitterly	1	3902	bubbles	1	3902	chaises	1	3902	cock	1
3902	blackbird's	1	3902	Bucer	1	3902	chalk	1	3902	Cockermouth	1
3902	blades	1	3902	budding-time	1	3902	chamber-window	1	3902	coercing	1
3902	blameless	1	3902	buffoonery	1	3902	Chambord	1	3902	coffins	1
3902	Blanc	1	3902	builder	1	3902	chamois	1	3902	Coker's	1
3902	bland	1	3902	builders	1	3902	Chamouny	1	3902	collar'd	1
3902	blasphemy	1	3902	buildings	1	3902	champion	1	3902	collected	1
3902	blasted	1	3902	builds	1	3902	chance-comer	1	3902	collegiate	1
3902	blaz'd	1	3902	burden	1	3902	chancing	1	3902	collisions	1
3902	blaze	1	3902	burghers	1	3902	changing	1	3902	colloquies	1
3902	blazon	1	3902	Burgundy	1	3902	channels	1	3902	colour'd	1
3902	blazon'd	1	3902	burial-place	1	3902	chaos	1	3902	colouring	1
3902	bleat	1	3902	burning	1	3902	chaplet	1	3902	colt	1
3902	Blencathra's	1	3902	burnish'd	1	3902	charcoal	1	3902	comates	1
3902	blend	1	3902	burnished	1	3902	charg'd	1	3902	combination	1
3902	blended	1	3902	bursting	1	3902	chariots	1	3902	combinations	1
3902	blighted	1	3902	bursts	1	3902	charitable	1	3902	combine	1
3902	blithe	1	3902	bury	1	3902	charity	1	3902	combines	1
3902	Blois	1	3902	bush	1	3902	charms	1	3902	combs	1
3902	blood-red	1	3902	busier	1	3902	charnel-house	1	3902	comedy	1
3902	bloody	1	3902	bust	1	3902	charter	1	3902	comely	1
3902	bloom	1	3902	bustle	1	3902	chartered	1	3902	comers	1
3902	blossoms	1	3902	butterflies	1	3902	chas'd	1	3902	comfortless	1

Wordsworth's Vocabulary in *The Prelude*

3902	commanding	1	3902	contamination	1	3902	crudest	1	3902	denounced	1
3902	commendable	1	3902	contemplations	1	3902	crush'd	1	3902	dens	1
3902	commendation	1	3902	contemplative	1	3902	cry	1	3902	denunciation	1
3902	comments	1	3902	contents	1	3902	culling	1	3902	depart	1
3902	commingled	1	3902	contention	1	3902	culprits	1	3902	depended	1
3902	commiseration	1	3902	contentious	1	3902	culture	1	3902	dependency	1
3902	commission'd	1	3902	contents	1	3902	Cumberland	1	3902	depicted	1
3902	committed	1	3902	continence	1	3902	Cumbria's	1	3902	deprav'd	1
3902	commix'd	1	3902	continent	1	3902	cunning	1	3902	depravation	1
3902	commonly	1	3902	continu'd	1	3902	cur	1	3902	dereliction	1
3902	common-place	1	3902	continually	1	3902	curfew-time	1	3902	deriv'd	1
3902	commonplaces	1	3902	continues	1	3902	curling	1	3902	desarts	1
3902	commonwealth	1	3902	contrarieties	1	3902	current	1	3902	descended	1
3902	commotions	1	3902	contrast	1	3902	currents	1	3902	desert	1
3902	commune	1	3902	control'd	1	3902	cushion	1	3902	deserted	1
3902	communed	1	3902	conventicle	1	3902	custody	1	3902	deserv'd	1
3902	communing	1	3902	convention	1	3902	customs	1	3902	deserve	1
3902	Como	1	3902	conversed	1	3902	cyphers	1	3902	deserves	1
3902	Como's	1	3902	conversion	1	3902	cypress	1	3902	design'd	1
3902	companionless	1	3902	convey	1	3902	daffodils	1	3902	desir'd	1
3902	companionships	1	3902	convictions	1	3902	daisies	1	3902	desireable	1
3902	comparative	1	3902	convinced	1	3902	dales	1	3902	desolate	1
3902	comparing	1	3902	convocation	1	3902	damp	1	3902	desolated	1
3902	comparison	1	3902	convoked	1	3902	damps	1	3902	desperation	1
3902	compeer	1	3902	coombs	1	3902	danc'd	1	3902	despis'd	1
3902	compeers	1	3902	coop'd	1	3902	danger's	1	3902	despised	1
3902	complacently	1	3902	coppice	1	3902	dangle	1	3902	dependency	1
3902	complaint	1	3902	copse	1	3902	dangling	1	3902	despotic	1
3902	complex	1	3902	copying	1	3902	darker	1	3902	destroyer	1
3902	compose	1	3902	cord	1	3902	dark-eyed	1	3902	destruction	1
3902	comprehension	1	3902	Corin	1	3902	darkly	1	3902	detach'd	1
3902	comprehensiveness	1	3902	corn	1	3902	dart	1	3902	detached	1
3902	compunction	1	3902	coronal	1	3902	dash'd	1	3902	detain	1
3902	concave	1	3902	corporeal	1	3902	dashing	1	3902	detains	1
3902	conceal	1	3902	corps	1	3902	daunt	1	3902	detect	1
3902	conceited	1	3902	correction	1	3902	day-dream	1	3902	detects	1
3902	conceiv'd	1	3902	correspondence	1	3902	daylight	1	3902	determin'd	1
3902	concise	1	3902	corrupted	1	3902	day-light	1	3902	determined	1
3902	conclude	1	3902	cost	1	3902	day-spring	1	3902	devilish	1
3902	conclusions	1	3902	costly	1	3902	day-thoughts	1	3902	devout	1
3902	concourse	1	3902	cotes	1	3902	day-time	1	3902	devoutest	1
3902	concussions	1	3902	cottagers	1	3902	dazzle	1	3902	devoutly	1
3902	condemnation	1	3902	couching-time	1	3902	deadening	1	3902	dews	1
3902	condescension	1	3902	countenances	1	3902	deadly	1	3902	diadem	1
3902	conduct	1	3902	counteract	1	3902	deafen'd	1	3902	diagrams	1
3902	conductor	1	3902	countermarch'd	1	3902	dealing	1	3902	diamond	1
3902	confederate	1	3902	counterpoise	1	3902	deals	1	3902	dictates	1
3902	confederated	1	3902	counter-turns	1	3902	deans	1	3902	dictators	1
3902	confession	1	3902	counterview	1	3902	dearly	1	3902	diet	1
3902	confident	1	3902	counter-winds	1	3902	deathless	1	3902	differ'd	1
3902	confiding	1	3902	country-playhouse	1	3902	debarr'd	1	3902	differing	1
3902	confine	1	3902	coupled	1	3902	debase	1	3902	difficulty	1
3902	confined	1	3902	courageous	1	3902	debasement	1	3902	diffidence	1
3902	confirm'd	1	3902	cours'd	1	3902	debts	1	3902	diffusive	1
3902	confirmation	1	3902	courser	1	3902	decanters	1	3902	dignified	1
3902	confirmed	1	3902	courtesy	1	3902	decaying	1	3902	dilatory	1
3902	conflict	1	3902	courtiers	1	3902	deceit	1	3902	dimm'd	1
3902	conflicting	1	3902	courting	1	3902	deceive	1	3902	dimple	1
3902	conflicts	1	3902	cove	1	3902	decision	1	3902	dinners	1
3902	confluence	1	3902	covenant	1	3902	decisive	1	3902	Dion	1
3902	conform	1	3902	cover	1	3902	deck	1	3902	dire	1
3902	conformity	1	3902	covertly	1	3902	deck'd	1	3902	directing	1
3902	confronting	1	3902	coverts	1	3902	declared	1	3902	directions	1
3902	confusion-stricken	1	3902	coward	1	3902	declin'd	1	3902	disappear'd	1
3902	congenial	1	3902	cowardice	1	3902	declining	1	3902	disappearing	1
3902	congratulation	1	3902	cowardise	1	3902	decoration	1	3902	disappointed	1
3902	congregated	1	3902	coy	1	3902	decoy'd	1	3902	disapproved	1
3902	congregating	1	3902	crack	1	3902	dedicated	1	3902	disarm'd	1
3902	congress	1	3902	cradles	1	3902	deduced	1	3902	disasters	1
3902	conjectures	1	3902	craven's	1	3902	deep-dale	1	3902	disbelieving	1
3902	conjecturing	1	3902	craves	1	3902	deeps	1	3902	discharg'd	1
3902	conjured	1	3902	craving	1	3902	deer	1	3902	discomfiture	1
3902	conjurors	1	3902	crawl	1	3902	defeated	1	3902	discountenance	1
3902	connect	1	3902	cream	1	3902	defenceless	1	3902	discouraged	1
3902	connection	1	3902	creator	1	3902	defenders	1	3902	discover'd	1
3902	conning	1	3902	credit	1	3902	deferr'd	1	3902	discoveries	1
3902	conquer'd	1	3902	creeks	1	3902	definite	1	3902	discretion	1
3902	conqueror	1	3902	crept	1	3902	deformities	1	3902	discriminate	1
3902	conquerors	1	3902	crescent	1	3902	defrauded	1	3902	discursive	1
3902	conquest	1	3902	cressets	1	3902	defrauding	1	3902	disdain	1
3902	conscience	1	3902	crest	1	3902	dejected	1	3902	disguis'd	1
3902	consecrate	1	3902	crested	1	3902	Delecarlia's	1	3902	dish	1
3902	consecrated	1	3902	crests	1	3902	delegates	1	3902	disjoin'd	1
3902	consecrates	1	3902	crevices	1	3902	deliberate	1	3902	disjoining	1
3902	consequence	1	3902	cried	1	3902	delicacy	1	3902	disjointed	1
3902	consisted	1	3902	cries	1	3902	delirious	1	3902	disliking	1
3902	consistory	1	3902	criminal	1	3902	deliver'd	1	3902	dislocated	1
3902	consoled	1	3902	critic	1	3902	deliverer's	1	3902	dislodg'd	1
3902	consoling	1	3902	crocodiles	1	3902	deluded	1	3902	dismally	1
3902	consorted	1	3902	crocus	1	3902	delusions	1	3902	dismay'd	1
3902	consorting	1	3902	crosses	1	3902	demanded	1	3902	dismounting	1
3902	constancy	1	3902	cross-legg'd	1	3902	demanding	1	3902	disobedience	1
3902	constellations	1	3902	crouches	1	3902	demeanor	1	3902	disown'd	1
3902	constitution	1	3902	crow'd	1	3902	demure	1	3902	display	1
3902	consummate	1	3902	crowds	1	3902	den	1	3902	dispos'd	1
3902	contagious	1	3902	crucibles	1	3902	denied	1	3902	disposes	1

Appendix 183

3902	dispositions	1	3902	elbowing	1	3902	essay'd	1	3902	falsly	1
3902	disquiet	1	3902	elders	1	3902	essences	1	3902	faltering	1
3902	disquietude	1	3902	elder-tree	1	3902	essential	1	3902	famed	1
3902	dissolves	1	3902	eldest	1	3902	establish	1	3902	fan	1
3902	distinctness	1	3902	elegances	1	3902	establish'd	1	3902	fane	1
3902	distinguish'd	1	3902	elegy	1	3902	estate	1	3902	fann'd	1
3902	distracted	1	3902	elevate	1	3902	esteem'd	1	3902	farewells	1
3902	distraction	1	3902	elevating	1	3902	estimates	1	3902	far-fetch'd	1
3902	distress'd	1	3902	elfin	1	3902	etcetera	1	3902	farm	1
3902	districts	1	3902	eloquent	1	3902	etesian	1	3902	farms	1
3902	disturb	1	3902	emanations	1	3902	ethereal	1	3902	far-secluded	1
3902	disturbance	1	3902	emancipated	1	3902	etherial	1	3902	far-travell'd	1
3902	diurnal	1	3902	embalm'd	1	3902	Etna	1	3902	fascination	1
3902	dividually	1	3902	embark'd	1	3902	Euclid's	1	3902	fashioning	1
3902	divin'd	1	3902	emblazonry	1	3902	Eudemus	1	3902	fasten	1
3902	divined	1	3902	embody	1	3902	Europe	1	3902	fasten'd	1
3902	divinely	1	3902	embodying	1	3902	European	1	3902	fastening	1
3902	diviner	1	3902	embosom	1	3902	evangelist	1	3902	faster	1
3902	divinity	1	3902	embraced	1	3902	evangelists	1	3902	fastnesses	1
3902	divorced	1	3902	embracing	1	3902	eventide	1	3902	father'd	1
3902	dog-day	1	3902	emerging	1	3902	ever-flowing	1	3902	fatter	1
3902	dogs	1	3902	emigrants	1	3902	evergrowing	1	3902	favour'd	1
3902	domes	1	3902	Emont	1	3902	everlasting	1	3902	feast-days	1
3902	dons	1	3902	emotions	1	3902	ever-living	1	3902	feather'd	1
3902	dotards	1	3902	empedocles	1	3902	ever-varying	1	3902	features	1
3902	doubly	1	3902	emperor	1	3902	every-day	1	3902	federal	1
3902	doubts	1	3902	emphatically	1	3902	everyone	1	3902	feeding	1
3902	dovedale	1	3902	employs	1	3902	evil-minded	1	3902	feelingly	1
3902	dower	1	3902	emporium	1	3902	exactness	1	3902	fellow-beings	1
3902	down-bending	1	3902	empress	1	3902	exalts	1	3902	fellow-countrymen	1
3902	downs	1	3902	emptied	1	3902	examinations	1	3902	fellow-labourer	1
3902	downy	1	3902	emulation	1	3902	example	1	3902	fellows	1
3902	doze	1	3902	enable	1	3902	examples	1	3902	fellow-travellers	1
3902	dragging	1	3902	enclosures	1	3902	exceeding	1	3902	fells	1
3902	dramas	1	3902	encourager	1	3902	exchange	1	3902	fenc'd	1
3902	dramatic	1	3902	encreas'd	1	3902	excitation	1	3902	fenced	1
3902	drayman's	1	3902	encreased	1	3902	excite	1	3902	fermentation	1
3902	dreamer	1	3902	endeavour	1	3902	exclaim	1	3902	fern	1
3902	dreamers	1	3902	endeavoured	1	3902	exclusion	1	3902	ferryman	1
3902	dreamless	1	3902	endow'd	1	3902	exclusive	1	3902	fervently	1
3902	dreamt	1	3902	endowment	1	3902	exclusively	1	3902	festal	1
3902	dreariness	1	3902	endues	1	3902	excursion	1	3902	festivals	1
3902	drench'd	1	3902	endur'd	1	3902	excursively	1	3902	festoons	1
3902	dressing-gown	1	3902	endur'st	1	3902	excuse	1	3902	fetch	1
3902	dried	1	3902	endurance	1	3902	executions	1	3902	fetching	1
3902	drift	1	3902	endures	1	3902	exempt	1	3902	fetters	1
3902	drifted	1	3902	enemies	1	3902	exercised	1	3902	feuds	1
3902	drinks	1	3902	enflame	1	3902	exerts	1	3902	fever	1
3902	dripp'd	1	3902	enflamed	1	3902	exhalations	1	3902	field-ward	1
3902	dripping	1	3902	enfold	1	3902	exhausted	1	3902	fiercest	1
3902	drivellers	1	3902	enfranchis'd	1	3902	exhibited	1	3902	fiery	1
3902	drives	1	3902	engender'd	1	3902	exhibition	1	3902	fife	1
3902	drizzling	1	3902	engines	1	3902	exhibitions	1	3902	fifteen	1
3902	droop	1	3902	engraven	1	3902	exhortations	1	3902	fifth	1
3902	drove	1	3902	engross'd	1	3902	exist	1	3902	figuring	1
3902	drown'd	1	3902	engulph'd	1	3902	existed	1	3902	filch'd	1
3902	drowning	1	3902	enhanced	1	3902	existing	1	3902	fill	1
3902	Druids	1	3902	enjoy'd	1	3902	expanse	1	3902	filled	1
3902	dubious	1	3902	enmities	1	3902	expectancy	1	3902	filling	1
3902	dukes	1	3902	Enna	1	3902	expectations	1	3902	fills	1
3902	dulness	1	3902	ennobled	1	3902	expense	1	3902	finding	1
3902	dunces	1	3902	enormities	1	3902	experienc'd	1	3902	finely	1
3902	dupe	1	3902	enquiring	1	3902	experiments	1	3902	fingers	1
3902	dupes	1	3902	enshrine	1	3902	explain	1	3902	finish'd	1
3902	during	1	3902	ensigns	1	3902	explain'd	1	3902	fire-like	1
3902	duteous	1	3902	enslave	1	3902	expos'd	1	3902	fires	1
3902	dying	1	3902	ensu'd	1	3902	exposed	1	3902	fireside	1
3902	dynasty	1	3902	ensues	1	3902	express	1	3902	fireworks	1
3902	dythyrambic	1	3902	entail	1	3902	exterior	1	3902	firmament	1
3902	eagle	1	3902	entangle	1	3902	extraordinary	1	3902	firmest	1
3902	eagle's	1	3902	entangled	1	3902	extravagance	1	3902	first-born	1
3902	earth's	1	3902	enterprize	1	3902	extravagant	1	3902	firth	1
3902	earthquake	1	3902	entertain'd	1	3902	extremes	1	3902	fishermen	1
3902	earthquakes	1	3902	entertainments	1	3902	exultations	1	3902	fissures	1
3902	earthward	1	3902	enthrall'd	1	3902	exulted	1	3902	fitness	1
3902	eastward	1	3902	enthralment	1	3902	eyed	1	3902	fitting	1
3902	eat	1	3902	entomb'd	1	3902	eyesight	1	3902	fixed	1
3902	eating	1	3902	entrancement	1	3902	fabled	1	3902	fixedly	1
3902	ebbs	1	3902	entreated	1	3902	fabulous	1	3902	flagelet	1
3902	echoed	1	3902	entrust	1	3902	fact	1	3902	flagg'd	1
3902	eclips'd	1	3902	entwine	1	3902	factionists	1	3902	flame	1
3902	ecstasy	1	3902	environ	1	3902	facts	1	3902	flar'd	1
3902	eddy's	1	3902	enwrought	1	3902	fade	1	3902	flashing	1
3902	edged	1	3902	eolian	1	3902	faded	1	3902	flatter	1
3902	edges	1	3902	ephemeral	1	3902	fading	1	3902	flattered	1
3902	edict	1	3902	equality	1	3902	fainted	1	3902	flatteries	1
3902	edifices	1	3902	equally	1	3902	fainting	1	3902	fledged	1
3902	Edinburgh	1	3902	equestrians	1	3902	fairer	1	3902	fleecy	1
3902	effeminately	1	3902	equipages	1	3902	Fairfield's	1	3902	fleeting	1
3902	efficacious	1	3902	equipment	1	3902	fairies	1	3902	fleshly	1
3902	efforts	1	3902	Erasmus	1	3902	fairly	1	3902	flood	1
3902	effulgence	1	3902	ermined	1	3902	fairy's	1	3902	floor	1
3902	eglantine	1	3902	Erminia	1	3902	fallacious	1	3902	Florizel	1
3902	eight-days'	1	3902	err	1	3902	falling-off	1	3902	flourish'd	1
3902	elaborately	1	3902	escape	1	3902	false-seeming	1	3902	flourishing	1
3902	elbow	1	3902	escapes	1	3902	falsest	1	3902	flown	1

Wordsworth's Vocabulary in *The Prelude*

3902	fogs	1	3902	Gehol's	1	3902	greenland	1	3902	heap	1
3902	foil	1	3902	gems	1	3902	greets	1	3902	heap'd	1
3902	foil'd	1	3902	generations	1	3902	Greta	1	3902	heart's	1
3902	fold	1	3902	Genevieve	1	3902	grieved	1	3902	heart-bracing	1
3902	foliage	1	3902	genii	1	3902	grimace	1	3902	heart-depressing	1
3902	folios	1	3902	gentleman's	1	3902	grimacing	1	3902	heart-experience	1
3902	follower	1	3902	gentlemen	1	3902	grin	1	3902	hearth	1
3902	followers	1	3902	geometry	1	3902	grinds	1	3902	hearts'	1
3902	foot-bound	1	3902	George	1	3902	Grisdale	1	3902	heartsome	1
3902	footing	1	3902	gewgaw	1	3902	Grisdale's	1	3902	heart-stricken	1
3902	foraging	1	3902	ghostly	1	3902	groan'd	1	3902	heavenly	1
3902	forbade	1	3902	ghosts	1	3902	grooms	1	3902	heavier	1
3902	forbear	1	3902	giant-size	1	3902	grosser	1	3902	heaviest	1
3902	forbearance	1	3902	gibbet-mast	1	3902	grossest	1	3902	heaving	1
3902	forcibly	1	3902	gifted	1	3902	grossly	1	3902	hedge	1
3902	fords	1	3902	gigantic	1	3902	grotesque	1	3902	hedgehog	1
3902	fore	1	3902	gilded	1	3902	grots	1	3902	hedge-row	1
3902	forego	1	3902	gilding	1	3902	grotto	1	3902	hedges	1
3902	forehead	1	3902	girlish	1	3902	grunsel	1	3902	heedeth	1
3902	forerunners	1	3902	girt	1	3902	guard	1	3902	heeding	1
3902	foretasted	1	3902	giv'n	1	3902	guards	1	3902	heedless	1
3902	foretold	1	3902	giv'st	1	3902	guesses	1	3902	heels	1
3902	forgers	1	3902	giver	1	3902	guest	1	3902	heifer's	1
3902	forgets	1	3902	gladden'd	1	3902	guests	1	3902	heinous	1
3902	forgiven	1	3902	glade	1	3902	guildhall	1	3902	heirs	1
3902	forming	1	3902	glancing	1	3902	gulph	1	3902	hemisphere	1
3902	forsaken	1	3902	glare	1	3902	gushes	1	3902	hemm'd	1
3902	forsook	1	3902	glassed	1	3902	gust	1	3902	hen	1
3902	forsworn	1	3902	glassy	1	3902	Gustavus	1	3902	herbs	1
3902	forth-breathing	1	3902	gleam'd	1	3902	gusty	1	3902	Herculean	1
3902	fortunatus	1	3902	glean'd	1	3902	ha	1	3902	Hercynian	1
3902	fortune's	1	3902	glimpses	1	3902	habiliments	1	3902	herd	1
3902	foul	1	3902	glistens	1	3902	habitude	1	3902	herded	1
3902	foundation	1	3902	glister'd	1	3902	hackney	1	3902	herds	1
3902	founded	1	3902	glitter'd	1	3902	hair-breadth	1	3902	herdsman	1
3902	fountains	1	3902	globe	1	3902	half-absence	1	3902	hereby	1
3902	fountain-side	1	3902	Glocesters	1	3902	half-and-half	1	3902	hermitage	1
3902	fourteen	1	3902	gloomier	1	3902	half-frequented	1	3902	heron	1
3902	fowl	1	3902	gloried	1	3902	half-hour	1	3902	hers	1
3902	fowler's	1	3902	glorying	1	3902	half-hour's	1	3902	hewn	1
3902	fox	1	3902	gloss	1	3902	half-inch	1	3902	hides	1
3902	foxglove	1	3902	glossy	1	3902	half-infant	1	3902	hiding-places	1
3902	fractur'd	1	3902	glow-worm	1	3902	half-insensate	1	3902	hie	1
3902	fracture	1	3902	gluttony	1	3902	half-insight	1	3902	high-seated	1
3902	fractured	1	3902	goadings	1	3902	half-learn'd	1	3902	highway	1
3902	fragments	1	3902	goatherd	1	3902	half-mile	1	3902	high-wrought	1
3902	frail	1	3902	goat-herd	1	3902	half-possess'd	1	3902	hillocks	1
3902	frailties	1	3902	godhead's	1	3902	half-rural	1	3902	hill-top	1
3902	frames	1	3902	godlike	1	3902	half-shelter'd	1	3902	hill-tops	2
3902	Francis	1	3902	god-like	1	3902	half-sitting	1	3902	hindrances	1
3902	frank	1	3902	gods	1	3902	half-standing	1	3902	hinge	1
3902	frank-hearted	1	3902	goers	1	3902	half-yearly	1	3902	hiss'd	1
3902	frankly	1	3902	goggling	1	3902	half-years	1	3902	hissing	1
3902	fraught	1	3902	goings	1	3902	hallelujah	1	3902	hit	1
3902	fray	1	3902	gondolas	1	3902	halloos	1	3902	hoard	1
3902	freaks	1	3902	goodly	1	3902	hallow	1	3902	hobbled	1
3902	freer	1	3902	good-natured	1	3902	hallow'd	1	3902	hollowness	1
3902	Frenchmen	1	3902	Gorsas	1	3902	hallowed	1	3902	homage	1
3902	frequented	1	3902	Goslar	1	3902	hallowing	1	3902	homeless	1
3902	fret	1	3902	gossamer	1	3902	halls	1	3902	homeliness	1
3902	fretful	1	3902	gowned	1	3902	halting	1	3902	homely-featured	1
3902	friendlessness	1	3902	graceful	1	3902	halts	1	3902	homer	1
3902	fronted	1	3902	gracefully	1	3902	hamlets	1	3902	hoop	1
3902	frontier	1	3902	graciously	1	3902	handle	1	3902	hootings	1
3902	fronts	1	3902	graciousness	1	3902	handmaid	1	3902	horns	1
3902	froze	1	3902	gradation	1	3902	hap	1	3902	horseman	1
3902	fruitfulness	1	3902	gradations	1	3902	happen'd	1	3902	horsemanship	1
3902	fruitless	1	3902	gradual	1	3902	happily	1	3902	horsemen	1
3902	fuel	1	3902	grafted	1	3902	haranguers	1	3902	hose	1
3902	fugitive	1	3902	grain-tinctured	1	3902	harbinger	1	3902	hospitably	1
3902	fugitives	1	3902	grammars	1	3902	harbours	1	3902	hospital	1
3902	fulgent	1	3902	grandame	1	3902	harder	1	3902	hotel	1
3902	full-blown	1	3902	grandest	1	3902	hardihood	1	3902	hour's	1
3902	fumes	1	3902	grandsire's	1	3902	hardship	1	3902	hourly	1
3902	funereal	1	3902	grant	1	3902	hardships	1	3902	hours'	1
3902	furnace	1	3902	Granta's	1	3902	hare	1	3902	housekeeping	1
3902	Furness	1	3902	grapple	1	3902	harlequins	1	3902	houseless	1
3902	furtherance	1	3902	grappling	1	3902	Harmodius	1	3902	housewife	1
3902	galaxy	1	3902	grasp	1	3902	harmonising	1	3902	howe'er	1
3902	gale	1	3902	grasps	1	3902	harp	1	3902	howl'd	1
3902	gales	1	3902	grass-plot	1	3902	Harry	1	3902	howling	1
3902	Galesus	1	3902	grassy	1	3902	harvest	1	3902	howsoever	1
3902	gallantry	1	3902	gratify	1	3902	hastening	1	3902	huckster's	1
3902	gallery	1	3902	gratuitous	1	3902	hastily	1	3902	huddled	1
3902	gallop	1	3902	gratulant	1	3902	hater	1	3902	human-heartedness	1
3902	galloping	1	3902	gratulatest	1	3902	hatred	1	3902	humming	1
3902	game	1	3902	Gravedona	1	3902	hauntings	1	3902	humourists	1
3902	gaming-house	1	3902	graven	1	3902	haven	1	3902	humours	1
3902	Ganymede	1	3902	gravest	1	3902	hawker's	1	3902	hunger	1
3902	garden-gate	1	3902	gravitation	1	3902	haycock	1	3902	hunger-bitten	1
3902	garish	1	3902	gray	1	3902	hay-grounds	1	3902	hunger-press'd	1
3902	garland	1	3902	grazed	1	3902	hazards	1	3902	hungry	1
3902	garnish'd	1	3902	Grecian	1	3902	headlands	1	3902	hunted	1
3902	gawds	1	3902	Greece	1	3902	heady	1	3902	hunter-Indian	1
3902	gaze	1	3902	greedily	1	3902	healing	1	3902	Huntingdon	1
3902	gazed	1	3902	green-house	1	3902	healthy	1	3902	hurdy-gurdy	1

Appendix 185

3902	hurry	1	3902	inference	1	3902	irreconcilable	1	3902	lawless	1
3902	husbanded	1	3902	infernal	1	3902	irregular	1	3902	lawn	1
3902	hush	1	3902	infinitude	1	3902	irresistible	1	3902	lawns	1
3902	hymn	1	3902	influx	1	3902	irresolute	1	3902	lays	1
3902	hyperboles	1	3902	influxes	1	3902	Isaiah	1	3902	lazily	1
3902	icy	1	3902	informs	1	3902	islanded	1	3902	lazy	1
3902	idea	1	3902	infus'd	1	3902	issues	1	3902	Le Brun	1
3902	identity	1	3902	infused	1	3902	issuing	1	3902	leaded	1
3902	idlers	1	3902	ingender'd	1	3902	isthmus	1	3902	leader	1
3902	idolater	1	3902	ingrate's	1	3902	Italy	1	3902	leafless	1
3902	idols	1	3902	ingress	1	3902	Jacobins	1	3902	leagu'd	1
3902	ignominy	1	3902	inhabitant	1	3902	James	1	3902	league's	1
3902	ill-fated	1	3902	inherent	1	3902	jealousies	1	3902	leagued	1
3902	illimitable	1	3902	inhuman	1	3902	Jew	1	3902	leagues	1
3902	ill-sorted	1	3902	injustice	1	3902	Jewish	1	3902	lean'd	1
3902	ill-suppress'd	1	3902	inlets	1	3902	job	1	3902	leap'd	1
3902	illustrated	1	3902	inmates	1	3902	jog	1	3902	leaping	1
3902	illustration	1	3902	inn-keeper	1	3902	John	1	3902	leaps	1
3902	imaged	1	3902	innocuously	1	3902	join'd	1	3902	lear	1
3902	imbecile	1	3902	innumerable	1	3902	joining	1	3902	learnings	1
3902	imbibed	1	3902	inobtrusive	1	3902	joint	1	3902	learns	1
3902	imitate	1	3902	inordinate	1	3902	joint-labourers	1	3902	lecturer's	1
3902	imitations	1	3902	inquired	1	3902	joints	1	3902	lectures	1
3902	immaturity	1	3902	inroads	1	3902	jostling	1	3902	legalized	1
3902	immeasurable	1	3902	insane	1	3902	journeyed	1	3902	legends	1
3902	immensity	1	3902	insatiably	1	3902	joust	1	3902	lengthening	1
3902	immunities	1	3902	inscrib'd	1	3902	judicious	1	3902	lent	1
3902	impart	1	3902	insensible	1	3902	Juliet	1	3902	lesson	1
3902	imparted	1	3902	inseparable	1	3902	jumbled	1	3902	level'd	1
3902	impatience	1	3902	inside	1	3902	June	1	3902	Leven's	1
3902	impeach'd	1	3902	insidious	1	3902	Jupiter	1	3902	libations	1
3902	imperceptibly	1	3902	insignificant	1	3902	justifies	1	3902	liberal	1
3902	imperfection	1	3902	insinuated	1	3902	justly	1	3902	liberties	1
3902	impersonated	1	3902	insisted	1	3902	jutting	1	3902	licence	1
3902	impervious	1	3902	insolent	1	3902	juvenile	1	3902	licens'd	1
3902	impious	1	3902	inspir'd	1	3902	keepest	1	3902	license	1
3902	impiously	1		inspirèd		3902	keeping	1	3902	liege	1
3902	implore	1	3902	instantaneously	1	3902	Kendal	1	3902	liest	1
3902	imply	1	3902	instead	1	3902	kettle-drum	1	3902	lieu	1
3902	importunate	1	3902	instil	1	3902	kinder	1	3902	life-like	1
3902	impose	1	3902	instinctive	1	3902	kindled	1	3902	lift	1
3902	imposed	1	3902	institutions	1	3902	kindles	1	3902	lifting	1
3902	imposing	1	3902	instructed	1	3902	kindliness	1	3902	lighter	1
3902	impossible	1	3902	instruction	1	3902	kindlings	1	3902	lightning	1
3902	impostors	1	3902	instructor	1	3902	kingdom	1	3902	lillies	1
3902	impotence	1	3902	instrument	1	3902	kirk-pillars	1	3902	limited	1
3902	impotent	1	3902	insuperable	1	3902	kiss'd	1	3902	lingerer	1
3902	impregnate	1	3902	intellects	1	3902	kissed	1	3902	linking	1
3902	impregnated	1	3902	intensely	1	3902	kitchens	1	3902	links	1
3902	impregnations	1	3902	interchanged	1	3902	kitten	1	3902	liquid	1
3902	impresses	1	3902	interdict	1	3902	knapsack	1	3902	lisping	1
3902	impression	1	3902	interfere	1	3902	knaves	1	3902	listless	1
3902	impressive	1	3902	interlunar	1	3902	knees	1	3902	listlessly	1
3902	imprison'd	1	3902	intermeddlers	1	3902	knife	1	3902	listlessness	1
3902	inaptitude	1	3902	intermeddling	1	3902	knight's	1	3902	literature	1
3902	inasmuch	1	3902	interminable	1	3902	knitting	1	3902	litter	1
3902	inaudible	1	3902	intermingles	1	3902	knock'd	1	3902	little-ones	1
3902	inbom	1	3902	intermitting	1	3902	knocking	1	3902	livelier	1
3902	incapable	1	3902	intermittingly	1	3902	knoweth	1	3902	liveliest	1
3902	incarnation	1	3902	intermix'd	1	3902	knowingly	1	3902	liveliness	1
3902	incense	1	3902	intermixture	1	3902	label	1	3902	liveried	1
3902	incensed	1	3902	internally	1	3902	labors	1	3902	liveries	1
3902	incidental	1	3902	interpose	1	3902	labours	1	3902	livery	1
3902	incited	1	3902	interposition	1	3902	labyrinths	1	3902	liveth	1
3902	incline	1	3902	interregnum's	1	3902	lac'd	1	3902	loath'd	1
3902	inclines	1	3902	interrupt	1	3902	lacking	1	3902	loathing	1
3902	incommunicable	1	3902	interrupting	1	3902	lad	1	3902	Locarno	1
3902	inconsiderate	1	3902	intertwine	1	3902	ladder	1	3902	Locarno's	1
3902	incumbent	1	3902	intervene	1	3902	lady's	1	3902	locks	1
3902	incumbrances	1	3902	intervening	1	3902	laggards	1	3902	locusts	1
3902	indecent	1	3902	interventions	1	3902	lair	1	3902	lodger	1
3902	indecision	1	3902	interview	1	3902	lamb's	1	3902	lodges	1
3902	indecisive	1	3902	interwoven	1	3902	lambs	1	3902	loiter'd	1
3902	indefinite	1	3902	intimation	1	3902	lame	1	3902	loiterer	1
3902	index	1	3902	intoxicate	1	3902	landing	1	3902	loitering	1
3902	Indians	1	3902	intrigue	1	3902	land-warriors	1	3902	long'd	1
3902	Indian-wise	1	3902	introduc'd	1	3902	lane	1	3902	long-back'd	1
3902	indications	1	3902	intruder	1	3902	languages	1	3902	long-continued	1
3902	indigenous	1	3902	intuition	1	3902	languid	1	3902	longings	1
3902	indigent	1	3902	invaders	1	3902	languish'd	1	3902	lookers-on	1
3902	indirect	1	3902	invest	1	3902	languor	1	3902	looketh	1
3902	indiscreet	1	3902	invested	1	3902	lank	1	3902	loop-holes	1
3902	indiscretion	1	3902	invests	1	3902	lap	1	3902	loosely	1
3902	indisposed	1	3902	invigorate	1	3902	larger	1	3902	loquacious	1
3902	indisputable	1	3902	invigorating	1	3902	lark	1	3902	lorded	1
3902	indolent	1	3902	inviolable	1	3902	lark's	1	3902	lords	1
3902	in-door	1	3902	invitations	1	3902	lascars	1	3902	lore	1
3902	induce	1	3902	involuntary	1	3902	lass	1	3902	lorn	1
3902	induced	1	3902	inwoven	1	3902	lassitudes	1	3902	lose	1
3902	indulgence	1	3902	irksomeness	1	3902	latch	1	3902	loses	1
3902	indulgent	1	3902	ironic	1	3902	latent	1	3902	losses	1
3902	ineffable	1	3902	irons	1	3902	laugh	1	3902	louder	1
3902	inert	1	3902	irradiate	1	3902	laughing	1	3902	loudly	1
3902	inexperience	1	3902	irradiates	1	3902	laughters	1	3902	lounging	1
3902	infants	1	3902	irradiation	1	3902	lavish	1	3902	love-beacons	1
3902	infection	1				3902	lawgivers	1	3902	love-knot	1

Wordsworth's Vocabulary in *The Prelude*

3902	lovelier	1	3902	men's	1	3902	mower's	1	3902	Odin	1
3902	loveliest	1	3902	mercies	1	3902	multifarious	1	3902	odious	1
3902	love-liking	1	3902	mercy	1	3902	mumbling	1	3902	off-and-on	1
3902	lover's	1	3902	merit	1	3902	murder	1	3902	offences	1
3902	lovest	1	3902	merits	1	3902	murderer's	1	3902	offensive	1
3902	loveth	1	3902	merlins	1	3902	murmur'd	1	3902	officiously	1
3902	low-hung	1	3902	merriment	1	3902	murmurs	1	3902	oftener	1
3902	lowliness	1	3902	merry	1	3902	muse	1	3902	omit	1
3902	lows	1	3902	messenger	1	3902	museum	1	3902	omitted	1
3902	low-standing	1	3902	metal	1	3902	music's	1	3902	opened	1
3902	Lu	1	3902	mettlesome	1	3902	musical	1	3902	opera	1
3902	Lucretilis	1	3902	middle	1	3902	muslin	1	3902	opportune	1
3902	lull	1	3902	migration	1	3902	mustered	1	3902	opposites	1
3902	lump	1	3902	mildest	1	3902	mutter	1	3902	oppress	1
3902	lure	1	3902	mildness	1	3902	mutter'd	1	3902	oppressed	1
3902	lurking-place	1	3902	milestone	1	3902	mutual	1	3902	oppressor	1
3902	lurks	1	3902	militant	1	3902	myriads	1	3902	oppressors	1
3902	lusters	1	3902	milk	1	3902	myrtle	1	3902	opprobrious	1
3902	lustily	1	3902	milk-white	1	3902	mysterious	1	3902	opprobrium	1
3902	lustre	1	3902	mill	1	3902	mystical	1	3902	oracular	1
3902	lute	1	3902	millions	1	3902	narrative	1	3902	orange	1
3902	luxurious	1	3902	mill-race	1	3902	narratives	1	3902	orations	1
3902	lyre	1	3902	mills	1	3902	narrowing	1	3902	orator	1
3902	machine	1	3902	Milton's	1	3902	nation	1	3902	oratory	1
3902	madding	1	3902	miner	1	3902	national	1	3902	orchards	1
3902	magician's	1	3902	mines	1	3902	nave	1	3902	orders	1
3902	magistrate	1	3902	miniature	1	3902	necessary	1	3902	organic	1
3902	magnanimity	1	3902	ministers	1	3902	necessities	1	3902	orient	1
3902	magnanimous	1	3902	ministration	1	3902	nectar	1	3902	oriental	1
3902	magnified	1	3902	minstrels	1	3902	needless	1	3902	orifice	1
3902	magnitude	1	3902	minstrelsies	1	3902	neglect	1	3902	original	1
3902	maid's	1	3902	minuet	1	3902	neglectful	1	3902	originate	1
3902	maiden's	1	3902	miracles	1	3902	negligence	1	3902	originates	1
3902	mail	1	3902	miraculous	1	3902	neighbouring	1	3902	Orion	1
3902	maim'd	1	3902	miscellaneous	1	3902	nests	1	3902	orphan	1
3902	Malays	1	3902	mischance	1	3902	net	1	3902	orphans	1
3902	manacles	1	3902	misdeem	1	3902	never-failing	1	3902	Orphean	1
3902	management	1	3902	misfortunes	1	3902	newcomer	1	3902	Ossian	1
3902	maniac's	1	3902	misguiding	1	3902	new-fallen	1	3902	ostentatious	1
3902	manifested	1	3902	misplaced	1	3902	Newton's	1	3902	ostrich-like	1
3902	manliness	1	3902	misrule	1	3902	next-door	1	3902	others'	1
3902	many-headed	1	3902	miss	1	3902	niceties	1	3902	outbreak	1
3902	map	1	3902	misses	1	3902	night's	1	3902	outcast	1
3902	maple	1	3902	mission	1	3902	night-wanderings	1	3902	outcry	1
3902	maps	1	3902	mistake	1	3902	Nile	1	3902	outer	1
3902	march'd	1	3902	mistaken	1	3902	noiseless	1	3902	outlast	1
3902	mark'st	1	3902	mistress	1	3902	noisier	1	3902	out-o'-th'-way	1
3902	market	1	3902	misty	1	3902	noisy	1	3902	outrage	1
3902	Mars	1	3902	misus'd	1	3902	noon's	1	3902	outrun	1
3902	martial	1	3902	mithridates	1	3902	noon-day	1	3902	outset	1
3902	martyr's	1	3902	mitred	1	3902	noos'd	1	3902	over-anxious	1
3902	martyrs	1	3902	mobs	1	3902	north	1	3902	over-arch'd	1
3902	marvel	1	3902	mock'd	1	3902	northwards	1	3902	overbless'd	1
3902	masquerade	1	3902	mocks	1	3902	notic'd	1	3902	overblown	1
3902	massacre	1	3902	model	1	3902	noticeable	1	3902	overborn	1
3902	massacres	1	3902	moderated	1	3902	notwithstanding	1	3902	overbridged	1
3902	masses	1	3902	modified	1	3902	nourished	1	3902	overcame	1
3902	massy	1	3902	Moloch	1	3902	nourishment	1	3902	overcome	1
3902	master'd	1	3902	monarch	1	3902	November	1	3902	overflow'd	1
3902	masters	1	3902	monarchs	1	3902	novice	1	3902	over-fondly	1
3902	mastery	1	3902	monasteries	1	3902	noviciate	1	3902	over-great	1
3902	match'd	1	3902	monastery	1	3902	nowise	1	3902	overhung	1
3902	materials	1	3902	monastic	1	3902	number	1	3902	overloaded	1
3902	maternal	1	3902	monk	1	3902	numberless	1	3902	overlove	1
3902	mates	1	3902	monkeys	1	3902	numbers	1	3902	overmuch	1
3902	mathematics	1	3902	monkies	1	3902	nun	1	3902	over-near	1
3902	matin	1	3902	monkish	1	3902	nuptials	1	3902	overpass'd	1
3902	matins	1	3902	monster	1	3902	nurse's	1	3902	over-pressure	1
3902	matron's	1	3902	monstrous	1	3902	nursed	1	3902	overpriz'd	1
3902	matrons	1	3902	Mont Blanc	1	3902	nursing	1	3902	overruns	1
3902	matures	1	3902	Mont Martyr	1	3902	nurslings	1	3902	overstepp'd	1
3902	maugre	1	3902	months'	1	3902	o'erhanging	1	3902	over-sternness	1
3902	Maximilian	1	3902	monuments	1	3902	o'erpower'd	1	3902	overtake	1
3902	may-bush	1	3902	moody	1	3902	oaken	1	3902	over-toil	1
3902	mayor	1	3902	mooring-place	1	3902	oaks	1	3902	overweeningly	1
3902	may-pole	1	3902	morality	1	3902	oaks'	1	3902	overwhelm'd	1
3902	maze	1	3902	mortality	1	3902	obduracy	1	3902	overwrought	1
3902	mazes	1	3902	Morven	1	3902	obedience	1	3902	owe	1
3902	meadow	1	3902	Moses	1	3902	obeisances	1	3902	owls	1
3902	meadow-ground	1	3902	moss	1	3902	obey'd	1	3902	ox	1
3902	meal	1	3902	motherly	1	3902	obligation	1	3902	pacing	1
3902	meals	1	3902	motive	1	3902	obliquities	1	3902	pack	1
3902	meanings	1	3902	mound	1	3902	obolus	1	3902	pageantry	1
3902	measured	1	3902	mounds	1	3902	obscurities	1	3902	pages	1
3902	measures	1	3902	mountain-echoes	1	3902	observance	1	3902	painfully	1
3902	mechanic	1	3902	mountaineer	1	3902	observation	1	3902	painter	1
3902	meditated	1	3902	mountain-ground	1	3902	observations	1	3902	painter's	1
3902	medley	1	3902	mountainous	1	3902	observes	1	3902	painting	1
3902	meeker	1	3902	mountebank	1	3902	obstacle	1	3902	palate	1
3902	meekness	1	3902	mountings	1	3902	obstruct	1	3902	pale-fac'd	1
3902	meeting-point	1	3902	mounts	1	3902	obtain	1	3902	pales	1
3902	meets	1	3902	mourn'd	1	3902	obtain'd	1	3902	palfrey	1
3902	Melancthon	1	3902	mournful	1	3902	obviously	1	3902	paling	1
3902	mellow	1	3902	mouths	1	3902	occasional	1	3902	palms	1
3902	melodies	1	3902	mov'st	1	3902	occasions	1	3902	pamper'd	1
3902	melody	1	3902	moveables	1	3902	ode	1	3902	pampering	1

Appendix

3902	pamphlets	1	3902	pike	1	3902	precipitated	1	3902	proving	1
3902	Pan	1	3902	pil'd	1	3902	preconceptions	1	3902	provokes	1
3902	pang	1	3902	pilfer'd	1	3902	precursor	1	3902	prudence	1
3902	pangs	1	3902	pilgrimage	1	3902	predestin'd	1	3902	prying	1
3902	panoply	1	3902	pilgrim-friars	1	3902	pre-eminence	1	3902	puff'd	1
3902	panted	1	3902	pilgrims	1	3902	pregnant	1	3902	puffs	1
3902	panting	1	3902	pillowy	1	3902	prelibation	1	3902	puissant	1
3902	pantomimic	1	3902	pilot	1	3902	prelude	1	3902	pull	1
3902	paper	1	3902	pinfold	1	3902	pre-occupy	1	3902	pulpit	1
3902	parading	1	3902	pink-vested	1	3902	pre-ordain'd	1	3902	punctilios	1
3902	parcel	1	3902	pinnacles	1	3902	prepar'd	1	3902	puny	1
3902	parcell'd	1	3902	pins	1	3902	prepare	1	3902	puppet-shows	1
3902	parent's	1	3902	piping	1	3902	prepares	1	3902	purchas'd	1
3902	park	1	3902	pitch	1	3902	prepossession	1	3902	purifying	1
3902	parliament	1	3902	pitch'd	1	3902	presage	1	3902	purple	1
3902	parlour	1	3902	pitcher	1	3902	prescience	1	3902	purses	1
3902	parrot's	1	3902	piteous	1	3902	prescrib'd	1	3902	pursuing	1
3902	parties	1	3902	piteously	1	3902	prescriptive	1	3902	pursuit	1
3902	parting	1	3902	pitiably	1	3902	presented	1	3902	putting	1
3902	partisan	1	3902	pitied	1	3902	presenting	1	3902	puzzle	1
3902	partner	1	3902	placable	1	3902	presents	1	3902	puzzled	1
3902	party-colour'd	1	3902	plain-living	1	3902	preserved	1	3902	quaint	1
3902	passed	1	3902	plainly	1	3902	presidents	1	3902	Quantock's	1
3902	passenger	1	3902	planet	1	3902	presides	1	3902	quarrel'd	1
3902	passive	1	3902	planning	1	3902	presiding	1	3902	quarrels	1
3902	pastime's	1	3902	planted	1	3902	presses	1	3902	quarrelsome	1
3902	pastimes	1	3902	planting	1	3902	pressure	1	3902	quarry	1
3902	patch	1	3902	plants	1	3902	presumptuously	1	3902	quarry-man	1
3902	patch'd	1	3902	Plato	1	3902	prettiest	1	3902	quarter	1
3902	pathway	1	3902	Platonic	1	3902	prevail'd	1	3902	quarter'd	1
3902	patriarchal	1	3902	play-fellows	1	3902	price	1	3902	queen	1
3902	patrimonial	1	3902	playmate	1	3902	priestly	1	3902	queens	1
3902	patriot's	1	3902	playmate's	1	3902	primaeval	1	3902	quell'd	1
3902	Patterdale	1	3902	playthings	1	3902	primrose	1	3902	questioning	1
3902	pattern	1	3902	playtime	1	3902	primrose-time	1	3902	quickens	1
3902	Paul's	1	3902	pleaded	1	3902	princes	1	3902	quicker	1
3902	paused	1	3902	pleas	1	3902	print	1	3902	quickly	1
3902	pauses	1	3902	please	1	3902	printed	1	3902	quiescent	1
3902	pavèd	1	3902	pleasingly	1	3902	prism	1	3902	quietly	1
3902	pavement	1	3902	pleasure's	1	3902	privation	1	3902	quite	1
3902	paw'd	1	3902	pleasure-ground	1	3902	prizing	1	3902	quits	1
3902	pay'd	1	3902	plebeian	1	3902	probation	1	3902	quitting	1
3902	peacefully	1	3902	pledge	1	3902	probe	1	3902	quivering	1
3902	peals	1	3902	pledges	1	3902	proceeds	1	3902	quoth	1
3902	pears	1	3902	plenteous	1	3902	processes	1	3902	rabblement	1
3902	peat-fire	1	3902	plied	1	3902	processions	1	3902	raged	1
3902	pebbles	1	3902	plight	1	3902	proclaim'd	1	3902	ragged	1
3902	pedestal	1	3902	plots	1	3902	proclaims	1	3902	rainbow	1
3902	peep'd	1	3902	plough	1	3902	proclamation	1	3902	rainy	1
3902	peeping	1	3902	ploughman	1	3902	proclamations	1	3902	raise	1
3902	pelican	1	3902	pluck	1	3902	procured	1	3902	rake	1
3902	pendant	1	3902	plumage	1	3902	prodigal	1	3902	rambled	1
3902	penetrate	1	3902	plunderer	1	3902	prodigies	1	3902	rampart's	1
3902	penetrates	1	3902	plunged	1	3902	prodigy	1	3902	Ranelagh	1
3902	peninsulas	1	3902	ply	1	3902	produc'd	1	3902	rank'd	1
3902	penny	1	3902	plying	1	3902	producing	1	3902	ranks	1
3902	pennyless	1	3902	pocketed	1	3902	profane	1	3902	ransacks	1
3902	pension'd	1	3902	poems	1	3902	profess'd	1	3902	raree-show	1
3902	pensioner	1	3902	poetry	1	3902	professedly	1	3902	rarity	1
3902	pensively	1	3902	points	1	3902	profit	1	3902	rash	1
3902	penury	1	3902	polar	1	3902	profitable	1	3902	rashly	1
3902	peopled	1	3902	pole	1	3902	profusion	1	3902	rattles	1
3902	peradventure	1	3902	policies	1	3902	projections	1	3902	rattling	1
3902	perceiv'd	1	3902	polish'd	1	3902	projects	1	3902	raving	1
3902	perch	1	3902	pompous	1	3902	Promethean	1	3902	reached	1
3902	Perdita	1	3902	pope	1	3902	prominent	1	3902	reaching	1
3902	perfection	1	3902	popinjays	1	3902	promiscuous	1	3902	readiest	1
3902	perfectly	1	3902	populous	1	3902	promising	1	3902	readily	1
3902	perfidious	1	3902	pored	1	3902	promote	1	3902	realiz'd	1
3902	perfidiously	1	3902	port	1	3902	promoted	1	3902	reaper	1
3902	perishable	1	3902	portals	1	3902	prompter's	1	3902	reappear	1
3902	perk'd	1	3902	porter's	1	3902	promptest	1	3902	reaps	1
3902	permanence	1	3902	porters	1	3902	promptings	1	3902	reascend	1
3902	perpetually	1	3902	posies	1	3902	pronounc'd	1	3902	reascending	1
3902	perplex	1	3902	possessed	1	3902	pronounce	1	3902	reason's	1
3902	perplexity	1	3902	possibly	1	3902	prop	1	3902	reasonable	1
3902	Persepolis	1	3902	posting	1	3902	propagate	1	3902	reasoning	1
3902	persisted	1	3902	posts	1	3902	properties	1	3902	rebellion	1
3902	pertain'd	1	3902	posture-masters	1	3902	prophecy	1	3902	rebellious	1
3902	pertains	1	3902	potentates	1	3902	prophesy	1	3902	rebound	1
3902	perturb'd	1	3902	potter's	1	3902	prophet	1	3902	rebuild	1
3902	perusal	1	3902	pound	1	3902	prophet's	1	3902	recall'd	1
3902	perused	1	3902	pourtray'd	1	3902	prophetic	1	3902	recedes	1
3902	pervade	1	3902	powder	1	3902	propositions	1	3902	receiver	1
3902	perverse	1	3902	practice	1	3902	propping	1	3902	recently	1
3902	perverseness	1	3902	practis'd	1	3902	prose	1	3902	receptacle	1
3902	perverted	1	3902	prancing	1	3902	prosper'd	1	3902	recipient	1
3902	pervious	1	3902	prate	1	3902	prostrate	1	3902	reckless	1
3902	pest	1	3902	prattlers	1	3902	prostrated	1	3902	reckoning	1
3902	Peter's	1	3902	prattling	1	3902	protecting	1	3902	reclining	1
3902	Phillis	1	3902	pray	1	3902	protection	1	3902	recognised	1
3902	philosopher	1	3902	preach'd	1	3902	protects	1	3902	recoil	1
3902	phoebe	1	3902	preamble	1	3902	proudest	1	3902	recoil'd	1
3902	physiognomies	1	3902	preceding	1	3902	prov'd	1	3902	recollected	1
3902	pictured	1	3902	preceptress	1	3902	proves	1	3902	reconcil'd	1
3902	pig	1	3902	precipitate	1	3902	provide	1	3902	reconcilement	1

Wordsworth's Vocabulary in *The Prelude*

3902	reconciles	1	3902	resolutions	1	3902	rounds	1	3902	scythe	1
3902	records	1	3902	resort	1	3902	rous'd	1	3902	sea-fight	1
3902	recovering	1	3902	resorted	1	3902	routs	1	3902	seal	1
3902	rectified	1	3902	resound	1	3902	row	1	3902	seams	1
3902	recusants	1	3902	resounded	1	3902	royalists	1	3902	search'd	1
3902	redbreasts	1	3902	respiration	1	3902	royalties	1	3902	sea-shells	1
3902	redeem'd	1	3902	respirations	1	3902	rubbish	1	3902	sea-shore	1
3902	redemption	1	3902	respired	1	3902	ruddy	1	3902	sea-side	1
3902	redounding	1	3902	respite	1	3902	rude	1	3902	seasonable	1
3902	redounds	1	3902	respites	1	3902	rudely	1	3902	seasoned	1
3902	reduce	1	3902	resplendent	1	3902	rudiments	1	3902	seated	1
3902	reduced	1	3902	responsive	1	3902	ruffian	1	3902	secluded	1
3902	redundancy	1	3902	restlessly	1	3902	rugged	1	3902	seclusion	1
3902	reel'd	1	3902	restor'd	1	3902	ruin	1	3902	seclusions	1
3902	re-establish'd	1	3902	restorative	1	3902	rul'd	1	3902	second-sight	1
3902	reference	1	3902	restraints	1	3902	ruminate	1	3902	secrecy	1
3902	refin'd	1	3902	resum'd	1	3902	ruminating	1	3902	secreted	1
3902	refine	1	3902	resume	1	3902	rumour	1	3902	sects	1
3902	refined	1	3902	retainers	1	3902	rumours	1	3902	sedan	1
3902	reflect	1	3902	retaineth	1	3902	rush'd	1	3902	sedate	1
3902	reflecting	1	3902	retains	1	3902	russet	1	3902	sedentary	1
3902	reflections	1	3902	retire	1	3902	Russian	1	3902	seeds	1
3902	refresh	1	3902	retiredness	1	3902	rustic's	1	3902	seed-time	1
3902	refresh'd	1	3902	retrac'd	1	3902	rustled	1	3902	seemliness	1
3902	refreshments	1	3902	retreating	1	3902	Sabine	1	3902	seest	1
3902	refuge	1	3902	retrograde	1	3902	sabra	1	3902	seizing	1
3902	regain'd	1	3902	retrospect	1	3902	sacred	1	3902	select	1
3902	regal	1	3902	returned	1	3902	sacrificed	1	3902	selected	1
3902	regenerated	1	3902	reunite	1	3902	Sadler's Wells	1	3902	self-applauding	1
3902	regent	1	3902	revelation	1	3902	safer	1	3902	self-blame	1
3902	regiment	1	3902	revelation's	1	3902	sagacious	1	3902	self-command	1
3902	register	1	3902	reverberated	1	3902	sages	1	3902	self-conceit	1
3902	register'd	1	3902	revered	1	3902	sail	1	3902	self-congratulation	1
3902	regretted	1	3902	reverenc'd	1	3902	sailor's	1	3902	self-created	1
3902	regulate	1	3902	reverenced	1	3902	sails	1	3902	self-defence	1
3902	regulation	1	3902	reverential	1	3902	saint	1	3902	self-destroying	1
3902	regulations	1	3902	reverentially	1	3902	sainted	1	3902	self-devotion	1
3902	rein	1	3902	reverie	1	3902	saints	1	3902	self-forgetfulness	1
3902	rejoic'd	1	3902	reverse	1	3902	sakes	1	3902	self-knowledge	1
3902	rejoicing	1	3902	reverted	1	3902	Salisburys	1	3902	self-pleasing	1
3902	rejoicings	1	3902	reviewing	1	3902	sallying	1	3902	self-possession	1
3902	related	1	3902	reviving	1	3902	salt-box	1	3902	self-presence	1
3902	relation	1	3902	revolution	1	3902	salutes	1	3902	self-presented	1
3902	relationship	1	3902	revolutionary	1	3902	sanative	1	3902	self-respect	1
3902	relaxing	1	3902	revolutions	1	3902	sanctifying	1	3902	self-restraint	1
3902	relent	1	3902	revolve	1	3902	sanction'd	1	3902	self-rule	1
3902	relick	1	3902	revolved	1	3902	sanctuaries	1	3902	self-sacrifice	1
3902	relief	1	3902	revolving	1	3902	sanctuary's	1	3902	self-slaughter	1
3902	religion	1	3902	Rhine	1	3902	sandal	1	3902	self-submission	1
3902	reliques	1	3902	Rhone	1	3902	sanguine	1	3902	self-sufficing	1
3902	relish	1	3902	ribaldry	1	3902	sapp'd	1	3902	self-taught	1
3902	reluctance	1	3902	ride	1	3902	Sarum	1	3902	self-transmuted	1
3902	remedies	1	3902	ridges	1	3902	satire	1	3902	self-will'd	1
3902	rememberable	1	3902	ridicule	1	3902	satisf'd	1	3902	semi-Quixote	1
3902	remiss	1	3902	ridiculous	1	3902	satyrs	1	3902	senators	1
3902	remissly	1	3902	riding	1	3902	saucy	1	3902	send'st	1
3902	remissness	1	3902	rife	1	3902	sauntering	1	3902	sending	1
3902	remonstrances	1	3902	righteous	1	3902	saving	1	3902	sensation	1
3902	remoulds	1	3902	righteousness	1	3902	savings	1	3902	sensibly	1
3902	remounted	1	3902	rimy	1	3902	Savoyards	1	3902	sensual	1
3902	removal	1	3902	rioted	1	3902	Scafell	1	3902	September	1
3902	render'd	1	3902	riots	1	3902	scamper'd	1	3902	sequel	1
3902	renders	1	3902	ripe	1	3902	scandal	1	3902	seraphic	1
3902	renovated	1	3902	ripens	1	3902	scanty	1	3902	seraphs	1
3902	renovation	1	3902	rippling	1	3902	scar'd	1	3902	Sertorius	1
3902	repair	1	3902	rises	1	3902	scare-crow	1	3902	servant	1
3902	repass'd	1	3902	risings	1	3902	scared	1	3902	services	1
3902	repast	1	3902	ritual	1	3902	scatterings	1	3902	servile	1
3902	repasts	1	3902	rival	1	3902	scavenger	1	3902	serving	1
3902	repeat	1	3902	rivalship	1	3902	scenery	1	3902	settle	1
3902	repeating	1	3902	river's	1	3902	schemed	1	3902	settler	1
3902	repetition	1	3902	river-sides	1	3902	schemers	1	3902	settling-time	1
3902	repining	1	3902	rivet	1	3902	scholar	1	3902	seven	1
3902	replied	1	3902	rivulet's	1	3902	scholar's	1	3902	seventeenth	1
3902	reply	1	3902	road's	1	3902	schoolboy	1	3902	sever	1
3902	reportest	1	3902	roaming	1	3902	schoolboy's	1	3902	sever'd	1
3902	repos'd	1	3902	roars	1	3902	school-boys	1	3902	severer	1
3902	reposed	1	3902	robe	1	3902	schoolfellows	1	3902	severest	1
3902	representative	1	3902	Robin Hood	1	3902	schoolmen	1	3902	severing	1
3902	reproach'd	1	3902	rock-like	1	3902	scoff	1	3902	severings	1
3902	reproaches	1	3902	Roland	1	3902	scoffers	1	3902	shading	1
3902	republican	1	3902	romances	1	3902	scoffs	1	3902	shadings	1
3902	repute	1	3902	Romeo	1	3902	scolding	1	3902	shadow'd	1
3902	reputed	1	3902	Romish	1	3902	scope	1	3902	shadows	1
3902	requesting	1	3902	Romorentin	1	3902	Scotch	1	3902	shallows	1
3902	requiem	1	3902	romping	1	3902	Scotland	1	3902	shalt	1
3902	requir'd	1	3902	roof'd	1	3902	scratch	1	3902	shameless	1
3902	require	1	3902	rooted	1	3902	scratches	1	3902	shaping	1
3902	rescue	1	3902	rope-dancers	1	3902	screaming	1	3902	shared	1
3902	resemblance	1	3902	Rotha's	1	3902	screams	1	3902	sheaf	1
3902	resembled	1	3902	rotted	1	3902	scribbled	1	3902	sheds	1
3902	resembling	1	3902	rotten	1	3902	scrolls	1	3902	shells	1
3902	reservoir	1	3902	rough-cast	1	3902	scruple	1	3902	sheltering	1
3902	resistance	1	3902	roughest	1	3902	scrupulous	1	3902	shewn	1
3902	resolute	1	3902	roundabouts	1	3902	scrupulously	1	3902	shewy	1
3902	resolution	1	3902	roundly	1	3902	scudding	1	3902	shields	1

Appendix

3902	shift	1	3902	snake	1	3902	stammerer	1	3902	sturdy	1
3902	shifting	1	3902	snakes	1	3902	stamp'd	1	3902	style	1
3902	shines	1	3902	snaky	1	3902	standard	1	3902	subdu'd	1
3902	shipp'd	1	3902	snatch	1	3902	standers-by	1	3902	subduing	1
3902	shoal	1	3902	snatches	1	3902	star'd	1	3902	subjected	1
3902	shock'd	1	3902	snatches	1	3902	stare	1	3902	subjoin'd	1
3902	shod	1	3902	sneers	1	3902	staring	1	3902	sublimer	1
3902	shooting	1	3902	Snowdon	1	3902	startling	1	3902	sublimest	1
3902	shortening	1	3902	snowdrops	1	3902	starved	1	3902	sublimity	1
3902	short-flighted	1	3902	snowy	1	3902	starving	1	3902	submission	1
3902	short-lived	1	3902	Soane	1	3902	stationary	1	3902	submissive	1
3902	short-sighted	1	3902	soareth	1	3902	stationed	1	3902	submissively	1
3902	shoulder	1	3902	sobbings	1	3902	statists	1	3902	submit	1
3902	shouldering	1	3902	soberly	1	3902	statue	1	3902	subservience	1
3902	shouting	1	3902	sobs	1	3902	statues	1	3902	subsist	1
3902	showing	1	3902	sod	1	3902	statute	1	3902	substances	1
3902	showman	1	3902	sod-built	1	3902	stays	1	3902	substantially	1
3902	showman's	1	3902	sodden	1	3902	steadied	1	3902	substitute	1
3902	shrewd	1	3902	soe'er	1	3902	steadiest	1	3902	subterfuge	1
3902	shrill	1	3902	soften	1	3902	steadily	1	3902	subterraneous	1
3902	shrillest	1	3902	softening	1	3902	stealth	1	3902	subtile	1
3902	shrine	1	3902	sojourn'd	1	3902	steam-like	1	3902	subtler	1
3902	shrines	1	3902	solacing	1	3902	steel	1	3902	subtlest	1
3902	shrink	1	3902	soldier's	1	3902	step'd	1	3902	subtlety	1
3902	shrouded	1	3902	soldiership	1	3902	steeple	1	3902	subversion	1
3902	shrub	1	3902	solemniz'd	1	3902	steeples	1	3902	subverters	1
3902	shrubs	1	3902	solemnized	1	3902	steeps	1	3902	succedaneum	1
3902	shudder'd	1	3902	solicitude	1	3902	steer'd	1	3902	succeeded	1
3902	shuddering	1	3902	soothe	1	3902	stem	1	3902	succeeding	1
3902	shuffling	1	3902	soothes	1	3902	stemm'd	1	3902	successful	1
3902	shun	1	3902	sooty	1	3902	stepp'd	1	3902	successively	1
3902	shunning	1	3902	sore	1	3902	sternly	1	3902	suck'd	1
3902	sibyl	1	3902	soul's	1	3902	sternly	1	3902	suffer	1
3902	Sicilian	1	3902	soulless	1	3902	sternness	1	3902	sufferers	1
3902	Sicily	1	3902	sounded	1	3902	steward	1	3902	suffic'd	1
3902	sickliness	1	3902	sounder	1	3902	stewards	1	3902	suggestions	1
3902	sideway	1	3902	sour'd	1	3902	stick	1	3902	suiting	1
3902	Sidney	1	3902	sources	1	3902	sticks	1	3902	sullen	1
3902	sifts	1	3902	south	1	3902	stiff	1	3902	sultry	1
3902	sigh'd	1	3902	sow	1	3902	still'd	1	3902	summer-time	1
3902	sightless	1	3902	sp[l]endid	1	3902	stipend	1	3902	sun's	1
3902	signboard	1	3902	spades	1	3902	stole	1	3902	Sunday	1
3902	signet	1	3902	Spain	1	3902	stone-abbot	1	3902	Sunday's	1
3902	silently	1	3902	span	1	3902	stone-axe	1	3902	sun-rise	1
3902	silvery	1	3902	Spaniard	1	3902	stone-eater	1	3902	superadded	1
3902	simple-mindedness	1	3902	Spanish	1	3902	stoop'd	1	3902	superfluous	1
3902	simpleness	1	3902	span'd	1	3902	stop	1	3902	supernatural	1
3902	simplified	1	3902	spar'd	1	3902	stopping	1	3902	superstition	1
3902	sincere	1	3902	speaks	1	3902	stores	1	3902	super-tragic	1
3902	sincerely	1	3902	spear	1	3902	storm'd	1	3902	supper	1
3902	sinews	1	3902	spears	1	3902	straggle	1	3902	suppers	1
3902	sing	1	3902	special	1	3902	straightforward	1	3902	supplanted	1
3902	sing'd	1	3902	specially	1	3902	strained	1	3902	supporters	1
3902	singers	1	3902	specimens	1	3902	straining	1	3902	suppress'd	1
3902	singing	1	3902	specious	1	3902	strand	1	3902	surety	1
3902	singleness	1	3902	spectre	1	3902	strangely	1	3902	surf	1
3902	singular	1	3902	spectres	1	3902	strangeness	1	3902	surfaces	1
3902	singularity	1	3902	sped	1	3902	strawberries	1	3902	surmise	1
3902	sinning	1	3902	spell	1	3902	strays	1	3902	surmounted	1
3902	sinuous	1	3902	Spenser's	1	3902	streaks	1	3902	surpass	1
3902	sire	1	3902	spent	1	3902	streaming	1	3902	surplice	1
3902	Sirius	1	3902	sphered	1	3902	streamy	1	3902	surprise	1
3902	sirocco	1	3902	spied	1	3902	strengthen'd	1	3902	surpriz'd	1
3902	sisters	1	3902	spinners	1	3902	strengthened	1	3902	surrounding	1
3902	site	1	3902	spinning	1	3902	strengtheners	1	3902	survived	1
3902	sixty	1	3902	spiritless	1	3902	strew	1	3902	suspected	1
3902	skeletons	1	3902	spirit-stirring	1	3902	strew'd	1	3902	suspicion	1
3902	Skiddaw's	1	3902	spiry	1	3902	stricken	1	3902	suspicions	1
3902	skies	1	3902	splendor	1	3902	strictly	1	3902	suspicious	1
3902	skilful	1	3902	splendour's	1	3902	striding-edge	1	3902	suspiciously	1
3902	skill'd	1	3902	spoil'd	1	3902	strike	1	3902	swains	1
3902	skirts	1	3902	spoiler	1	3902	strikes	1	3902	swallow	1
3902	sky's	1	3902	spoils	1	3902	string'd	1	3902	swallowing	1
3902	slack	1	3902	spontaneously	1	3902	strip	1	3902	swallows	1
3902	slacken'd	1	3902	sported	1	3902	stripling's	1	3902	swan	1
3902	slackens	1	3902	sporting	1	3902	stripp'd	1	3902	swarms	1
3902	slackness	1	3902	sportive	1	3902	stript	1	3902	sway'd	1
3902	slate	1	3902	sportively	1	3902	strode	1	3902	Swede	1
3902	slaughter	1	3902	spotted	1	3902	stroll'd	1	3902	sweeping	1
3902	slave	1	3902	spousals	1	3902	strolling	1	3902	sweeten	1
3902	slaves	1	3902	spray	1	3902	strongly	1	3902	sweeter	1
3902	sleety	1	3902	springes	1	3902	structure	1	3902	sweets	1
3902	slippers	1	3902	spring-tide	1	3902	structures	1	3902	swell	1
3902	slippery	1	3902	springtime	1	3902	struggle	1	3902	swift	1
3902	slipping	1	3902	sprinklings	1	3902	struggles	1	3902	swiftness	1
3902	slumber'd	1	3902	spungy	1	3902	struggling	1	3902	sycamore	1
3902	slumbering	1	3902	spurious	1	3902	stuck	1	3902	syllogistic	1
3902	slumbers	1	3902	spurring	1	3902	studded	1	3902	sylvan	1
3902	slung	1	3902	squares	1	3902	student's	1	3902	symbol	1
3902	sly	1	3902	squires	1	3902	studied	1	3902	synod	1
3902	smiles	1	3902	stable	1	3902	stuff	1	3902	synthesis	1
3902	smites	1	3902	staggering	1	3902	stumbling	1	3902	Syracuse	1
3902	smoke	1	3902	staid	1	3902	stung	1	3902	system	1
3902	smoothly	1	3902	stale	1	3902	stun'd	1	3902	tailors	1
3902	smoothness	1	3902	stalking	1	3902	stupefied	1	3902	tak'st	1
3902	smote	1	3902	stall	1	3902	stupendous	1	3902	talents	1

Wordsworth's Vocabulary in *The Prelude*

3902	talks	1	3902	thriven	1	3902	triumph'd	1	3902	unfenc'd	1
3902	tame	1	3902	thrives	1	3902	Trompington	1	3902	unfenced	1
3902	tamed	1	3902	throttled	1	3902	troop	1	3902	unfetter'd	1
3902	tamer	1	3902	throw	1	3902	trophies	1	3902	unfilial	1
3902	tamper	1	3902	throwing	1	3902	troubled	1	3902	unfold	1
3902	tapers	1	3902	thrush	1	3902	truly	1	3902	unfolded	1
3902	tarn	1	3902	thrusts	1	3902	trumpets	1	3902	unforewarn'd	1
3902	tarried	1	3902	thumps	1	3902	trumpet-tones	1	3902	unfrequent	1
3902	tarrying	1	3902	thunder	1	3902	trunks	1	3902	unfruitful	1
3902	Tartar	1	3902	thunderer	1	3902	tuft	1	3902	ungenial	1
3902	tassell'd	1	3902	thunderstricken	1	3902	tumblers	1	3902	ungovernable	1
3902	tassels	1	3902	thwart	1	3902	tumbling	1	3902	ungracious	1
3902	tasted	1	3902	thwarting	1	3902	tumultuous	1	3902	ungratefully	1
3902	tatters	1	3902	tie	1	3902	tuneable	1	3902	ungreeted	1
3902	taunt	1	3902	tigers	1	3902	tuneful	1	3902	unhabitual	1
3902	taunting	1	3902	tight	1	3902	turbulent	1	3902	unhappiness	1
3902	taunts	1	3902	tillers	1	3902	Turk	1	3902	unhealthy	1
3902	tavern	1	3902	tilth	1	3902	turmoil	1	3902	unhonour'd	1
3902	teaches	1	3902	timbrel	1	3902	turnings	1	3902	unhous'd	1
3902	teeming	1	3902	timid	1	3902	turret's	1	3902	uniform	1
3902	teems	1	3902	timidly	1	3902	tutelary	1	3902	unimpair'd	1
3902	teeth	1	3902	Timoleon	1	3902	twain	1	3902	unimportant	1
3902	telescopes	1	3902	Timonides	1	3902	twelvemonth's	1	3902	uniform'd	1
3902	temper'd	1	3902	timorous	1	3902	twig	1	3902	uninformed	1
3902	temperament	1	3902	tingled	1	3902	twigs	1	3902	uninhabited	1
3902	temperance	1	3902	tinkled	1	3902	twin	1	3902	uninvited	1
3902	temperately	1	3902	tints	1	3902	twinkle	1	3902	unions	1
3902	temperature	1	3902	tiresome	1	3902	twinkles	1	3902	unison	1
3902	tempering	1	3902	titled	1	3902	twinkling	1	3902	unites	1
3902	tempests	1	3902	title-page	1	3902	types	1	3902	unkindness	1
3902	temple's	1	3902	Tivoli	1	3902	tyrant	1	3902	unlaborious	1
3902	temporal	1	3902	to-day	1	3902	tyrant's	1	3902	unlike	1
3902	tempt	1	3902	toe	1	3902	tyrants	1	3902	unlock'd	1
3902	temptation	1	3902	toilette	1	3902	ultimate	1	3902	unloos'd	1
3902	tempting	1	3902	tolerant	1	3902	umbrage	1	3902	unlovely	1
3902	tenacious	1	3902	tolerated	1	3902	umbrageous	1	3902	unluxuriant	1
3902	tenanted	1	3902	toll'd	1	3902	unabated	1	3902	unmerited	1
3902	tended	1	3902	tomb	1	3902	unaccustom'd	1	3902	unmoving	1
3902	tendencies	1	3902	tombstone	1	3902	unacknowledg'd	1	3902	unnam'd	1
3902	tenderest	1	3902	to-morrow	1	3902	unadorn'd	1	3902	unnecessary	1
3902	tending	1	3902	tones	1	3902	unadulterated	1	3902	unneighbourly	1
3902	tenets	1	3902	tongue-favor'd	1	3902	unaffecting	1	3902	unnoticed	1
3902	tens	1	3902	tool	1	3902	unaim'd	1	3902	unnumber'd	1
3902	tent	1	3902	tooth	1	3902	unalarm'd	1	3902	unobserv'd	1
3902	tenth	1	3902	topmost	1	3902	unambitious	1	3902	unorganic	1
3902	tepid	1	3902	torches	1	3902	unamusing	1	3902	unpaid	1
3902	termination	1	3902	torpid	1	3902	unassuming	1	3902	unpeaceful	1
3902	terrace	1	3902	toss	1	3902	unbaffled	1	3902	unprepared	1
3902	terrestrial	1	3902	tottering	1	3902	unbewilder'd	1	3902	unproclaim'd	1
3902	terrible	1	3902	tournament	1	3902	unbias'd	1	3902	unprofan'd	1
3902	terrier	1	3902	toward	1	3902	unblinded	1	3902	unprofaned	1
3902	terrifying	1	3902	towering	1	3902	unborn	1	3902	unprofitable	1
3902	terrors	1	3902	traced	1	3902	unburthen'd	1	3902	unprofitably	1
3902	tether	1	3902	traces	1	3902	uncertainty	1	3902	unpropp'd	1
3902	Thames	1	3902	tracing	1	3902	unchasten'd	1	3902	unquenchable	1
3902	thankfulness	1	3902	tradesman's	1	3902	unclaimed	1	3902	unrais'd	1
3902	thanksgivings	1	3902	tradition	1	3902	uncomplaining	1	3902	unreasoning	1
3902	that's	1	3902	traditions	1	3902	unconquerable	1	3902	unrecogniz'd	1
3902	thaws	1	3902	traffickers	1	3902	unconsciously	1	3902	unrecorded	1
3902	theatres	1	3902	tragedies	1	3902	uncontrol'd	1	3902	unregarded	1
3902	their's	1	3902	trampling	1	3902	undecaying	1	3902	unrelentingly	1
3902	thenceforth	1	3902	trances	1	3902	undelighted	1	3902	unrespited	1
3902	thenceforward	1	3902	tranquillised	1	3902	undepress'd	1	3902	unrestrain'd	1
3902	Theocritus	1	3902	tranquillity	1	3902	under-agents	1	3902	unsaluted	1
3902	theories	1	3902	tranquillizing	1	3902	under-countenance	1	3902	unscour'd	1
3902	thereat	1	3902	transit	1	3902	under-coverts	1	3902	unsettles	1
3902	therefrom	1	3902	translated	1	3902	undergone	1	3902	unshar'd	1
3902	thereof	1	3902	transmigration	1	3902	undermine	1	3902	unsheltered	1
3902	thereon	1	3902	transmitted	1	3902	under-powers	1	3902	unshrouded	1
3902	therewith	1	3902	transparent	1	3902	under-presence	1	3902	unsightly	1
3902	Thespian	1	3902	transplanted	1	3902	under-sense	1	3902	unsinged	1
3902	thickening	1	3902	transports	1	3902	understanding's	1	3902	unsleeping	1
3902	thick-entangled	1	3902	trappings	1	3902	under-thirst	1	3902	unsoil'd	1
3902	thick-ribbed	1	3902	travail	1	3902	underwent	1	3902	unsoul	1
3902	thirsted	1	3902	travellers'	1	3902	undiminish'd	1	3902	unsound	1
3902	thirteen	1	3902	travels	1	3902	undischarged	1	3902	unsubstantial	1
3902	thirty	1	3902	travers'd	1	3902	undisciplin'd	1	3902	unsuccessful	1
3902	thitherward	1	3902	treacherous	1	3902	undisguis'd	1	3902	unsung	1
3902	tho'	1	3902	treasonable	1	3902	undismay'd	1	3902	unthought-of	1
3902	Thorn	1	3902	treasur'd	1	3902	undisorder'd	1	3902	untill'd	1
3902	thoroughfare	1	3902	treasures	1	3902	undisturbed	1	3902	untoward	1
3902	thoughtful	1	3902	treatise	1	3902	undoing	1	3902	untrain'd	1
3902	thoughtfully	1	3902	tree-tops	1	3902	undomestic	1	3902	untrod	1
3902	thoughtfulness	1	3902	tremble	1	3902	undress	1	3902	untroubled	1
3902	thousands	1	3902	trembled	1	3902	undulation	1	3902	untun'd	1
3902	thraldom	1	3902	tremendously	1	3902	unencroach'd	1	3902	untutor'd	1
3902	thrall	1	3902	tribe	1	3902	unexalted	1	3902	unused	1
3902	thread	1	3902	tribunals	1	3902	unexampled	1	3902	unutterable	1
3902	threaten'd	1	3902	tribune	1	3902	unexpected	1	3902	unwearied	1
3902	threatening	1	3902	trick	1	3902	unexpectedly	1	3902	unwelcome	1
3902	threats	1	3902	trick'd	1	3902	unextinguish'd	1	3902	unwholesome	1
3902	three-years'	1	3902	trickling	1	3902	unfading	1	3902	unwithered	1
3902	thrill'd	1	3902	trifling	1	3902	unfaithful	1	3902	unwoo'd	1
3902	thrilling	1	3902	trim	1	3902	unfamiliarly	1	3902	unworldly-minded	1
3902	thrills	1	3902	trimm'd	1	3902	unfather'd	1	3902	unworthily	1
3902	thrive	1	3902	Trinity's	1	3902	unfeeling	1	3902	upbraiding	1

Appendix

3902	upbraids	1	3902	vineyard	1	3902	weakest	1	3902	wished-for	1
3902	upheaved	1	3902	violating	1	3902	wealthy	1	3902	wishing-cap	1
3902	upholder	1	3902	virtual	1	3902	weapons	1	3902	withering	1
3902	upholders	1	3902	visages	1	3902	weariness	1	3902	wizard	1
3902	upholds	1	3902	visit	1	3902	wearing	1	3902	wold	1
3902	upholstery	1	3902	visitor	1	3902	weaves	1	3902	wolf-skin	1
3902	up-leaping	1	3902	vistos	1	3902	wedlock	1	3902	wolves	1
3902	uplooking	1	3902	vivifying	1	3902	weekday	1	3902	woman's	1
3902	uprear'd	1	3902	voiceless	1	3902	weekly	1	3902	wond'rous	1
3902	upris'n	1	3902	voluble	1	3902	weeks'	1	3902	wonder'd	1
3902	uprose	1	3902	volumes	1	3902	weighs	1	3902	wondrous	1
3902	up-shouldering	1	3902	voluptuous	1	3902	welcom'd	1	3902	wood-built	1
3902	upturning	1	3902	voluptuously	1	3902	well-born	1	3902	woodcocks	1
3902	useful	1	3902	vomit	1	3902	well-match'd	1	3902	wooden	1
3902	usefully	1	3902	vomiting	1	3902	well-spring	1	3902	wood-honey	1
3902	uselessly	1	3902	votary	1	3902	welterings	1	3902	work'd	1
3902	usurpation	1	3902	vouchsaf'd	1	3902	Westminster	1	3902	workmanship	1
3902	usury	1	3902	vouchsafe	1	3902	Westmoreland	1	3902	workmen	1
3902	Utopia	1	3902	vow	1	3902	westward	1	3902	world's	1
3902	vacancy	1	3902	vow'd	1	3902	wetting	1	3902	worm	1
3902	vacation	1	3902	voyage	1	3902	wheel	1	3902	worm-like	1
3902	vagaries	1	3902	voyager	1	3902	wheel'd	1	3902	worshipp'd	1
3902	vagrants	1	3902	Vulcan	1	3902	wheeled	1	3902	worshipper	1
3902	vain-glory	1	3902	wading	1	3902	wheels	1	3902	worthiest	1
3902	Valais	1	3902	wain	1	3902	whencesoe'er	1	3902	worthiness	1
3902	vallies	1	3902	wains	1	3902	whensoe'er	1	3902	woven	1
3902	vane	1	3902	waist	1	3902	whensoever	1	3902	wrap	1
3902	vanish'd	1	3902	waiting	1	3902	whereabout	1	3902	wreath	1
3902	vanquish'd	1	3902	wallowing	1	3902	whereby	1	3902	wreath'd	1
3902	vapour'd	1	3902	wan	1	3902	whereof	1	3902	wreck	1
3902	varieties	1	3902	wanderer's	1	3902	whereunto	1	3902	wren	1
3902	variety	1	3902	wanderers	1	3902	whip	1	3902	wrench'd	1
3902	vassalage	1	3902	wands	1	3902	whirl	1	3902	wren-like	1
3902	Vauxhall	1	3902	waning	1	3902	whirl'd	1	3902	wrinkles	1
3902	veer	1	3902	wanton	1	3902	whirling	1	3902	writhing	1
3902	veering	1	3902	wanton'd	1	3902	whirlwinds	1	3902	writing	1
3902	vehicle	1	3902	warbling	1	3902	whispered	1	3902	wrote	1
3902	vein	1	3902	warblings	1	3902	whispering	1	3902	year's	1
3902	velvet	1	3902	wardens	1	3902	whispers	1	3902	yearn	1
3902	vender's	1	3902	warehouse	1	3902	whist	1	3902	yearning	1
3902	ventriloquists	1	3902	warfare	1	3902	whistle	1	3902	years'	1
3902	venturous	1	3902	warmer	1	3902	Whittington	1	3902	yellings	1
3902	Venus	1	3902	warmest	1	3902	wholesome	1	3902	yellowing	1
3902	verge	1	3902	wars	1	3902	whoso	1	3902	yester	1
3902	verified	1	3902	wash	1	3902	wicked	1	3902	yesterday	1
3902	vermin	1	3902	wast	1	3902	wicker	1	3902	yew-tree	1
3902	vers'd	1	3902	water's	1	3902	widely-parted	1	3902	yoke-fellows	1
3902	vest	1	3902	waterfall	1	3902	widening	1	3902	Yordas	1
3902	vested	1	3902	waterfalls	1	3902	wide-scatter'd	1	3902	Yorkshire	1
3902	vestiges	1	3902	water-falls	1	3902	wide-spreading	1	3902	Young	1
3902	vexation	1	3902	waterspout	1	3902	widest	1	3902	yourselves	1
3902	vexations	1	3902	water-weeds	1	3902	widow	1	3902	Zacynthus	1
3902	vexatious	1	3902	waved	1	3902	wield	1	3902	zealously	1
3902	viands	1	3902	wavering	1	3902	wielded	1	3902	zephyrs	1
3902	vices	1	3902	waving	1	3902	wilfulness	1	3902	zest	1
3902	victims	1	3902	wax'd	1	3902	wily	1			
3902	victories	1	3902	waxen	1	3902	Winander	1			
3902	victorious	1	3902	wax-work	1	3902	wind-mill	1			
3902	vile	1	3902	wayside	1	3902	window's	1			
3902	villager	1	3902	way-side	1	3902	window-garlands	1			
3902	vine-clad	1	3902	waywardness	1	3902	wing	1			
3902	vines	1	3902	weaker	1	3902	wins	1			

Subject Index

A
'A of B' structure 31
'A of B' phrase type 84
abstract locative noun 83, 84
abstract noun 12, 13, 15, 28, 82, 83, 125
abstract word 12, 13, 60, 82, 83
accelerator 19
acoustically motivated expression 101
active and passive "voice" 115
adversative conjunction 109
alliteration 32, 75
anacoluthon 119, 120
antonym 18, 24
appositional element 94, 95, 98, 99, 101, 102, 111, 114, 121
appositional double expression 98
appositive 1, 35, 49, 93, 94, 102 121
approach to Nature 19
articulate sound 93, 94
artifact 102
Asahi Shimbun Newspaper 1
auditory expression 93, 94, 107
the axis of selection 95
the axis of space 27, 91
the axis of time 27, 91

B
back-and-forth movements 79
behind-the-scenes story 4
the Bible 42
bidirectional 94
bipolarization 70
brake 19
broad category 49
The Brown University Corpus of American English (*Brown*) 26, 78, 95

C
The Canterbury Tales 79
centripetal tendency 122
classification 7, 9, 10, 12, 20, 22, 23, 24, 34, 37, 60, 69, 76, 126
close adhesion 74
coinage 120
Collins COBUILD Wordbanks Online 43
Collins Dictionary of the English Language 41
Collins Dictionary of Quotations 31, 41
combination of words 1, 43
comparative degree 25, 69, 70
conceptual diagram of chapters 2, 3
concrete noun 28, 82, 83, 84, 95, 102, 125
concrete word 13
configuration of verbs 118
conjunction 7, 25, 103, 109, 113
connotation 14
conventional use 31
convergence 41, 112, 114, 116, 119, 122
content word 27, 77, 79
copulative 109
core of expression 112
co-referential double structure 109

D
"Daffodils" 59, 68
deepening 97, 98, 101, 102, 103, 116, 121, 126
degree of abstraction 12
depth-ordered or "recursive" structure 103
determiner 24, 66, 114
deviational usage 31
diagrammatic illustration 103
distinctive characteristic 7
diphthong 32
divergence 78, 112, 114, 116, 119, 122
downward vector component 44
double-layered structure 114
double structure 98, 109, 110, 114, 115, 116, 120
dual and reciprocal meaning 115

E
elegant variation 108, 112
element 97, 98, 99
end focus 110
end-weight 111
'enduring thing' 99, 100
enhancing 97, 98, 102, 103, 116, 121, 126
epithet 44, 61, 66, 69, 115, 116
equivalent structure 106, 110, 112, 113, 118
'exterior form' 52, 58, 70
exterior form of things 62
'external forms' 69

F
finite verb 40, 55
foregrounded expression 92
foregrounded regularity 93
foregrounding 98
four-layered structure 101
French Revolution 57, 63, 90, 98
frequency count 7, 9, 13, 15, 21, 24, 29, 36, 45, 71, 126
function word 27, 77, 79

G
general word 51, 52, 60, 64, 65, 125
grouping 24, 34
Gutenberg Files 42

H
Hamlet 72
handling of words and phrases 112
head word 49, 108, 109, 111, 114, 116, 121
'high object' 99

193

'the horizon of his mind' 58, 127
hypernym 9, 28, 52, 70
hyponymous subdivision 9
hyponymy 8, 9
hyponym 12, 70

I

identical adjectives 25, 29, 125
idiosyncratic 43, 78
idiosyncratic multi-layered structure 120
the indescribable 1, 126
image schema 90, 94, 95
'imagination of the whole' 28, 92, 105, 110, 122
inarticulate sound 94
individual attribute 12, 14
'intellectual eye' 58
intensifier 41
interactive action 94
interjection 7, 25
interrelationship 61, 77
interrelationship between man and Nature 106
International Thesaurus 7
interrelation 28, 77, 79, 92-95, 125, 126
intransitive verb 103
inversion 106
inverted object 113, 114
invisible 22, 24, 52, 54, 59
'inward eye' 59, 102
isotopy 106, 110, 111

J

juxtaposition 74

K

Kadokawa's New Dictionary of Synonyms 24, 49, 82, 95
key word 36, 68, 94

L

The Lancaster-Oslo/Bergen Corpus of British English (LOB) 26, 78
language code 115
laws of chance 27, 79
lexical item 2, 4, 13, 17, 21, 24, 36, 37, 44, 53, 104, 110
'life and nature' 99
life is a burden 33, 37, 39, 42
the literature of knowledge 72
the literature of power 72
Longman Lexicon of Contemporary English 7, 34
Lyrical Ballads 20, 37

M

major sentence 103, 121, 123
marked 13, 28, 29, 32, 41, 92, 109
marked deviation 95
metalanguage 55
metaphor 19, 41, 43
'mighty mind' 5, 24, 25, 57, 62, 73-75, 95, 105, 113, 114, 117, 123, 125-127
'mighty forms' 21, 25, 29, 62, 70, 73, 74, 86, 96, 127
minor sentence 103, 108, 109, 110, 114, 117, 121-123
mirror-image relationship 72, 73, 106, 116, 126
'motions of delight' 1, 57, 87, 95
multi-layered expression 98, 102, 103, 121, 122, 126
multi-layered structure 3, 4, 6, 97, 98, 99, 103, 108, 114, 116, 120, 121
mutual interaction 125
mutual relationship 17, 29, 120, 121
mystical experience 98

N

National Institute for Japanese Language 2
the natural world 17, 98, 127
nature poet 18, 83
Nature's outer world 73
Nature's outward movements 87
'Nature's secondary grace' 73
near-synonym 93
negative value 34, 35, 37, 42
network 2, 7
neutral value 34, 35, 37, 41
new information 110
Nineteenth-Century Fiction: Full-Text Database 44
nominal equivalent structure 113, 118
non-finite verb 55
non-sentence 119

O

object 12, 28
OED2 16, 32, 34, 35, 66, 88, 93, 94, 111, 115, 117
Oedipus Rex 43
optically motivated expression 101
orientational metaphor 41, 43
the outer world of Nature 17, 28, 29, 75, 79, 91, 95, 125, 126
'outside of our human life' 58
'outward face of things' 56, 58, 105, 117, 118, 123
Oxford Advanced Learner's Dictionary 40
The Oxford Dictionary of Quotations 31
oxymoronic combination of words 43
oxymoronic word combination 44

P

PALA 5, 6
parallel linguistic structure 117
parallel relationship 13
parallelism 93, 116
paronomasia 75
participial phrase 111
passive voice 49
past participle 47, 55
past perfect tense 110
philological circle 48, 79
phonetic value 32
pluperfect tense 117
poet of love, joy, and passion 18

Subject Index 195

poet's inner world 24, 28, 29, 73, 79, 95
poetic craft 95
point of articulation 75
polyptoton 111
polysyllabic adjective 32
positive degree 70
positive image 24, 59
positive-image words 24
positive value 34, 35, 37, 39, 42
post-modification 15, 25
pre-modification 15, 25
preamble 97
present tense 47, 115
primary charm 73
probabilities of occurrence 27, 79
prominence 111
prototype 2
proximity 74
punctuation 4

Q
quantitative classification 22, 69, 76, 126

R
real state of adjectives 25
rearrangement of adjectives 71
relationship between man and Nature 106
relative clause 13, 15, 31, 59, 62, 94, 102, 108
the Revolution 92
retreat from Nature 19
Roget's II The New Thesaurus 34
Roget's Thesaurus 59
Romanticism 5, 6

S
saw → heard → felt 21, 28, 66-68, 126
scales of abstraction 82
selectional restriction 44
semantic affinity 40
semantic component 4, 21, 86, 88, 95
semantic feature 113
semantic field 7, 69, 106, 110

SEMES 106
sensor 17
signifiant 52
signifié 52
the Snowdon passage 55, 75, 92, 95, 97, 103, 104, 106, 110 112, 114-116, 119, 121-123
'something' 52
'sounds of undistinguishable motion' 61
sound structure 75
'speaking face of earth and heaven' 17, 73, 87
'spots of time' 38, 116
stratificational network 7
struggle toward definition 94, 102
stylistic characteristics 98
stylistic deviation 78
subcategory 49, 60, 82
subdivision 9, 12, 13
sublimity of nature 73
subject complement 113, 114, 119
subject-object relations 45
subordinate clause 49, 103, 113, 119-121
superficial appearance of affairs 25, 71
superficial beauty of Nature 70, 76
'superficial thing' 50, 53
superlative degree 25, 69, 70, 98, 102, 108
superordinate 9, 12, 70, 71
superordinate word 51, 52, 60, 64, 65, 68, 70
symmetry 100
synonym 17, 34-36, 42, 93, 117
syntactic movement 103
syntactic structure of *The Prelude* 126
syntagmatic relationship 8, 15, 25
syntax 36, 37, 57, 97, 103, 104, 106, 121, 126

T
that-clause 114, 115, 116, 119

theme 15, 44, 98, 106, 127
theory of imagination 16, 28, 55, 92, 98, 106
'thing' 12, 28, 60
threefold structure 97, 98
the time difference 27, 78
"Tintern Abbey" 13, 31, 33
'to-and-fro' movements 87
token 7
transitivity 56, 117
triple appositive structure 102
triple structure 4, 97, 98, 103, 109, 126
triple-layered structure 108
triple-structured expression 108
type 7, 12, 25, 49, 70, 71, 98, 126

U
'unassuming things' 50, 53, 68 126
unidirectional 94
'undistinguishable motion' 1, 61
undistinguishable sounds 62, 68, 126
'undistinguishable world' 87, 101
'unknown modes of being' 1, 20, 61, 99
upward vector component 44

V
variation 93, 94, 108, 109, 112, 115, 121
verbal equivalent structure 118
verbs of auditory perception 5, 46, 48, 59, 60, 63, 64, 66, 68, 126
verbs of cognition 20, 28, 45, 46, 48, 66, 125
verbs of motion 21, 86, 88-90
verbs of perception 3, 20, 21, 28, 45, 46, 47, 54, 66, 125, 126
verbs of visual perception 3, 5, 45-46, 48-50, 54, 59-60, 62-63, 66-68, 90
visible 22, 52, 54, 59, 117

'visionary power' 61
visual and auditory verb 45
vocabulary of emotion 18, 19, 36

W

wandering poet 27, 88, 92
word combination 13, 24, 42, 44, 75
Word List by Semantic Principles 7, 8, 15, 17, 18, 20, 25, 46
Word Frequencies in Written and Spoken English 26
Wuthering Heights 79

Number

13 words 2

Personal Name Index

A
Austin, Francis 68, 79

B
Beaupuy, Michael 57
Beethoven, Ludwig van 44
Bolton, Whitney French 106
Brontë, Emily. 79

C
Carroll, John Bissell 78
Carter, Ronald 35
Chatman, Seymour Benjamin 83
Chaucer, Geoffrey 42, 79
Chesnutt, Charles Waddell 43
Close, R.A. 91
Conrad, Joseph 83

D
Darbishire, Helen 4
Davie, Donald 121
Davies, Hugh Sykes 27, 68, 79
Defoe, Daniel 43
De Quincey 72
Dickens, Charles 79
Dickinson, Emily. 79

E
Empson, William 68, 77

G
Gavins, Joanna 5
Gill, Stephen 68, 96

H
Halliday, M.A.K. 17, 108
Hardy, Thomas 42
Havens, R.D. 36, 72
Hayashi, Shiro 2
Hofland, Knut 78

J
Jakobson, Roman 75, 95
Johansson, Stig 78
Johnson, Mark 41, 43
James, Henry 83

Jones, Robert 106

K
Kanno, Masahiko 5
Kunihiro, Tetsuya 8, 12
Kanou, Hideo 19

L
Lakoff, George 33, 41, 43
Leech, Geoffrey 78, 79, 83, 84, 93
Lewis, Cecil Staples 68, 88
Lindenberger, Herbert 83, 98, 102, 115

M
Masui, Michio 1
Matsuo, Masatsugu 7
Miles, Josephine 18, 36, 68
Miyagawa, Kiyoshi 52, 68
Miyazaki, Yukou 68

N
Nakamura, Hiroko 68
Nida, Eugene A. 8

O
Otsuka, Takanobu 103

P
Pottle, Frederick A. 52

Q
Quirk, Randolph 115

R
Read, Herbert 116
Riffaterre, Michael 106

S
Saito, Toshio 5
Sebeok, Thomas A. 95
de Selincourt, Ernest 4
Shakespeare, William 33, 42, 72, 88
Schiller, Friedrich von 43
Short, Michael 79, 83, 84
Spitzer, Leo 48, 79

Suzuki, Shigetaka 7

T
Tokugawa, Ieyasu 33
Turner, Mark 33

W
Wales, Katie 93, 97, 103, 106, 111
Ward, J.P. 56, 68
Watanabe, Toshiro 33
Wells, John C. 32
West, Michael 13, 14

Y
Yamauchi, Shouichi 68